To Rachel

Happy Christmas 2008 from your wonderful friends Sara, [...] Ned and Graham. We hope you enjoy reading these books about our home.

With all our love.

THE HOUSE OF STRIFE

By the same author

FICTION
The New Zealanders
Summer Fires and Winter Country
Among the Cinders
The Presence of Music
This Summer's Dolphin
An Ear of the Dragon
Strangers and Journeys
A Touch of Clay
Danger Zone
Figures in Light
The Lovelock Version
Season of the Jew
Monday's Warriors

AUTOBIOGRAPHY
One of Ben's: A New Zealand Medley

DRAMA
Once on Chunuk Bair

NON-FICTION
New Zealand: Gift of the Sea (with Brian Brake)
The Shell Guide to New Zealand
Love and Legend
The Reader's Digest Guide to New Zealand (with Brian Brake)
Voices of Gallipoli

THE HOUSE OF STRIFE

Maurice Shadbolt

BLOOMSBURY

First published 1993 by Bloomsbury Publishing Ltd, London,
and Hodder & Stoughton Ltd, Auckland, New Zealand

Copyright © 1993 by Maurice Shadbolt

The moral right of the author has been asserted

Bloomsbury Publishing Ltd, 2 Soho Square, London W1V 5DE

A CIP catalogue record for this book
is available from the British Library

ISBN 0 7475 1616 2

10 9 8 7 6 5 4 3 2 1

Typeset by Graeme Leather, Auckland
Printed in Hong Kong

*The sweetest sound in the world is
the music of what happens*
— Finn McCool

*Do what you will, this life's a fiction
And is made up of contradiction*
— William Blake

Author's Note

The House of Strife is the third in a trilogy of novels — beginning with *Season of the Jew* and continuing with *Monday's Warriors* — deriving from the New Zealand wars (1845-72). Though the three novels are independent of each other in terms of character and locale, the common thread is 'the strangest war that ever was carried on', as it was styled by one mystified British observer.

I should like to acknowledge the contribution made to this trilogy by two people in particular — first by military historian Christopher Pugsley, for walking me over battlefields to ensure that I at least got the warfare right; second by fellow novelist Elspeth Sandys for ensuring that I finished the trilogy. To the first I dedicate *The House of Strife*; to the second I dedicate the entire trilogy.

Thanks are also due the Arts Council of New Zealand and the English Departments of the University of Waikato and University of Auckland for fellowships which enabled me to research and write the trilogy.

One

The first time I saw John Heke he was no disappointment. Heralded by hoofbeats and baying dogs, he rose shadowy out of New Zealand forest on a misty midwinter morning. As he took potent shape he might well have been mistaken for the young Alexander among hounds, horses and kinsmen in the mountains of Macedonia. Heke's beast was a picturesque piebald. A silver-plated musket sat across his saddle. Hard behind him, a rowdy retinue of tribesmen led a team of pack-horses labouring under the carcasses of wild pig. Huntsman Heke appeared to take no joy in his bloody trophies. When he sighted me he mustered no pretence of pleasure either. Indeed there was something akin to pain in his features when I dismounted and rather breathlessly drew attention to myself.

'Ferdinand Wildblood, sir,' I informed him.

He said nothing. He sat haughtily high in the saddle, straight-backed, and lean. He wore tweed English trousers, a seaman's tunic, and a light Maori cloak loose across his shoulders. His face? The fairest I can say is that his sharp nose, long jaw and eloquent eyes were to bewitch many a portraitist. I remained breathing hard.

'I have been looking for you,' I explained.

He looked left at one lieutenant, right at another. Finally his eyes found a place of rest forward of his horse. At no point did they meet mine.

'I have not been looking for you,' he disclosed.

He rode on with his boisterous escort. I was left gazing at the soiled rumps of their beasts. It was not a stirring encounter. It would be better unremembered.

Forty years have gone since that meeting. Memory has become a creaky conveyance. Yet it delivers dew on fern, the jingle of harness, the smell of blood, the beat of my heart. With hindsight I see I was the last person John Heke needed that morning, or perhaps on any other of his spirited life. Yet there I was; here I am. Ferdinand Wildblood, no less.

True that mine is not a name to quieten a crowded room. Even Londoners familiar with the literary productions of Messrs Lovelady and Pettiworth, late and unlamented of Covent Garden, would have difficulty identifying my person, familiar though they might be with my work. The fact is that I failed to use it in connection with toil beneath my calling, and the publications of Messrs Lovelady and Pettiworth for the most part were. They were a cut above penny dreadfuls and less pernicious than shilling shockers. They were also popular. There was a time when no Englishman packed for a coach or sea journey unaccompanied by a selection of Lovelady and Pettiworth narratives, not a few of them mine. Some even say that the firm's racy reputation, and consequent collapse, owed much to me. I remind the reader that Messrs Lovelady and Pettiworth cheerfully published my work of their own wish; and that I had no part in their ill-starred refusal of a manuscript by a young *Morning Chronicle* scribbler named Dickens. Besides, who was I to know that the South Pacific would so fast go out of fashion? That such homely sagas as *The Old Curiosity Shop,* for argument's sake, would soon supplant my own *Monarch of Maoriland* in the Englishman's carrying bag?

I leap too far. When I began youthfully with Messrs Lovelady and Pettiworth, it was in a humble and indifferently paid editorial capacity; my income was enough to retain an attic room in Grub Street. I had no intention of camping long in that nomad neighbourhood; nor of an impecunious career with Messrs Lovelady and Pettiworth. The fact was that I fancied myself first and last as a poet, not as a lacklustre journeyman in the jungle of London letters. It was my ambition to prove that the melodists of our language — the mighty likes of Shakespeare and Shelley — were not all gone; that there were golden tunes yet to be plucked from the lyre of old England, most fetchingly by me. How could I have known that Tennyson was waiting in the wings? But erudite regret has no place in this narrative. Lord it though he may over his lessers, Alfred Tennyson has never seen the half of life. Our laureate may have written of 'the long wash of Australasian seas'; he has never seen such seas, other than in his lofty imagination. He may sing of his gallant six hundred in the valley of death; he has never heard the authentic sound of shot and shell.

My future began to unfurl when old Mr Pettiworth summoned me to his chambers on a dank December morning in 1836. I was not altogether sure that Mr Pettiworth was aware of my existence; I was flattered to find myself standing before his desk. At length he looked up.

'Ah,' he said. 'Young Wildblood. You must have been with us some months now.'

'Some years, sir,' I pointed out.

'Just so,' he agreed. 'And you find your position with us tolerable?'

'I should have made my misgivings plain, sir, if my terms of employment were altogether so.'

'Nevertheless,' he suggested, 'you may well aspire to cut your teeth on something sterner.'

Presumably he meant something more robust than repairing the punctuation and spelling of his half-literate authors; and running errands to our drunken printers. I no longer kept tally of the Lovelady and Pettiworth publications I had conscientiously groomed. It was not for me to suggest to Mr Pettiworth that my menial situation was unworthy of my talent. I remained modest.

'This,' he proposed, 'may be your chance.'

'This, sir?'

'This,' he said. He was referring to a shaky mountain of manuscript beside his desk. 'It has come our way, I know not how, from a man who purports to have terrifyingly intimate knowledge of his subject. It may well be so. There are some two thousand pages testifying to his intimacy. To be frank, Wildblood, Mr Lovelady's stamina is not as it was. Nor is my eyesight as keen as it might be. Determining the quality of this author's saga is a daunting prospect. The man seems only lately to have become familiar with pen and ink. It is by far the most dishevelled manuscript to have come to this firm in many a year; some pages are impossible to decipher.'

'And what is the nature of his narrative, sir?'

'Of rousing kind, if I am not misled. According to the man's own information, in an accompanying letter, he recounts what, on the civilised face of things, is an extraordinary tale. It seems the fellow was shipwrecked in the South Pacific some years ago. The lone survivor of the disaster, he drifted on a raft to New Zealand where he fell in with native Maori, embraced the savage life as the lieutenant of a cannibal chief, and became, in due course, an antipodean warlord. With, he tells us, a harem of lascivious Maori maidens.

What more could one ask?'

'Something less than two thousand pages, sir,' I ventured.

'Something intelligible,' he said.

My optimism grew. I could see an editor's rank, a rise in remuneration. 'You are asking me, sir, to undertake this task?'

'I am asking you to copy the manuscript in a fair hand. Mr Lovelady and I will thus be in a better position to contemplate this author's worth. Mr Lovelady is in two minds about the prospects of the story, though the promise of libidinous material appears to give him pause. I am not, on the other hand, giving you licence to remove offensive passages from the narrative. Rest assured that such passages will be for our eyes only.'

'So you wish me to copy all two thousand pages?' I was not altogether downcast. Ladders, after all, have rungs.

'Shall we say by the month's end?' Mr Pettiworth asked.

'That gives me less than three weeks,' I protested.

'By my tally too,' Mr Pettiworth said.

It took me no more than three difficult nights to realise that neither my life nor my position with Lovelady and Pettiworth was being enhanced by my toil. I burned midnight oil and bent over backwards to make the manuscript more promising. It refused the most acrobatic of attentions. It was not just that it was near incomprehensible; legibility was the least of my woes. The fact is that from the first page I was aware that I was in service to a shameless mountebank. Deceit is no bad thing in a novelist — novels being as they are, a debased form of literature, designed by and for ill-disciplined daydreamers — but in this instance the book proposed itself as a verbatim record of high adventure. As such it was miserably counterfeit. Narrative interest was negligible; the man could not even tell a tale. High adventure became a low yawn. Most crucially, however, there were clues — in the form of abrupt changes in the colour of the prose — which made me suspect that the alleged author, one James Dinwiddie, was an incompetent plagiarist. Research on my part was desirable. At that date literature pertaining to the South Pacific, and particularly New Zealand, was not large. Such as sat informatively on library shelves began with the journals of Captain Cook, as published by Hawkesworth, some five decades earlier. There was a gap thereafter; it seems voyagers in those latitudes, after surviving a massacre or two, thought to live and let live; especially to live. Not until my native century did accounts of mariners, adventurers and explorers who had risked New Zealand begin to appear. Few were sober; many were overwrought. I drew the conclusion that the visitor to New Zealand had reason to be feverish. More to the point, I did not have to delve far into such literature to find paragraphs ostensibly by James Dinwiddie looking me in the face. He had pilfered much of his manuscript shamelessly from such sources; seldom had he changed a comma. Moreover, his story of a white warlord among fierce Maori was far from original; stories akin to it had been told not just once but several times. Only the harem of lascivious Maori maidens seems to have been his own seedy supplement to the tale. Otherwise the man was an impostor. The discovery robbed me of another night's sleep. One way or the next, doubtless due to the colourful nature of the literature I had been perusing, I seemed to have aged several years. I dreamed of Dinwiddie's confounded harem, of unmentionable pagan practices, and not least of a land far from London.

It was time to brave Mr Pettiworth's chambers and confide my findings. He was slow to look up. Then he considered me for some time. 'Tell me, Wildblood,' he said. 'Are you always like this?'
'This, sir?'
'Do you always shake so?'
'Not to my knowledge, sir.'
'Good Lord, man. Your arms and legs promise to part company from your torso.'
'I remain unaware of it, sir.' This was to toy with truth. I had never not been aware that God had placed me in an ungainly frame, one at odds with my harmonious nature.
'Extraordinary,' he observed. 'And your legs manage to carry you from one place to another?'
'On the whole, sir.'
He shook his head in wonder. 'Well?' he asked. 'What is it?'
'It is in reference to this manuscript, sir,' I informed him.
'Finished, are we?'
'I have second thoughts about the enterprise, sir.'
'You are not employed to have second thoughts, Wildblood. Or, so far as I can determine, any thoughts at all. You are to produce a fair copy as directed.'
'Nevertheless, sir,' I protested.
'What is it, then?' he demanded. There were manuscripts on his

desk ready to be rushed to Britons starved of adventure.

'I have given this book my time, my patience and my sleep, sir. It would be remiss of me not to draw your attention to the fact that it is the work of a cheeky charlatan.'

'Authors,' Mr Pettiworth sighed, 'are an unreliable breed. Much the same was said, I am given to believe, of the author of *Robinson Crusoe*. It was published, nevertheless, to some profit.'

'Then I hasten to be frank, sir. The book purports to be a truthful chronicle of a man's personal experience as a castaway in New Zealand. It is my suspicion that the author has never been south of Surrey. Should you wish, I can produce chapter and verse to that effect.'

Mr Pettiworth didn't blink. 'That is called literary licence,' he informed me. 'We have never made a point of subjecting our authors to an inquisition in respect of their bona fides. Where, Wildblood, would literature then be? Above all, where would Lovelady and Pettiworth be? Are you ready to sit before me and argue that Homer told an honest tale?'

I wasn't sitting. I was standing. But I let that pass. I played my most powerful card.

'Furthermore,' I said, 'publication of this book could have unfortunate consequences. Financially perhaps, and certainly for the reputation of Lovelady and Pettiworth. Unscrupulous journalists of the penny press could have a cruel carnival in exposing your audacious author James Dinwiddie as a retired clergyman in the Cotswolds. The ensuing scandal could obscure your good intentions as a publisher.'

Mr Pettiworth could be detected listening at last. 'Continue,' he said.

'Dinwiddie is not only a liar, but a cheat. The few pages of interest in his manuscript are thieved from his literary betters. He makes no attempt to disguise his plagiarism, even when stealing from volumes published well within the memory of our readers.'

'You are sure of this, Wildblood?'

'Unshakeably, sir.'

There was a substantial silence.

'A damn shame,' he finally said.

'Just so, sir.'

'And a great disappointment.'

'Indeed, sir.'

About to put vexation to his rear, he observed, 'You have failed to enlighten me in one respect. You pass no judgement on the narrative worth of the work.'

My reply proved my undoing. Perhaps poetry would be the poorer. Who, in modesty, am I to say?

'I could, sir,' I argued, 'tell a better tale myself.'

'You could?'

'In a manner of speaking, sir.'

'In what manner of speaking, Wildblood?'

'Mine, sir. Mr Dinwiddie's manuscript is written with small respect for the bricks and mortar of our trade. In short, for the English language, sir. I pride myself on workmanlike prose.'

There was a more considerable pause. Mr Pettiworth placed the tips of his fingers together and contemplated his rainy window.

'Pray do so,' he said wearily.

I was not sure I heard right. I was not sure I wished to. 'Sir?' I inquired.

'Pray write a better one,' he said.

'Me, sir?'

'You,' he confirmed. 'Meanwhile, Wildblood, you may recall that you have a desk elsewhere on these premises.'

Thus, with no toll of bell, was *Monarch of Maoriland* begun. I returned to the library shelves I had lately used to launch my lethal salvoes at James Dinwiddie's mediocre work. This time I did not have the thrill of the hunter, the smell of blood in my nostrils; I read my way through disheartening December into joyless January. As volume after volume blurred before me I became one of the better informed citizens of the British Isles in respect of that remote land called New Zealand. I knew every cove of its perilous coast. I knew the country's formidable flora. I was familiar with its fickle climate. Above all I was intimate, as few before me, with its native inhabitants. As warriors they made the heroes of *The Iliad* seem playful apprentices to the killer's craft. Toward the end of that melancholy month I took up my pen in earnest and became deaf to the world. Brown armies surged around me in red-blooded battle. I tasted human flesh hot on my tongue. Shapely tribal belles, suppliant in the light of my campfire, waited on my warrior whim. London, for four weeks of dream, ceased to exist. On the last day of foggy February, with my lamp burning low for lack of fuel, and rain rattling through my roof into a strategic bucket, I laboured down the last page of the manuscript. Then, returning to the first with a sigh, I appended the only title possible for the work. *Monarch of Maoriland* it had to be. It would be imprecise to pretend that the title owed nothing to James Dinwiddie's (*Monarch of the Man Eaters*) or that the manuscript was not indebted to Dinwiddie's inventive sortie into the South Pacific. On the other hand there was not an adjective which could be identified as other than my own. (As for the nouns, James Dinwiddie was not heard from again; he failed to request the return of his magnum opus.)

Mr Pettiworth was awed. Mr Lovelady was ravished. There was a chair ready for me in Mr Pettiworth's chambers when I presented myself to them one morning in March. A manservant brought tea. There was shy spring sunlight beyond the window. My employers considered me warily, and in silence. My face may have made it plain that I didn't need their approval; I had a sure sense of my worth.

'We scarce know what to say,' Mr Lovelady finally confessed.

'Bewitching,' Mr Pettiworth agreed.

'And all your own work,' Mr Lovelady marvelled.

'We were thinking,' Mr Pettiworth said, 'of something of the order of ten pounds.'

'For the copyright?'

'It is not this firm's policy to pay royalties,' Mr Pettiworth said. 'Nor to let authors get above themselves.'

'I was thinking,' I confessed, 'of twenty or thirty.'

'Thirty it shall be,' Mr Pettiworth promised, skipping a score of pounds with interesting haste.

'On first publication,' I added experimentally. 'Further printings shall require payment of the same order.'

Mr Pettiworth and Mr Lovelady sought each other's eye in the same second. They nodded as one.

'Agreed,' Mr Pettiworth said. 'We will expect, of course, that you submit future work to us on the same terms.'

'Future work?' I said cautiously.

'There will be future work, will there not?' Mr Lovelady asked. There was a tremor in his tone.

'I have not been contemplating it,' I explained.

'Come,' Mr Pettiworth said. 'You cannot stop here. Your manuscript is gold. There is more to be mined in the same location.'

'I have not been thinking further than promotion to a more lucrative and livelier editorial role within this firm. The book was written to make a point, certainly to make good a boast.'

'You cannot continue to hide your light under a bushel,' Mr Pettiworth said firmly. 'If that is your intention, we will not collaborate.'

'It would be a shame and a disgrace,' Mr Lovelady agreed.

'And a loss to English letters,' Mr Pettiworth added.

'So publish my poetry,' I challenged.

As chance arranged, my verses (under the title *London Lyrics*, a volume coloured by my Grub Street sojourn) and *Monarch of Maoriland* were published the same month. That is to say, in May of 1837. Of the first publication, little can be said. It did find one reviewer. In a poisonous paragraph, a certain Sebastian Goodfellow, no friend of literature, and especially not of rival rhymesters, reported that 'All that can be said about Mr Wildblood's feeble collection of verse is that the author's surname promises much and delivers little. There is nothing of the wild in his lacklustre lines; they are all totally bloodless.'

The same could not be said, of course, of *Monarch of Maoriland*. It was untamed from the first line to the last. As for blood, the book was all but dripping. In this instance, however, it was impossible to make play with my surname. Authorship of the book was attributed to Henry Youngman, a pseudonym which seemed to suit my fledgling rank in the republic of letters. Messrs Lovelady and Pettiworth, after testing the manuscript on their favoured booksellers, ordered a first printing of ten thousand copies. It seemed I had been short of astute in my negotiation with the firm. This was confirmed when a second printing of ten thousand proved necessary within a week. The rest of the tale now resides in the annals of popular literature. No matter that reviewers, those willing to confess they had finished it, found the book repellent. Their diatribes merely provoked further printings. Enriched booksellers were soon inquiring after Henry Youngman's next book. And the grimy premises of Messrs Lovelady and Pettiworth were cleaned and refurnished. I should be last to deny, despite my first financial chagrin, that my own circumstances were also improved. I moved to a modest dwelling at World's End less at the mercy of the elements, something less than a gentleman's residence and something more than a tradesman's. I replenished my wardrobe in a style dashingly fashionable, thereby putting Grub Street still further to my rear. Regular nourishment also did wonders; flesh began to gather more adequately on my form. As for professional matters, I not only took tea with Mr Pettiworth as a regular arrangement; there was cake in evidence too.

'Far be it from me to press you,' he said, 'but we are all breathless.'

'Breathless, sir?'

'Awaiting your new manuscript. What else?'

'In that case, sir, I confess myself out of wind too.'

'Come,' he said. 'We cannot stop now.'

'We, sir?'

'Henry Youngman, if you must. And do call me George.'

'With pleasure, sir. Meanwhile Henry Youngman, as you well know, is a fiction. He does not exist. Ferdinand Wildblood, on the other hand, does. Unlike Henry Youngman, he has convincing evidence of his birth and baptism. Moneylenders' records might further confirm his existence.'

'You trifle with me,' Mr Pettiworth protested.

'Not in respect of moneylenders,' I told him.

Mr Pettiworth was not slow to get my drift. 'There would be, as you know, a worthwhile bonus paid upon early delivery of the manuscript.'

I didn't know. But I was not tempted to quibble. 'Worthwhile, sir?'

'Certainly of the order of fifty pounds.'

'I note a decent hesitancy, George, to leap into larger figures.'

'Very well, then. One hundred.'

'And fifty.'

'Of course,' he said warmly.

'I shall whisper the sum in Henry Youngman's ear,' I promised. 'Should he show signs of rebirth, I shall report accordingly.'

Two

George Pettiworth saw me as trifling with his firm. The reader may likewise think me coy about coupling with fate. The truth is that Henry Youngman already had his knife at the throat of Ferdinand Wildblood. Unknown to Messrs Lovelady and Pettiworth, Henry Youngman had commandeered my desk. There were two works in progress there. One was already titled *Sirens of a Savage Shore*. The other would become known as *Murder Most Maori*. Rather than bundle his favoured themes into one book — or his eggs into one basket, as in *Monarch of Maoriland* — Henry Youngman endeavoured to keep combat and copulation separate, the better to oblige dissimilar classes of reader. Those who sought warfare, thinking coitus an interruption, were slaked; those whose preference was for the prurient were as amply fulfilled. One way and another, 1837 was Henry Youngman's halcyon year. Henry and I heard remotely in that same twelve month that a young Queen had been enthroned; and that the Victorian era had thus begun. At first we were not suffered any interference. *Sirens of a Savage Shore* was the rage of London's newly literate until *Murder Most Maori* supplanted it soon after. Ferdinand Wildblood humbly continued to serve Henry Youngman as minion. He saw Henry was fed, clothed, and comfortably housed; and that there was always an ample quantity of ink on his desk, pen and paper ready. He even made it a weekly chore to hire women for Henry in order that his work continued in hand. There was little that Ferdinand failed do for Henry; as bedfellows they were better matched than commonplace pairings. It is true that Henry might have been more chivalrous toward Ferdinand, perhaps even grateful, as book followed book. But Ferdinand was never disposed to remind his partner that without his devotion and dedication Henry Youngman would literally be nothing. 1838 — the year of *The Maori Magdalen* and *Triumph of the Tribesman* among others — flashed into 1839. By that time frail Mr

Lovelady had taken leave of life, and even spindly George Pettiworth looked not long for this world. Some thought he persisted only to relish the profits of Henry Youngman's next prose endeavour. *The Belle of Blackguard Beach* did not disappoint the firm. The many familiar with the story will recall that it is set in an especially infamous location in New Zealand's Bay of Islands, where whalers disported themselves after months of sea-weary hunting and harpooning. Against this noisy and noxious backdrop Henry Youngman placed the tale of two lovers, a runaway seaman and an agreeably immodest tribal princess. Their two very different worlds promise to tug them apart. They take to the tall greenery of the New Zealand interior and there, for a time, amid waterfall and wildflower, live out a poignant and passionate idyll. It has to be said that Henry lavished his noblest prose upon the luckless duo. The unhappy climax, as capricious fate takes a hand, and tribesmen of evil temperament and murderous mariners join in hunting them down, showed Henry at his finest too. The grief provoked by the death of the princess rivalled that spent on Dickens's Little Nell. Perhaps the largest tribute paid to the book — though I was to learn this too late to be of use — is that the love affair was purloined (in a romance titled *Typee*) by a seafaring American scribbler of no lasting reputation named Melville. The Dinwiddies of this world are legion.

Henry Youngman's prose continued to race unbridled. There were shadows, nonetheless. I fancy that it was in the vicinity of 1840 — with *The Tattooed Trojans* the toast of the current season — when George Pettiworth produced a volume for my inspection. It was wrapped in some dun-coloured material without lettering or illustration. Puzzled, I removed the wrapper and found within one of Henry Youngman's later epics, one which leaned to the licentious side of pagan life.

'What,' I asked George Pettiworth, 'does this mean?'

'In brief,' George said,'we have a new monarch. A young Queen. An innocent, Wildblood.'

'I am not blind,' I told him. 'Nor deaf.'

'We would do well to serve her best interests,' George informed me. 'I am talking of the need for a moral atmosphere suitable for one of her years. God knows that this fancy German she has wed will be thrusting the crueller facts of existence on her soon enough. The lecher may be at work at this very moment.'

Mr Pettiworth's eyes had a disturbingly loyal glow.

'It is a little late in the day to save her,' I suggested.

'Perhaps. Perhaps not.'

'Besides,' I argued, 'we are not legislators. We are, are we not, literary men.'

'Nevertheless,' said George gravely.

'Are you trying to tell me that our beloved monarch's virtue is served by marketing Henry Youngman in drab?'

'I am not alone in this. Who wars against purity and wins? It is not for me to pronounce on the public mood.'

'Any moment now you will be trying to tell me that Henry Youngman must rein his imagination in.'

'You oblige me greatly by saying it,' George said. 'But only in respect of lewd custom. There is no objection to slaughter. Make use of New Zealand, by all means, but in a manner more seemly.'

'Dear God in heaven,' I sighed.

'I should prefer piety in your tone,' George Pettiworth said.

That was the first blow. There was one worse when I returned home and sat Henry Youngman at his desk. For the first time I noted symptoms of imaginative fatigue. The narrative on which he had been labouring (*The Vengeance of The Tattooed Trojans*) refused to move more than a sentence; long sighs became audible. I walked him to a nearby hostelry in the hope that convivial company and a warm fire might revive my valued friend. He remained sullen. Not even the promise of a reliable wench restored him. Henry seemed to be telling me that his day was done; that the 1840s were not for the likes of us. In panic I tipped tumbler after tumbler of mature malt whisky down his throat. The one perceptible result was that I had to pick him up from the pavement several times on our homeward journey.

Next morning Henry Youngman woke with a hellish head; Ferdinand Wildblood was equally bedevilled. Henry made no move to return to his desk, nor to his manuscript. 'New Zealand?' he seemed to be saying. 'Where in God's name is that?'

For once Ferdinand found no lucid reply. Then it struck me (distressed Ferdinand and truculent Henry) that we had been living on leavings. We needed to feed fresh grist to the muse. It was years since I had paused long in a library. Fiction generates itself; one fabrication begets another. Henry Youngman's New Zealand was no slave of history, no knickknack of geographers. It was a world unto itself, needing no underpinning from fact. Yet that, after all, was where we began. It was time to return the pitcher to the well. Henry and I resorted to libraries again, and the dustier shelves in bookselling establishments. It was in one such location that I first happened on the name Hongi. Or, to give the great warrior his full name, Hongi Hika. His name leapt at me from the pages of an illustrated work by an artist who had boldly sauntered through the South Pacific. This peripatetic fellow had fetched up in New Zealand in the 1820s and there met Hongi Hika near his dying hour; he had even painted Hongi as he succumbed to the pains of the world unbaptised, unredeemed, and unashamed. As I looked further into Hongi's terrible tale, I began cursing my lackadaisical ways as a scholar, not to speak of days indolently spent entertaining Henry in low haunts. Hongi Hika and Henry Youngman had long been made for each other; it was my failing that they had never met. As I read on, I felt Henry looking over my shoulder; he was all accusation. Why, he asked, had we been wasting our time? Hongi made Henry's recent fiction look emaciated.

In short — for it is all there with next to no embellishment in *Death By a Thousand Muskets: The New Zealand Napoleon*, should the reader wish to stomach the story in full — Hongi Hika was a warrior of commanding vision and considerable appetite. At the dawn of the century he had been one chief among many, a competent campaigner, skilful in surviving battle, but otherwise a run of the mill mechanic of murder. What lifted him above fellow belligerents was his impassioned interest in the European vessels beginning to appear on the Pacific horizon. Where myopic tribesmen saw such vessels as a source of loot, to be left blazing after plunder, Hongi identified them as stockpiles of power. He promised their skippers a haven.

Among the many trade goods soon on offer to his people, in exchange for timber and tribeswomen, nothing took his eye more than the muskets the voyagers brandished and tended to discharge in fright. Hongi tested one on a slave to his satisfaction. As the echo of the shot faded, and the slave twitched on reddening sand, Hongi's thought was that the musket would prove a reliable means of showing time-tested enemies their place. Why labour at cracking open skulls — with all the punishing procedure of hand to hand duel — when powder and shot could do the work from a distance? As a warrior Hongi was bound to serve vengeance, more for insult than injury. Injury was of the flesh; insult was of the spirit. Injury might be repaired; insult was indelible. Ancestors had been mocked and shamed. New Zealand had a wealth of Maori who, in the near or far past, had called Hongi's tribe a collection of cowardly old women. There were those still bold enough to compare Hongi with a pig's arse. These Maori were now doomed. Any even tempted to think lukewarm of Hongi were to be unlucky.

Meanwhile Christian missionaries made a timely appearance with news of a faith asking peace and goodwill to all fellow humans. To the surprise of many, Hongi offered these sheepish arrivals his protection. Though not disposed to encumber himself with their faith, he worked them into his larger plan. Peace had its place in that programme. Serene missionary settlements meant more mariners calling. More mariners meant more muskets. Hongi had especial goodwill for men dealing in muskets.

His quest for mastery took him far. On missionary invitation he voyaged to England. In Cambridge, among awed scholars, he helped compile a Maori dictionary. In London he shook the hand of George IV. 'How do you do, Mr King George?' Hongi asked. 'How do you do, Mr King Hongi?' the King of England asked. Unable to resist the awkward question, Britain's monarch asked if Hongi was as much a cannibal as rumour said. Hongi cheerfully confirmed that such was sometimes the case. There was a long and shocked pause, with the lips of palace underlings pursed. Finally George IV beamed reassuringly. It was his understanding, he said, that British mariners, marooned after shipwreck, not infrequently made a nourishing meal of their own. That calmed matters considerably.

Made familiar with Hongi's needs, generous King George unveiled the royal armoury and presented his South Sea colleague with a suit of chain mail, a helmet, cutlasses, antique pistols, and muskets of historical character. Hongi would have preferred firearms in better working order but was gracious enough not to complain. Hongi proved a shrewd student of British culture and custom. The notion of monarchy intrigued him. So did British military organisation. He had much to reflect on during the return voyage to New Zealand. In Sydney, a few days' sail from home, he traded in most of his gifts for weapons of recent manufacture, and for reliable gunpowder. Missionaries reliant on Hongi turned a blind eye. They saw no inconvenience in an antipodean tyranny, and much gain; they would then treat tidily with one ruler, not with confusing tribal committees.

Home again, Mr King Hongi's acquisitions continued apace. When he tallied ten hundred muskets, he launched war. For tribal honour, or mana, he laid waste to fellow Maori most of the length of the North Island of New Zealand. Many rivals disappeared forever, their distinguished warrior lineages lost. As Hongi's volleys boomed across their shores, tribe after tribe was panicked into flight, or paralysed into unsuccessful submission. Panicked or paralysed, thousands perished. Those who survived battle were penned up for methodical slaughter, and finally consigned to earth ovens. Hongi worked as a terrier in sniffing out his foe. One hitherto invincible tribe fled the coast, as Hongi's armada closed with their territory, and set up an island bastion on a lake forty miles inland. That proved no problem to Hongi and his drilled executioners. They portaged their canoes up hill and down dale into the interior and, in one smoky morning's work, left the island lifeless. Yet poetic justice persists even in the unlettered antipodes. Injury rather than insult undid him; the man was flesh too. A stray shot through the lung lowered Hongi himself in the year 1827; he lingered on for another year with a whistling voice and a gift for anguished prophecy. His remaining enemies breathed again and embraced Christianity with fervour. Never in the Maori story had there been a warrior more formidable; never again would New Zealand know his peer.

Ferdinand Wildblood thought the tale too terrible to be borne; it lost him night after night of sleep. That was Henry Youngman's cue. While Ferdinand tossed, Henry turned. In the morning Henry was bright-eyed at his desk while bleary Ferdinand recuperated with coffee. *Death By a Thousand Muskets* was begun. This was not to be the work of a mere three or four weeks, like most Henry Youngman manuscripts. It was to be Henry's masterpiece in the genre he had fathered. The reader may conclude that Henry had by this time a life of his own. The reader would be right. Literary ambition had this far not been one of Henry's vices. Monetary return was more to the point. Baffled Ferdinand became a bystander, watching his former protégé succumb day by day to the sins of aestheticism. Henry's prose no longer ran amok; the search for the *mot juste* could lengthen excruciatingly. Most of a morning might pass in fashioning a phrase; even then it might be discarded as imperfect. Three or four weeks became three or four months, then three or four years. George Pettiworth was demented, with his largest money-spinner locked in the topmost reach of his ivory tower. Henry was not of a mind to placate his publisher with tales of a makeshift nature, as many another author might. Nothing but his best would satisfy him now. It was a relief to all concerned when Ferdinand judged the tale told. Even then, or until Ferdinand wrested the manuscript from him, Henry continued pecking away at it with his pen.

Ferdinand Wildblood could barely bring himself to read it. Worse, George Pettiworth was in difficulty too.

'Far be it from me to pass a verdict on the literary merit of this work,' he said. 'If anything, its calibre quickens my dismay.'

'Dismay, George?' Ferdinand and Henry alike were stunned.

'What am I to make of it?' our publisher pleaded. 'What, Wildblood?'

I shrugged.

'Even fiction must live within tolerable limits,' Mr Pettiworth pronounced.

'I can vouch for its truth, sir.'

'Even of such nonsense as a blood-crazed savage travelling twelve thousand miles to London to ask armaments of our late monarch?'

'Indeed, sir. And receiving them. There is not an incident confected.'

'Truth must sometimes be trimmed of its excesses, Wildblood. I see surfeit on every page. Besides which, I have found myself prey to nightmare while I pondered this manuscript.'

He shuddered impressively at the recollection.

'What are you telling me?' I finally asked.

'I thought never to hear myself say this,' Mr Pettiworth replied at length. 'It is an unhealthy book, Wildblood. Unhealthy; and base. I see no redeeming quality.'

'I regret that you find it so, George.'

'This Hongi Hika of yours, this Maori Napoleon — there is no way, I suppose, in which he might ask forgiveness toward the end of his intolerable tale?'

'In the eyes of heaven, baptised in the Christian faith?'

'Just so,' Mr Pettiworth agreed.

'Not without damage to truth, sir.' I felt obliged to demonstrate that Henry Youngman, however patchy his past record, also had principle.

'I feared as much,' Pettiworth said. 'I imagine you are familiar with the book that wretched fellow Fielding called *Tom Jones*.'

'I have perused it,' I admitted.

'You may not recall the consequences of its publication. London was shaken by earth tremors. There was only one construction to be placed upon that occurrence. Divine disapproval, Wildblood.'

'And you are suggesting an encore should my modest manuscript find print?'

'It is not for me to tell our Creator his business.'

There was a long pause.

'And you would prefer not to publish it?' I finally asked.

'I should prefer you not to press it upon me. We have had a satisfying partnership over recent years. May there be more.'

'I hear rejection,' I observed.

'Dejection,' he insisted. 'I have not been looking forward with enthusiasm to this conversation. I have been some days wrestling with my conscience.'

'I daresay,' I said. My publisher's tone suggested that his new sense of civic responsibility had a godly cause.

'Times are not as they were, Wildblood.'

'Indeed not,' I agreed, and fired a ranging shot. 'I am given to understand churches are filling again.'

'Some would say not before time. Society needs uplift.'

My range was accurate. The shot found him in his Sunday best.

'Elevation, I take it, is not to be found in Henry Youngman's new manuscript?'

'Not in any narrative which irresponsibly revels in human evil — without, that is, the promise of blessed deliverance.'

'Heathen life was never handsome,' I argued.

'Nonetheless,' Mr Pettiworth said.

That same day I parted company with Lovelady and Pettiworth and left the manuscript with a Soho publisher of lesser repute, but even better known for swindling his authors. On the strength of Henry Youngman's name this plebeian fellow was prepared to take it. 'On the other hand,' he warned, 'this kind of thing is going out of fashion.'

'Literature?' I asked.

'The exotic,' he said. 'The dark side of the globe is now known. There is no novelty. Imitators of Henry Youngman have seen to that.'

'Imitators?' I said weakly.

'By the score. The public has been sated. Where have you been living?'

A good question. Life with Henry left me with little time to contemplate the unsophisticated marketplace.

'A temporary eclipse,' I argued, 'is sometimes the fate of the literary pathfinder.'

So was daylight robbery.

The final and near fatal blow fell while *Death By a Thousand Muskets* was with the printer; it made the peril of earth tremors appear puny. Having imbibed hazardously, as had become their melancholy custom, Ferdinand and Henry were making heavy weather of their return home that summer dusk. A figure rose before them: an unkempt fellow, surely a beggar, with a hand outstretched. 'Sixpence for an old seafarer,' he suggested.

He was ignored. Such creatures could become a pestilence in our neighbourhood. As we passed him by, however, he said to our rear, 'A shilling, then.'

This reverse of beggarly routine was startling. We had to look back. It was a seasoned face we saw. There was polar storm in it, tropic sun, and the seven seas. The fellow's eyes weren't winning. His build was powerful, his tattooed arms bulky with muscle. His toothless smile was also far from friendly. What made him more unpromising was that he seemed to be sober.

'Try me with a pound,' he proposed, perhaps to confirm that we heard him right. Certainly to ensure that he had our attention.

We hesitated, Henry and I, and were lost.

'You'd be Henry Youngman, then,' the fellow observed, in displeasingly familiar tone.

It had to be hoped that Henry had a happy reader before him.

'Who asks?' I challenged.

The man mustered his breath.

'James Dinwiddie,' he said.

I trusted I had not heard right. 'Dinwiddie?' I said faintly.

'James Dinwiddie, the same. Don't pretend you never heard of me.'

It was most of a decade since the name had significance. On the other hand it was unforgettable. In Dinwiddie's indifferently plagiarised manuscript Henry Youngman had his gauche beginnings. I had once tried to persuade George Pettiworth — and myself, for that matter — that Dinwiddie was an untravelled Cotswolds clergyman with too much time on his hands. This was not proving the case. The unrefined rogue moving to bar our path home had certainly been south of Surrey. Plagiarist he may have been, but his salty appearance argued truth to his tale. Whether he was ever a ruthless warlord might be moot; his capacity for grievous bodily harm was not.

'What about *Monarch of Maoriland* then?' he challenged.

'Monarch of what?' I pleaded unhappily.

'You stole my yarn,' he asserted.

'Stole what?'

'My yarn. You, Henry Youngman.'

'I fear you have the wrong man,' I told him. 'My name is Ferdinand Wildblood. Ask after me in this vicinity, and my neighbours will be delighted to identify me as such. As it happens, I am indeed a literary fellow. But a poet, and the celebrated author of *London Lyrics*. Meanwhile I wish you well in your quest for Henry Youngman. Now do be a good fellow and stand to one side.'

Dinwiddie was slow to shift. He announced with menace, 'Don't think I'm fooled. Mr Pettiworth told me where to find you, what you looked like. A skinny and dreamy young fellow, he said, all arms and legs. And dressed, at his best, like a London rake.'

There was nothing in this description easy to refute.

'Mr Pettiworth told you this?'

'When I lifted him by the collar and backed him to his window.'

My position was no better. To my rear was low embankment wall and the Thames in high tide. There were no bystanders to heed my circumstances. Dinwiddie could deliver me to Neptune with no interference.

'Perhaps,' I suggested resourcefully, 'you could spell out the nature of your complaint more temperately. With more light shed on the subject I might even, who knows, be of assistance in locating the murky Henry Youngman.'

Dinwiddie remained all suspicion. Reluctantly, he said, 'Ten years ago I told the story of my life. I left it with Lovelady and Pettiworth. As things happened, I had business elsewhere.'

'I can see,' I ventured, 'that you are a man with more than one iron in the fire.'

'This business was in Van Diemen's Land,' he said.

That was no surprise. 'You were transported?' I said with polite interest.

'Ten years.'

'I am told Australia's penal colonies leave much to be desired.'

'There was two off for good behaviour. If I hadn't kept my nose clean I might never have known.'

'Known what, Mr Dinwiddie?'

'About *Monarch of Maoriland*,' he said. 'After I got my ticket of leave, I worked for a farmer back of Hobart. I had a hayshed for sleeping. The last fellow there had been a forger, a man with a great liking for words. He left some of his books behind. And there it was in a ragged cover. My story. Mine. Fancied up something foul by this Henry Youngman.'

I was about to object to this description of Henry's sprightly prose, but thought better. Dinwiddie was shaking with grievance.

'I don't mind telling you,' he whispered, 'that I never had a purpose in life to speak of. Not till that day. Then I did. On my honour I did.'

I was not one to dispute James Dinwiddie's intimacy with honour. 'And what,' I inquired sympathetically, 'was that?'

'To roast Henry Youngman's arse and fry his balls,' he said. 'That's when I've finished emptying the bugger's pockets.'

'I see,' I said.

'He must have made a mint from me,' Dinwiddie explained.

'Tragic,' I whispered.

'When I get him by the throat it will be time to talk tragic,' he announced.

No one could say Henry hadn't been warned.

'And you reckon you're not him?' he added.

'Mercifully,' I agreed.

'It would be a terrible thing to get the wrong man,' he confessed. 'It's not the noose that worries me. It's the thought of that thief walking free.'

Even vengeance, it seemed, had an Achilles heel. Meanwhile the thought of Henry walking free was also much on my mind.

'I suggest you pursue your enquiries in another location,' I said. 'The man must be known. London, intimidating though it may seem to a mariner, is just a large village.'

'I'll turn it upside down,' he promised. 'I'll shake him out.'

'It may be thirsty work,' I suggested. I opened my purse and removed several coins. 'Here,' I explained, 'is a pound to expedite creature comfort.'

He had no cavil with the sum offered. To ensure his continued serenity, I warmly added a few further shillings. My highly strung hands began acting of their own volition. More and more currency of the realm spilled from my purse and rolled free on the embankment. Dinwiddie gathered it up briskly.

'It's fair decent of you,' he said.

'My pleasure,' I claimed.

'And if you see Henry Youngman, you can tell him I'm coming for him. Maybe not today. Maybe not tomorrow. But one day.'

Henry was already under no misapprehension on that score.

Finally I shook hands with the wretch and, with a deep breath, walked clear. I tried not to look back. When I did, I saw Dinwiddie more or less as I had left him; he was regarding my rakish rear with wonder. When I looked back a second time, he seemed to have moved several paces in my direction. I sensed a man slowly succumbing to second thoughts. A third sighting of James Dinwiddie confirmed that he had begun to follow me with urgency. It was my luck that I had some fifty paces to the good. Nevertheless he was gaining. I soon had the impression that my feet were not touching ground, that I was more aerial than earthbound with James Dinwiddie in soaring pursuit. My home and castle lifted abruptly before me; the lock on my door magically opened with the first twist of key. I had barely time to bolt the door from within before Dinwiddie began to beat fervently upon it. If the truth be known, I collapsed to the floor in a flood of fright. Between assaults on my door Dinwiddie's heavy breathing could be heard; also messages for Henry.

'I should have bloody known,' he roared. 'I let my good nature get the better of me.'

Exhaustion worsted him in the end. After dark the blows on my door diminished; bitter shouts became hoarse whispers. Toward midnight both ended. I slept briefly and badly. To see what first light said, some fidgety hours later, I stealthily eased apart the curtains of my upstairs window. Daylight informed me that James Dinwiddie, now sitting wakeful on my step, was likely to become a lasting presence in my life. I coolly examined my situation. Common sense said I had the advantage, even under siege. Sooner or later Dinwiddie must defecate or doze, even seek liquid sustenance with my cash. At that point I could contrive an exit. But to where? Common sense also said that Dinwiddie, having been within reach of Henry Youngman's neck, was not one to give up the hunt now. He would turn London twice over in rage. There was no safety in the city.

'You see?' I said to Henry. 'You see what you've got us into?'

Henry's reply was indistinct.

'Think of something,' I urged.

If Henry had something in mind, he wasn't making it known.

'Look,' Ferdinand Wildblood said, 'you got us into this. You get us out.'

So far as Henry made his feelings plain, it was to the effect that this was not a fair statement of the position; Ferdinand had also had the pleasure of Henry's triumphs, over the years.

'Besides,' Ferdinand added unkindly, 'you're the one for high adventure. Mine is for the lyrical side of life, when you've allowed it. My sonnets are no help to us here. A modicum of your swashbuckling just might.'

I eased the curtains apart again. At that moment, some fifteen feet below, Dinwiddie heaved himself upright, yawned, and stretched. Then he let loose a lethal fart. Satisfying himself on that score, he resumed a fresh position on my step. I shuddered.

'Henry, old fellow,' Ferdinand announced. 'I have a surprise for you. New Zealand.'

Henry was pure panic. New Zealand?

'On the next free vessel.'

Henry refused to entertain this as a serious suggestion. Not even when I pointed out that the earnest gentleman at our front door meant to inconvenience us further.

It appeared that Henry had no objection to liberating himself discreetly from Dinwiddie. New Zealand, however, was taking things too far.

'Correct me if I'm wrong, Henry, but you have been heard claiming that no man in England knows New Zealand better.'

For narrative purpose, Henry had to agree.

For the first time in their liaison Ferdinand sensed that he had the upper hand. 'You may,' he surmised, 'soon have tales more trustworthy to tell.'

With, Henry protested, the Pacific out of fashion? Where was the future in it? Hadn't Ferdinand heard his pinch-penny publisher?

'Henry,' Ferdinand explained with patience, 'we are not talking literature. We are talking life.'

To confirm it, Dinwiddie began beating on the door again. Shouts rose too. Soon every resident in the street would be roused. It promised to be a long day. Henry ended his silence.

New Zealand, he appeared to agree, had something to be said for it.

Three

The *Integrity* was not the most comfortable vessel in maritime history, and far from the least leaky, but it had the virtue of sailing on an ebb tide from Tilbury an hour or two after I left my affairs in the hands of a lawyer and completed a small transaction with a gunsmith. Disadvantages were three. The *Integrity* was sailing only so far as Sydney. And it had a cargo of convicts. The third was that the corrupt skipper forced me to bid rashly for his only remaining accommodation, a rancid rabbit hutch of a cabin. He claimed to have my interests at heart. 'Our ship isn't for the likes of yourself, sir,' he announced.

'Meaning what?'

'A gentleman needs luxury, sir, and elegant company.'

'I remain the best judge of my need,' I told him. I noted that I was looking over my shoulder, watching for Dinwiddie to make a demonic appearance on the dockside. The largest need of my life was the *Integrity* under sail. My final offer won the skipper's approval. He pocketed my pound notes with a reluctant sigh. 'It's your funeral,' he warned.

'On the contrary,' I reported. 'A funeral is what it is not.'

I trod the port deck and looked toward the coast of England until it was a thin shadow on the horizon. Certainly until it was impossible for a hard-rowing Dinwiddie to manifest in a dinghy.

There was a presence at my shoulder. 'Excuse me, sir,' a voice said. Nervous by nature, and no less so of late, I tended to jump. Then I determined that the voice belonged to the pleasant-faced major in charge of the detachment of soldiery guarding the convicts. 'Cyprian Bridge of the Rutlandshire regiment,' he said, extending his hand. 'Her Majesty's 58th Regiment of Foot.'

'Ferdinand Wildblood,' I announced, 'late of London.' Henry Youngman might have been showier. It was my conviction, however, that Henry was better kept under lock and key for his own health.

I shook Major Bridge's hand warmly. I might be in need of a martial shield before the voyage was done. The skipper was scurvy company, and his cutthroat crew no better than the crop of bad apples they were shipping to Sydney.

'I had no notion,' Major Bridge said, 'that there was to be a civilian aboard the *Integrity*.'

'It is a surprise to me too,' I confessed. 'My decision to make the voyage was distressingly sudden.'

'It would have to be, if you'll forgive me saying so, a matter of life or death to make me choose this vessel.'

'Death, most certainly,' I agreed. 'I learned of a well-to-do bachelor uncle expiring in Australia, and of his sheep-grazed acres lacking an heir. It seemed tactful to pursue his acquaintance with urgency.'

I regretted the fiction. Major Bridge had an uncomfortably honest face. He was also gracious enough not to point out that a wait of a few days would have given me a vessel faster.

'The skipper,' he observed, 'is under the impression that you have a literary bent.'

'How so?' I said uneasily.

'He noted the number of books in your cabin, and not least what appears to be manuscript.'

The skipper was a spy, in brief.

'I dabble in the sphere of letters,' I admitted.

'Does that require you to be possessed of a two-barrelled pistol?'

'There is murderous malice and lethal envy in the literary world. Even men of small reputation must look to their rear.'

'To be frank,' the major said, 'our skipper is troubled. The pistol, which he asked me to confiscate, suggests that you may be a wolf in sheep's clothing. His urgent worry is that you may be of misguided humanitarian persuasion, a journalist determined to make much of the horrors of this vessel's business on the high seas. Of the convict traffic, in short. It would be harmful to him, and more so his employers, should that be the case. Indeed he is noticeably short-tempered about that prospect already.'

'And sent you to sound me out?'

'With no wish to. On the other hand it is better that such fears are aired sooner rather than later. It is a long voyage. On the open sea misfortune is never more than a minute away.'

'Especially in storm? With the cry of man overboard decidedly faint?'

'You take my meaning,' Major Cyprian agreed with relief. 'This, you must understand, is not a conversation of my making.'

Dinwiddie began to seem less objectionable company after all. I had no distinction as a swimmer.

'The skipper can rest easy,' I rather rushed to say. 'Be so good as to inform him that his apprehension is mistaken. My inclination is to compose pleasing verses rather than expose ugly scandal. My dreads are elsewhere, and of my own making.'

This was more than a breezy army man could hope to comprehend. Fortunately he didn't try.

'Good,' he said. 'My second chore is more agreeable. It is to invite you to mess with me, and my lieutenants, so long as the voyage lasts. I cannot guarantee the character of our victuals should search for wind lengthen intolerably; but even the least of our repasts should prove more civilised than those on the captain's table. He is never seen to nourish himself on more than biscuit and rum.'

'This is most generous of you,' I said.

'It is in our interest too,' Cyprian claimed. 'A little literary conversation will enliven days otherwise devoted to backgammon. We are keen readers, one and all, in our mess. If you're interested, I can lend you Henry Youngman's last.'

'I think not,' I was heard to say.

The happiest estimate for the Sydney journey was one hundred days. The unhappiest partook of eternity. The difference was not noticeable. Intestinal sorrow was rife. Seasickness was no respecter of reputation or rank. Henry Youngman was no hero on the high sea; he lived day to day in wordless misery. Even Ferdinand Wildblood had difficulty keeping his lyrical chin up as waves lofted giddily overhead. The skipper's appearances at the wheel were few and villainous; otherwise he trusted the fate of his ship to his mate. Underfoot there was low groaning from the embezzlers, pickpockets and harlots with whom the Australian colonies were soon to be seeded. In his few lucid moments, Ferdinand saw the voyage — and the vessel — as an instructive parable; civilisation was a patchy crust over a cesspit, and a literary gentleman off the beaten path chanced faecal matter on his footwear. Roaring Atlantic refused the *Integrity* a sighting of the Cape of Good Hope. It finished, in fact, on the wrong side of the ocean, putting in for repairs at Rio de Janeiro. The heat of the vessel mounted in those latitudes. Its timbers, long seasoned with shame and sorrow, gave up odours more rank. A number of our travelling companions, below deck, thought it time to terminate the voyage; they unhelpfully slipped their shackles and rioted. Major Cyprian established his martial proficiency by calling on his men to train their muskets in venomous fashion.

'Fire,' he said calmly, fighting not to avert his eyes.

Three dead and a dozen wounded made his point sufficiently. Flogging of survivors followed. Reburbished and replenished, the *Integrity* gulped up a kind wind and breezed out of Rio on to the world's wild highways again.

Major Cyprian, through the worst weather, seemed the soul of serenity, succumbing neither to *mal de mer* nor to malt whisky. I was therefore surprised, as the voyage resumed, to find him morose. Circumstances said he was entitled to a smile. As we closed with the Cape of Good Hope birdlife became plentiful; we sweetened shipboard routine with some shooting. Even a bag of three albatross and twice as many mollyhawk failed to gladden him. What weighed on Cyprian was his ancestry. For two centuries Bridges had been soldiers and sailors fighting Britain's battles. The gallantry of the Bridges, however, had come to a distinguished halt at Waterloo. That was thirty years past. There had been no worthy war since. In all the 58th Regiment, there were now no more than four or five grizzled rankers who remembered Napoleon's rout. And of officers, none but their decrepit and absentee colonel. The rest had never heard shot whistle wickedly overhead or ducked a deadly spear. This was true of moody Cyprian too. Without war a Bridge was an orphan. Cyprian had prayed for regimental posting of more combative character. Even garrison duty on a fever-ridden Indian frontier would be eligible, so long as there was promise of a fanatic uprising. He feared he would one day sell off his commission without sight of an acceptable foe or a tale to tell the sons of his sons.

'This,' he said in poor humour, training a fowling piece and tightening its trigger, 'is not my notion of soldiering.'

A further albatross thumped down on our deck.

Warmed by his claret, I saw fit to observe, 'You are telling me something.'

'This is a vile business,' he confided.

'This?' My mind on the ill-fated albatross, I imagined Cyprian might have recalled Coleridge's nautical rhyme and now be repenting.

'The transport of these wretches from one side of the earth to another. What end does it serve? What good?'

I sensed sedition, of sorts.

'It is not for me to say,' I replied warily.

'I am not a humanitarian, you understand,' he went on in lowered voice.

That was an unnecessary preface. I had seen him draw his sword and call up the volley in Rio.

'Indeed,' he added, 'it would be much the same to me if all wrongdoers went to the gallows. Humanitarianism is not, however, the point. Daily commerce with the criminal class is. The problem, Wildblood, is that we are soon degraded as much as they. Once proud soldiers of the line are made mere warders. Our regiment is debased. We are not serving honour.'

'I take your meaning,' I said.

'Filling Britain's scum with the Queen's lead is not honest soldiering. War would be a liberation. A fitting antagonist still more so.'

It was apparent that the Rio affray had not left him unscarred. At that moment Cyprian was so despondent that I wondered recklessly if he might enjoy Henry Youngman's company more than peaceful Ferdinand Wildblood's. Fortunately I thought better.

'What is it?' I asked. 'What really ails you?'

'That I have been twenty years in the army and have, for the first time, called upon my men to kill. Think on it. Have you heard a tale more absurd?'

'And this grieves you?'

'It torments me,' he owned.

'The thought of three rogues less in the world cannot rest on your conscience,' I argued. 'There is more to your mood.'

'The future,' he agreed. 'When the voyage is done, I take command of the 58th's headquarters in Sydney, thereby responsible for law and order in the colony of New South Wales until my colonel makes a creaky appearance. True that I will have generous quarters and as many convict servants as comfort requires. True also that I will have the company of my good wife, my dearest Louisa, when her vessel follows mine. Otherwise, Wildblood, I must expect more of the same. I see my fortieth year looming with no occasion for pride, soon my fiftieth and sixtieth too.'

I saw that as no cause for alarm. Save for some imperishable if so far unwritten sonnet, my own prospects were no more elegant. To my credit, however, I did my best to cheer Cyprian as we investigated another bottle of claret.

'Think more of your lovely Louisa,' I urged.

That failed to extinguish his mood. It tended to fan it.

'I do,' he grieved. 'Dear God I do. There are times, I confess, when I cannot get enough of her.'

'And she, perhaps, of you,' I said shrewdly.

'Her demeanour often suggests it,' he allowed.

'All to the good,' I said, not without envy. 'She would surely prefer a loving husband to a deceased hero.'

Cyprian chose not to hear. He was placing shot in the path of another albatross.

It was our fortieth day at sea. We had ninety more.

I would be last to deny Sydney Cove a picturesque aspect, with its inlets, islands, and bizarre specimens of tree. But human handiwork, thus far in its history, fell short of enchanting. Its buildings were random and mostly of rock; streets straggled and often, on close acquaintance, gave up the ghost. It was as if a gang of drunken stonemasons had been launched on the land. Terra Australis was not for the likes of me, nor for Henry. This was confirmed when I walked the town the morning after our arrival. James Dinwiddie seemed to grin at me from every corner, from every shop door. Sydney was filled with facsimiles of the fellow. Tattooed arms and toothless smiles advertised men lately freed from convict irons. It was not a restful morning. What made it worse was the thought that Dinwiddie might have already have picked up my spoor. My leisurely voyage out made it possible for him to be awaiting my arrival. Thus it was that I walked back to the *Integrity* in rising alarm. I did my best to conceal my state from Major Cyprian. Fortunately he was preoccupied with ridding the vessel of his unwholesome charges and sprucing up his sea-weary soldiers so that they might do credit to the 58th as they marched through the streets of Sydney.

Before we parted, however, he remembered to present me with my sequestered pistol. 'I trust you will never need this,' he said with some emphasis.

'The need may have gone,' I informed him. 'I suspect literary commentators and penny-a-line assassins are thin on the ground in this hemisphere.'

'Look me up when you have won the heart and fortune of your

ailing relative,' he urged. 'Perhaps we can kill a few kangaroo together.'

My lie involved me in further fabrication.

'I have just had the worst of news,' I reported. 'It seems he expired while I was at sea. His land and lucre have fallen into the hands of the London whore who kept house for him.'

'See a lawyer,' Cyprian suggested.

'I think not,' I said.

'Why not?'

'I have a philosophic nature,' I claimed.

'So you will take a boat home?'

'Not in haste. I am tempted to prolong my stay in this vicinity. I think, for example, that I might contemplate New Zealand at close quarters before succumbing to civilisation again. It may mean only another week under sail.'

'New Zealand?' Cyprian's face evinced no enthusiasm.

'What is the matter?'

'It is surely no place for a poet,' he said.

'On the contrary,' I said. 'I see a place of rough-hewn character ready to be awoken to rhyme.'

'What does that mean?' he asked with awe.

'A land awaiting a scribe,' I interpreted.

'You should read Henry Youngman,' he said.

I was tempted to familiarise earnest Cyprian with the facts of the matter.

'Why?' I asked.

'He's done it already,' Cyprian said.

Four

Less than a fortnight later I watched New Zealand mounting moist from the ocean in the cool light of dawn. This loneliest of lands had much in its favour. Dinwiddie was not an imaginative man; he would never fancy Henry Youngman fleeing to the locale which engendered their misunderstanding. I might never have to defend my person with a pistol; my family jewels were surely less at risk here than in any other earthly venue.

My exhilaration rose as we closed with the coast and skirted New Zealand's northernmost limb. No matter that Henry had often elaborated, in his heartiest prose, on such a scene. It was a morning of music — of mysterious mists, crying seabirds and wave-lapped wilderness — fashioned for Ferdinand Wildblood. I regretted only that I no longer had Major Cyprian on hand, an intimate with whom I might share finer feelings. My rum-swilling shipboard companions were indifferent to the spectacle unfurling to starboard. Indeed they appeared to scorn it.

'New Zealand,' one lucid voice said. 'Who sodding needs it now?'

I might have informed him that I sodding did, rather direly. Events, however, were to prove I was missing his point.

Next day we were sailing into the Bay of Islands. It needed no introduction either. Henry had made much of its merits as a sanctuary for seafarers. All the world's navies could shelter there safely, and most of the planet's merchantmen too. Lofty hills soared all about, arcadian coves, and islets dripping with spray. Furthermore it was the busy setting of *The Belle of Blackguard Beach*. For three decades the Pacific's mighty whaling fleets had moored off Blackguard Beach (otherwise known as Kororareka). They had taken paradise by storm, providing custom for booze dens and bawdy houses, and sin for the missionary mill. It was toward this corner of the vast Bay we were now proceeding. There was more reason for *déjà vu* as wave-whitened reefs and rocky capes rippled past. This was also the realm of Hongi Hika. In this marine Eden the Maori Napoleon had mustered his warriors and weapons. It was here his war canoes had sailed south to serve death as maligned ancestors required. Even Ferdinand Wildblood could not resist a twinge of nostalgia. Henry, revived by the powerful whiff of terra firma, was a wistful spectator too. In his mind's eye were canoes powered by a hundred paddles and club-wielding commanders calling the beat. Such visions may not have been vouchsafed to ordinary mortals. So much for ordinary mortals. Henry Youngman was home.

Leaving large vistas astern, we rounded a headland and there Blackguard Beach was, or should have been. The first surprise was that the mild waters of the haven ahead were not packed with the Pacific's whalers. There was a storm-battered barque or two, and a solitary schooner moored offshore. The settlement itself was a medley of cottages and huts. There were dinghies and canoes hauled up on the shore. But where were the roistering crewmen, where the rowdy grog-shops, the gaming dens, the bustling houses of ill repute, the tribesmen making wily deals on muskets? There were no bold Maori tribeswomen diving into the tide and swimming out to us with promise of pleasure. Indeed there was little depravity of any kind noticeable ahead. The ship's anchors hit water and chains rattled away. A stroller on the foreshore paused to consider our arrival, yawned, and walked on. The place had all the zest of a righteous Welsh village on a wet Sunday. Henry was dumbfounded by the lack of pandemonium, and Ferdinand no more articulate.

Finally he turned to the Yankee bosun. 'What,' he managed to ask, 'has happened here?'

'Happened?'

'To Blackguard Beach.'

'That's what's bloody happened,' said the bosun.

He nudged Ferdinand's gaze higher. Above the settlement, on a hill of some substance, a Union Jack drifted from a flagstaff. Ferdinand was slow seeing its significance.

'Civilisation,' the surly bosun said. 'Customs duties. That's bloody what. The place has been priced out of business. Skippers don't call.'

Ferdinand felt Henry's quiver of indignation.

'You are telling me,' Ferdinand ventured, 'that Blackguard Beach is no more?'

'A long time no bloody more,' the bosun said.

'There is something amiss here,' Ferdinand argued, on Henry's behalf.

'What's amiss,' insisted the bosun, 'is that flag.'

'It can seldom have flown on so picturesque a promontory,' Ferdinand suggested.

'It's buggered the Bay,' the bosun averred. 'When the Maoris was running the place we knew where we stood. Five pounds for anchorage and protection.'

'What is so different? Is the Bay not still in their care?'

The bosun gave Ferdinand a withering stare and spat to starboard. 'Where,' he asked, 'have you been?'

It was soon plain. Where Henry and Ferdinand had been was lost in Henry Youngman's noisy narratives. We were deaf to the fact that there was a bona fide New Zealand in business elsewhere. This New Zealand, as distinct from the land of Henry's remunerative fancies, had been four years ceded to Britain by Maori chieftains; they had appended their signatures or marks to a treaty which granted them the rights of British subjects and promised protection from predatory outsiders. Had we read *The Times*, perhaps, we should have been better prepared for the law-abiding vista before us. But Henry and I were not noticeably afflicted by the outer world when Henry was telling a tale. So here we sea-wearily were. We had rounded the planet to be enlightened by a foul-mouthed bosun when twopence worth of London print might have told us as much.

'Are you giving me to understand,' I asked, 'that New Zealand is a colony now?'

'Understand what you like,' the bosun replied in even poorer temper. 'It's no odds to me.'

'I fail to see the appurtenances of British government,' I protested.

'There's the flag,' he said irritably.

'But where is the governor's residence? Where the aides, the offices, the edifices of imperial rule?'

The bosun, who knows with what justice, was observing me even more leerily. 'That's because there aren't any, are there?'

'No?'

'They farted off south as soon as they got their treaty signed. They reckoned the Bay of Islands too far out on a limb to govern the country proper. And too full of bloody Maoris. You want the governor, you go to Auckland. That's where the best people are. The governor, the ladies and gents.'

'Auckland?'

'The capital. Two hundred miles south.'

I felt a powerful melancholia coming on.

'You want to go ashore?' the bosun asked. 'Or do you want to bugger about?'

The latter was uninviting; I was going ashore. At the least an amiable tavern might help Henry and me contemplate our diminished circumstances. A whaleboat manned by muscular locals put out from the beach. Half the oarsmen were of brown hue, their faces ferociously tattooed. There was no mistaking them. After years of literary sport with their race we were seeing our first Maori tribesmen. A decade or two earlier such a sight would have occasioned a voiding of bowels. Meanwhile sighing Henry was counting the losses rather than the gains of antipodean civilisation. Brawny oarsmen, addressing their obscenities to all and sundry, were no substitute for Maori temptresses frolicking about our vessel.

My situation was sundry. The barefoot oarsmen thumped aboard, manhandling my trunks down to their craft, and as robustly disposing of me over the side; I swung perilously on a rope ladder, finding poor grip, until a couple of fierce creatures with potent breath took me in charge as I dropped. My ducking was slight. The timbers of the whaleboat did me more damage as I was dumped aboard. Henry appeared to be informing me that I was making a scene of myself. By the time I retrieved my wits the oarsmen were closing with the shore and beaching their boat. It cannot be said that Henry and I voluntarily kissed New Zealand soil as we staggered the last yards to land. Presently the shore ceased to sway; the scene before us settled. Palm, fern and salt-loving coastal vegetation — not to speak of the human prospect — said we were at world's end. At the least we were a long way from London's homely version.

'Say hello, Henry,' I urged.

Henry's first need was liquor. The grog-houses offered small choice. All were empty and quiet. All were makeshift, dim and dirty. All retailed rum of a colonial kind. We settled on the least joyless. Mine host was a bulky man by name of Turner, a pockmarked individual with a ruffian's laugh. There was no mistaking him for anything but another boorish graduate of Australia's criminal academies.

'You looking to settle?' he asked.

'Certainly to find my land legs,' Ferdinand informed him. 'After that my plans are, shall we say, in the lap of the gods.'

'What's your business?' he asked.

'Of a sedentary nature,' Ferdinand admitted.

'What would that mean, then?'

'Pushing a pen rather than a plough,' Ferdinand explained.

'You'd be a clerk, then,' Turner decided.

'I write in a fair hand,' Ferdinand agreed. 'I take dictation, and can even turn a phrase of my own.' This was not untrue. He saw no point in alarming Turner further.

'Lucky for you,' Turner scowled. 'You might have a future.'

'You are overly sombre,' Ferdinand concluded. 'Am I to understand that others do not?'

'Not around here. See for yourself.'

'You're talking Queen Victoria,' Ferdinand suggested, 'and colonial rule.'

'I'm talking turnip heads,' Turner said. 'Bastards buggering up a good country.'

'I take it you mean missionaries,' Ferdinand said.

'And fools in naval uniform sent out to govern this place. Honourable willies who think they know what's best for the Maori.'

'And you do, sir?'

'I ought to,' Turner said. 'I bloody married one.'

He made a stiff-armed gesture which could not be interpreted as other than lewd.

Though Henry appeared to be getting the taste for it, the rum was failing to clarify Ferdinand's situation. 'I have the impression, Mr Turner, that I know what is best for me. At the head of my list is a bed not hostage to the sea's commotion. Perhaps you could suggest a reputable inn near at hand?'

'I got a bunk in a back shed,' Turner revealed.

Next morning Ferdinand woke to pure Pacific sky beyond murky window with the impression that his situation was similarly scrambled. (Henry, slow recovering from single-handed debauch, had nothing notable to contribute.) On the one hand it was necessary to keep a distance from Dinwiddie so long as the fellow remained out of countenance. On the other it was desirable that, if only for Henry's sake, this excursion be made productive. Sauced with the authentic, served up as new, Henry's South Sea tales might even enjoy a fresh vogue. Certainly something useful should be salvaged from this geographical jumble. But where to begin?

With Turner, perhaps.

Breakfast was greasy bacon and greasier eggs served up by Turner's ungraciously cursing Maori wife in a kitchen reeking of pig fat. Grim Turner found rum a helpful condiment in combating his wife's culinary excess. Overcoming his personal nausea — hungry Henry, further down his alimentary tract, having no such problem — Ferdinand swallowed food with difficulty and managed to say, 'It is time to be honest with you, sir. My arrival here is no accident.'

That gambit made no impression. Morose Turner barely looked up from his plate. His wife slammed mugs of questionable tea on the table.

'No?' Turner finally grunted.

'The fact is, sir, that I may not be as I seem. I am no gentleman adventurer in the South Sea. No dilettante traveller.'

'Is that what you seem?' Turner said.

'I may well leave that impression.'

'It never crossed my mind,' Turner confessed, and gustily slurped down tea. 'I was worried you was a new bugger from the government. A spy here to see who's smuggling what.'

This failed to humble Ferdinand. 'In that case it is desirable that there is no further subterfuge on my part. The fact is, Mr Turner, that I am a poet.'

Turner was uneasy. 'A poet?'

'Just so.'

'I suppose it's better than a fucking forger,' Turner decided.

That was close to the bone, Henry's literary career considered. On the other hand it was neither the time nor place to let Henry loose on New Zealand.

'Furthermore,' Ferdinand went on, 'I have a long unslaked fascination with the antipodes.'

'With the antiwhat?'

'With New Zealand.'

'Why didn't you say so? It's got a name.'

'The furthest place on this planet deserves a designation better than that unimaginatively left by a fearful Dutch discoverer.'

'Is that right?' Turner asked, with small show of curiosity.

Ferdinand persevered. 'I am here for my health. In particular, Mr Turner, I am looking for creative refreshment. Others might style it inspiration.'

Turner wasn't styling it anything. 'What's it to me?' he said with unease.

'I should be obliged if you were to point me in the right direction,' Ferdinand proposed.

'And what direction would that be?'

'I am, for example, interested in those whose warrior domain this was. Not least in those who inherit the cloak of such as the proud and fierce Hongi. I am interested in the tales told and songs sung. Legend and lore are food and drink to the poet.'

'Bugger me dead,' Mr Turner exclaimed. He spilled tea down his front and rose with a roar.

'Something troubles you,' Ferdinand deduced.

'Better a government bastard,' Turner explained, spluttering away from the table.

Ferdinand thought it timely to walk Blackguard Beach and take stock of this once notorious niche of New Zealand. The atmosphere of this erstwhile hell-hole was dauntingly sanitary. The sun was bright, the air autumnally brisk. Dogs barked, pigs grunted, and fowls squawked. There were few other sounds of commerce with the morning. Fishermen were putting out nets. A dinghy was ferrying artisans out to a vessel in need of repair. Architecturally the town gave itself few airs. Some cottages were neat, with well-groomed gardens, and roses wrapped round their front doors. Others were prematurely decrepit. There was a simple wooden church, with a churchyard already in business; rough stones and crude crosses told of drowned mariners and infants early in the arms of Jesus. It proved as spirited a location as any in the village. Ferdinand felt Henry's candid yawn rise within him. Henry unfairly appeared to be holding Ferdinand responsible for their present plight.

Wait, Ferdinand suggested.

For more of the same? Henry asked.

It was a fair question. Admitting defeat, Ferdinand directed himself toward Turner's unkempt establishment again. As fortune arranged it, another lone figure lifted from the shore, a stolid and bespectacled individual in clerical black with a collar in keeping. Freshly arrived by water, he carried dripping seaboots in one hand, a leather-bound Bible in the other. Despite these impediments he was advancing diligently on Ferdinand. Ferdinand looked left and right and saw nowhere to flee. He endeavoured to put a pleasant face on the encounter as they closed.

'I heard rumour of an arrival on yesterday's vessel,' the fellow said, with unpromising vigour. 'You must be the new face in our community.'

'The name is Wildblood, sir,' Ferdinand confessed.

'And mine is Williams,' the fellow said, adding needlessly, 'The Reverend.'

As we shook hands I was obliged to stifle Henry's heartfelt groan. The Reverend Williams pressed on.

'Idle curiosity brings few to the Bay of Islands now,' he said. 'I take it you have business here.'

'Of sorts,' I agreed with decent reticence.

'Perhaps of mercantile nature?'

'To be honest, sir, no.'

'A pity,' said Williams. 'A man of commercial acumen might give this neighbourhood interest in life. Perhaps even save it.'

'I should have thought saving was more in your line of work, Reverend.'

'The salvation I offer, Mr Wildblood, is a long term affair. I speak of the short. Material welfare, in missionary endeavour, must go hand in hand with the spiritual. Faith is no lasting substitute for a full belly.'

'Why not,' I asked riskily, 'leave things as they are, sir? Or were?'

'You mean leave this land full of dangerous heathen?'

'On the extreme view of things. My understanding is that the natives of these islands formerly lacked nothing in nourishment.'

'Of an often unspeakable kind,' Williams pointed out.

'That might be seen as a matter of taste,' I argued, or perhaps Henry. 'In their eyes we may have customs as foul. Young felons dancing on a rope's end are not an elevating spectacle.'

Though given pause, Williams was unwilling to agree. He sighed, 'Do you think, Mr Wildblood, that I have not — in my larger moments of despair — contemplated the self-same question? That it might have been better for all concerned had these islands never been discovered? I am not unfamiliar with the notion of the noble savage. If nothing else, it is well-meaning. It takes a charitable view of mankind. But let me tell you, sir, it is no help to us here. These islands have been discovered. The sweets of civilisation have been tasted by its inhabitants. They wish iron and steel; they wish the wheel and the written word. They wish our medicines, our agriculture, our clothing.'

'And the musket,' I interposed stealthily.

'The recent past was unfortunate,' Williams allowed. 'We must trust old grievances buried, the scars of battle healed. With God's grace the worst is past.'

'How far past?' I inquired.

'A year. Hardly more.'

My interest quickened. 'In this locality?'

'Virtually in view of this shore. It was boisterous but mercifully lacking in corpses. In short, there was more shouting than shooting. It encouraged the hope that the warrior spirit may be on the wane among my parishioners.'

'But there was battle.'

'Indeed,' Williams said.

Just a year gone? All was not lost; there was hope for Henry still.

'The cause?' I enquired. 'Women or land?' Henry's encyclopaedic knowledge of New Zealand was helpful here; these were the most revered motives in the Maori code.

'Land, in one sense,' Williams said cautiously.

'In another?'

'The hot-heads of one tribal group contested sale of land to the government by another. The latter took the unhelpful view that it was theirs to sell.'

'My sympathies are somewhat with the hot-heads,' I confessed.

Williams, perhaps not surprised, was wary.

'My understanding,' I explained, again exploiting Henry's bookish knowledge of the subject, 'is that there is a sacred bond between the savage and his soil. Once lost to outsiders, the bond is broken, the spirit of the land flown. I take it that the former wished the land to remain in Maori hands.'

'In an ideal world, perhaps so.'

'Meaning?'

'Their wish was for a share in the proceeds.'

'For mere monetary gain?'

'Alas,' Williams said. 'The noble savage is now an accomplice of Mammon.'

I left Henry to accommodate this. I pressed cordially on. 'All the same, sir, it is good to see things of the spirit watered and tended in this forsaken spot.'

'Forsaken is the word,' the Reverend Williams said. 'The government is not only indifferent to our situation. It daily worsens it. First customs duties which deter shipping and mean no market for Maori vegetables and meat. Then a decree against the indiscriminate felling and sale of timber, which provided much employment. To the fury of many Maori, the Governor sees the forest as a resource to be harvested with discretion. As salt in the wound, a needy Maori now finds he cannot sell off fertile acres to arriving colonists. Such sale can only be made to the colonial government. The notion is to protect innocent natives from the unscrupulous.'

'A worthy notion, if I may say so.'

'It would be as well not to say so loudly, Mr Wildblood. The problem is that the government shows disinclination to buy a square foot of local soil. Resentment is rife. Maori cannot sell their produce, their labour, timber or land. Some villages are sinking into dire poverty. Chiefs with once respectable appearance are falling back on old blankets and native mats as garb. Small wonder that such as John Heke have begun to flourish.'

'John Heke, sir?'

'A rowdy young man, and a sore trial to us all. Though the first to sign the treaty in question, he now fires up his neighbours with the assertion that Maori are no longer their own masters, with fewer and fewer rights in the land of their fathers.'

'John Heke,' I said thoughtfully.

'That is correct.'

'I shall remember the name, sir, should it prove necessary to keep a distance.'

'Pray do,' Williams urged.

'Meanwhile I trust that missionaries prevail upon Providence to smile,' I suggested.

'Missionaries must,' he sighed.

I made my way back to Turner's establishment. Turner, as unlovely as ever, made an appearance as I approached.

'I been thinking over what you said,' he reported.

'Enlighten me,' I suggested. 'What did I say?'

'About what you was wanting of the Bay of Islands, and Hongi and all.'

'And what is your thought, Mr Turner?'

'You might be looking for John Heke.'

'Remarkable you should mention it,' I said.

Five

I know what catchpenny chroniclers say. I know what inky historians will. In setting this down, four decades on, it is not my intention to sacrifice good drinking time merely to corroborate the lacklustre fancies of others. At my advanced station in life drinking time is precious; I can count few years of it left. What sobers me undesirably is duty to the dead. They are all gone now, all those who have begun peopling these pages or are preparing to: the rebel John Heke, the Reverend Williams, the execrable Turner, and not least that honest toiler in martial fields named Cyprian Bridge. Even those who have yet to leap all too human from my pen are long in the grave: such as Kawiti the last pagan (alias the Duke), the despairingly gallant Philpotts and the disgraceful Despard. The battlefields which rang with their gunnery and their homicidal cries are now empty of all but English grass and grazing beasts. New Zealand is no longer a land lost in Oceania's mists. The new species of steamer on the route means a voyage of no more than four or five weeks. My former and much mourned acquaintance Anthony Trollope, a visitor to the colony before his demise, informed me that all the conveniences of civilisation welcome the traveller in that once unruly corner of Victoria's realm: clubs of more than mediocre quality, grand houses with ballrooms, and oysters and champagne. He noted that even the meanest towns had libraries where books by Carlyle, Dickens and Macaulay (and of course A. Trollope) might be found much thumbed. The populace, he also reported, is most gratifyingly British, rather more John Bullish than John Bull. The Britannic lion has not roared there in vain. 'All good things have been given to this happy land,' he wrote. 'When the Maori has melted, here will be the navel of the earth.'

Melted? I never saw the inhabitants of that warrior land as likely to liquefy. And the navel of the earth? I could nominate another aperture. But it is not for me to belabour the distinguished dead of my profession.

What of the less distinguished? What of such as James Dinwiddie and Henry Youngman? Though I have often imagined his bones dwindling in convict quicklime, Dinwiddie's demise cannot be verified. Henry, on the other hand, manages a phantasmal existence. I have felt him nostalgically looking over my shoulder as I pen this memoir. Otherwise his narratives are sometimes to be found shop-soiled in the bargain stalls of booksellers along the Charing Cross Road. Threadbare bindings ensure that they will know no further posterity.

Autumn sunset colours my window. It tells me that it is time to take my usual and comfortably cushioned hansom cab to my club, past homeward crowds and the bright braziers of chestnut sellers. Before I dispatch my first brandy let me say this. The melancholy fact is that when I first met him John Heke, for all his reputation as a malcontent, didn't have an uprising to his name. He was a rebel without a rebellion, a warrior without a war. He spent his best years looking for both. And when he had his heart's wildest wish he failed to see what he could do with it. Let truth make a showing. I still lament that warloving lad whose affection was never reciprocated.

According to the best information available John Heke presently sulked inland, beyond the Bay's salty shallows. 'Look for a good place to make trouble,' Turner advised. 'That's where the loud-mouth will be.' I was no authority on places to make trouble, nor necessarily in search of them, but New Zealand was never for the faint-hearted. Henry warmed to my bold decision to know Heke better. The day following my first brackish sample of Blackguard Beach I found an unenthusiastic Maori boatman prepared to transport me a mile or two up the Bay for a sum which might have bought me half a passage to London. If I couldn't afford it, he said, it was all the same to him; he didn't want to go anywhere. I found I could afford it.

Midway across the water, with my companion still lacking interest in the enterprise, I ventured, 'Tell me about John Heke.'

'Who?'

'Heke. John.'

That brought him to life. 'That bugger,' he said.

I thought not to pursue the matter. He, however, did.

'What do you want to know about him for?' he asked.

'I hear much of the man,' I explained.

'Much?'

'To his discredit. I thought another view helpful.'

'He is noise,' the fellow said.

'Noise?'

'Noise.' My taciturn confidant, after an uncivil grunt, failed to enlarge on that judgement.

At least opinion in the Bay was undivided on the audibility of John Heke.

My boatman's leaky sailing dinghy left me damp-footed on a long strip of sand backed by more durable dwellings than Blackguard Beach boasted. There was a conspicuous church and a barn of a building alongside. Within, the zealous singing of psalms informed me that I was in the vicinity of the village school. I had been inconsiderately deposited on devout terrain; I was in a mission community. All the scene lacked was a missionary. The Reverend Williams's impeccable sense of timing made good the lack. He lodged in the corner of my right eye, refusing to budge as I endeavoured to drift away from the settlement on a port tack. He was not alone. Walking with him was a young woman sedately English in dress, rather prettily bonneted. Her face, nonetheless, was Maori.

Williams hailed me, of course. I pushed my slow feet toward him. His dusky companion hung back as he moved on me with fervour.

'This is a pleasing surprise, Mr Wildblood,' he told me. 'You are wasting no time making yourself familiar with our corner of the colony.'

'Beguiling as the Bay of Islands is from sea level, sir, I require an inland perspective on the place.'

'To what end?' Williams inquired.

'I cannot keep a secret long,' I confessed. 'The fact is, sir, I am a literary man. I imagine I may, as is my nature, one day pen impressions of this sublime locality.'

There was a subterranean sigh from Henry.

'In what form?' Williams asked.

'Who knows, sir? Perhaps a stanza of verse. Perhaps a paragraph of prose. Perhaps something more substantial.'

Williams puzzled. 'The name Ferdinand Wildblood is not familiar,' he decided.

'It promises to be. Even my least generous critics allow that I have a powerful sense of vocation.'

'Hence today's excursion?'

'I have hopes of hiring a horse this side of the Bay and pushing further.'

Fast, Henry instructed me.

'One might be arranged at no expense to yourself,' Williams said.

'That is most handsome,' I said.

'Meanwhile you must meet my god-daughter. Come, Angela. Say hello to Mr Wildblood of London.'

The girl moved nearer. 'Hello Mr Wildblood of London,' she said rather winningly. She performed a surprisingly proficient curtsy.

'Angela,' Williams explained, 'is by far the most agreeable of my charges in the Bay. She has been in my physical and spiritual care since her christening. Her parents, I regret to say, perished pagan in a measles plague. On the other hand the joy is that she demonstrates what, in Christ's care, a Maori might be.'

She did indeed. Her cool grace was worthy of a native-born Englishwoman. Though not necessarily unfriendly, her eyes were those of a woman easier wooed than won. Certainly she was determined not to be impressed by Ferdinand Wildblood of London. She was perhaps in her twenties, and, so far as her garments allowed a view of the matter, of pleasing form. She was also familiar. She was the ethereal belle of Blackguard Beach in the flesh. Life, in its pedestrian fashion, was again aping art.

Meanwhile Williams was waiting on my approval.

'My congratulations, sir,' I said. 'It is worth voyaging twelve thousand miles to set eyes on so elegant a creature.'

My gaze roved back to his ravishing god-daughter. I was stunned and unmanned. Angela was no longer a model of rectitude and refinement. Her faint smile had taken on a cheeky twist. Her eyes were bold and candidly Maori and making no secret of their interest in a footloose Londoner. All nonchalance was gone; I had never seen a more provocative face. Then I understood. Henry was pirating my powers of perception, seeing a female more to his need than my maiden. While I viewed the belle of Blackguard Beach he saw a siren of a savage shore. To be fair — though I fail to see why I should be — we had been months in the loveless company of hairy mariners and were thus more than a little excitable. Angela might have left my heart *hors de combat*; she had won rather more of Henry's anatomy. Was I expected to play dispassionate chaperon?

'Perhaps tea?' Williams asked. 'My residence is near.'
I hesitated.
Yes, Henry urged.
'How could I say no, Mr Williams?' I replied.

More of the day than I might have wished was then given to social intercourse. Tea was presented in the best of bone china; there were wholesome mission scones lavishly buttered. Angela flitted about silently and efficiently. The occasion was free of incident, other than when, taking further stock of her form, I reached clumsily for cup and saucer; and found both beyond reach in a tide of tannin. She mopped up the moisture deftly; that chore brought her in proximity to my outlying limbs. For a moment her gaze met mine. Mine? Henry's. She found cause to dab solicitously at spots of tea left on my trouser legs. It was her accomplishment, within minutes of a most innocent encounter, to see that there was more to Ferdinand Wildblood than met the eye.

Reverend Williams, more ponderously, seemed to suspect as much too. 'Surely, Mr Wildblood,' he said, 'you have not come to this outpost of England merely to meditate on the making of literature?'

'Literature is where one finds it,' I proposed. 'I have reason to think less of worth is produced in the fleshpots of civilisation than is commonly thought. Besides, who knows that this far colony will not need a poet to celebrate its finer qualities in decades to come?'

'A poet. Here, sir?'

'And why not?' I argued.

'We have enough of that kind of thing at home,' Williams said.

I was perplexed. 'Meaning what, sir?'

'Meaning I see no call for it here.'

I affected dismay. 'No?'

Williams became even more terse. 'I have some feeling for my native flock, Mr Wildblood. Enough corruption has beached here without exposing them to more. Better that latter-day Lord Byrons, with their unnatural loves and offensive vices, linger in London.'

'You appear to be telling me that you have no large liking for literature, sir.'

'I see myself as in service to the Author of All Things,' he explained.

'As his publisher, sir?'

'So to speak. I like to see this land as the finest in his collected works. May it remain immaculate.'

'Let me race to reassure you, sir. There is nothing of the unnatural in my sentiments; my vices are of a small and commonplace kind.'

'That is as may be,' Williams said. 'Yet the fact is that by your example you could encourage others to follow. It might become a fashion.'

'There are the seven seas to say otherwise. The *longueurs* of shipboard life do not lend themselves to song.'

'Am I free to deduce, then, that you are talking of extended residence?' Williams asked.

'I have not given thought to its duration,' I asserted.

If Dinwiddie died, on the other hand, it could be of remarkably brief character. But how, beached here, would I know? Meanwhile I rose to my feet. 'You mentioned an available horse,' I recalled, fearing that Williams might now have second thoughts.

'Indeed,' Williams said. 'And how far do you plan riding?'

'I anticipate no long exertion.'

'Dark could catch you early,' Williams said. 'What then?'

'I daresay I might, with promise of remuneration, find some well disposed Maori to give me lodging.'

'And you might not,' Williams said. 'You are aware, of course, that John Heke presides inland.'

'That is my understanding,' I confessed.

'He is lawlessly exacting a toll on travellers through his territory. My blunt advice is to put on a brave face and pay up. He is looking for provocation. Life is hazardous enough in this colony without giving Heke new cause for offence.'

'Are you talking conflict, sir?'

'I am talking commotion, Mr Wildblood. Fortunately most tribesmen side with common sense rather than Heke. They are not unanimously of the opinion that Britons need to be put in their place. They fear fray with rival tribesmen more. Queen Victoria's annexation of these islands may be a mixed blessing, but it does foster peace between Maori and Maori.'

'Your warning is appreciated, sir.'

'It is needed,' Williams said.

I made my goodbyes. 'I hope I may take advantage of your company again soon,' I told Angela.

Her face was aloof, her smile small and reserved. Henry could make what he liked of that; he was never apologetic about taking advantage.

I rode inland under noon sky. The route to the interior, rutted by wagons, was largely uphill, winding among scraggy vegetation, charred stumps and patchily pastoral land. The lone jewel in this prospect was a body of water hurtling down from the hills and fanning out over a precipice in silky tapestry. There were bold rocks at its foot, ferns shiny in a faint mist of spray. It was a flawless setting for lovers. Needless to add, I had myself in mind as one of the parties; Angela, even if late met, seemed admirably suited as a companion in bliss. Otherwise it was a dull-coloured journey. Sight of other travellers would have been welcome. Not even a footsore native was in evidence for most of the afternoon. With sun warming my face, I had to remind myself that this was no English summer; this was antipodean winter. Towards the cool end of day I sighted the smoke of a Maori village. There was nothing else for it. Placing my trust in the milk of Maori kindness, I pointed my horse toward rest and sustenance. Ten minutes later I was picking my way into the village through tidy potato plantations and patches of Indian corn past their season. Palm-thatched dwellings were without pretension. Cooking fires burned here and there. I dismounted and led my horse toward the centre of the place. Women and children gazed at me with interest; I tipped my hat politely at those along my path. Males were few in number, and mostly too juvenile to be troubling or too venerable to be alarming. Even men betwixt and between failed to look believably barbarous. No weapons were evident, and no menace; it was as bucolic a community as one might encounter in an English rural ride. I directed my inquiries to the most intelligent looking fellow on show. He was bulky and dressed in patched seaman's garb; he looked as if he had seen more than a little of the world. Aside from his cosmopolitan air, his face was moderately cordial.

'Your toll,' he asked.

I dropped the required number of pennies in his hand, then several more for good measure. 'I should be grateful if you could direct me toward John Heke,' I said.

'Heke?'

'The same.'

He shrugged.

'Are you telling me you don't know?'

'I am telling you I speak no English,' he announced.

'That answer sounds more than adequate,' I protested.

'I speak no English to strangers,' he explained. 'And never to men of the government.'

'And I seem such to you?'

'Who else would come looking for Heke?'

'Then let me assure you that this is not the case. I come as friend.'

'They all say that, all men from the government bearing bad news.'

'Think on this, then,' I suggested. 'I am informed that there is bitter feeling abroad in the Bay of Islands. In these circumstances would a man from the government ride here alone, late in the day?'

It was supposition on my part that government men would not. For all I knew they could be arriving in Maori villages near nightfall all over the Bay of Islands. Nevertheless conversation became milder in character.

'Why do you wish Heke?' he asked.

'That is more difficult to explain,' I told him.

'Explain,' he proposed amiably.

'I am told he inherits the warrior cloak in these parts.'

'What is it to you?'

'I might wish to shake his hand,' I suggested.

'Why should Heke wish to shake yours?'

A good question. Before I could answer he added, 'Are you American?'

'Is that an advantage?'

'Heke finds much of interest in conversation with Americans. He learns of what the British have done elsewhere, in China, India and Australia, and further places. He learns of people made slaves. From Americans he likes to hear of the tea tipped in Boston harbour, and of battles with the British. When the mood takes him he flies the Stars and Stripes from his canoe, the better to anguish Britons.'

That needed thought.

'I cannot claim intimacy with events in the Americas,' I confessed.

'A pity,' my interlocutor sighed.

'On the other hand,' I informed him, 'I hope to make the acquaintance of happenings here.'

'For what?'

'To write of them, perhaps.'

'Write?'

'Such is my calling,' I explained.

'This is true?'

'As I can tell it,' I said. 'I own to no loyalty other than to my pen.'

'That is helpful,' he judged.

'I shall say as much to Heke,' I said.
'And you now expect Maori hospitality?'
'I am no pauper,' I said. 'I can pay my way.'
'Did I talk money?' the fellow asked fiercely.
'Not that I heard.'
'Good,' he said. 'My christened name is Moses.'
'But Heke?' I asked.
'Tomorrow,' he promised.

When he finally saw fit to enlighten me, Moses explained that Heke was away hunting with a party of young fellow tribesmen; his return was not expected until morning. 'Set out early,' Moses advised. 'Meet them on the way home. I will point the path to take.'

'That seems needlessly complicated,' I protested. 'Why may I not wait on him here?'

'It may be one of his bad days.'

'What does that mean?

'You may trouble him less as a lost traveller.'

'If it is one of his good?'

'Little better,' he advised.

Meanwhile sociable Moses made it his business to brace me for the rendezvous. My horse was fed and watered; he irrigated me with rum of stalwart quality. He was also not averse to sharing his thoughts.

'You may have luck with Heke,' he disclosed. 'He could be interested in a writer.'

'Why so?'

'He likes to read, and especially to be read to. He speaks English well, but reads it less well. Reading to him is thus often my task.'

'And what is his favoured form of print?'

'Skippers sometimes leave books behind.'

'Of what character?'

'Adventurous. Heke likes especially the works of Henry Youngman.'

There was a long pause. Henry, still musing on the memorable Angela, began taking more interest in proceedings.

'Why this Henry Youngman?' I asked.

'He tells a fair story. Also Heke thinks he once met the man. When in New Zealand Henry Youngman called himself Dinwiddie. Might that be so?'

I felt a chill.

'I know neither name,' I claimed loftily. 'From my point of view this fellow Youngman belongs to a low order of literature.'

'Low?'

'Unworthy. Lacking virtue and veracity.'

'Try telling Heke,' Moses suggested.

I grew quiet, partaking perhaps too hastily of rum. In the process I also numbed Henry.

A bed must have been found for me soon after; at least I woke on flax matting and under a patched rug next morning. Moses had his hand on my shoulder; he was shaking me awake.

'It is time for your travel,' he said.

My head was of another opinion. My vision was shaky too.

'Come,' Moses said with authority. 'Heke awaits you.'

Breakfast was a lump of bread unleavened and unbuttered. There was morning mist on the hills. We rode a mile or two south, following a path flattened by many horses, until forest of ferny character began rising around. Moses, riding bareback, finally reined in. 'Follow this path slowly,' he said, ' and you will surely meet Heke riding home. I hope the hunt has him in good humour.'

'If not?'

He offered me his hand. 'Good luck,' he said.

With his hoofbeats gone, I found myself in an unedifying situation. With no more than sixty hours passed in New Zealand I was alone, defenceless and as good as lost in foggy and unfriendly forest, hoping to meet up with God knew what irritable species of half-tamed Maori. It was a circumstance worthy of one of Henry's wilder tales. The difference was that Henry always knew where his hero was heading; he knew the next chapter. I had not the dimmest notion of Ferdinand Wildblood's direction. As trees closed in and the path became faint, I found my interest in the enterprise waning. The morning was no warmer. I was attacked by shivering fits, more so when sounds canine, equine and finally human grew ahead. I crammed my chattering teeth together and arranged myself for the encounter to come.

I began this memoir with an account of the meeting which then failed to materialise. There is no delight in dwelling on it further. Sufficient to say that on that lonely forest trail John Heke took no interest in Ferdinand Wildblood's modest endeavour to introduce himself as such. Heke grandly brushed past. His demeanour would have done credit to British royalty. I had just enough time to note that John Heke, unlike most of his retinue, had no festively carved face. There was a token tattoo on his young chin; the rest, so far as his scowl allowed it to be seen, was unblemished. I would later learn that Heke had been received into the Christian church before his tribe's tattooers had done the job respectably. Thereafter, in theory at least, there was no call for pagan adornment.

'I have been looking for you,' I told him.

'I have not been looking for you,' he informed me.

His retinue hurtled past too. Their sound faded. I was left, more or less, where I stood. So much for a tactful ambush. Twelve thousand miles of travel made the slight harder to take. I mounted my horse in poor humour, discovered it lame, and finally limped from the forest, leading the wretched creature, most of the day later. There was no welcome awaiting me in Heke's village. There was, however, Heke. Amiable Moses was standing beside him on the approach to the village. He must have put in a kind word for me. Though Heke's face was no happier, this time he took the view that I had an existence. He even held out a hand.

'Whom is it I address?' he asked.

There was no long pause before my reply. The day's exertion had undone me. The temptation was fatal.

'Henry Youngman,' I said.

Six

Confusion ruled. Heke gazed on me for some time.
'You do not look like Dinwiddie,' he concluded.
'Mercifully,' I agreed.
'And yet you call yourself Youngman. How can this be?'
'Because I am,' I insisted.

He remained reluctant to free Henry Youngman from James Dinwiddie. He recalled Dinwiddie as a dismal ship's deserter given shelter by his tribe. Dinwiddie had been a slave fed with scraps in return for latrine duties and the repair of mischievous muskets. He had certainly been no man-eating potentate. On the other hand his claim of a personal harem was not without foundation. It had been one of his chores to please elderly widows of the tribe. On expeditions of bellicose character, Dinwiddie had remained at a prudent distance from the killing and the ovens of the victors. What endeared him to tribesmen was his talent for turning his unpretentious part in proceedings into rousing campfire narratives. In these tales, to their vast delight, James Dinwiddie was a two-fisted tribal fighter, club gripped in one hand, pistol in the other. Even seasoned storytellers of the tribe were awed; they had never heard a liar like him. Heke was no more than a boy in the shadows of the tribe when Dinwiddie was in residence. He had disappeared between one day and the next, abducted from New Zealand by a skipper short on crew. Heke identified the man's tales when he encountered *Monarch of Maoriland*. He recognised Dinwiddie's contribution down to the last trickle of gore.

'Let me confess it,' I told Heke. 'I knew James Dinwiddie. It is faintly possible that some of his anecdotes rubbed off on to me.'

'Ah,' Heke said.

'The fact is that I now make it my business to avoid the fellow,' I explained with conviction.

Heke grunted.

'Furthermore,' I continued, 'it cannot have escaped your notice that Henry Youngman's later works are distinctly superior.'

'They are not perfect,' he argued fastidiously.

'What in this world is?' I challenged.

He was not to be deflected. Common sense continued to tell him that Henry Youngman could do better than reside in Ferdinand Wildblood's inoffensive person.

'I am he,' I insisted, with growing certitude.

'Prove it,' Heke commanded finally.

'How?'

'Tell me *Triumph of the Tribesman*.'

'Now?'

'All,' he commanded, and pointed me to a campfire.

Darkness had not long fallen when I began. Firelight coloured attentive faces. We were half way to midnight before I rushed through the tale's powerful climax to its elegaic close.

'Now *Murder Most Maori*,' Heke suggested.

'All?' I whispered.

'Now.'

That took us to midnight. The faces about our campfire were no fewer. Then *The Tattooed Trojans* took their bow. It was no use attempting to telescope the stories for the sake of my sanity. Heke was swift to protest when I took liberties with the text; and helpful when my memory faltered. It was suddenly long past midnight.

'There are more,' Heke pointed out.

'Perhaps,' I said hoarsely.

'Perhaps one I have not read?'

My depleted condition left me liable to folly. 'There is,' I admitted, '*Death By a Thousand Muskets*. It was being set in type when I made my departure from London.'

'And what is its nature?'

'It tells of the New Zealand Napoleon, the rise and tragic fall of the great Hongi.'

The silence about the fire was impressive.

'You said Hongi,' Heke observed.

'That is correct.'

Moses was looking anxious. It was possible to interpret the silence as menacing.

'What is it you say of my mighty forebear?' Heke challenged.

'Forebear?' I asked uncomfortably.

'That is so.'

'I have,' I answered, 'tried to be just.'

'Just?'

'From the viewpoint of both friends and enemies.' This was to trim truth. The one viewpoint Hongi's enemies had was from a prostrate position, waiting upon *coup de grâce* from club or musket.

'I trust you have offered his memory no insult,' he warned.

'One day you may be able to judge for yourself.'

'I will judge now,' he decided.

'Now?' I appealed.

'Begin,' he decreed.

There was a lone solace this time; I was not confined by a text known to my listeners. I could nip Hongi back here, spruce him up there, without Heke protesting errors and omissions. My editing became more fervent when I chanced to glimpse Heke's moody face.

The eastern sky was paling as Hongi royally skirmished his last with life and called his lamenting wives and children to his side. I milked his deathbed for every tear. There was a twinkle of moisture on face after tattooed face around me; I didn't dare look at John Heke's. In point of fact my condition was close to incurable too. My voice was gone, and most of my wit. In sympathy with Hongi I pitched into coma. I was aware of attempts being made to return me to narrative health; of Moses vainly trying to rejuvenate me with rum.

I was most aware, however, of John Heke's sturdy voice as I was borne away. True that he spoke Maori to his fellows; but the meaning was unmistakable.

'This,' he pronounced, 'is Henry Youngman. Let no one say different.'

No one was heard to.

I remained a further forty-eight hours recuperating in Heke's camp. Most passed in feverish sleep. Moses, who kept watch on my horizontal form, later swore that I had muttered entire passages from *Death By A Thousand Muskets* as I dreamed — thus offering further compelling evidence of my identity. It was fortunate that Heke felt he had his pound of flesh from Henry Youngman; I could not have survived a curtain call. He seemed unhappy to see me leave, calling me to his side after I shakily saddled my horse.

'I wish to confess something,' he said. 'I wish you to know that I sleep with Henry Youngman under my pillow.'

I was aghast. Under his pillow? To what end? That Henry's tales would rub off? True that Alexander, triumphing into Asia and back, slumbered with Homer under his head between battles. To be frank, John Heke deserved better; at least something lilting.

'Storytellers are precious among men,' he informed me.

It was news to Henry Youngman, as much so to Ferdinand Wildblood. Henry's ornamental fictions had never been fairly valued by Lovelady and Pettiworth. 'That is a pleasure to hear,' I replied.

'They keep treasure safe,' Heke explained.

'On one view of the matter,' I agreed.

'There is no other view,' he said forbiddingly. 'What are we, if not our stories?'

I had to think.

'Have you found yours?'

'Perhaps in those of others,' I suggested.

'A man must have his own,' he argued. 'Otherwise he walks the world a shadow.'

'You are in conversation with yourself,' I judged.

'I,' he agreed pleasantly, 'am still looking for mine. Or my story for me.'

'I shall watch with interest,' I promised.

The journey back to the Bay of Islands lacked much in serenity. Having earlier shammed lame, my horse bolted homeward with the first sniff of salt air. Then the already familiar armada of sunlit islands leapt into view. I steered downhill and nursed my sensitive rump from the saddle outside the Reverend Williams's residence. There was relief on his god-fearing face as he helped me to ground.

'I was about to urge a search party,' he said. 'I surmised that you might have met trouble.'

'I met Heke,' I confessed.

'There is no perceptible difference,' he said. 'How was his mood?'

'It improved on acquaintance.'

'You saw nothing of menace?'

'I saw an appetite for celebrity.'

'That is John Heke,' Williams sighed. 'Would that he had some laurels to rest on.'

'Meaning what, sir? '

'Had he been born ten years earlier, before tribal warfare lost its fascination, the Bay of Islands might now know fewer alarms. As things are, much of his grumbling seems due to the fact that he feels warrior glory gone from the world. He thinks his people too obsessed by trade goods and trivia to observe their true calling. I daresay he gave you an extensive list of native grievances, real and fancied.'

'He was more concerned to enlighten me in respect of his ancestry.'

Williams laughed dryly. 'He told you the great Hongi was his antecedent?'

'Warned me, so to speak.'

'Hongi was a far cousin of Heke's father. A tenuous bond. Hongi is hardly more an ancestor of Heke's than is Adam of us all. When younger, Heke tended to be poor of temper when this was pointed out by fellow tribesmen. He finally raced into a marriage with one of Hongi's more robust daughters, to establish a more illustrious connection.'

'I see,' I said, though my view of the matter was impaired by the sight of Williams's spellbinding protégée looking on from a distance. Attempting to hear Williams out, I tried not to let my eyes roam too far towards her. It became an even more heroic exercise as Williams rumbled on.

'Heke was a scamp from the first,' he said. 'At mission school I caught him thieving paper from the classroom. I thought it hunger for literacy. Alas, he confessed that he needed the paper to manufacture cartridges. He aspired to follow Hongi on one of his more fearful expeditions of conquest. That ambition was absurd, of course. He was barely past infancy. As a youth he was no improvement. In one scatter-brained skirmish with rival tribesmen he suffered a wound in the throat. The lion became an overnight lamb, reluctant to take the field again. He even resumed acquaintance with the church. For a time I was led to think he might prove an eminent soldier of the Lord amongst his less fortunate fellow countrymen. When he and his wife were baptised, however, there was a curious response. He wept.'

Williams had my attention in full. 'Wept, sir?'

'Not to put it too strongly, he sobbed. It was the cause of some consternation in the church. Naturally I allowed him time to regain his composure. His wife, of sturdier stuff, dried his tears.'

'The Heke I have just encountered is not conspicuously lachrymose,' I argued.

'I fear I am past making sense of John Heke,' Williams said.

'It would seem Heke has a problem of a similar nature.'

'It now interests me only so far as he interferes with the well-being of my parishioners. When Heke sniffs, they sneeze. I would be last to deny that they have a just list of woes. But Heke is less help than hindrance with his constant clamour for deference. He was one who signed this land over to Britain and urged wavering fellows to append their marks too. A little late in the day, he now wishes to withdraw. Fortunately, more senior chiefs stand by their word.'

Angela was winning my gaze again, not to speak of Henry's. He refused to be kept in his place; I had to haul my saddle-sour breeches higher.

It was too late to return by water to Blackguard Beach, and Turner's uncouth establishment. Williams insisted that I remain overnight at his residence in Paihia (the native name of his domain). He wished to regale me with further intelligence of the difficult John Heke over a dismaying meal of mutton and a frustratingly small glass of claret. His god-daughter fluttered about, proving a most competent servant; Mrs Williams, whose eyes seldom lifted from the ungarnished repast, was as modest a missionary wife as might be found in a hundred mile hike. If I learned anything new of Heke, I have no recall of it. I have more memory of Angela leaning agreeably near my shoulder as she placed my plate; and of brushing yet closer as she bore it away. I hoped for brandy to relieve my parched palate. None arrived at the table. I pleaded fatigue early. It was no less than the truth; I was entitled to sleep for a week after my symposium with Heke. I teetered alarmingly as I rose from the table and allowed lamp-bearing Angela to lead me to guest quarters. Her remote and composed face gave nothing away. My feeling for her could not disclose itself as other than honourable; carnality of a comprehensive character could not be further from mind. My need was for oblivion, as soon as decent.

Angela, however, had other thoughts on the matter. So, I detected, did Henry.

'This is your room,' she said, lighting my candle. 'You will have a pretty view of the sea in the morning.'

'Thank you,' I said. To my dismay I heard Henry add, 'It could not be prettier than the one before me.'

If she blushed, her complexion hid it well. 'Not so loud,' she whispered.

'I was not aware that my voice was raised.'

Nor was her gaze lowered. 'Later,' she said.

Before I could interpret this pledge she was gone. I barely had the competence to shed my clothes, perform quick ablutions, and extinguish the candles. Then I pitched myself between sheets with a sigh. For Ferdinand Wildblood, that New Zealand night, the world was well lost.

As it happened this was a misapprehension; creation was still in business. I woke to find considerable use being made of my person. On the one hand unclothed and uncurbed Angela was covering it with caresses. On the other Henry was bent on deploying it to his own self-centred ends; he was about one of his characteristically nimble performances as a lover. Neither took me into consideration. Given my depleted state their rampant conduct was callous. My reservations unheard, I remained a beleaguered bystander as passion mounted. In extremity, hoping to nullify Henry, I tried to fix my mind on my first virtuous vision of Angela. This proved luckless. Mercifully Henry failed to make more of the enterprise than was necessary for his satisfaction. I was soon sighing too, if with relief rather than accomplishment; peace seemed at hand again. I slid toward sleep, hoping to take Henry with me.

Angela asked, 'Do you love me?'

'Of course,' Henry said, via my lips.

'Show me again,' she suggested.

Dear God, I prayed.

Angela, need I say, set about giving Henry further opportunity to excel.

She was right in one respect. The island-studded sea was a superb sight as it coloured with morning. I might have been more appreciative of the vista had my night been less demanding. As things were, I met dawn red-eyed. My rodent-like companion left me to it; he was far gone in repose before Angela made a circumspect return to her own room. Heke and Henry could be the death of me.

At breakfast I lifted tea to my lips with a shaky hand. I made no attempt to meet Angela's eye. For once I succeeded in keeping Henry in harness.

'Have you plans for the future, Mr Wildblood?' Williams persisted in asking.

Henry no doubt had. Ferdinand did not.

'When I catch up with my feet, sir, I will no doubt be thinking hard on my prospects. In the meantime it must be said that I have hardly arrived in New Zealand.'

In my experience it is hazardous to take the name of the future in vain. Ambuscade is its favoured tactic. Seconds later it arrived with the sound of hoofbeats. Then there was a young Maori tethering a hard-ridden horse at the Williams gate. Williams rose without haste from the breakfast table; I finally followed him outdoors. The Reverend, speaking Maori, was in earnest, somewhat agitated converse with his visitor. Williams's face told me that urgent matters were pending.

He sent the young man indoors for refreshment. Then he turned to me.

'It is all my fears confirmed,' Williams said. 'That young man is one of the more fervent in my flock. I have no reason to doubt what he tells me.'

'About what, sir?'

Williams was too preoccupied to answer. 'Did you,' he went on, 'observe unusual activity in Heke's camp?'

'Of what nature, sir?'

'Serious nature.'

'I am an ill-fitted judge, sir. I have too little first-hand experience of the Maori world to distinguish the serious from the frivolous. As a race they seem most remarkably to manage a keen sense of both.'

Williams had no interest in this finding. 'Let me ask again,' he said. 'Did you have an impression of looming belligerence?'

'Most Maori, in my short experience, seem to be pugnacious in character.'

'Did you hear wild words, then?'

'Some less amiable than others, perhaps.'

This was still no help to Williams. 'What is the difficulty?' I asked.

'Heke,' he sighed. 'Not for the first time, and I fear not the last. This new intelligence, however, is the most alarming yet. It seems he is suddenly calling younger sympathisers to his side and urging them to ready their firearms.'

'I cannot confirm that. I saw nothing.'

'Nothing, Mr Wildblood?'

'Whatever,' I insisted.

That might have been because I was recumbent. For much of my time in Heke's camp a cannon could not have roused me. On the other hand I had the uneasy suspicion that Henry Youngman's narratives — and not least the luminous version of Hongi's life in *Death By a Thousand Muskets* — might have some complicity in the affair. What heroic fancies might have started to stir again in brown breasts? What lion-hearted age was roaring anew in their ears?

'Nevertheless,' Williams said. 'The boy is reliable. His information is to be trusted.'

'What else did he say?'

'That Heke makes no secret of his intentions. He means to fell the flagstaff from which the British ensign flies.'

'Above Blackguard Beach?'

'There is no other useful,' Williams said. 'He wishes to level it today or tomorrow.'

'Are we talking war, Mr Williams?'

'We must trust not. Heke tells his people that he means no threat to life; he wishes the ensign lowered and no more.'

'And thereafter?'

'Customs duties ended and Maori charges for anchorage resumed. The right to fell their own trees for financial gain, and sell their own land to whomsoever has cash.'

'That is more serious,' I had to agree. 'Perhaps best to let him have the flag.'

Williams was shocked. 'The British flag?'

'Better that than British lives.'

'Correct me if I err, Mr Wildblood, but as I understand it poets have a fine feeling for symbols. That flag is such. It means law and order; it is a bulwark against bedlam. No one knows it better than Heke.'

'A poet is also aware, sir, that we are talking of a length of New Zealand timber and a measure of coloured calico. Both can be replaced with small labour.'

'Nevertheless I shall attempt to urge Heke toward a more pacific course. I must keep you company this morning.'

'To Blackguard Beach?'

'I shall await Heke's arrival there. No doubt there will be argument of a tedious kind. It must be suffered.'

'You would interpose yourself between the flag and inflamed tribesmen?'

'I know Heke of old. A boo to a goose is the most he could manage even on his best day.'

'All the same, sir, might it not be safer to call out the guard?'

'Guard?' Williams said.

'To make a stout showing,' I explained.

'There is,' Williams informed me, 'no soldier within two days' sail. In these parts our destiny is in God's care.'

That was dismaying intelligence.

'You mean there is no protection for the lawful?'

'Aside from the flag. And a pistol here, a cutlass there. Mine has long rusted.'

'Dear God,' I sighed.

'As I said, Mr Wildblood.'

'In the absence of soldiery it sounds all the more desirable to leave Blackguard Beach — and not least the flag — at the Almighty's disposal.'

'We must do our best to interest him,' Williams proposed.

Inside the hour Williams's sturdy mission craft was running across the Bay before a wintry breeze. The missionary settlement of Paihia dwindled behind our bucking stern. The last thing visible there was the lone figure of Angela wistfully farewelling her industrious paramour. Meanwhile chill spray drenched us. Williams was busy polishing and repolishing his glasses and peering apprehensively toward Blackguard Beach. As we neared it we saw a community losing its lethargic character. Inhabitants were clustering on the shore. One or two were even running to greet us. There were faint shouts too.

'Rumour has reached them also,' Williams judged.

The mission vessel grounded on Blackguard Beach. We were soon surrounded. The crowd was of one mind and many voices: all asserted that Williams was best equipped to put peril in its place.

'Patience,' Williams pleaded. 'I know your fears.'

These were evident in Turner's person. He had a pistol in his belt and a musket in hand. He was not the only one armed. Briton and Maori alike were primed for brutish business.

'You will oblige me by returning all weapons to their customary location,' Williams said. 'First, however, you will favour the Almighty with a brief prayer.' He dropped to his knees. One by one, two by two, his makeshift congregation followed suit. Turner was noticeably reluctant. Finally even Ferdinand Wildblood marshalled himself for worship. With only lapping sea audible, Williams began making himself heard.

'Our Father,' he pleaded, 'let today pass tranquil. Let our dreads be seen as unworthy of those in your charge. Let storm blow itself out. Let goodness and mercy prevail.'

Sceptics with a wary eye on the world's actual weather discerned that goodness and mercy were not materialising out to sea. Whimpers of fright and bellows of consternation heralded the appearance of Heke's first warrior-filled vessel on the waters of the Bay. Williams finished his prayer in strikingly succinct fashion. By the time the inhabitants of Blackguard Beach had risen to their feet there were several similar vessels on view. The locality was about to be overwhelmed by visitors. Let Henry Youngman lament lack of uproar now.

'Return to your homes,' Williams ordered calmly.

The citizens of Blackguard Beach were disappearing right and left, most of the view that valour was undesirable.

'We are entitled to defend life and property,' Turner protested.

'We are entitled to live, sir,' Williams announced.

Then there was the ruddy-faced police magistrate, a man in powerful anguish, fearful that a show of civil authority was expected.

'Get yourself out of harm's way, Mr Beckham,' Williams advised. 'Place your constables under lock and key too.'

Soon I was Williams's one companion on the shore.

'I mean to wait on Heke,' Williams explained.

'You are a bold man, sir,' I suggested.

'Christ gives me courage,' Williams argued. 'Also knowledge of John Heke. At the least I might give him pause.'

'Pause, sir?'

'I may urge a prayer upon him too.'

I thought on that; and on the approaching canoes.

'I observe unease,' Williams said.

'Interest in events,' I argued.

'Events may take a daunting interest in you. There is no reason to remain.'

'With your permission, sir, I hope also to stand my ground.' Was that Ferdinand speaking, or Henry? No matter now. It was said.

'Please yourself,' Williams told me.

Heke's fleet closed with the beach. There was no race ashore. Wading tribesmen heaved their vessels above the tide line. Then they clustered to light their pipes, gossip, and laugh. They certainly took up no offensive posture with their firearms. The deserted appearance of the settlement entertained them hugely. Every door on the seafront was shut and bolted. Heke himself was slow to arrive and advance on Williams. There was a tremble in his limbs; his eyes were shiny with elation. His lieutenant Moses remained slightly to his rear. Moses' eyes met mine knowledgably; he had a faint smile.

'What is this nonsense, Heke?' Williams challenged.

'Bad words are said of me here,' Heke explained.

'What bad words, Heke?'

'That I do not mean what I say,' Heke explained.

'Thus this?' Williams queried.

'It may be seen that I do not merely boast and brag. Those who insult me may now see different.'

'I am sure they shall,' Williams said. 'Your point is therefore made.'

Heke had no inclination to embrace this limiting view; he had two hundred tribesmen looking for lively endeavour. 'What is it you wish, Reverend Williams?' he inquired finally.

'That you now travel peacefully home. What else?'

'For the same bad words to be said when I depart?'

'This sortie, if nothing else, must win a healthy respect. Let it end here, Heke, before matters get out of hand.'

'But matters are in my hand,' Heke pointed out stubbornly. 'I allowed them to escape once. Never again.'

'My understanding is that you hope to lower the British flag above the Bay.'

'I do not mean it to remain,' Heke admitted.

'There is no need for me to remind you that Britain is strong and New Zealand small.'

'I have heard it said,' Heke allowed.

'More Britons arrive in the colony daily,' Williams observed.

'Alas,' Heke said.

'Nevertheless most Maori give the newcomers reason to think they are welcome. More to the point, they may soon outnumber the natives of these islands.'

'What are you telling me?' Heke asked.

'You behave dangerously,' Williams pronounced.

'As I must,' Heke claimed.

Williams sighed. 'A prayer could cool matters,' he suggested.

'When poisonous tongues are quiet,' Heke said. 'When this place is cleansed.'

Williams looked fearful. He had reason to. Heke gave out abrupt orders to Moses and his other lieutenants. Armed warriors disposed themselves along the foreshore in two muscular ranks, the community of Blackguard Beach defenceless before them. Williams thought it unwise to make further representations. He whispered, 'It would seem we are to witness something not seen on this strand for years.'

'What is that?' I asked.

'A haka. A Maori war dance.'

'And a war?' I asked faintly.

'Don't speak the word,' Williams whispered.

Heke's lone chant was taken up by two hundred throats, followed by a thumping of feet and a flourishing of weapons. This exercise did not speak of moderation. I recognised it as the militant rite, designed as a preface to disembowelment, which sent European voyagers tacking away in terror for decades after New Zealand's discovery. Even to my unseasoned eye, however, something was missing. For one thing the choreography was of the sketchiest. For another the dancers could have done with more painstaking rehearsal. Though there was some shrewd improvisation, they crashed into each other clumsily and did each other damage with weapons; several were soon sprawled. As for the rest, many had forgotten their lines. It was possible to see this as a promising omen. It was also possible to see that Christianity had something to be said for it. Years of baptisms, sermons and psalms had taken their toll of battlefield etiquette.

'They ask an enemy,' Williams explained.

Despite the theatrical flaws of Heke's challenge, candidate foemen were steadfastly refusing to show fight. Residents of Blackguard Beach not only chose to remain indoors; they were not disposed to make themselves visible at their windows either. The performance passed off without an appreciable audience. It deserved better. The rousing rush to bare their buttocks, the time-honoured tactic for terrifying opponents, was no cheap spectacle.

With the last syllable of ceremony heard, Heke's men were at a loss until tradition again took over. If proceedings lacked something in glory, at least there was loot. In efficient if informal fashion the unruliest tribesmen advanced on the settlement; and particularly on mercantile establishments. Heke made no attempt to call them back. Windows began breaking; doors were battered with musket butts. Such doors were soon unbarred by obliging merchants. Hogsheads of rum, casks of twist tobacco, and sacks of sugar and flour were among the items soon in the care of their clientele. Clothing was especially favoured by threadbare tribesmen. Jackets, tunics, trousers and footwear were tried for size and worn from that moment forward; proceedings at least took on a more stylish turn. Meanwhile no offensive plan was apparent. Having commandeered Blackguard Beach, Heke appeared bereft of larger strategies. He could be glimpsed now and then attempting to make sense of his circumstances. Sometimes he was in earnest conversation with Moses and other lieutenants. Often he was gazing at his men with awe. Though he remained aloof from the plundering, he cannot have been unaware of the material advantage attendant on rebellion. On the other hand, he was also surely contemplating the first law of human conflict: that the affairs of men have their own momentum and a mysterious itinerary. Which means, in short, one damned thing after another.

Williams and I escaped the melee ungrazed. 'We must trust,' he said, 'that Heke sees that no resistance is to be offered. Let him now get on with felling his confounded flagstaff, if he must.'

'If he must?' I asked.

Williams's change of heart was surprisingly sudden, perhaps due to a vision of what might be.

'Much as I deplore his target, Wildblood, better that than this. One spark might ignite a powder keg. It only needs Turner or some other maddened merchant to present a weapon. Then where are we?'

No aggrieved merchant presented so much as a carving knife. As sack of a settlement went, it was tolerably tranquil. Buildings other than those occupied by prosperous merchants were unplundered. The village church was left alone too. No fires rose. Dead and dying did not litter the lanes. There were no sorrowing cries from stricken widows, no captive virgins dragged off by the hair. The only butchery was of pig and fowl. It would not have done for the terrible Hongi Hika, and never for a Henry Youngman narrative; Henry would have lost most connoisseurs of carnage then and there. By noon there were harmless cooking fires along the seafront, and cheerful insurgents lunching amply and filling their pipes with tobacco of quality. Mugs brimming with rum also did much to muffle sounds of civil disorder. These now amounted mainly to warriors testing newly obtained muskets by discharging shot in a seaward direction. Heke's force was happy to live off Blackguard Beach until otherwise ordered.

Finally John Heke took note of the Reverend Williams's protestations.

'You have done your worst,' Williams argued. 'Why not leave off now?'

'I am thinking,' Heke said.

'As are we all,' Williams said. 'Prayer would be timely.'

'What is today?' Heke asked, with seeming irrelevance.

'Saturday, I believe,' Williams answered.

'Tomorrow is therefore the sabbath,' Heke pointed out.

'That is so,' Williams had to agree.

'Let today look after itself,' Heke proposed. 'Tomorrow is for prayer.'

'I have your word?' Williams asked.

'And my men,' Heke said.

'I should like it on one further matter,' Williams said. 'That you will not fell the flagstaff today. Or, for that matter, tomorrow.'

For a moment Heke seemed in difficulty. The moment passed. He blinked; he smiled. 'You have that too,' he promised.

An appeased Williams began gathering up his more afflicted parishioners for informal if fervent devotions. Rather than eavesdrop on his editorial suggestions to the Author of All Things, I persisted in Heke's vicinity.

'What is your feeling?' he asked.

'My feeling is that the inhabitants of Blackguard Beach may now think long and hard before even whispering your name.'

'That,' he said modestly, 'is my feeling also.' He lifted his eyes skyward, to a point somewhere above my head. 'You fail to enlighten me on one matter.'

'What might that be?' I asked warily.

'What Henry Youngman thinks.'

'The day has not been devoid of interest,' I acknowledged. 'Fortunately the drama has not been of a full-blooded kind.'

'But it is a story.'

'And this far, if I may say so, yours.'

'You may say so,' he informed me.

By nightfall din had dwindled to a few half-hearted rebel shouts and poor-tempered colonist curses. I finally sought rest in Turner's diligently looted residence. The picture of a man ruined, Turner sat at his table, a lone candle burning low, his head in his hands. The slightest sound outdoors left him shuddering.

'I should have known New Zealand would end badly,' he confided.

'In what respect?' I asked.

'My wife's gone off to cook for Heke,' he said.

That was not good news for Heke.

Sunday was cool again, sunny and clear. The citizens of Blackguard Beach peered warily from windows and doorways and found their community magically intact. Though panes of glass were sometimes missing there was not a rafter out of place. Heke's army was sleeping off surfeit along the shore. Celebration and thanks seemed due. Family after family bestirred itself. Men buttoned themselves into their Sunday suits and women made themselves modest in bonnets. Children were washed shiny and combed, and soon had hymnals in hand. In the spirit of things, I looked out sober attire; Turner, a robust heathen, regarded me with suspicion.

'You look like another bloody preacher,' he said.

It was not for me to tell Turner that six days of the week were sufficient for sin.

Soon every lane in the village led to the church. There, however, matters became perplexing. Competing for the attention of Providence were John Heke, his lieutenants, and as many score tribesmen as he had been able to rouse. To win entry to the church it was necessary to run a rebel gauntlet. Warrior weapons were stacked tidily in the churchyard. Warrior faces had a melancholy in tune with the sabbath. When Williams's customary congregation was seated, Heke and his colleagues began filing in. The place was far from spacious; there was pushing and shoving, and less than standing room for those at the rear. I found Moses beside me in the crush; his eyebrows lifted heavenward.

When quiet prevailed, Williams took the pulpit. 'Let us consider Proverbs chapter fifteen, verse one, as our text for today,' he suggested. 'A soft answer turneth away wrath.'

There was a rustle here, a whisper there, and silence. John Heke must have wondered what he had done wrong.

He was first to the communion rail, not noticeably moist-eyed.

Would that I could report more reliably. The fact of the matter is that I drank more than my due of commandeered liquor on that sabbath. Say what you like of him; John Heke was never a man mean of spirit when filling a glass.

I found nerve to say, 'How would you see this as ending?'

He answered with a difficult question. 'How would Henry Youngman?' he said.

'With the noble nature of the victor disclosed,' I suggested.

Heke gave the proposition thought. 'That is the story I am looking for?'

'It is not for me to say,' I argued modestly.

Moses was a less exacting companion. Dusk found us on the shore before a cheery fire.

'What now?' I asked.

'Heke has a problem,' Moses explained.

'Rebels famously do,' I pointed out.

'His is his own. How to be a Christian warrior.'

'Britons experience no such difficulty.'

'No?'

'When the sword is drawn the ten commandments take a holiday.'

'Interesting,' Moses said. 'We have yet to see the sword of the red tribe drawn.'

'Don't wish it,' I warned.

Before retiring early to bed I persuaded myself that Heke would now see wisdom in withdrawal from Blackguard Beach. Prayer and intemperance had done their worst; his contingent was in drowsy disarray. There should be no further cause for local laments.

Nevertheless I woke on the Monday to far shouts. It was some time before I could distinguish one from another. They proved to have an identical message. A bellowing Turner took up the incoherent chorus as he burst in my door.

'He's done it,' he said. 'The pisser's been and done it.'

'Done what, Mr Turner?' I yawned.

'Felled it,' he reported. 'Heke's dropped the bloody flagstaff. The Union Jack is in the dust.'

I appeared to be wide awake. Heke was a man of his word. He had promised Williams he would not interfere with the flag on Saturday or Sunday. He therefore sensibly reserved the enterprise for Monday.

To see for myself I toiled up the hill with Turner to join a subdued gathering of locals. Heke's axemen had worked at the bulky base of the staff with wild vigour; woodchips crunched underfoot as we approached. The toppled timber was a powerful sight; the flag had been shredded by neighbouring growth as it fell. Voices were whispered. From that height the Bay of Islands had a wintry blue sheen. In the middle distance the canoes of John Heke's flotilla were paddling home; the fallen flagstaff was his dumbfounding farewell.

'He's gone too far this time,' Turner announced with satisfaction. 'He'll find what Britain is all about.'

That might be so. It was more to the point that John Heke was finding what he was all about.

Seven

Dispute draws chroniclers as fast as dung does blowflies. Many and capricious are the tales of John Heke's uninhibited weekend. Every lettered man in the Bay of Islands raced to his pen as loot-filled canoes put off from Blackguard Beach. These accounts lacked nothing in colour, and everything in candour. It was claimed that Heke, in the course of promoting riot, had announced his intention of slaying every white arrival in New Zealand. If so, he had made an indifferent beginning. Blackguard Beach could count as many souls resident on the Monday as it had on the Saturday, even if many were packing. There was not so much as a fatal instance of apoplexy, though Turner came close. It was also said that Heke and his frisky young followers had made it their business to expose their persons lewdly to the innocent women of Blackguard Beach. It was not acknowledged that unworldly females were few in the Bay of Islands; or that bare buttocks were a less injurious spectacle than smoking firearms. Even more earnestly it was asserted that Heke was in league with disreputable Yankee traders, perhaps Papist Frenchmen, and looking for an alliance with the United States of America. His expedition — in this account — had been to demonstrate to the United States that he was a rival worth respect in the matter of humbling Britain. All reports had something in common. They agreed John Heke was harmful to the health of the colony.

Bureaucratic braying was heard when news of the felled flagstaff, in one lively form and the next, journeyed down the coast to the new capital of Auckland. Governor FitzRoy, a good-hearted fellow, was urged to look to his firepower. Looking, he found some seven dozen armed men at his disposal. Enough to outlast martial ceremonial, but hardly a battle. FitzRoy was a circumspect fellow, as well he might be after skippering the *Beagle* in its now infamous voyage around the planet in the company of that humourless heretic Charles Darwin. FitzRoy may have had no firm view on survival of the fittest; he certainly had on durability of the wisest. He took the temperate stance that native woes might well be considered before shot began flying. Lest prudence not prevail, however, he informed the colony of New South Wales of his modest circumstances. Within weeks there were another eight score soldiers under sail from Sydney Cove.

Though it is not my intention to play conscientious chronicler (preferring the informal manner of the late Henry Youngman) it must also be said that Maori of the Bay of Islands were in as much a panic as the most fretful servant of Queen Victoria. John Heke's brazen behaviour, so long an embarrassment, now menaced the well-being of judicious tribesmen. Longer in the tooth than the upstart flagstaff-feller, and considerably more scarred, they knew what battle meant. Their young dilettante fellow tribesman did not. Like Heke, they knew what Britons had been about in Kabul, Canton, and Calcutta. Unlike Heke, they were not aroused by such information. On the contrary, news of so zealous a fighting clan had a sobering effect on senior tribesmen. They deduced, for example, that Britain's muskets were many. Nor had they desire to see the Stars and Stripes — or for that matter the tricolore of France — fluttering in the stead of the Union Jack; better the devil they knew.

Gathering in sedate conclave, they agreed that Heke had to be muffled. When Governor FitzRoy arrived in the Bay of Islands with his hastily mustered Sydney force — on the prophetically named vessel HMS *Hazard* — they tumbled over themselves in their race to reassure him of their best intentions. This was timely. Aboard the *Hazard* was a bellowing bullock of a colonel named Hulme, of the 96th Regiment of Foot, all for war there and then. 'Where are the buggers?' he roared on first sight of Blackguard Beach.

Failing to identify a suitable sodomite, he suggested to FitzRoy, 'We shall have to shoot anything brown that moves.' The thoughtful FitzRoy differed. This was fortunate. Had Hulme been given his head, he might have levelled every respectable, reverent and Queen-loving Maori in the Bay of Islands, thus presenting Heke with a war beyond his most robust fancy. This possibility cannot have escaped FitzRoy either; he was certainly aware that a British governor was still a twig in a brown tide. He therefore listened with gravity when loyal Maori undertook to keep Heke in his place. In return, he promised that customs duties would no longer be levied in the Bay of Islands; that Blackguard Beach could henceforth be considered a free port. He further announced that Maori were relieved of the obligation to sell off their lands only to the government; that it was theirs to dispose of as they pleased. Finally and reluctantly he even allowed that tribesmen might be entitled to fell their own trees for profit.

So much for the larger grievances in John Heke's roster of wrongs. At least he now had a leaf of laurel to rest on. Though he failed to present himself to the Queen's representative, he was reclined on long enough by his muscular elders to dispatch a contrite apology to FitzRoy. By way of compensation for Heke's misdemeanours FitzRoy asked only that the assembled chiefs present him with their muskets and tomahawks. This they did in dignified fashion. Quite as solemnly FitzRoy returned their weapons. Fortunately for his equilibrium, Heke had no part in this mummery.

FitzRoy was guilty of just one indiscretion. Before he returned to Auckland, with the Bay of Islands apparently at peace, he ordered the flagstaff raised and the Union Jack hoisted again. When report of this reached Heke, he declined to believe it. Britons, as he understood it, were men of honour. Likewise as Christians they abhorred false witness. They would not claim victory where victory was not. The flag would say Britain had triumphed. Governor FitzRoy, he said, could not be so inconsiderate of tribesmen's feelings. Heke misjudged matters. No colony was founded on tact.

What then of Ferdinand and Henry? The truth is that the latter found his first honest experience of high adventure heady, and the promise of extensive assault and battery likewise. In the hope of further furore, garnished with the attentions of Angela, he wished to prolong his presence in the Bay of Islands. As usual, it was for Ferdinand to manage the commonplace world. Following Heke's raid, and the flight of many colonists, there was an excess of accommodation in the vicinity of Blackguard Beach; Ferdinand took up the rent of a cottage vacated by a panicked Scots carpenter. With a sigh he arranged chair and table, pen and ink, and bid Henry do his worst. For most of a week Henry stared unproductively at the sea through dusty glass; his pen seldom did more than twitch in his hand. In such somnolent intervals Ferdinand contrived to give himself to study of the Maori tongue in the hope that he might find its cadences helpful in making sense of his circumstances; he also composed a seemly sonnet or two.

These were meant to call the attention of Angela to his person (he foresaw a volume called *South Sea Sonnets*). The problem was outflanking Henry.

As it happened our mutual inamorata knocked on the door of our cottage a week after we moved in. She had escaped the pious realm of Williams on the pretext of visiting an ailing aunt at Blackguard Beach. Less than a minute after the door opened Henry and Angela were vigorously entwined. Ferdinand, as usual, was brushed aside in their haste to make the most of each other. That enfeebling rendezvous was the first of many. Through the rest of winter and most of spring Angela's visits to her indisposed relative were regular. Rumour of war failed to divert besotted Henry. Even the menacing appearance in the Bay of Islands of the corvette called *Hazard* — with eighteen influential guns on show — made no impression. He was delirious in a philanderer's Eden. Making more and more indifferent company, he pined for Angela poignantly between trysts. I failed to interest him in the course of events beyond the lovers' couch: in Governor FitzRoy's arrival, for example, and in the concessions that worthy made to return serenity to the Bay of Islands after Heke's riot. Even a musket shot to the rear of his active rump might not have reminded Henry of his vocation. When detected in the creative act, rather than the reproductive, he was inclined to return to the maudlin mode rather than the manly — to the sentimental like of *The Maori Magdalen* and *Sirens of a Savage Shore*. The truth is that Henry Youngman had lost his nerve as a storyteller. The legitimate Bay of Islands, as distinct from the lusty bastard sired by his London fancies, appeared to have left him in shock; his prose was listless, his palette muddied by an excess of the authentic.

It was left to me to sally out, make the acquaintance of fellow countrymen and win news of the world. When I rowed to the *Hazard* I was hauled ungraciously aboard by a couple of ugly jack tars.

'Who have we here?' a voice of authority was heard asking. 'Yet another colonial yokel asking our sympathy?'

There was a tall, lean and beardless young man in half-buttoned naval attire examining me through his monocle. A lieutenant, if I was not mistaken. I was not mistaken. The supercilious fellow had the appurtenances of authority and none of the distinction.

'By no means, sir,' I assured him with vehemence. 'My name is Ferdinand Wildblood, late of London.'

'And a gentleman, I'll be bound.'

'That is as may be,' I said.

'I hear New Zealand already has more than Mayfair. They say the place fair swarms with fellows of freshened pedigree.'

'It is not a problem which preoccupies me,' I informed him.

'Is it true,' he asked, 'that the Maori has likewise begun to give himself righteous airs? Is that what this confounded business is all about?'

'My impression, sir, is that what most occupies the Maori is the riddle of remaining Maori in a land losing its uncivil character.'

'You are a solemn fellow,' he judged.

'Affairs here make for gravity,' I explained.

'And for guns?'

'It must be hoped not.'

'Pity,' he said. 'Not even a practice shoot?'

'Even a practice shout might be inflammatory.'

He finally offered his hand. 'The name is George Philpotts.' His smile, after all, was quite winning. Certainly his hand was firm. 'What would you say to a civilised game of backgammon?'

I reminded myself of my mission. 'In the business of ferrying men at arms, you have not, I suppose, encountered Cyprian Bridge?'

'Major Bridge? There's a noble fellow for you. No; I regret not. The 58th remains on garrison duty in Sydney. Cyprian was breaking his neck to join this foray, in the hope of turmoil of interest, but it was not to be. Our superiors did not consider New Zealand a nut worth cracking by the 58th. Cyprian, when given this news, went into steep decline. What is your interest? Is Major Bridge a friend?'

'We survived a thirsty voyage together.'

'Bravo,' said George Philpotts. 'A friend of Cyprian Bridge's must be a friend of mine. I have a fairish bottle of claret uncorked in my cabin. Would you care to chance it?'

'With dispatch,' I said.

'I expect fair exchange,' George Philpotts explained, warmly leading the way to his quarters. 'I wish intelligence of this fellow Heke. Is he a fiend?'

'In the eyes of some, perhaps.'

'In yours?'

'For the most part he is as pleasing of countenance as many an Englishman.'

'What then is his affliction?'

'The world,' I said.

'That is a considerable malady.'

'Or a foe worth a fight,' I suggested.

'Now you interest me,' George said, adjusting his monocle with one hand and filling my glass with the other. 'Tell me more.'

'Would that I could.'

'Try,' George urged.

'For a start,' I explained, 'he is a Christian.'

'Then, poor fellow, he wins my sympathy.'

'What is that supposed to mean?'

'Merely that I was bred by a bishop.'

I was shocked. 'Informally?'

'Well within wedlock, more is the pity. Otherwise I might not have been cast out as the irreligious black sheep of the family and incarcerated in the navy. The world's seas give me much time to reflect on my doctrinal differences with Pater.'

'I see.'

'As for Heke's being a Christian, I take it you are telling me that he is not to be seen frivolously as such.'

'That is for the Lord to judge,' I suggested.

If I failed to enlighten George Philpotts further on the conduct and character of John Heke, it was not through design. The fact is that Heke's silence had become impressive. One rumour had him in jaunty mood; another spoke of his melancholy. Possibly one version was as true as the other: he was a mountain of mixed feelings. In asserting their loyalty in their transactions with the Governor, his fellow tribesmen had dismissed him as a mere mischief maker. He could now be forgotten, they argued. This was in error. Whatever else Heke was, he was no longer in large peril of leaving this life unremembered. To be fair, this may have been reason for Henry's difficulty. A story which starts with flagstaff crashing to earth has everywhere to go.

Nonetheless the meeting with George Philpotts proved amiable, as several uncorked bottles soon testified. It was the first of many mellow encounters. I was sorry when the *Hazard* finally hoisted sail and Governor FitzRoy and his soldiery left the Bay of Islands to its familiar devices.

The task of restoring the flagstaff, following FitzRoy's departure, fell on police magistrate Beckham. Conscientious in arresting, fining and confining residents of the Bay of Islands for their shortcomings as citizens, he had less stomach for his larger duties as caretaker of civilisation. Certainly he proved in no speed. Selection of a suitable length of timber took time. It could not be too green or too weathered, too large or too small. His indecision on this score persisted for weeks. When aspersions on his character grew loud, he conscripted a raucous team of residents to heave a likely pole uphill. No one was in a greater lather than Beckham. He could be seen looking over his shoulder in a seaward direction, presumably in fear of Heke's canoes making another colourful visit. When the hilltop site was reached Beckham announced work done for the day.

Always in the thick of affairs, Turner protested, 'Why not put the bloody thing up?'

'Because we lack a flag,' Beckham informed him. 'A pole without a flag suggests we are half-hearted.'

'Stitch up the old bugger,' Turner proposed.

'Impossible,' Beckham announced. 'Stitches could serve as displeasing reminder of recent events. And should they come apart, superstitious natives might see an omen.'

So the new flagstaff was dumped among the debris of the old until an ensign of suitable dimension could be fetched from Auckland. Turner grumbled off downhill, followed by Beckham and other nervous colonists. It was left to Ferdinand Wildblood to note that the waters of the Bay of Islands were less empty than they were an hour before. A small canoe was stationed off Blackguard Beach, its occupants too distant to be identifiable. Sun glinting on glass suggested a telescope in use. Soon thereafter the canoe was inconspicuously paddled across the Bay again. It had to be a party reporting to Heke. Ferdinand thought not to make an account of this sighting. There was apprehension enough in the Bay.

When a replacement flag finally arrived from Auckland Beckham judged it too faded and threadbare to see out the lively breezes of the Bay of Islands long; he sent for another. The second was said to be soiled, though stains were not apparent to any but Beckham; he passed it to his wife for lengthy laundering.

Before Beckham could procrastinate further, the people of Blackguard Beach were unnerved again by visitors. A short, bull-necked and much tattooed Maori tramped into town with an unwholesome score of armed men breathless behind him. There was no mistaking his authority. He halted outside the police magistrate's dwelling. 'Where,' he bellowed for all to hear, 'does the flag fly,

Mr Beckham?'

Beckham tumbled out his door, hauling on braces and tucking away shirt tails.

'Where, Mr Beckham?' the loud Maori repeated. 'Where is the Queen's flag?'

'There have been difficulties,' Beckham claimed.

'I am here to end them,' the Maori announced. 'Show me the timber. Show me the flag.'

'What for?' Beckham asked.

'That the flagstaff will stand and the flag fly.'

'Today?'

'Today.'

'This is irregular,' Beckham judged.

'Does Heke still cause you to piss your breeches?'

'It is not that simple. We lack armed protection.'

'You will have it,' the Maori promised.

By this time most inhabitants of the town were watching from a wary distance. Flustered Beckham was not an attractive sight. His face reddened with humiliation.

'Must I be,' the Maori asked, 'the Queen's man here?'

There was a shamed silence.

'I gave my word to the governor that the flag could fly again,' the Maori said. 'I find that the flag is not flying. What does this say? It says that Heke prevails. It says my word is empty.'

Such was my first sight of Tamati Waka Nene — or Timothy Walker Nene, in the more comprehensible version of his name. By nightfall the flagstaff stood tall on the hill above the beach. And the Union Jack flapped again in brisk Bay of Islands wind. Below the summit a party of Nene's tribesmen made camp. They proposed to protect the flag as long as necessary. Having expressed himself lengthily on the cowardly character of colonists, Nene took himself inland again. Blackguard Beach was as eerily quiet as it had been after Heke's departure. Beckham resolutely remained indoors.

Turner passed judgement. 'There is only one Briton worth the name in these parts,' he announced. 'His name is Nene.'

Nene must have been at least sixty years old then, and looked nearer eighty. There was no Maori more possessed of rank and respect in the north of New Zealand. He was famous for not having missed a reputable war in five decades. He did not mean that record to be impaired. His was one wiry wing of the powerful Ngapuhi tribe; Heke's was the other sinewy appendage. When not slaying and enslaving traditional foes north and south, they were in rehearsal, which meant feuding with each other. There was even less love lost in these clan quarrels. Another was in the making. Nene had declared for the Queen, insisting that Maori must acknowledge the presence of other peoples on the planet. Besides, he added, he had no complaint about the price Britons had been prepared to pay for indifferent land; commotion of Heke's kind imperilled the market. Treaties were treaties; there was no turning back. Heke was no more than a hiccup on enlightenment's highway. Or so it then seemed.

Spring in the Bay of Islands can be confused with summer. It was true the morning I set out to refresh my acquaintance with Heke. The sky was cloudless, the sun warm, the sea calm; my hired sailboat had to search out feeble zephyrs to find the far shore. More than a month had passed since FitzRoy's visit; a week since Nene's. John Heke had been given sufficient time for sullen reflection. I hoped to determine how matters now stood. And, more to the point, where Heke did.

First, however, Williams's missionary settlement at Paihia had to be survived. For lustful Henry and longing Ferdinand there was compensation in sight of Angela. She bustled brightly about us, seeing to refreshment, while Williams pondered aloud on capricious humankind.

'I do not see this ending well,' he said. 'Warn Heke, if you will, not to be precipitate.'

'I shall carry that message,' I promised.

'I have a fearful sense of fresh trouble.'

'You are not alone, sir.'

'Horse stealing and petty theft are reaching epidemic proportion inland. The guilty parties may be Heke's men; they may be mere felons. But all such acts are now bound to be laid at his door. I foresee the return of soldiers should troublemaking persist.'

'And should the flag,' I suggested.

Williams sighed. 'You might note the numbers in his camp,' he suggested. 'I have heard of sympathisers afoot in his direction. Even some of Nene's people. Which may account for Nene's intervention; who knows? Nothing would enrage Nene more than Heke promising to usurp his prestige in these parts. News of Heke's numbers might help us interpret our present situation.'

'Do I understand you correctly, sir? If I am not mistaken, you are asking me to play spy.'

'Reliable observer,' Williams suggested.

'I fail to see the difference,' I protested.

'Sober information rather than giddy rumour would be for the welfare of all. Understand this, Mr Wildblood. There are still old rivalries, jealousies and enmities looking for expression in this vicinity. Even, for that matter, obstinate pagans with dead of past decades unavenged. The clock could be turned back. Christ could be crushed underfoot in the commotion.'

'You paint an unhappy picture, Reverend.'

'You see my life's work unravelled,' Williams sighed.

'Very well, then. If I note anything out of the ordinary, I shall bring it to your attention. I cannot say fairer.'

'Thank you,' he said.

Concentration was difficult in the Williams household. I was preoccupied with the problem of placing a sonnet discreetly in Angela's hand before I withdrew. What made it difficult was that Henry's eyes were signalling her lecherously. Finally I rose to depart. Hardly recognising myself, and no doubt undone by despair, I took a bold step toward her.

'It is a splendid morning,' I announced. 'And a long journey alone. You would sweeten it by riding with me a little of the way.'

'Me?' she said with surprise.

'Until the path grows steep,' I proposed.

Williams's face was not encouraging. 'Angela has duties,' he announced.

'No doubt,' I said.

'And is a shy girl,' he added. 'She is not in the custom of riding with visitors from the outer world. In any case it would not be fitting.'

'It is not every day a mission girl in the Bay of Islands has the chance to share an hour with an English man of letters.'

'Most might think that a mercy,' Williams grumbled.

'It cannot but help give her confidence in the social graces,' I argued. 'You have my word that my motives are of the seemliest. I promise not to remove her from sight of civilisation. I stake my reputation on Angela coming to no harm.'

This was not a substantial wager. Nevertheless my eloquence appeared to leave Williams in difficulty. Angela was poised for disappointment; perhaps he foresaw a vexing god-daughter should he refuse her permission to ride. By way of preliminary there was a crash of chinaware. Cups and saucers last seen in Angela's hands were now in fragments. Her guileless face rose above the wreckage. 'I am sorry,' she said with no conviction.

'An hour, then,' Williams said.

'No more,' I promised.

To Angela he added, 'You will turn back at the falls. No further. You understand?'

Angela appeared to. She left a daughterly kiss on Williams's silvering head.

The morning could hardly have been brighter. Angela rode sidesaddle, in authorised Englishwoman's manner, with parasol shading her head. The effort of winning an hour with her left me with little to say. In the event she spoke first.

'What is it you wish today, Mr Ferdinand?' she asked.

I was slow to say.

'You have not been shy before,' she pointed out.

'I am a gentleman today,' I explained.

She saw fit to laugh.

I persuaded my horse nearer hers, taking my heart literally in my hands; and slipped her my *billet doux*.

'There may be more,' I warned.

She halted her horse to puzzle over the missive. 'Words?' she said with wonder.

'In the literal sense.'

'This is a letter?'

'Of loving nature. I should prefer it seen as song.'

She failed to be impressed.

'Inspired by you,' I persisted.

'Me?'

'It is not unknown for poets to lavish their gift upon objects of adoration. The greatest English songster, William Shakespeare, composed dozens of sonnets to his mysterious Dark Lady. You seem to be mine.'

'I must turn back,' she announced in panic.

In even larger alarm, I reached for her hand. On horseback this manoeuvre was hazardous. Her mount veered away; likewise her hand. I lost stirrups and saddle, and found myself resuming acquaintance with the world on rocky ground. Angela was kneeling near, her face misty above mine.

'My love,' I whispered, perhaps prematurely.

'Do you hurt, Mr Ferdinand?' she asked.

'Abominably,' I complained. 'My greatest pain is here.'

I placed my hand on my heart, leading hers there too.

'That is not where you have complained of an ache before.'

'I have to confess it. There is an irresponsible side to my character. You could yet tame it.'

She was not impressed. 'You are ready to stand on your legs,' she judged.

I did, rather slowly. My bones were bent, but not irreparably buckled. Angela retrieved the horses, and held my reins ready.

'My ache remains,' I informed her.

I found no sympathy. 'I know where it dwells,' she insisted.

'You misunderstand,' I pleaded.

My Dark Lady thought not.

We rode a mile further. Each silent yard was a nail in Ferdinand's coffin; she refused to be wooed. The sound of rushing waters grew loud. As we neared the falls I found, after all, little picturesque in their character; the place held no charm for a foiled suitor.

'It is time for me to turn back,' she announced.

'If you must,' I sulked.

'I must,' she said.

I made my last throw. 'A parting kiss, then,' I suggested.

She laughed cruelly, and pointed her horse back toward the Bay. 'Next time,' she said over her shoulder.

'Next time?'

'When you are more manly.'

'Meaning less gentlemanly?'

'That is for you to decide.'

Nevertheless euphoria buoyed me the rest of the day, and most of the way.

On first sight of Heke's village my chest seemed to fill out, with Ferdinand Wildblood fading away; this was Henry Youngman's domain. As I passed outlying dwellings men nodded with respect. In the centre of the settlement others gathered to greet me and relieve me of my reins. Among them was genial Moses. John Heke, however, put in no appearance.

'He is away visiting,' Moses explained.

'Allies?'

'Friends,' Moses said.
'Are we talking of social courtesies?'
'Perhaps,' Moses said.
'How is his mood?'
'Poor,' Moses reported.
'He knows of Nene's visit?'
'He knows,' Moses acknowledged.
'And that the Queen's flag flies again?'
'Who does not?'
'Does Heke mean to let matters stand?'
Moses shrugged. 'That is not for me to tell you.'
'Meaning?'
'Heke doesn't know either.'
'He has won much of what he wanted,' I pointed out.
'Except to persist as we wish. Today the governor can say yes. Tomorrow he can say no.'
'Is that Heke's thought?'
'It is what the flag tells him,' Moses said.

There was little left to say. Playing reliable observer was profitless too. There was no unusual number of males or increase in horse numbers in John Heke's village. Nor were firearms more evident. That might do much for Williams's peace of mind.

'You are disappointed,' Moses judged.
'I should have liked to have seen Heke,' I confessed.
'For what purpose?'
'To think on his story.'
Moses was thoughtful. 'Then he may wish to see you,' he surmised.

Next morning I rode inland with Moses, in a more or less southerly direction. We threaded through fernland and forest, and crashed through swamp. Towards the end of the day we tethered our beasts and used a small canoe to cross a river which spilled greasily through mangroves. We beached our craft on a smelly mudbank and hauled it to dry ground. Thereafter we hiked into hill country. Another mile made an old Maori stronghold apparent. It crowned a small plateau, its once powerful earthworks crumbling, its palisades weathered silver. Backed by dark bush, it was an inhospitable place. It was also an unpromising locality for loyalty to the British crown to flower. Smoke rose from cooking fires. There was the sound of chickens and children.

'Kawiti's,' Moses explained.

'Kawiti?'

'Better known as the Duke.'

'A Maori duke?' I attempted not to smile.

'When sailors first came to the Bay of Islands they knew the great Hongi as a king. Kawiti was the wildest of his fighting followers. There was no lord of war more feared. Therefore he was called Duke.'

'You fail to tell me what this nobleman is doing here.'

Moses was in no rush with information. 'He is now an old man,' he said.

'A wise one?'

'Perhaps. Perhaps not.'

'What are you telling me?'

'The Duke is no Christian,' Moses explained. 'He may live to be the last pagan. One by one he has seen other warriors of rank succumb to the missionaries, some on their deathbeds. He has scorn for them all.'

'Is that why he dwells far from his fellows?'

'He wishes not to see what is happening to his tribe,' Moses agreed. 'He sees others who think only of selling land, chiefs who now feud with each other over which hills and valleys are theirs to market. He chooses to reside here with his family until he is needed.'

'Needed by whom?'

'Those who wish his wisdom,' Moses said obscurely.

'In other words Heke,' I interpreted.

'Who knows?' Moses shrugged. His face was sly.

'Heke appears to have nothing against colonist cash.'

'That is a problem,' Moses acknowledged.

'Nor does he turn his face from Christ,' I pointed out.

'That is a difficulty too,' Moses allowed.

The settlement was unguarded; we were met with no challenge. Nor was I much noticed. Mangrove forest had left me muddy enough to be taken for Maori. John Heke and a man of unmistakably ducal character sat together on a roughly carpentered wooden bench, outside the settlement's largest dwelling, in late afternoon sun. Moses and I eased ourselves into an inconspicuous location nearby. Heke appeared a frivolous fledgling beside the old campaigner. Looking every year of his three score and ten, Kawiti alias the Duke was white-haired and lean, all sinew and scarred skin, his dark shanks especially spindly. His features were buried under beard and bold tattoo. Neither man looked elated by the company he was keeping. Weariness was in evidence. Conversation consisted of spurts of eloquence ventilated by momentous silences.

When it suited him, Moses translated for me. 'He tells Heke that the British fish is only to be battled in deep water. Heke wades only up to his ankles. Fighting a flagstaff has no distinction. Any fool could fell it.'

'He tells Heke he is a fool?'

'In a most civil way. He informs Heke that he might be more willing to talk if there were a real war to fight. Meaning with the redcoat men of Britain. Heke must boast less, prove himself more, and produce the red tribe at an agreed hour.'

John Heke looked even more downcast. With more than enough said, the Duke rose, looked loftily over those present, and returned to the interior of his dwelling. A long silence ensued.

'So that is that,' I suggested.

'Altogether,' Moses agreed.

John Heke was no conversationalist on the slow journey home. With darkness, and the terrain too unruly for travel, he ordered camp made. Finally he called me to his fire.

'How is Henry Youngman?' he asked.

'Perplexed,' I informed him.

'You saw Nene?'

'And the new flag flying.'

'Might it seem that Nene has the better of me?'

'It might,' I said cautiously.

'If you were a Briton of senior station, what would your thought be?'

'The same,' I reluctantly reported.

'Might it also seem that the Duke does not take me seriously?'

'He certainly appears content with retirement.'

'So what does that say?'

It was not for me to answer.

'You would say it is not much of a story,' Heke grieved.

Eight

As midsummer arrived it might have been thought that John Heke was even more on the wane. But 1845 was less than a fortnight in the making when he felled the flagstaff a second time. Nene's men had grown bored with the commonplaces of guard duty. They wandered off to bed their women and weed their gardens. The new-minted flagstaff was left in the care of a signalman and his son. The two were woken an hour before dawn by a barking dog. They found their door fastened against exit; at a distance they heard the sound of axe on wood. At first their cries went unheeded. Then a voice they knew as Heke's was heard cordial beyond their barred door.

'I much regret interrupting your night's sleep,' he informed them. 'Does someone within smoke?'

'You want tobacco?' the shivering signalman asked.

'Matches,' Heke said.

These were promptly passed through the window. Outside there was the groan of timber in trouble. Cries of fulfilment heralded the thump as the flagstaff toppled. Finally there was the crackle of flame. This time the demolition of the flagstaff was comprehensive; they were torching it too. The terrified signalman and his son were freed. Hands were shaken and in the course of further apologies Heke did much to explain his fascination with the flagstaff. 'It is not made of flesh,' he said. 'It neither bruises nor bleeds. Better still, it does not cry out in pain. This battle is won. Tell your fellows there is no cause for fear.'

This appeared true. Heke and his boisterous party made no advance on the dwellings of Blackguard Beach. They ambled back to their canoes as the last of the flagstaff smouldered. There was no jubilant shot fired, and, aside from an axeman with split shin, no blood shed. As a raid, it was magically free of rancour. The community merely woke to find itself flagless again.

'Now,' said Turner, 'it begins.'

'It?' I asked.

'The real thing,' he predicted.

'War?'

'And no mistake.'

Looking back, I see that was John Heke's notion too; he was arranging a rendezvous with the red tribe which the Duke would not be able to resist. In this respect he found recruiting officers busy on his behalf on the far side of the planet. Long-winded legislators in the British House of Commons had begun denouncing treaties and agreements with the New Zealand Maori as sinful folly. To meet with South Sea natives in solemn ceremony gave brown scoundrels an overblown notion of their station. It was unsanctioned by experience and common sense. Like natives elsewhere, they were best shown their predestined place with a firm show of force and, if need be, with a brisk cannonade. As for their soil, that which they cultivated might remain their own. Land left wild, on which they merely hunted or fished, might rightfully be considered Britain's, with no monetary compensation necessary. John Heke was privy to this news before most in the Bay of Islands. After picking it up from a passing skipper he did not think on it long. He threw himself on a horse and hurtled into the high terrain of the interior, outdistancing his lieutenants, and placed the intelligence at the feet of the Duke. According to Moses, who arrived at the old warrior's upland eyrie a breathless second, the Duke was silent for some time. Finally he turned a cold eye on Heke.

'This is all you have to tell me?' he asked.

Heke dwindled. 'Much land you think yours could now be theirs.'

'True,' the Duke said calmly.

'And more.'

'As I warned.'

'I see no anger,' Heke protested.

The Duke sighed; his tone remained that of parent to petulant child. 'I am old,' he explained unnecessarily.

'And content to sit?'

'And wait.'

'Until light is gone from the Maori sky?'

'Until the war that wants me.'

'Which is that?' Heke asked bitterly.

'My last,' the Duke said quietly.

'Mine might serve you well,' Heke suggested.

The Duke was silent.

Heke twisted the knife. 'How long can you live, old man?'

The Duke refused a forecast. Heke produced his *coup de théâtre*. With a flourish he presented the Duke with a small package of dressed native flax tied with a cord.

'Untie the cord,' Heke proposed.

As onlookers grew quiet the Duke did so. Cord and covering fell away to reveal an ancestral jade club precious to their tribe. Daubed with human excrement, however, it was an unsavoury sight. The Duke was not perplexed. The meaning could not have been plainer. The weapon stood for the Maori. The excrement stood for insult heaped on their tribe. It was for the Duke to say whether the club was to be cleansed or left soiled. To the surprise of some, the Duke backed off and pleaded need for rest; the club was left on the ground, where it drew flies as the Duke dozed in his dwelling.

Thwarted Heke, in the hour or two which then passed, paced from one quarter of the Duke's stronghold to another; he seemed to be looking for something and not finding it. At times he appeared in visceral pain. There was even, imagined Moses, a trace of tears. Toward sunset the Duke reappeared. First he stood silent outside his dwelling. He looked at the sky, then at his visionary junior. Finally his gaze fell on the befouled club. Waving away flies, he took it up without flinching.

'Bring water,' he ordered.

'I will clean it,' Heke offered.

'The task is mine,' the Duke insisted. 'I can make your war work.'

It was still high summer in the Bay of Islands. The season might have been conducive to indolence, but there was little languor to be seen. After the second rout of the flagstaff, one day was never like another. In the week following there was alarm after alarm, all of them false, with fearful householders scurrying this way and that. Some brandished weapons; others flourished petitions to the government concerning life and limb. Rumour appeared to be preparing the way for the final ruination of the town. Merchants of gloom were finding it expedient to set up shop in Auckland or Wellington, the further south the better. Itinerant skippers were making the most of this harvest; none left without human cargo. From my window on the world I watched vessels take the tide on the ebb and their sails unfurl as they found wind. To be frank, I was impatient. Fate surely had something more substantial in mind than the rumps of merchant shipping. Was it my destiny to be the last citizen of Blackguard Beach, in nostalgic conversation with Henry Youngman?

In the meantime Angela made it her business to ensure that Henry had little breath left for social intercourse. If truth be told, and sometimes it must be, his amorous spirit had begun to flag behind his flesh; the condition was that virulent form of boredom known as accidie. If he had the new-found conviction there was more to life than lust, who would gainsay him? This left the door ajar for Ferdinand. More often than not, now, Angela was perplexed by a tea party arranged in her honour. With prose pleasantries terminated she was ambushed by a selection of sonnets. She correctly identified these rhapsodic tributes as preliminaries to the real business of the encounter; the problem was that Henry rather than Ferdinand remained the beneficiary of the transaction. Ferdinand, by and large, was left cooling his heels.

Williams was another and frequent visitor to Blackguard Beach. He comforted those in most need; he did not refuse communion to the meanest sinner, or for that matter to Wesleyans of fraying faith.

'At least you show no inclination to panic,' he observed.

'I know Heke,' I claimed.

'Would it were still that simple. You have heard, I imagine, of the alliance the wretch has made with Kawiti.'

'With the Duke?'

'As they call the ugly old villain,' Williams said with distaste.

'I believe I have heard some such account,' I said vaguely. It was not for me to inform Williams that I had a handy source.

'It means, sir, that old ghosts may be awoken. The Duke is of the old warrior caste, one which never blinked at butchery. There is safety in Heke's less single-minded generation. For all our present woes, we are not numbering dead.'

'Are you saying Heke's toil with the axe is to be encouraged?'

Williams was not saying. 'I fear the worst,' he reported, and went his unhappy way.

At dusk the same day my handy source knocked on my door. It was Moses, whose furtive appearances in the town had become regular when evening fell. Heke had assigned him the duty of keeping watch on the place and reporting on hearsay. This was not onerous. Much of his time was spent enjoying my hospitality, depleting my supply of spirits, and besting me at cards.

'News from Auckland?' he asked.

'Of a confusing nature. Gossip says Governor FitzRoy is at his wits' end. Nevertheless his rejoinder is certain.'

'Guns.'

'And as many soldiers as he can interest in a fight. He cannot be feeble this time. Or generous. I trust Heke knows.'

'He knows,' Moses announced, and reflectively shuffled the cards.

'And you mean to stay with him?'

'With never a dull day,' Moses agreed.

Governor FitzRoy's reaction, of time-honoured nature, did no more than befog matters. In poor temper he placed a bounty of one hundred pounds on John Heke's head. This was a blunder. For the first time Heke had a sure sense of his own worth; no Maori had been priced higher the length of the land. It was a challenge to prove himself worth every penny.

Further tribute followed. FitzRoy sent thirty soldiers north, and summoned more from Sydney. Beckham was optimistically ordered to swear in all able men as constables and issue them with arms and ammunition so that they might swiftly arrest Heke should he make a repeat appearance at Blackguard Beach. Knee deep in new orders, Beckham was also instructed to raise a fresh flagstaff and to protect it from predatory axemen by sheathing its base in iron and caging it with tough palisades. A blockhouse was to be built about it, its guard on watch day and night; another grew downhill, to cover the approach to the first. Provision was made for women and children, the aged and infirm, in the form of a bulky stockade. Maori were warned of the punishing consequences of comforting Heke, and above all of slighting the Union Jack. 'Great Britain will never allow her Flag to be displaced,' FitzRoy scribbled to Beckham. By January's end there were fifty soldiers ensconced in the neighbourhood, and more due from Sydney. Early in February my new friend Lieutenant Philpotts made a welcome return when the *Hazard* resumed station off Blackguard Beach. Ratings and marines took charge of the blockhouses; a field gun was placed to train fire on intruders. Other pieces were tactically planted around the town. Tribesmen who gathered to marvel at martial bedlam were warned away. Many were merely waiting for Governor FitzRoy to make a showing. They had never yet heard of a leader who viewed war from afar. What kind of chief, they asked, left it to subordinates to do battle? To be fair, FitzRoy had a choice of evils. To travel to the Bay of Islands, and there wait on a rebel of humble rank to do mischief, might equally lower his status in the eyes of the Maori and elevate his foe. He handed field command, therefore, to Police Magistrate Beckham. This ensured folly. In an indifferent martial career, Beckham had never ranked higher than ensign. He had no notion of how to manage armed men in number, nor what to do with an eighteen-gun corvette.

I expected Beckham to come knocking. I was not disappointed.

'I am empowered to enrol you as a special constable,' he announced.

'I feared as much,' I answered.

'And to issue you with a weapon,' he explained.

'I have a handsomely crafted pistol of the two-barrelled kind,' I said, presenting it for his inspection.

'A toy,' he judged. 'It would never blow a hole in a Maori hide.'

'There is, I suppose, no respectable way I can be excused duty.'

'You suppose right. What kind of man are you, Mr Wildblood?'

'An imaginative one,' I informed him.

He grunted in unfriendly fashion.

'Furthermore,' I pressed on, 'I see no large need for war.'

'You echo Williams,' he said.

'It is true that I sometimes listen to Mr Williams more than is good for me. It is also true, however, that I have reached this conclusion without benefit of clergy.'

'You would see our community defenceless?'

'I should certainly like to see it milder of temper. Heke must see cause to increase his numbers. Where will that end?'

'Against British steel,' Beckham promised.

'May I confess myself less than enthusiastic about that prospect?'

'By all means,' Beckham said patiently.

'And that I have mixed feelings in this matter? What do you say to that?'

'Drill tomorrow at nine,' Beckham told me. 'Daily until further notice.'

Turner turned out to be my drill sergeant. As a sometime chain gang overseer, promoted from irons because of his gift for bluster, he was an effective choice as a martial bully. His language was fittingly foul, his humour of the gallows kind.

'What are you doing with your arse?' he bellowed brutishly, after

I attempted to wheel in accord with his order. That left me marching solo while several score companions trooped elsewhere.

'Locating it to my rear,' I protested.

'If I see it off in another direction, I'll boot it,' he promised.

He reckoned without the worst. Musketry practice, and my skittish firearm, converted him fervently to the view that poets had no place in the defence of Blackguard Beach; he was lucky to escape with no more than a fragment of his left ear lost. He reported to Beckham that Constable Wildblood was better reserved to duties less stirring.

'Chin up,' George Philpotts said compassionately in his naval cabin that night. 'It isn't given to all of us to challenge a savage foe face to face. Who knows that you might not yet have some sturdy role to play? I shall suggest to my commander that you might usefully be seconded to me.'

'To what end?' I asked warily.

'Perhaps to communicate with the town's defenders,' he said. 'Someone will have to bear information back and forth. We may need intelligence in the matter of training our guns reliably. That is, if the worst prevails. Or, dare I say, the best. Our present show of strength may ensure that it does not. That could be a disappointment for all.'

'Perhaps,' I said thoughtfully. 'There is no word yet, I suppose, on Major Bridge and his regiment.'

'Cyprian has been summoned,' George reported. 'Communication with Sydney is infernally slow. I gather that shipowners are unwilling to risk their vessels in this vicinity until an extortionate price is paid for the transport of troops. I too will rejoice when we have the 58th on the horizon rather than the bumbling odds and sods of less enlightened regiments. It has never been more needed. It is my feeling, by the way, that this subject deserves another bottle.'

'Amen,' I agreed.

Somewhat later I was rowed ashore by a rating. But for an oil lamp in a window here and there, the town was dark; it was also powerfully quiet. A lonely pair of sentries patrolled the shore. If this was to be an antipodean Troy, I could see candidates for the roles of Achilles and Agamemnon; neither John Heke nor the Duke would much surprise Homer. The problem was seeing a helpful Hector. Beckham nobly dedicated to the death? Turner gloriously felling the enemy at the gate? Alas.

I turned into my quarters. Before I lit a candle I knew there had been a visitor. The place was perfumed with fresh tobacco smoke. An exhausted bottle and empty glass confirmed that Moses, rather than Angela, had been my shadowy caller. There was a gift too. The parcel bore the inscription *To Henry from Heke*. Within the wrapping I found a bottle of good quality ink, three virgin pens, and a useful stockpile of paper. A loaded musket could not have been more eloquent.

Nine

*F*our days have gone since I last put my shoulder to this pen. And I still fail to find strength. Is it because I want to to cry stop? Never. One must listen to the past, not shout it down. Speaking of shouting, it seems to me that man had a problem in New Zealand. Save for birdsong the land was stirringly soundless. The first humans saw its untamed terrain as rubble left by feuding gods. Man had to fill it with his own din to feel at home. Nothing served better than battle. Firearms lifted the sound of mortal tumult even more satisfyingly. In the time of which I write the place was home to one hundred thousand tribesmen, with thousands of white colonists beginning to wade ashore. Nevertheless there was still a square mile of silence for every man, woman and child in the land. This suggested even more uproar in the making. Though it is forty years in the past, I find myself listening again for the first shot in the war they call Heke's.

He displayed himself on the northern shore of the Bay in the first mellow week of March. Two hundred men kept him company. From Blackguard Beach, on the southern shore, the smoke of many fires was visible; they glowed nightlong. If Heke's intention was to leave Britons feeling unloved, this stratagem was no fiasco. The more so when news came from the interior that the Duke was rallying scores of seasoned men to his side; further news said the old aristocrat was already on the march. Absence of news was just as demoralising; there was still no word on the arrival of the 58th under the command of Cyprian Bridge. Given all this, and not a little more, Ferdinand's inclination was to take to bed and cover his head with a blanket. Circumstances, however, made no provision for malingering. Angela, for example, was still determined to enliven the remainder of Henry Youngman's earthly span. Moses continued his nocturnal visitations in the course of collecting intelligence of the red tribe's troubles. To be fair, he no longer tempted me into disloyalty by pressing me for information; he merely divined what he needed from my apprehensive countenance.

Finally there was Williams.

'Heke and the Duke could join forces any day now,' he reported to me.

'No doubt,' I said.

'The thought is not to be borne. Heke might still charitably be seen as a boyish nuisance. There is no kindly view to be taken of the wicked old warrior with whom he makes common cause.'

'You are about to put a proposition to me, sir,' I decided.

'I have in mind a last chance to bring Heke to his senses,' Williams agreed.

'Involving me?'

'Your good offices. Heke has requested me to conduct divine service in his camp. It would be churlish to refuse. In his heart of hearts he remains a Christian of conscience.'

'I trust you have a serviceable text in hand.'

'I had in mind the epistle of James. Chapter four, verse one. From whence come wars and fightings among you?'

'And you mean to make a rejoinder in that respect, sir?'

'As does James. War begins in the members of men. It begins, as does all evil, in our lusts. Resist the devil, says James, and he will flee from you.'

'I confess myself at sea, sir. Is it abstinence you are suggesting, or emasculation?'

'Purity of heart,' Williams said. 'I hope to provoke lengthy discussion. Better untidy discourse than untimely death. The longer matters are drawn out, the better the chance for Christian virtue to prevail.'

'You are a tenacious man, sir.'

'A vexed one.'

'You have still to tell me how I might serve your purposes.'

'It is not that I fear journeying alone to Heke's camp. It is merely that a lay presence is desirable. Better still, a familiar of Heke's. Ideally, such a personage might have a pacifying effect when my message is heard.'

'You ask much, sir.'

'I think not,' Williams said. 'Your acquaintance with Heke, though you might wish it otherwise, is no secret. Nor, for that matter, is your identity. You had me believe your name was Wildblood, a harmless poet. Native gossip tells me that this is not altogether the case. You are more widely known as Youngman, a promiscuous scribbler of trifles. Please don't protest innocence.'

'In my capacity as Henry Youngman I seldom do, sir.'

'It may be,' Williams went on, 'that a tale of moral character could divert Heke's hot-heads. And at least persuade them to delay matters.'

'With a Henry Youngman tale?'

'Why not?' Williams looked quizzical over his glasses.

'It is plain that you are unfamiliar with his work. Through no wish of my own Henry Youngman tends to make a case for heroic enterprise.'

'Then it is time to tell a new story,' Williams suggested. 'One which honours compassionate pursuits.'

I feared as much. 'In the present noisy climate,' I argued, 'such a message must surely fall on deaf ears.'

Williams himself failed to hear me. 'The more we detain Heke, the more time he has for second thoughts. Should he fall into the Duke's clutch all is lost.'

'The old man may have more to fear from Heke's embrace. It was he who summoned the Duke from hiding.'

'Rumour says Heke is beginning to rue it. He may have begun to see that he has unbottled a genie. Worse still, from Heke's point of view, the Duke promises to become a rival. The Duke's notoriety makes him, not Heke, the man of the hour. Vintage warriors are more inclined to look to the old rogue as a leader than untried Heke. Jealousy could work in our favour, given time.'

'How much time do you have in mind, sir?'

'For your new tale? Between now and Wednesday.'

'Wednesday,' I protested, 'is the day after tomorrow.'

'That is my impression too,' Williams said.

The composition of a saga drenched with sweetness and light made Henry's past literary chores look puny. They were. He was a novice in the trade of hammering prose swords into ploughshare parlance. On the first of the two nights left to preserve Britain's most distant domain his lamp burned until dawn. It promised to glow as long on the second too. With no more than a flatulent phrase on show, Henry faded wraith-like from the field and left the literary dilemma to Ferdinand Wildblood. For hour upon hour there was an urgent crackle of pen on paper. One stanza gave birth to another; one rhyme rang in the next. Never had Ferdinand Wildblood been heard to more resonant effect. By promising miracle he was attired, shaven and ready for the Reverend when he appeared at his door on Wednesday morning. Williams's countenance was dishearteningly dour.

'The Duke,' he disclosed, 'is no more than a day's ride away at last report. And still gathering men as he travels. Worse, white colonists are fleeing before him. And for good reason. The wretches are killing colonist livestock, and then looting and firing barns and dwellings. The bad news is that they are like some biblical plague. The good is that no loss of life is reported.'

'That is more than a small mercy,' I argued.

'I hope for another. Heke cannot be happy. He wishes no war against Christian colonists. For one thing, they remain a ready source of money. His is a fight with the flag and those who will it to fly. May his differences with the Duke flourish.'

An obliging breeze whisked us toward Heke's camp. Unarmed tribesmen lined the shore and ushered us on to dry ground. With an expressive roll of eyes in my direction, Moses led us to Heke. Most of his two hundred were already seated in an attentive semi-circle.

'All awaits you, Reverend Williams,' Heke said with a faint smile.

Shaky Williams contemplated the Bible in his hands. He may have been in circumstances more cheerless; his face did not suggest that such was the case.

Silence grew.

'Come, sir,' Heke urged. 'You have a congregation before you ready to give of their lives. A message of comfort might do much for their happiness.'

'Is that why you wish me here?' Williams asked. 'For purposes of morale?'

'Do British soldiers not ask blessing before battle?'

'On occasion,' Williams allowed with unease.

'Then why not we? Do we not rank equal in the eyes of God?'

Heke, it has to be said, had a point.

'Proceed,' he ordered.

Williams began. His discomfort did not diminish. Rather than elaborate on one text, he used his ammunition too liberally, leaping from one biblical injunction to another. His sulky congregation appeared unimpressed with the proposition that they had best turn another cheek to British authority; they looked mutinously of the view that warmakers had as much right as peacemakers to be blessed. Much as he tried to bend it, Williams could not even persuade the golden rule to fit present circumstances. His audience was only too willing to do unto others as they would be done unto; otherwise zest was lacking.

After a desperate hour Williams gave in to exhaustion. His audience, it seemed, had no more to ask of him than communion. Heke was first to kneel for wafer and wine.

'It is your turn, I fear,' Williams said to me as he finished moving through the brown throng.

As it proved, communion's end was Heke's cue. Rising above his fellows, he said, 'We thank our brother in Christ for moving fearless among us. We know he will also give blessing to the soldiers we fight. This is fair. We wish a foe bold, strong and noble. If we fail, there will therefore be no disgrace in defeat.'

I had to assume that he meant every word. Warriors notoriously do.

Williams shuffled unhappily. 'I had not counted on this,' he whispered. 'He is using me to fire his rabble.'

Heke overheard. 'Have you more to say, Reverend Williams?' he asked with interest.

'Perhaps my companion has,' Williams said.

'Henry Youngman?' Heke said.

'As Mr Wildblood sometimes chooses to style himself,' Williams said. 'I have persuaded him that a literary work might not be out of place on this occasion.'

'We are always happy to hear from Henry Youngman,' Heke said generously; it was more than many a publisher might now say. When Heke signalled me to his side, and I looked over the horde of heads before me, the blue amphitheatre of the Bay beyond, I felt Ferdinand Wildblood's hour had come. It is open to few fabulists to fashion events; to give poor humankind pause in its folly. There was never a bard born who would not envy my circumstance. I coughed, clearing my throat in the style of Maori orators, and lifted my arm expressively; there was a gratifying murmur of approval and anticipation from tribesmen squatted near.

Then I was launched. While Moses interpreted with suspicious fluency, I drew the attention of fellow creatures on this planet to the pleasures of the flesh, to the virtues of a full belly and a good woman. To phrase it modestly, they were hearing a song of affection for the world: one which took cognisance of sunrise and sunset, the fragrance of flowers, the music of birds. There were no subterfuges. It argued that life was good, and death undesirable. Even heaven, it hinted subversively, might not be all it was rumoured to be.

It was some time before I risked examining faces. Williams's was unsurprisingly cool. Heke's was intrigued. Elsewhere, abetted by Moses' long-winded translations, my stanzas were having a usefully enfeebling effect. Beyond the fiftieth many warriors were in difficulty with the waking world.

Finally and reluctantly I arrived at the end of my lines. The last of Moses' hoarse translation lifted away on the breeze. The silence was powerful. It was not that I expected applause. Urgent whispering, and sage nodding of heads, would have been sufficient; declarations of love for life could follow in the fullness of time. But tribal eyes were on Heke rather than me; they were looking to see what their leader made of my message. Even those lately battling oblivion were now open-eyed.

As it happened, Heke had much to make of it. He rose, cleared his vocal passage, and looked over his people; he seemed to be contemplating face after face. He addressed his first words to me.

'You tell us that the world is rich,' he said.

'That is so,' I agreed.

'And good.'

'For the greater part,' I allowed cautiously.

'What you say is true also of New Zealand?'

'Especially so,' I said.

'Is not such a land worth fighting for?'

Heke had led me on to tricky terrain. I looked in appeal to Williams, to no helpful effect.

'On one view of the matter,' I finally said.

'Is there another?' he challenged.

I found myself silent.

'As for life,' he added, 'the sweeter it is, the braver the warrior ready to risk its loss.' He turned to his force. 'Let me,' he asked, 'hear if my men agree.'

His youthful followers leapt loud to their feet, their firearms making a perilous appearance; their response roared over us. Fearful seagulls fled high in the air. It was some time before the sound of rustling sea returned.

'You hear?' Heke said.

Williams and I allowed that we did.

'Is there more to say?'

Williams at least thought not. Our verbal exertions, mine no less than his, had gone for nothing. He shook Heke's hand sadly and silently and began to make abject return to his boat. I followed at reflective pace.

'Wait,' Heke called.

'For what?' Williams said.

'I want you to know that I wish no misfortune to fellow men.'

'You fail to convince me,' Williams said.

'Mine is a quarrel with a serpent,' Heke argued. 'As soon as I cut off its head it grows another. Rumour tells me that it is now a monster, with skin of iron, kept in a cage; I wish to view this rare and wonderful creature which needs men in bondage.'

'You are talking of Britain,' Williams said.

'Its flag. I wish you to pray for me.'

'If I must,' Williams sighed.

'I also wish your companion to linger at my side.'

He meant, it seemed, me. My interest in proceedings became less detached.

'As hostage?' Williams asked.

'I have need of him,' Heke explained.

'It could go ill with you if he is harmed.'

'I would miss him too,' Heke claimed.

'Nevertheless he is entitled to be heard on this subject.'

I found my voice faint. Henry also proved to be in hiding. 'I am happy to be of service,' I suggested.

'You will be,' Heke promised.

My overnight woes might have been worse. The largest was surviving Moses' roaring snores in a roughly thatched bivouac. Morning revealed more serious discomfort in the making. Angry smoke on the horizon signalled the arrival of the Duke's arsonists. Soon there were three hundred armed men streaming down coastal hillside, the Duke riding lean at their centre. Few were under forty, and some all of sixty. Tattooed faces and bullet-scarred bodies announced them as battlefield veterans. Some led horses already burdened by the spoils of war. They looked with condescension on Heke's less robust band and halted at a distance. The Duke rode the last score of yards to Heke alone. There was a silence as the two faced each other.

Heke was first to speak. 'You are here,' he said, never one to neglect the obvious.

'That is so,' the Duke said, replying in kind.

'Your skirmishers have been busy,' Heke observed.

'As ordered,' the Duke agreed.

'Were they ordered to put peaceful families to flight, to loot and destroy dwellings? Did you woo men to your side with promise of prizes?'

'I pledged them no more than did my fighting father, and his father before him.'

'When Maori chastised Maori.'

'Perhaps so,' the Duke allowed.

'This is different,' Heke said. 'Now we war for fellow Maori.'

'For all?' The Duke had difficulty with this notion.

'All,' Heke confirmed.

'Even Nene?'

'Maori can no longer afford to fight Maori. That is a bygone pleasure .'

The Duke considered cloudy sky for a time. This was not the world he knew.

'Tell Nene,' he suggested dryly.

'Our guns could persuade him to hear.'

'And join us?' the Duke mocked.

'Perhaps to stand to one side.'

The Duke evinced no joy in that prospect either.

Heke persisted, 'We punish only those who would have us without right to the land we called ours.'

'Therefore we war with all of fair skin,' the Duke asserted.

'Let virtue be seen. There are many such who mean us no harm. Men who plough fields and fatten cattle make a poor enemy.'

'Christians?' the Duke asked with suspicion.

'Fellow men. What is your grievance against them?'

'That they are here,' the Duke said.

'Our tribe made them welcome.'

'They have been hungry guests,' the Duke said. 'You tell me yourself they promise to bite larger.'

'I offered you a war with the red tribe,' Heke pointed out. 'I offered you fight with the soldiers and sailors who now guard the flag. Not with those who give us no insult.'

'What do you tell me?' the Duke demanded.

'Let us be rebels, not robbers,' Heke asked.

The Duke, after long silence, pleaded need for thought among his fellows. Thus much of a day passed with the two armies camped separate, the two leaders testily so. It was dusk before they found need of each other again.

'I hear you,' the Duke admitted.

'And I you,' Heke said.

This meant the Duke would have his war and Heke have his. The Duke would duel with men of the red tribe drawn from the town. Heke would fell the flagstaff at his pleasure. The town was to be left intact and its inhabitants unharmed. High spirits and reckless deeds were not to be countenanced. It would be a short and dignified fight, followed by swift withdrawal. In other words they fashioned a clash mutually pleasing.

Heke had received Christian blessing. The Duke needed ceremony of a more inspiring kind. With the council of war concluded, he wished the interpreting of omens to see where death hid in the scheme. To this end he had in his entourage his favoured pagan priest, or tohunga, an aged soothsayer whose talents had been little tried for a decade. To divine the course of battle the priest used a pair of airborne darts. These had a sharp end and a blunt; when lofted in the air there was an auspicious and inauspicious way for them to return to earth. The sharp end pointing away from the thrower meant good fortune; pointing toward the thrower meant poor. Heke's prospects were contemplated first. One dart was thrown for him; a second for his foe. His dart fell propitiously, not so his enemy's. 'You will confound the red tribe,' the priest deduced. 'The flagstaff will fall.' There was a sigh of relief from spectators. Then the Duke's fortunes were considered. This time the darts took a perverse tack. The dart for the soldiers fell unpromisingly. So, on the other hand, did the Duke's. 'This means,' explained the priest helpfully, 'there will be a hard fight. For you, and for them.'

At first the Duke looked piqued. Neveretheless omens could not be gainsaid. He announced that the message met with his approval. 'I could not ask better,' he claimed. 'Who wants an easy fight?'

A good question. Shifty faces suggested that he would have found more than a few volunteers for an effortless encounter. Even his tougher tribesmen appeared to be thinking that there was something to be said for one-sided strife.

After formalities were finished, Heke asked me to his side. 'A canoe waits for you on the shore,' he informed me. 'You are now free to leave.'

'I understood you had need of me,' I said.

'That is correct,' he said. 'You will report what you have seen and heard in my camp?'

'If asked,' I confessed carefully.

'That is my need,' he explained. 'Our attack on Blackguard Beach will be made on Tuesday morning.'

'This Tuesday?'

'The eleventh of March,' he agreed.

He appeared to be serious.

'You wish me to report this?'

'Why else would I tell you?' he asked. 'The signal will be the rising of the dawn star. We will attack from three points. Two of the points will be the Duke's. He will attack through the pass to the west of the town and from the hills to the rear. The third attack will be mine. While the Duke tempts men from the town I move on the flagstaff. Have you questions?'

If I had, they failed to make themselves apparent. Labour as I will with this pen, I still fail to make this conversation sound likely. Followers of Henry Youngman's feasible fictions need read no further.

'It is not for me to tell a warrior his business,' I said. 'As I understand it, surprise is the essence of successful warfare. A forewarned foe is a dangerous one.'

'Perhaps so,' Heke shrugged.

'And yet you now scorn it.'

'Ambush is no honourable ally,' he explained.

On the one hand, he may have been refining his story. On the other, who knows? I took a deep breath. 'You are not,' I asked, 'using me for the purpose of deceit now?'

'I promise,' he said.

'I call that chivalrous,' I told him.

'I call it Christian,' he said.

Heke's canoeists ferried me to within forty yards of Blackguard

Beach, then suggested I swim; they were not taken with the notion of closing with a shore populated by bitter Britons. I protested lengthily, pointing out that I was no swimmer. Finally and roughly they dumped me in deep water and made off at speed. Turner, a witness to this inconsiderate proceeding, rowed out to my rescue in a dinghy. He allowed me no time for a change of clothes. He bundled me off bedraggled to Beckham.

'You bring news?' Beckham said.

'Of unhappy nature,' I shivered. 'Heke and the Duke plan their assault on Tuesday next, shortly before dawn.'

'You eavesdropped on their scheming?'

'I am no spy, sir. I have it from the horse's mouth.'

'From Heke?'

'Indeed, sir.'

Beckham laughed shortly. Turner guffawed.

'Let me hear this right,' Beckham asked. 'Heke, you say, confided their battle plan?'

'As much as he judged fit, I daresay. I thought it tactless to ask for detail.'

Turner gave further rein to amusement.

'At all events you believed him?' Beckham said.

'I had no reason not to,' I said.

'It did not occur to you, I imagine, that Heke is playing a devilishly devious game?'

'It most certainly did.'

'And?'

'I nonetheless believe him.'

'Tosh,' Beckham said. 'You are as gullible as Williams.'

'It would be remiss of me not to report my findings,' I argued. 'It is no business of mine whether you act on them.'

'Indeed it is not,' Beckham said. 'I should be grateful, Mr Wildblood, if this went no further. You will serve us best by not pressing your view upon uneasy citizenry. Is that understood?'

'You wish me to remain silent?'

'Just so. Less than level-headed citizens might promote a stampede from the town. Heke's intention would then be accomplished. He is trying to terrify us. He wishes us to abandon our community and our flag so that he can claim a conquest. In this procedure he has made you his agent. We are not to be terrified, Mr Wildblood. We are not fleeing. Furthermore John Heke, braggart though he may be, is no fool. He knows this place to be fortified and manned by disciplined soldiers of the Queen and dedicated citizens of our militia, not to speak of the *Hazard*'s marines; he would never chance a reckless attack. He knows that never has a makeshift native army had the better of British might. Never in this world, Wildblood.'

'That might be seen as a challenge, sir.' I warned.

'To devalue our good name?'

'Certainly to enliven the record, sir.'

'It is not my inclination to preside over an event of belittling nature,' Beckham explained.

'May I venture a suggestion, sir?'

Beckham's face was not enthusiastic. 'Of what character?'

'Practical,' I claimed. 'Call urgently on Nene.'

'Nene?'

'And his men. My understanding is that he remains hostile to Heke and the Duke. Their hope is that their fellow tribesman will remain neutral in the event of an armed clash. They think a triumph of sorts might persuade Nene to be, if not partner in their campaign, at least a thoughtful bystander.'

'You appear to have misheard me, Mr Wildblood. It is not my intention to allow Heke satisfactions of any sort.'

'Consider the possibility of killing two birds with one stone, sir. If Nene's men were to help man the town's defences, Heke and the Duke would surely refrain from hostile proceedings. No triumph could then be claimed. And no Nene persuaded of neutrality.'

'Out of the question,' Beckham announced. 'For one thing Britain has never had need to defend itself with unkempt natives. For another, there would be difficulty in distinguishing friend from foe in the unlikely event of a shot or two being fired.'

My clammy garments were still shedding moisture. Anxious for warmth, I deferred to Beckham. 'If that is how you see it,' I said wearily.

'Indeed I do, Wildblood. You will be much in my debt if you attempt to frighten the town no further with false intelligence. Is there more to be said?'

'Only that the proof of the pudding is in the eating, sir. My hope is that Heke's appetite is modest; any such hope for his ally would be vain.'

'Get away with you,' Beckham said.

'Back to your books,' Turner urged.

Of such is doom made; Blackguard Beach was baring its throat to history.

This was on Friday. Toward evening I rowed out to the *Hazard* to seek consolation from my friend Lieutenant Philpotts. He fitted his monocle gravely to his eye. 'I observe a man in need of a bracer,' he announced.

This was true. I suspected my ducking heralded a fever; I was still sneezing volcanically.

'I believe you have been trysting with the enemy,' he said.

'Trying to avert trouble,' I sniffed.

'You mean you want to spoil our sport? The *Hazard*, I must have you know, has never fired a serious salvo in its history.'

'I am aware of your affection for your guns. The fact of the matter, however, is that I have witnessed half a thousand rebels massing.'

'Good,' Philpotts said.

'Good?' I failed to comprehend him.

'Britons,' he explained, 'are at their best when outnumbered.' He lifted his glass. 'To the war,' he proposed.

Condemned to the company of madmen, I was slow to join him in the toast, though my first tot was finished rather sooner than his. My second merely left me thirsting for a third. It was soon clear, however, that the best naval rum was not going to banish my blacker misgivings; finally I confided them.

'Good God,' Philpotts said. 'Tuesday morning?'

'With the dawn star,' I said.

'Why are you telling me?'

'In the hope that someone will hear.'

'You have a ready listener. You think the warning credible?'

'Heke may be many things, but he is no liar. It would shame him to win by subterfuge.'

'Which Beckham judges it to be?'

'Entirely,' I agreed. 'A threat to make us take to our heels.'

'This is deuced serious after all,' Philpotts concluded. 'I begin to think my commander should know.'

'A word in his ear could pay dividends in terms of our well-being,' I argued.

'I have a problem with my superior,' Philpotts explained. 'Commander Robertson is a dashed fine fellow, in most respects, but given much to melancholy. He broods on the fact that his predecessor on the *Hazard* jumped overboard in despair of making sense of New

Zealand. He has a feeling that he may share the same fate before his term of service frees him of the place. His fervently held belief is that colonists are as asinine as the Maori. To be frank, Wildblood, he is a man haunted. Present circumstances do nothing to diminish his mood. He is depressed that the defences of the town are of poor quality, and the defenders are under the command of fools. He feuds daily with Beckham. Not a morning passes when I wonder if I will find him ripping a razor through his throat. I have no wish to contribute further to his condition — unless, that is, I must.'

'You must,' I insisted.

'Confound it,' Philpotts said.

At first light on Saturday Commander Robertson stormed ashore, with Philpotts at his side, to do business with Beckham. Robertson was a ferocious and bulky black-bearded Scot who even when sober looked in league with the devil. He was manifestly not in alliance with the angels that morning. It did not promise to be a comfortable awakening for Beckham. So it proved. Robertson hauled Beckham from bed by the collar of his night shirt.

Robertson asked, 'Is it or is it not the case that you have been apprised of a Maori attack on Tuesday next?'

'There has,' Beckham admitted, 'been dubious intelligence to that effect.'

'Which you have not seen fit to share?'

'I feel under no obligation to report every rumour that floats about the Bay. Good God, man, I should be everywhere at once.'

'Which you should be,' Robertson suggested. 'Rebellion is simmering around you, man.'

'Are you attempting to give me orders, Captain Robertson?'

'I am telling you that I shall not be taking them,' Robertson announced.

'I represent colonial authority here,' Beckham pointed out. 'This could be construed as mutiny.'

'Then mutiny it damn well shall be, sir,' Robertson promised deafeningly; and left Beckham to partake soberly of breakfast.

In the course of remaining aloof from events, I walked the shore and looked across the Bay. There was no smoke on show from the site where Heke and the Duke had been camped. The day before there had been dozens of fires burning. I made it my business to whisper as much in George Philpotts's ear as he returned to the *Hazard* with his cursing commander.

'How do you see it?' he asked.

'They may be moving their men around to this shore of the Bay. Wouldn't you, if you had Tuesday in mind?'

George was thoughtful. 'God damn it,' he said finally. 'Is there no sanity in this place?'

It seemed not. Finally Captain Robertson was persuaded to give less thought to disembowelling Beckham and more to the mystery of the missing fires.

'Perhaps they are short of livestock to roast,' Robertson said.

'Perhaps, sir. Perhaps not.'

'Then, damn you, get out on the water and see. Look along shore to the west of the town. Note menace if it exists. Then report back here, if you can find me.'

'Where are you likely to be, if not on the *Hazard*, sir?'

'Drunk,' Robertson vowed.

George took a pinnace a mile or two up the Bay, investigating coastal terrain the Duke and Heke might cross in the course of making themselves forceful. So far as George judged it, the shore was empty of nuisance. The day was warm. Lassitude soon overtook his oarsmen. Finally he called a halt in a ferny cove and ordered men ashore to reconnoitre and rest. After the cove was found harmless some men dozed on the sand; others picked oysters. George himself dutifully clambered from the cove and looked for birds fluttering from vegetation, footprints, any sign of humans abroad in number. Having satisfied himself that there was nothing significant to be seen in the locality, he was nonplussed when his arms were grabbed from behind and held vigorously. His peaceful oyster-pickers were similarly astonished. Others woke with muskets pointed in their faces. Cries were few and muffled. They were made prisoner without a firearm discharged or a tomahawk swung. After debate among their captors they were marched a short distance inland. Heke and the Duke were seated under a large tree consuming cold mutton and dried shark with their senior lieutenants.

'What is it you want?' Heke asked George.

'Intelligence,' George reluctantly confessed.

'You have it. Our appointment is on Tuesday.'

'As I am given to understand,' George agreed shakily.

'So why,' Heke sighed, 'am I to be pestered today? Is your need to be a hero?'

George decided it wasn't. His gaze wandered to the Duke. The Duke's face said that it was a matter of no interest whether Philpotts and his party were slain now or three days hence. In hope that Heke would be slower to countenance cold-blooded killing, George looked hastily toward the younger rebel again.

'May I ask leniency for my men?' he asked. 'They were merely following orders.'

'And for yourself?'

'It is not for me to instruct you in your best interests.'

'Has war begun?' Heke said with an air of innocence.

'Not to my knowledge,' George said, rather mystified.

'Good,' Heke said. 'If you undertake not to disrupt my meal further, you are free to leave.'

'You have my word as a gentleman.'

'Go,' Heke ordered. 'We meet on Tuesday.'

'On Tuesday,' George agreed.

In some disrepair he arrived back at Blackguard Beach toward dusk. After reporting to irate Commander Robertson, he sought me out, knocking briefly on my door before pushing it open. His timing was unfortunate. It so happened that with Henry weary of his rakish ways — and absent without leave since his humbling failure with the pen — I was attempting to entertain Angela to the best of my modest ability. Through no fault of my own I was in an unbuttoned condition. It was no use endeavouring to disguise my circumstances or explain that in amusing a female acquaintance of some standing I was merely seeking to retrieve my colleague and collaborator Henry Youngman from limbo. George Philpotts saw what he saw, though he had to adjust his monocle to register details.

'Dear God,' he said, 'who would have guessed it? You are a sly devil of a fellow, Wildblood.'

He backed tactfully out.

'And so, by the way, is your friend Heke,' he informed me.

Sunday was fretful. Martial drill continued with no more than an hour's pause for church parade. Williams was persuaded that a sermon of a sunny nature served the occasion best. Commander Robertson continued trying to interest Beckham and his cronies in more heartfelt preparation for fray. The sabbath failed to muffle his nautical language. 'What kind of bloody men are you?' he asked.

'Soldiers,' Beckham claimed.

The army had never been high in Robertson's estimation. 'Don't expect me, you witless buggers, to pull your chestnuts from the fire,' he warned. 'I don't mean my men to perish for your tomfoolery.'

'You are threatening me, sir.'

'Telling you,' Robertson said.

Monday was melancholy. In the late afternoon two vessels, a sea-weary Yankee whaler and a leaky Sydney merchantman, dropped anchor offshore. Commander Robertson presented his respects to their skippers and alarmed them by asking them to remain outside the *Hazard*'s field of fire. They would further please him, he added, if they remained on hand to take non-combatants aboard in the event of difficulty ashore. He was swiftly followed by Beckham, who assured the uneasy skippers that Blackguard Beach was tranquil and meant to remain so. Their custom was welcome; they were not to be panicked into departure by talk of belligerence.

As for the militia and troops under his orders, he urged them to enjoy a hearty night's sleep. When this news was brought to him, Commander Robertson's countenance coloured even more darkly. If ever he was to remedy his situation with a razor it was surely that night. Instead, after much meditation, punctuated by the clinking of bottle on glass, he lifted a cutlass from his cabin wall and tested it bitterly on the *Hazard*'s nearest timber. With his free hand he grabbed up his bottle and warmed his interior further with his native fluid.

'Philpotts?' he roared.

George came running. He found his superior hitching himself into a kilt of clan MacDonald tartan; it was an occasion for awe.

'In my absence you will have command of the *Hazard*,' Robertson announced. By way of emphasis he swung again at his vessel's woodwork; chips flew.

'What, sir, does that mean?'

'It means,' Robertson explained wearily, 'that within the hour you will have half a hundred men ready to follow me ashore.'

'That is much of our complement, sir,' George observed.

'You will not be left defenceless,' Robertson pointed out. 'Have remaining men stand to our guns from midnight.'

George was a boy bewitched by a birthday treat. 'The guns, sir?' he asked breathlessly.

'What else, man? In the case of catastrophe you will discharge them to effect.'

'How is catastrophe to be judged, sir?'

'Dear God, man. When you see crazed savages running amok.'

'May I ask, sir, what you will be up to?'

'Crazing them,' Robertson promised.

Blackguard Beach slumbered. Must I confess it? Who was I to fan panic's fires? Fate needed no authorisation from me. Reader, I slept too.

Ten

Faithful to pledge, John Heke and the Duke encircled the town before dawn on Tuesday. They moved in three parties. The first, under the Duke, felt out the pass to the south of the town. The second, led by his lieutenants, clambered up steep terrain to the rear. The third, wholly Heke's, pushed on to the blockhouse built about the flagstaff. Since fair warning had been given stealth was seen as unnecessary. Warrior blundered blindly into warrior, with curses frequent and abrasions many. As they closed with the blockhouse, crawling through scrub and fern, Heke's men became more discreet, believing their luck suspect; they communicated with their fellows by mimicking the cry of a native owl. No wakeful Briton noted the surprising abundance of breathless birds of prey. Finally Blackguard Beach was invested from three sides; the one way out was by water. The first impediment to the rebel plan was marine mist. The dawn star, which should have signalled attack, failed to glimmer. A second hitch then made a showing. Commander Robertson had placed a small naval cannon to cover the pass while he established men on the town outskirts. When the Duke impatiently ordered his men forward they collided with this firepiece, and a five-man piquet.

There was the sound of a lone musket. It was followed by a fusillade and the rousing whistle of overhead shot. The shouting was even more fearful. It was Maori belief that warrior lungs should be emptied loudly in the first moment of attack. In that way, in the event of death proving instant, they would leap into the next world still fully functional. Battle for Blackguard Beach had been joined.

Military history is not my forte. In any case even cool-eyed Thucydides, raised from a Greek tomb, might be reduced to a mumbling dunce in attempting to explain the events of that day. Most of a thousand armed men were soon involved or doing their ingenious best not to be, largely the latter. Seldom have two groups of combatants been at greater pains to shun each other. The one thing genuine about the engagement was din. At modest estimate five thousand shots must have been discharged. With so much flying metal at large, some belligerents were bound to find the day fatal. There were between thirty and forty such unfortunates, most of them notched by their neighbours. On the other hand it was only the casualty list which made the affair formidable. That, and Commander Robertson.

When the survivors of his stricken piquet raced in to report disaster, and two of their number felled, he called his men to stand firm and meet intruders muzzle to muzzle. Having selected their mode of decease, he made no secret of his own preference. As the Duke's warriors hurled themselves out of the half-light, Robertson flew upon them with poor-tempered howl and flailing cutlass. They had never seen his like before; tribesmen in his path had no further chance to. For two decades enfeebled by the notion that warfare amounted to pointing a musket with malice and tugging a trigger, they were no longer comfortable with combat at close quarters. Also under the impression that Britons held life dear, they were poorly prepared for a hairy-legged and dangerously melancholic Gael who scorned firearms and fought hand to hand. As it happened, many were reloading with difficulty in the dark or finding it a problem to train their firearms in the crush. Four of their number were divided by his blade. Others prudently made way for him, backing into the path of an untypically harmful flight of their own shot. Tumult and recriminations were such that Commander Robertson felt free to argue with fate further by hounding a fifth victim through the Maori line. He was then lost to view of his men. Command was gone. As it proved, however, he decided the skirmish. Both attackers and defenders saw wisdom in separating themselves from suicidal intimacies; the rout was collective, with attackers fleeing as fast as defenders, sometimes shoulder to shoulder in the murk.

In roughly the same minute the men of the Duke's second party, arranged on wooded high ground behind the town, discharged their muskets in the hope of persuading Britons to wake and make targets. For the most part Britons spurned the invitation. Some two hundred men, soldiers and armed townsmen alike, raced for the stockade meant to house women and children, the ill and the old. Honest non-combatants, arriving more slowly, burdened by possessions, found space grudgingly surrendered. Beckham was admirably fitted to play commander among womenfolk and infants. As panic mounted he ordered all weapons and powder to be brought within the stockade and a magazine established. Small field guns were perched on platforms and pointed in the direction of danger. John Heke, whose men were now spread about the blockhouse on Flagstaff Hill, appeared to be waiting on furore to become more propitious before declaring his presence.

For a time I refused to let gunfire interfere with repose. The noise declined to become less noxious. Where was Henry Youngman at this hour? The fact is that he wasn't. Shaky Ferdinand had to survive the day solo. As I climbed into my breeches in the dark, with the flash of musketry lighting my window, my door was thrown open. A shadow stood on my step.

'Heke hopes you are careful not to get killed,' Moses said.

'I have a similar wish,' I assured him.

'On the other hand he trusts that you do not remove yourself too far from events of the day.'

'I had the bridge of the *Hazard* in mind,' I explained.

'Lucky for you,' Moses said. 'Other people have a war to fight.'

He shouldered his musket and dawdled off in the direction of warrior duty.

Daylight uncovered frustration on two smoky fronts. Shot was still being spent by men convinced that battles were in progress. Left to its own devices the war might have expired for want of gusto there and then. The Duke's contingent did not prove more distinguished than any other; his men had been living languidly on their reputation for a decade. There was, however, Heke's band. Romantic scribblers made much of his role that day. They attributed most of the day's drama to thespian Heke and no more than a supporting role to his elderly ally. The Duke's two-front attack, in their view, was a mere feint to allow Heke to make free with the Union Jack. They weren't to know that the Duke preferred to fight flesh and blood. Nor did they note that Heke was remarkably reticent about taking the field in earnest. The uproar below Flagstaff Hill failed to animate him. With a splendid view of the occasion, lit by the rising sun, he seemed dazzled and dazed by the colour and sound of the war he had spirited up. This dreamy inertia seemed likely to persist. Then events cruelly ended his reverie. The soldiers of the flagstaff blockhouse carelessly threw open their door to view proceedings down in Blackguard Beach. They were of two minds where duty lay. Was it with their blockhouse or their beleaguered fellows below? While they debated they discovered themselves marooned in a landscape filling with excitable Maori. In mortal fright many hurled themselves downhill in half-dressed condition, abandoning their weapons and leaving the flagstaff to fate. On their way to sanctuary they managed to stampede men in the lower blockhouse too; guns were unceremoniously spiked as more defenders took to their heels. War, as wars will, was looking after itself, with human beings mere grist to its mill.

In despair of hearing their commander's order, Heke's men finally crashed into the upper blockhouse and shot or otherwise silenced those showing resistance. So much for warrior work. Heke, so it was said, gazed aghast at the British dead at his feet. Presumably they were not as envisaged. While he woke from rousing daydream to the sight of authentic corpses his men continued with toil of a commonplace kind. The mechanics of felling a flagstaff were now familiar. The latest version required sweaty workmen to demolish the blockhouse, tear out protective palisading and finally lever away iron sheathing. That is, before axemen might begin their exertions. This took time and more than a little discussion. Meanwhile Heke's euphoric warriors were not tempted to involve themselves with graceless affairs downhill. Though some contributed a shot or two, to warn off impetuous Britons, most grounded their weapons, warmed themselves with rum retrieved from the blockhouse, lit their pipes, mocked axemen seen tiring, and boasted about their heroic role in the dawn's happenings. After an hour or two the flagstaff was seen to rock. It floated bewitchingly on its base for a few moments, as if looking out the least painful way to fall, and then pitched loud to earth. There were cries of triumph and sighs of satisfaction.

It was now the middle of the morning. Nervous shooting aside, the Duke's two contingents were sharing a standstill with Britons below. As reluctantly agreed, the Duke was not entangling himself with the town, but waiting for his foe to make a bold show on ground outside. His foe had no such fancy. The Duke's laments on this score rivalled those of foul-mouthed Britons. Their complaint was that the Duke's men were unfairly evading shot behind boulder and bush. Never having met an armed enemy before, they were under the impression that the latter were duty bound to display themselves. As for Heke, if he had fresh fields to conquer he seemed happier viewing them from afar. The day's work was done; the rest was domestic. He raised a flag of truce and had warriors bear British wounded to the shore, also two women whose nightly duty had been to comfort lonely men of the blockhouse. With them went a message to Magistrate Beckham suggesting he lift his head long enough to see that the flagstaff was no more.

My observation post on the *Hazard* was not bereft of comfort. George Philpotts was persuaded that primed guns worked best with primed gunners. To keep their spirits up, while fiasco flourished ashore, he spliced the mainbrace. The response from his men, when a cask of rum was rolled out, was ecstatic; the deck was soon awash with Dutch courage. George lubricated himself intemperately too. Then word arrived of Commander Robertson's apparent demise. George's change of circumstances dawned in his face. As he rose to the occasion he even looked an inch or two taller. The Bishop of Exeter's delinquent son looked riskily set on repairing his deficiencies. 'Damn it,' he announced. 'I am the commander now.'

He reminded me of my subordinate position. 'Take a dinghy, Constable Wildblood,' he ordered. 'Conduct some reconnaissance. If Beckham is inclined not to pursue hostilities, this day will end in disgrace for all concerned.'

'Through no fault of yours,' I pointed out.

'All will be tarred with the same brush,' George argued. 'Army, navy and local luminaries alike.'

'What do you wish Beckham told?'

'To give fight or get out. At least, if the second, we could get a shot or two in; the navy might then know less disgrace. Since the triumph of Trafalgar the British navy has not been in the custom of losing battles. It is not my intention to share in shame today.'

From which I made the deduction that command as well as rum had gone to his head; his misty monocle had become as opaque as Lord Nelson's eye-patch. I hastened to land and made my way to the stockade. The picture within was not ennobling. Children whimpered and women sobbed. Elsewhere men with cold muskets hid in corners, flinching as shot winged overhead. At one angle of the stockade I found Beckham masquerading as a gunnery officer; he was endeavouring to convince Turner that shells lofted into the hills would put the fear of God into Maori marksmen.

'Bloody needles in haystacks,' Turner growled.

Beckham observed me on hand. 'What have you to say for yourself?' he demanded.

'No more than we might all ask ourselves sincerely,' I suggested, and went on to report George's less inflammatory sentiments.

'Who,' Beckham asked, 'does Philpotts think he is?'

'At this moment, with Commander Robertson indisposed or dead, he has reason to think himself in command of the *Hazard*. At all events there are none willing to contradict him.'

'And he tells me to give fight?'

'Or get out, sir.'

Beckham was thoughtful. 'Be it on his head, then,' he decided.

'Women and children might be moved first,' I urged.

'Did I say otherwise?' Beckham asked.

A feminine undergarment became a truce flag. Women, children and the maimed were grouped and men shamming mortally stricken weeded out. I then steered this motley band down to the shore. We were dangerously visible to the rebels above. Peril dropped away, however, as I bundled my charges into small craft on the foreshore. First shooting stopped. Second, I suddenly had an unusual number of willing hands in the evacuation, most of them brown; they were busy commandeering canoes and small craft on my behalf. John Heke had sent his men down from the hills to speed woeful Britons on their way. As I marvelled at this Moses made an appearance.

'This is irregular,' I pointed out.

'Nevertheless,' Moses said.

'Warn Heke that Christian scruple can become tedious. War could lose its good name.'

'He has his own to consider. He is thinking of the Duke, and what thwarted warriors might do.'

'You are talking massacre?'

Moses shrugged. 'Heke does not know how this will finish. But he knows how it could.'

'Unhappily,' I suggested.

'Just so,' Moses said.

I had news for Magistrate Beckham. Affairs in the stockade, however, had been enriched by the return of Commander Robertson violent and vocal. Half filled with shot, he had hidden under a bush, until danger stampeded past, and then crawled slowly to safety. Preoccupied with his personal condition, he failed to note that defence of the town was now a profitless enterprise. Roaring at immobile men to take fight to the foe, he further informed them that failure did not figure in his scheme of things. His sincerity was respected; his request was not. His resurrection meant there were three giving orders. George Philpotts, desperate to give his guns an outing, was shouting shrilly from the deck of the *Hazard*; Commander Robertson was bellowing bullishly from death's door; and Beckham baying breathlessly from all quarters of the compass. Unanimity of a sensible sort came when Commander Robertson collapsed into coma toward noon. Philpotts and Beckham found themselves in agreement. The stockade was to be surrendered, defenders evacuated.

The decision made, Turner thought it timely to disclose pugnacity. 'We should have made this a fight to the finish,' he claimed. 'I can hear Heke laughing.'

Beckham said nothing, but extensively, between gritted teeth.

'You wouldn't read about it,' Turner sighed bitterly.

'On the contrary,' Beckham warned, 'you may, sir, and at intolerable length.'

Playful fate then confirmed matters. A pipe-smoking rating allowed sparks to drift into the garrison magazine; there was a comprehensive roar. More than the community's reserve munitions were lost. Worldly goods were flung about, and men aflame. In one respect the event paid a dividend. The swirling smoke of the conflagration covered our exit to the shore. Musketry subsided. Awed tribesmen had good reason to conclude that they had been witness to a formidable act of *felo de se*. Shouldering their arms, they began strolling down to the shore. Amused to find blackened Britons still at large, they helped carry our wounded and push our small craft off from the beach. Especial courtesy was extended to Commander Robertson's prone form; he was bedded comfortably in a canoe. I found Moses beside me again.

'How is Heke?' I asked.

'He will be more cheerful when Britons have gone.'

'So, I daresay, will Britons.'

'He fears the Duke may take it into his head to fall upon any slow to leave. This place will shortly be wild with the Duke's warriors. They have had a poor day. Also the Duke. The joy has been Heke's. He felled the flagstaff. The Duke saw no more than the rumps of the red tribe. His men will not be sociable.'

That information gave me powerful incentive to swing my legs into a dinghy. Ahead, a line of little craft was pulling toward the *Hazard* and the other vessels in wait. Beckham and Turner, beside me not a minute before, had magically evaporated; likewise all able-bodied men. It looked as if I wished the distinction of being last to leave. This was not the case.

'Tell him it was not a day to be forgotten,' I said.

'Especially by Henry Youngman?'

'Even by Ferdinand Wildblood.'

'That will keep Heke happy,' Moses promised.

Giving my craft a farewell shove, Moses waded back to land. I began rowing in earnest. I had not won more than twenty yards of water when I heard myself hailed by a familiar voice. With alarm I saw Williams beaching a mission vessel at the west end of the beach. In his company were two or three Maori helpmates in Christ, and, unbelievably, Angela. With the Duke's aggrieved warriors due to swarm over Blackguard Beach, this was a lunatic time for a man of the cloth to put in an appearance. Determined to tell him so, and to inform him forcefully that Angela was at risk, I changed course and rowed fervently in their direction. As I did so I heard a musket to port and, if I was not mistaken, shot passing in proximity to my left ear.

'Wildblood?' Williams called, as I closed with his party. 'Is sanity to be seen yet?'

'It is not making itself conspicuous, sir.'

'So it is all that I feared.'

'Worse,' I reported.

'Dead? Dying?'

'I have not been active in pursuing their acquaintance, sir. Nor, I suggest, need you.'

'I know my responsibility, Mr Wildblood.'

'And I know mine, sir. It is to warn you away.'

'Point me toward sorrow,' Williams said. 'There is no need for you to accompany me.'

'Nor is there any need for your god-daughter to be in peril.'

Angela, placing her arm in mine, smiled appreciatively as I helped her ashore.

Williams explained, 'The noble girl insists on remaining at my side to ensure my well being. If you can dissuade her, Wildblood, all to the good. Meanwhile there is Christian duty.' He turned to his Maori aides. 'Forward,' he ordered, hoisting a truce flag.

We fell in behind. 'I came for you,' Angela whispered. 'I thought you might be shot.'

'Not for want of providing a target.' It was more to the point that her saintly godfather was determined to give death a second chance on my person.

Our little procession shuffled up the shingle beach on to solid shore; we were presented with a view of the abandoned town. The prospect was tolerably placid. Scores of leaderless warriors padded back and forward, wondering at their windfall; the place had been surrendered to them intact. The abundance of loot was such that they didn't know where to begin. There was no great glee or commotion. Even our arrival failed to draw comment or ribald laughter. The silence was uncanny. Williams's step didn't falter even when confronted by the Duke's more fearsome colleagues. They tended to part and let him pass on his way.

Finally, at the end of a dusty lane, Heke and the Duke came into view, lieutenants alongside them. The Duke was conspicuously poor-tempered. The pair were feuding so resonantly they at first failed to notice our gentle group. Heke was pleading that the town be left in one piece. The Duke was declaring himself indifferent to the fate of the place. As it happened, it was about to be decided without reference to either.

Heke, welcoming diversion, sighted us at last. He raced free of the Duke to shake the hands of fellow Christians. 'It is finished,' he promised Williams.

Williams was cool. 'And not before time,' he suggested.

'You will conduct divine service?' Heke asked.

'Of what nature?'

'Thanksgiving,' Heke suggested.

'You ask too much,' Williams said.

'It was not my thought to take the town,' Heke explained. 'It was delivered to me by miracle.'

'That verges on heresy,' Williams observed.

Heke shrugged. 'If this is no miracle God has no son.'

Williams despaired. 'What is your thought now?'

'Colonists may return to collect their property. My men will ensure their safety.'

'I have your word?'

'My Christian word,' Heke reminded him. 'They may also return to their homes when guns cool.'

'That is magnanimous,' Williams had to concede.

'I cannot promise protection for soldiers and sailors. It saddens the Duke that they were indisposed to fight.'

With conversation taking so amiable a turn it seemed no risk to breathe freely again. That was a mistake.

First there were faint whoops from seaward. Seconds later the first salvo from the guns of the *Hazard* struck the town. George Philpotts and his gunners, after years of inoffensive rehearsal, had begun practising their profession. Dust and debris rose unhealthily right and left as Angela and I flung ourselves to ground. Timber took wing. Tottering chimneys became brutal avalanches of brick. Windows bulged and blew out, with evil shards of glass whistling near. There was battering round shot. There was whining grape. And lest the first salvo be thought a testy mistake there was an even more formidable barrage to follow. Angela hugged me tight; I gallantly hugged her tighter. We crouched under a solid doorway which seemed to offer shelter. Heke, a dozen yards off, was still staring at the sky in disbelief. The Duke was shaking his musket in rage.

Williams, toppled by a blast, rose filthy. 'This cannot be suffered,' he judged.

No one was heard to differ.

He further announced, 'I mean to show a flag of truce from the shore.'

'I think not,' Heke argued.

'I think so,' Williams said. He looked, as I feared he might, in my direction. 'Mr Wildblood? Would you be so good as to keep me company?'

'To what end?' I asked.

'Another English face might give emphasis to my message. And should one of us fall, the other can keep the peace flag flying.'

With my posterior already an ample target, I found it impossible to muster interest in the project. Nonetheless, Angela was looking on. 'Of course,' I noticed myself say.

'Good,' he said. 'Let us proceed.'

I divested myself of Angela's embrace. Heke considerately placed men on either side of us, lest warrior patience begin fraying. We proceeded to the shore unmolested and there took station. Williams heroically waggled his flag to win the attention of the *Hazard*'s gunners. A further shell or two sputtered overhead and boomed into the town. Then there was a significant pause. Presently a small dinghy detached itself from the *Hazard*. There were two aboard. A rating bent to the oars; and an ashen midshipman. As they closed gingerly with the shore, this earnest young messenger called, 'I come from Lieutenant Philpotts. He wishes to know whether your flag is to be construed as truce or surrender.'

'It stands for common sense,' Williams said bitterly.

That confused the unfortunate young fellow; it was not in his lexicon.

'Lieutenant Philpotts would appreciate a firm answer,' he shouted as his craft bounced on the waves. 'He will accept only unconditional surrender from John Heke and his allies.'

'Surrender?' Williams said with wonder.

'Indeed, sir.'

'Lieutenant Philpotts,' Williams observed, 'does not appear to be inhabiting the same war as we.'

'Nevertheless, sir, he finds truce unacceptable.'

'Otherwise?'

'He means to give the wretches a day to rue.'

'With his guns?'

'Indeed, sir.'

'Inform Lieutenant Philpotts that it is a little late for the navy to carry the day.'

'Sir?'

'Tell him to desist. In matters of compassion, things are proceeding favourably ashore. His salvoes spell ruin of hope.'

The messenger began drifting seaward again.

'Then it is not surrender?' he asked.

'Nor for me to suggest it,' Williams agreed.

'Then it is best you remove yourself,' the midshipman said.

'From my parishioners?'

'If you persist in styling our enemy such.'

'Were I not a servant of the Almighty, sir, I would tell you to go to blazes.'

That ended their *tête à tête*. The oarsman steadied the dinghy on the tide and then, on command, pointed it back to the *Hazard*.

Williams turned away tired.

'What now?' I asked him.

'Cover your head,' he suggested.

Five minutes later the guns of the *Hazard* resumed levelling the town. None but slow warriors were caught in the refreshed fire, and few to fatal effect. Most scrambled to safe elevations, the better to observe the spectacle. There were cheers of approval when an especially thrilling target was struck. Never had tribesmen witnessed foemen more forcefully engaged in shooting themseves in the feet. The notion of destruction proved infectious. As the *Hazard*'s salvoes grew ragged, adventurous warriors joined in proceedings by creeping back to the town to loot and raze buildings left standing. Heke was past quibbling. Giant gusts of flame did much to freshen war's panorama.

Williams, meanwhile, had more than enough dead to keep him at his trade. Heke provided the means, in the form of purloined shovels and idle warriors, to inter them tidily. This scribe was pressed into service as a pallbearer. Corpses were collected, wound in sheets, and rolled into the clay. I had not known there were so many ways to die, none of them pleasing. War is sweet to them that know it not. My chore might be seen as a penalty for living off immoral earnings — or, to put it more coarsely, pimping for Henry Youngman.

As the bombardment became fitful, and finally ceased, graveside hymns grew audible on the afternoon air. Not the least voice was John Heke's. He possessed a fine tenor; Angela had a fetching contralto. Out in the Bay three vessels low in the water with refugee cargo, hauled anchors, unfurled sail, and glided from view.

By nightfall Blackguard Beach was no more.

Eleven

'It is,' said Williams over supper, 'difficult to escape the conclusion that you entertain certain feelings toward my goddaughter.'

This was on return to his mission station. There was warmth, nourishment, and apparel uncoloured by blood. The debacle of Blackguard Beach was forty-eight hours behind us, though Williams was still mired in vocational gloom. Due to Angela's midnight ministrations, I was surprisingly sunny. Indeed, why not? Many never see the far side of their first battle.

'Sir?' I asked, playing for time.

'You heard,' he said irritably.

'It is, sir, a reasonable conclusion,' I conceded.

'That you entertain such feelings?'

'The fact is, sir, that I should be deficient in character if I failed to hold Angela in high regard.'

There was a difficult pause; Williams looked over his glasses in steely fashion.

'It would be a mistake,' he warned, 'to let such sentiments detain you longer in the Bay of Islands.'

'What are you asking, sir?'

'That you think on your personal welfare. By week's end there will be few white faces within fifty miles of the Bay. Most sensible colonists will already be riding hard for Auckland. This is not a wholesome place to be. Some will say it never was, and good riddance to Blackguard Beach. That is as it may be. What you have witnessed is a beginning, not an end. There will be more graves dug. It would be remiss if I failed to point out that one might be yours.'

I thought on that, and on Angela.

'I can spare a horse,' Williams went on. 'There is an overland route to Auckland, in parts quite tolerable. Very soon, if matters are inflamed further, there may not even be that. Musketry could close it off. My earnest advice is to depart now.'

I was not deceived. He had hit on war as a way to rid his household of a lovesick suitor. I stole a look at Angela as she glided to and from the table; that armoured me.

I said, 'May I ask your intention, sir?'

'I mean to remain,' he replied with reluctance. 'I have survived cross-fire before. I might again. Who knows, I may yet persuade the respective parties to talk rather than fight. I appreciate your contribution this far, Mr Wildblood. It would rest uncomfortably on my conscience were I to ask more of you. Better you return to your poems.'

'Your concern for my calling touches me, sir.'

'Sleep on it,' Williams urged.

Forfeiting repose proved more rewarding. Another indiscreet hour with Angela did much to persuade me that life beyond her arms could only be lacklustre. If she regretted or even noted the absence of Henry Youngman in these proceedings, it was not apparent. I pride myself on the notion that I gave her more to ponder upon. She was no longer the streaming-haired wanton who raided my bed in hunt of libidinous Henry. Lovemaking was now a roundelay of rich secrets and rhythmical sighs. As for Williams's funereal talk, the fact was that the prospect of an early grave alarmed me less than loss of my brown beloved. Let me say it then. All the Venuses ever moulded were but abominations beside her. There. Said. Such is the alchemy of love. Not only did I sleep dreamless. I was a different man. This was literal. Henry was gone.

I woke to fierce banging on my bedroom door. I opened it to find Williams in unholy disarray.

'There is a horse saddled for you,' he informed me. 'My advice is that you speed your ablutions and breakfast swiftly.'

'What has happened, sir?'

'Much that I foresaw. A messenger tells me that Timothy Walker Nene has begun to move against John Heke.'

'Nene?' I asked blearily.

'The old devil is furious. He sees his wing of the tribe suffering for Heke's misdemeanours. He judges it time to expel Heke from the Maori map before British vengeance begins to fall on loyal tribesmen as much as dissident. Aside from which he has old scores to settle.'

'With the Duke too?'

'The Duke's kin likewise had a penchant for killing Nene's. Old grudges have been biding their time. Their hour has now come. Take my word for it, Mr Wildblood. The ghost of ghastly Hongi walks again.'

'I hope you are mistaken, sir.'

'It is my fervent prayer too.'

'And where does Britain figure in this?'

'My hope is that it may not. I have a message ready for the governor; I urge him to forgo retaliation for the events at Blackguard Beach.'

'In favour of what, sir?'

'In favour of giving Maori time to put their house in order and speak with one voice. I am not willing to despair of Heke. Christian remorse could yet get the better of him.'

'Blood is up, sir. There is shame in the air. Such a message must fall on flinty ground.'

'Nevertheless, I ask you to bear it to Auckland.'

'Me?'

'And to deliver it to the governor in person.'

'This morning I find myself ever more of a mind to remain here, sir.'

'Then, Mr Wildblood, I must point you in the direction of duty.'

'I am not a talented horseman,' I protested.

'You will improve,' Williams promised.

Williams's intelligence said Heke was retiring inland, as though in fright, after the demise of Blackguard Beach. Remorse may have been at work, if not necessarily of a Christian kind. He surely knew that he had gone too far this time; retribution seemed sure. 'He is behaving as a man vanquished,' Williams mused, 'rather than as victor of the affray.' Heke had even conferred with the Duke's soothsayers in the hope that they had an attractive appraisal of his situation. As for simmering Nene, he was reported travelling at speed to check John Heke's retreat. His intention was to hinder and humiliate the young rebel until he could be delivered up to the British. In that way the Maori covenant with Britain's Queen would remain unblemished.

When it was pointed out to Nene that all Maori might soon have differences with the British, he replied shortly, 'Better the Queen than Heke.' He saw Heke as more than an upstart in the realm of the

Maori; he discerned a new native despot in the making. In trampling the wisdom of his elders, Heke was a menace to his own kind. The reckless young, ignoring the pleas of fathers, were racing to Heke. He had the glory, not to speak of hacked flagstaffs. What could their fathers offer? The netting of fish? The harvesting of potato? Anarchy and hunger would follow if sons scorned fathers. Tribe after tribe could be overturned, their traditional leaders spurned by the young. Heke therefore had to be curbed.

'And better by the Maori,' Williams said. 'I trust the governor heeds my plea. That message must reach him before he orders further soldiers to take the field.'

Thus I put the Bay of Islands behind me. Angela was bravely tearful. I confess myself stricken too. Along with loss I had two hundred miles of unknown terrain to disconcert me. My only reprieve would have been the sails of some Auckland-bound vessel miraculously on the horizon. Much as I willed one, there was no miracle. 'I am providing you with an escort,' Williams said. 'They will guide you until it proves impossible to do so.'

'What does that mean?'

'When they find themselves in the territory of old enemies.'

'What will I do, in that eventuality?'

'Win friends,' Williams suggested.

I climbed reluctantly into the saddle. The two mission boys chosen to keep me company slung themselves bareback on their beasts.

Angela sobbed again. Williams placed a fatherly arm around her. His other was lifted in blessing. 'Godspeed, Mr Wildblood,' he said, and meant it.

The first day went in freeing ourselves of the Bay of Islands, much of the second too. There was channel after salty channel to ford, mudbanks to survive, and melancholy forests of mangrove to fight. Campfire conversation was not enlightening, no matter how much of the Maori tongue I mustered. The boys were apprehensive. They led a sheltered life in Williams's Christian community; he familiarised them only with such of the outer world as he thought fit for their ears. Recent events, however, were no secret. They knew there was death abroad in the Bay. They knew the Queen to be displeased by the handiwork of cousins. They knew John Heke was about, and Timothy Walker Nene, and God knew what other free spirits with firearms in hand. Above all, they knew they would sooner be anywhere but in my company. I failed to entrance them by reciting lyric or recounting legend by our fire. When they fancied I wasn't looking they rolled their eyes at each other frequently, as if in mysterious code. This was not heartening; there was worse.

The third day and the fourth were free of incident, though not of cruel hills and malevolent vegetation. Leviathan trees, with thick clouds of leaf, let little light into the gloom. Lesser greenery, vine and creeper, grabbed our garments and whipped our throats. In their anxiety to bypass beaten paths and bellicose humans, my guides had lost themselves, and, for that matter, me. Our beasts were increasingly diffident. With promise of leaner times ahead, our food supplies, mostly of dried shark and eel, were soon on mean ration. I began contemplating the fleshy rump of my horse; by my reckoning it would be palatable in a day or two more.

On the fifth day, by chance, we met up with the woodland trail we should have been following in the first instance. Humans and horses had been shuffling through forest debris in number; there was a tapestry of footprints, and frequent mounds of fresh dung. Heke's army? Nene's? Whose? My companions were indifferent; it was all the same to them. The young ruffians even tried to hoodwink me into taking a northerly direction rather than a southerly; a route that would have returned us to the Bay again. I was not averse to this notion either; but it was not to be thought that I had never tried to locate Auckland. The peace of the realm might depend on me. Might? Did. I produced my compass. That ended argument. My companions persisted at my side in petulant silence.

On the sixth day we emerged into country more open. For the first time it was possible to see miles ahead. Our unkempt trail solidified into a cart track winding through scrubby vegetation. The land before us was undulating and ferny plain, with patches of flax and foliage and glimmers of lake and stream. Cooled volcanic cones swarmed beyond. Their terraced flanks said they had seen service as Maori fortresses in time past. It was not alluring landscape. Unlike most New Zealand vistas, however, it was intelligible.

We had not travelled a mile downhill when we heard a shot. My guides were not of a mind to determine its nature. In instant sweat they turned their horses. Had their beasts been birds, they would have been aerial.

'A duck shooter,' I argued calmly.

There was a second, less distant detonation.

'Two,' I judged. 'Perhaps we can borrow a fat bird for our pot tonight.'

They were not persuaded.

'Would you have it said,' I challenged, 'that grandsons of warriors did not venture where a lone Briton would?'

It appeared that they did not in the least mind what was said, so long as they were pointed home. There was only one other card to play.

'Your mission is for Williams, is it not?'

They agreed that this was the case.

'And who is Williams?' I asked.

A man of God, they were obliged to concede.

'Therefore you are about God's work,' I pointed out.

They were suspicious that catechism was about to take a doleful turn. They were correct in this assumption.

'God,' I informed them, 'will be grieved if you abandon me at this point. Not to speak of his only begotten son Jesus. There is also the Holy Ghost to be taken into account. The entire trinity.'

My robustly evangelical ring gave them thought. I allowed them no time to nit pick.

'I promise no war,' I added rashly.

They hesitated.

'Come,' I commanded.

They followed shyly. We ventured into war.

We had not journeyed another mile when a fusillade flew in from our right. Another, with as much abandon, stormed across our path from the left. Neither did us harm. On the other hand neither promised good. We dismounted and dived to earth. There was further thoughtless discharge of muskets before we understood that we were not targets. The cart track had been requisitioned as a rough boundary between belligerents. There was a Maori war party to our right; another to our left. Each was intent on distressing the other. The shots we heard earlier had been of prestigious marksmen establishing the range of their rivals. This determined, they were now experimenting with fire in volume. Engrossed in martial concerns, certainly in keeping their heads low, they were slow to observe tranquil travellers. A good deal more shot sped overhead before someone to the left called halt. Then someone with equally large lungs made himself heard to the right. A resentful last shot sang away. Nevertheless the truce was difficult to trust. Eventually and cautiously I found my feet. Williams's mission boys remained prone until sure of my survival.

'Proceed,' ordered someone in concealment to the left.

'Proceed,' commanded someone to the right.

I warily retrieved my horse. The boys finally and nervously gathered theirs. After heaving myself into the saddle I tipped my hat impartially left and right.

'Thank you, gentlemen,' I said.

Our benefactors remained steadfastly invisible. We rode on. I made it my business not to look behind. After a short interval the muskets began to bang out again. Whatever way we looked at it, and there were not many, we were not crossing terrain likely to serve longevity.

At a distance of some five hundred yards, a robust ridge lifted across our path, falling in easy stages to lakeside. But for patches of native flax and fern and solo cabbage palms the ridge rose from clear ground. It had possibly been fired for peaceful purpose, but never put to the plough. It was now being readied as an arena for war. Along its upper flank there was extensive industry; the sound of hammer and saw was conspicuous. Timber was being manhandled uphill and palisades were growing. We could also observe warriors digging. I was witness to a traditional Maori fortress being fashioned. In other circumstances I might have been fascinated by the spectacle. Circumstances, however, were not conducive to stopping and staring. I had a powerful sense that the intervening territory was alive with hunters looking for quarry. Volleys, followed by gusts of smoke, lifted to our rear, to our right, and presently to our left again. The smell of ignited powder wafted across the scene; there was the patter of exhausted shot dropping into fern. It was more and more desirable that shelter be sought. We pushed on to a spindly grove of trees, dismounted, and tethered our beasts.

I pointed to the fortress. 'Heke's?' I asked the boys. 'Nene's?'

The sober pair shook their heads. They also clung to me urgently. They appeared to hold me responsible for their well-being. This might prove a mortal mistake.

Our unauthorised appearance must have been noted. A horseman rode out from the fortress. He ducked once or twice, and sprinted when he perceived a gap in the shooting. His bulk was familiar. Then his face too. Moses arrived breathless.

'What are you doing here?' he demanded.

He might well ask. 'Upon an errand for Williams,' I explained.

'To Heke?'

'To Auckland.'

'There is a war on,' he pointed out.

'That has not escaped me,' I said.

'Well?'

'Show me the way out,' I suggested.

'That is more difficult,' Moses said.

'Then show me a place of less danger.'

'I have no notion either,' he confessed. 'It may be another week before battle is better organised. At the moment no one knows where it is. It is not even clear who is friend and who enemy. You may look along a barrel and see an uncle's face, or a cousin's. Until everyone knows what the war is about it is safer to exchange shot than salutations.'

'What is it about, then?'

'Heke needs to defeat Nene before the red tribe returns vengeful. He cannot fight two foes at once. On the other hand Nene wishes a triumph to show that British soldiers are not needed; that Maori is better fitted to vanquish Maori.'

'And that is to be settled here?'

'One way or the other,' Moses said.

'How soon?'

'This month or next. Someone must tire or think twice.'

'My errand is urgent,' I protested.

'That is your problem,' Moses shrugged. 'I have enough of my own.'

There was another in the form of a volley chipping overhead foliage. There was a compelling thump as Moses went to ground; I was not slow to follow. The mission boys competently buried themselves under fallen branches. Moses rolled on his back and considered western sky. 'Hardly an hour more,' he said breathless.

'Until what?'

'Sundown,' he informed me.

'What does that mean?'

'Enough for the day. Meals must be respected.'

'Meals?'

'It is also agreed that there is no night fighting, no dawn surprises, and no ambushes. Men with no rest and no food fight poorly.'

'What kind of war is this?'

'Ours,' he argued.

'It is an unusually charitable recipe.'

'We do our best to season it with Christ,' he admitted.

My incredulity remained plain.

'War,' Moses explained with patience, 'has enough hardship. Why make it miserable?'

We whiled away the rest of the day's fight with pipes, tobacco and Moses' muddy pack of cards. The mission boys made a magical reappearance when shot became less dense in our vicinity. Finally, wonderfully, gunfire stopped. For a fraught minute silence prevailed. Then scores of scrappily clad warriors leapt noisy from hiding. They fervently greeted those at whom they had been directing their fire, pressing noses together in the customary Maori manner, and asking news of the fallen; there were sometimes tears shed by both parties as deceased relatives and friends were tallied. Wounds were examined and bandaged. Christian prayers were offered up, here and there coloured with pagan chants. After sharing their tobacco, the adversaries shouldered their muskets and parted with promises to resume killing on the morrow. Though not without charm, this sporting spectacle was hardly a sight to tempt Hongi from the grave.

'Come,' Moses said, as burial parties roved out to recover the fallen. 'Time for home comforts.'

The ridge Heke was revising swelled up between swamp, forest edge and lake. Overlooking tribal trails, it neighboured a citadel of the tribe with a piquant past. Two decades earlier the great Hongi had chosen to lapse into his final coma at this location; it was said he had used his last breath warning his people to beware of the men in red garments he had seen parading in London. In less trustworthy versions of the tale he had even predicted that such future foemen might beneficially be met in this vicinity. As a deathbed story it was as felicitous as most. It certainly suited Heke. Where better to battle than where the brown Napoleon left off? War here might confirm Heke's right to wear the conqueror's cloak. Nene's object was to harass Heke and persuade his allies to think again. The Duke decided he had thought sufficiently on the subject. He had not risen from retirement to play at war. It was the red tribe or nothing. The red tribe absent, it was nothing. The Duke made it known that he had better things to do and marched his men home to their wives and cultivations. Before departure he made his contempt for Heke audible. The younger man, he announced, was still thrashing about in the shallows of war, waiting on the tide to come in. When it had risen nearer Heke's neck the Duke might be notified. In the meantime he wished neither hide nor hair of Heke. Moses saw the Duke's denunciation as due to the disappointments of Blackguard Beach; Heke had asked the Duke to hold off from the town and its people, even from its defenders. The result was that the town had fallen without him lifting a warrior finger. Triumph, such as it was, belonged to Heke. The flagstaff was again in the dirt; and the Bay of Islands emptied of Britons. Who would recall, or want to, that the Duke had been present? He had a story too. He did not mean to imperil it further.

The Duke's disappearance preceded my appearance. I found worry in warrior faces. Heke would have to build his fortress and hold off Nene's skirmishers without a seasoned adviser at his side.

Meanwhile the stronghold was half-finished. I was led uphill past gun pit and palisade and offered a makeshift shelter for the night. Then I was delivered to Heke. Still smarting from the Duke's insults, he was in dour mood.

'Is it for me to cry enough?' he asked.

I suggested that it wasn't for me to inform him so.

'Come,' he said.

'I observe you in difficulties,' I admitted.

'Of what nature?'

'Ominous,' I suggested. 'The Duke gone and Nene at the gate.'

'What would Henry Youngman have me do?'

I told him truthfully that I had no notion. Even had Henry been available he would likely have retired from the war in a state of expository confusion.

'If I withdraw men from this fortress, and order them to return home, what will be said?'

'That you have made your point,' I proposed.

That did not impress him greatly. 'Or Nene has.'

'Or Nene,' I had to agree.

'And that I feared the march of the British.'

'Perhaps,' I said judiciously.

'What kind of story does that make?' he asked.

There was a short answer. The tale of a wild and wandering warrior boy cantering sensitively away into the mists might be the stuff of a wistful ballad. It would never make a Lovelady and Pettiworth list.

I spent the night with Heke. At first, to his credit, he didn't press me for the nature of the message I carried. Finally curiosity, as well it might, got the better of him.

'Does it call for peace?' he asked.

'It argues moderation on the governor. As one would expect of Williams. He suggests you are best left to come to your senses.'

'And bow before Britain?'

'Williams does not use those words.'

'I do,' Heke said.

'You may,' I ventured, 'be in more danger of having to kneel before Nene. If this continues you may find British soldiers a welcome sight.'

'Welcome?'

'A breath of fresh air,' I insisted, 'for those alive to breathe it.'

Heke was thoughtful.

The next day began bright and surprisingly serene. There were no shots in the vicinity of Heke's fortress or for that matter anywhere; the silence was soon suffocating. His warriors failed to return to their daily chore of keeping Nene's loyalists at bay. They reclined lazily outside their shelters, smoking, chewing last night's leavings, scratching their bellies, and otherwise laughing, farting and reminiscing. This was not war as generally licensed by literature. Finally I made an enquiry of Moses.

'The sabbath,' he explained.

Heke read the text for the day to a sometimes attentive audience shortly before noon. The unexceptional sentiments were from the Psalms. 'Except the Lord build the house, they labour in vain that build it,' he informed those around them. He suggested that their fortress might be seen as the work of the Lord. On the other hand he forcefully drew their attention to the fact that labour on their defence works could not be left to the Almighty alone. Heke wished to see enterprise of a manual kind in the following week, not merely with muskets. It was a tired and unconvincing sermon and Heke seemed to know it. Men with moody faces drifted back to their placid sabbath pursuits.

Afterwards he requested my company again.

'If you bear Williams's message you can bear mine,' he proposed.

'To the governor?'

'To Nene.'

I was not taken with the sound of that. 'Of what nature?' I asked.

'Friendly,' he assured me.

That seemed unlikely; my face must have said so.

'A message from one warrior to another,' he explained. 'I wish Nene told that if he goes on this way, there will be no one to challenge the red tribe on their return.'

'I thought that was his notion.'

'Half of him thinks so. The other half wishes to see the red tribe at work with small guns and large, and with the bayonet. Especially the bayonet.'

'Everyone to his taste,' I said soberly.

'If the red tribe is good, Nene would like the prestige of fighting alongside them. But if he stops me here, that will never be. He needs an enemy. He needs me.'

This proposition may have had a droll logic. But that, for my purpose, was beside the point.

'And you wish me to inform him so?'

'Today,' Heke said.

With a truce flag fluttering overhead Moses steered our threesome in the direction of Nene's camp. Within a half mile of Nene's fires he turned his horse and passed me the flag.

'Good luck,' he said.

I rode on alone. Sabbath, it proved, was being observed in Nene's camp too. There was not a sentry in sight. Nor did warriors train their muskets when I presented a target. They merely stood to stare.

'Nene?' I asked.

There were sullen grunts and fingers pointed. Leading my horse between impermanent shelters, I found myself in an impressive and confusing congregation of chiefs. There was, however, no mistaking the tattooed and bull-necked man sitting at their centre. Warfare was not making Nene more winsome of feature. He failed to favour me with a smile.

'Well?' he asked.

'I come by way of Heke's camp,' I explained.

'A fool can see that,' he said.

'Only by chance,' I hastened to add. 'I bear a message from Williams to the governor in Auckland; it happened that while on my way I fell in with Heke's men first.'

'A message from Williams?' he said sourly.

'To the governor,' I confirmed.

'What does this message say?'

'It is not for me to disclose its nature,' I replied.

'If from Williams, it surely asks peace.'

'That,' I agreed, 'is a fair surmise.'

'Peace will never quieten Heke,' Nene growled.

'Perhaps not,' I agreed cheerfully. 'But then, what could?'

'The gun,' Nene informed me.

This was an unhappy start. I proceeded to my secondary chore.

'John Heke,' I began, 'has asked me to point out to you that should you defeat him here the British may make no appearance. Who will there be for them to fight? And who for you to win the Queen's favour?'

Rather surprisingly, Nene's face was lit by a laugh.

'He asks that?'

'He argues that you need him more than he does you.'

'Cheek,' Nene said, though with some admiration.

'Perhaps,' I said.

'His character does not improve,' Nene decided.

'Meaning?'

'He must be made to eat turd.'

That left a silence.

'Look around you,' he suggested.

I looked. One chiefly face was as forbidding as another.

'What do you see?'

'Men of distinction and, it must be wished, wisdom.'

'Just so,' Nene said with approval. 'More men of rank report to me every day. None wish to slay sons and grandsons who side with Heke. Nevertheless they will. There is no hope for Heke.'

'And no mercy?'

Nene shrugged. 'We mean only to wear away at his force until it disappears. That would be agreeable for all.'

'I see,' I said, with discomfort.

Nene added, 'My thought is that I also have a message to the

Governor. I ask you to bear it. It will tell the Governor that Heke must be punished. And to send troops soon. Heke must be shown he is nothing.'

I have to confess it. I detected a longing for the comprehensible company of fellow countrymen.

Twelve

To ensure my safety, Nene dismissed the mission boys, providing me with companions of a less retiring disposition. In their company I continued southward to Auckland with messages calling for peace on the one hand and war on the other. For a time it seemed unlikely that the governor would receive either. Tempting though it is to list my woes along the way, they belong to the annals of exploration rather than the chronicles of conflict. My guides made it their business to rescue me from river, ravine, and extremes of lassitude. Of a suspicious nature, and unwilling to let old adversaries sour our progress, they directed shot at anything two-legged on the skyline. It was two weeks or longer before I had Auckland in distant view. My mentors in New Zealand's ferny maze turned back with grunts which might be construed as goodbyes; I was left to ride solitary and saddlesore into the current capital of the colony.

Had I thought of a hero's welcome, as even the humblest of men might in such circumstances, my first sight of the place would have dimmed it. This outpost of Empire was little more heartening than Blackguard Beach on first acquaintance, and possibly as inflammable. Mercantile buildings ranged from squalid to unpretentious. Dwellings were wretched and wooden. Here and there the Union Jack flew without let or hindrance. Despite the onset of delirium I managed to observe that the locality was patched with red uniforms. There were piquets here, patrols there, and a soiled detachment of soldiery paddling along the mushy main street. Meanwhile I was making myself noteworthy. Slumping even lower in the saddle, reins trailing from my hand, I excited attention and comment. Pedestrian traffic came to a standstill as my horse wandered on whim. My problem was making myself understood by citizens and soldiers. Finally I mustered an intelligible whisper. 'The Governor,' I pleaded.

My voice must have suggested unhappy news from the hinterland.

At all events my horse was hauled in an uphill direction. A sentry or two stood guard outside the governor's residence. I was aware of a long, low building of credibly official character; and not much else. A bulky sergeant at arms loomed before me.

'Ferdinand Wildblood, late of London, wishes to present his respects to the governor,' I informed him.

I discovered myself bedded in a barracks infirmary; and in the hands of an inept and expedient army surgeon who judged my malaise as best served by large draughts of brandy. This enabled him to diagnose my condition as no more than delirium tremens.

Governor FitzRoy was terse.

'I am appreciative of the pains you have taken to bring me intelligence of the north,' he told me. 'The fact is, however, that your news is no longer so. While you meandered frivolously overland, ship after ship has brought similar tidings. Maoris and missionaries alike are bombarding me pestilentially with paper. I now dread the arrival of new vessels from the north. More messages. More pleas. Meanwhile I wish you a speedy recovery.'

That, it appeared, was that. A hero's welcome? Cowards have had kinder.

'May I ask a question, sir?'

'If it concerns pecuniary reward, Wildblood, I must inform you that the colony's purse is empty.'

'Remuneration could not be further from my mind, sir.'

'Then by all means ask your question,' he said generously.

'Is the issue to be forced?'

'You mean, is Heke to be tamed?'

'Just so, sir.'

'I fear he has to be, Wildblood. If fellow Maori cannot put him in his rightful place, Britons must.'

'And what would you judge his rightful place, sir?'

'Out of sight,' he reported fretfully.

So must Rome's consuls have wished their restless subjects. FitzRoy was a tall, lean, melancholy man. It was said of him that even when he did the right thing, which he sometimes miraculously managed to, he made it seem a disaster. Whether he behaved honourably or otherwise it all turned out the same. If there wasn't a pitfall in a policy, he was by temperament inclined to dig one himself. As a naval hydrographer he had been dutiful in mapping the world's deeps. In recognition of services rendered, with no other qualifications than a gift for gloom, he had been given a colony to caretake. Now dry land was looking more abyssal than any ocean. He turned a grieving gaze on me.

'It is all most miserable,' he said. 'Noisy colonists are calling for blood.'

'I imagine they are, sir.'

'Life is at a standstill. The capital is on a war footing. Many here believe Heke will attack any day.'

'I can put your mind to rest on that score, sir. Heke is himself besieged.'

'Am I right in understanding that you are acquainted with the fellow?'

'Heke and I are on talking terms,' I agreed.

'Then tell me. Does he still wish to divest himself of land for monetary gain? Now that his tribesmen have won carte blanche to do so, does he still wish to fell this colony's mighty forest?'

'When he has finished with flagstaffs, perhaps.'

'Is there no moderation in the man?'

'Of a righteous sort, sir.'

'Then let me phrase it differently. Is war what he wants?'

Untruth tempted me. I put it aside.

'Alas,' I said.

After the Governor departed I closed my eyes and sank into sleep. There was no useful choice. My clothing was threadbare; I had only pence in my pocket; the Bay of Islands was distressingly distant. My future was shy about showing its face.

'Wildblood, dear fellow,' a familiar voice said.

I swam upwards through mist. The voice became even more recognisable. A face took form too.

'Whatever have you been up to?' Major Cyprian Bridge was asking. 'Come on. Speak up. There's a good chap.'

To tell the truth, and I may soon make a habit of it, I was tempted to place a kiss on Cyprian's honest martial face. Certainly a tear of relief might well have trickled down my cheek.

'Now, now,' he said. 'No theatrics.' He went on to explain, 'I was just back from patrol when I heard that an emissary from the battle front by name of Wildblood had arrived in the town. It was not difficult to deduce that you and he must be one and the same. What great good luck, I thought. Soon I shall know everything I need know about John Heke.'

'I would rather you did not ask,' I sighed.

'Are we talking of indignities commited upon your person?' he asked with concern. 'If so, I promise we shall make the wretch pay dear. What is it, Wildblood?'

'Excess,' I said.

'Of what?' he asked.

'Almost everything,' I explained.

'Thus your reluctance to talk?'

'Until my mind clears.'

'Very well, then,' he promised. 'I shall press you no further. What vexes me, however, is how a peaceful poet got himself into such a pickle.'

'I marvel too,' I confessed.

'Do you realise, dear chap, that you now know more of war than I?'

I shrugged.

'Who would have thought it when our ways parted in Sydney?'

'Not I,' I admitted.

'You are a lucky fellow.'

'That is not how I should phrase it,' I said honestly.

'No? Yet rumour tells me that you behaved creditably in the unsavoury affray at Blackguard Beach.'

'Someone had to,' I proposed. 'The lion's share of good works was performed by a man of the cloth called Williams.'

'I have heard him called a confounded traitor — a cleric who consorts with the enemy.'

'A shepherd cannot be denied his flock.'

Cyprian thought on this. 'In ideal circumstances,' he suggested, 'feats of arms should herald the Christian faith, not follow it. Faith coming first suggests weakness. Worse, it confuses the natives. Conquest prior to conversion, on the other hand, leaves no one in two minds. Do I read the situation right?'

'If you are telling me that it is not ideal,' I agreed.

'They are certainly not for our mutual friend George Philpotts. He is facing a court of inquiry. Is it true, by the way, that he lost his nerve and that he and his men behaved as panicked drunks? In short, shamefully?'

'They behaved as dedicated gunners will. Their salvoes were

efficient. It is true that their target was unfortunate.'

'With any luck George will be acquitted of incompetence and cowardice. Witnesses are few and confused. His role in events may be left to rest on his conscience.'

'That would seem a satisfactory conclusion.'

'Perhaps,' Cyprian said reluctantly. 'Would that I were there with the 58th. It would surely have ended differently. Certainly with no disgrace to British arms.'

'Though perhaps with more bodies.'

'Death is no consideration in respect of dishonour,' he said.

'As Maori might say.'

That brightened him. 'So they should make a fight of it?'

'If they leave off felling themselves.'

'The devil take them,' he said.

'I think they are providing for that contingency,' I said.

Cyprian was back at my bedside next day. 'Good news on two fronts,' he announced. 'I have had a word with my commanding officer. You are welcome as a guest of the 58th. His hope is that you will be able to provide us with instructive intelligence when we reach the Bay of Islands. The other news may delight you still more. You will soon be back there. Our expeditionary force sails tomorrow.'

'Tomorrow?' I said weakly.

'You will be out of this cesspit of a capital and returned to healthier surroundings.'

I sighed with relief.

'That sounds most heartfelt,' Cyprian observed.

'I must declare an interest in the the Bay of Islands,' I explained.

'Are you talking land?'

'Love,' I said.

'I should have known. So you too have succumbed to the passions of these islands.'

'In humble form,' I argued.

'So who is she? And what?'

'Perfection,' I said.

'Say no more,' Cyprian told me. 'Your secret is safe.'

I thought to distract him. 'And your lovely Louisa?'

'She grows no less so. She means to follow from Sydney soon to divert me from matters military should need arise in the course of war.'

'That suggests a long campaign.'

'Not so,' Cyprian said. 'It merely means that in my case need arises frequently. The shortest separation from Louisa can be taxing; she finds it so too.'

'May you be as lucky in war,' I said.

'I have reason to hope so,' Cyprian said modestly. 'This time we shall have the measure of our insolent foe. We now have the men and munitions to make an impression on Heke, not to speak of a weapon hitherto unfamiliar in warfare.' He leaned forward and whispered confidentially, 'Rockets, Wildblood.'

'Rockets?' I said with disbelief.

'With the smell of hell. Sure to put the fiercest warrior to flight.'

'Extraordinary,' I ventured.

'Unlike less imaginative superiors I have long been of the view that science has something to offer the craft of warfare. This, Wildblood, will be a war worth watching.'

Cyprian's grey eyes were endearingly youthful again.

The force assembled on the Auckland waterside was some four hundred strong, three hundred regular soldiers from the 96th and Cyprian's beloved 58th; and a naval brigade of one hundred. Command was in the care of Colonel Hulme of the 96th. Hulme was then sixty years old. Though he had won honours under fire in India in younger and leaner form, he was now more famed for his martial punctilio than his pugnacity. After he had inspected the twenty score at his disposal, with a keen eye for poorly laundered tunics, I eavesdropped on his conversation with officers. 'There will be nothing unkempt about this campaign,' he promised them. 'Nothing cheap. Nothing shoddy. There are standards to maintain, here in the antipodes, and by God and the Queen we shall maintain them.'

His subordinates, for the most part, studied their feet. One among them, however, looked upward, as if conferring with Providence through his monocle. This was George Philpotts, that day hastily acquitted of cowardice and conduct unbecoming a naval officer, and restored somewhat soiled to his commission. I tried to meet his eye. He failed to meet mine.

'Who knows,' Hulme went on, 'that there might not be further campaigns in this colony?'

No one was willing to suggest not.

'Let our expedition set an example by which others shall be

judged,' Hulme proposed. 'Let us also scrub away the stain on British character left by recent events. Am I understood?'

He was. Lieutenant George Philpotts continued to suffer in silence.

'Otherwise, gentlemen,' Hulme finished, 'it is not my intention to refer further to those events. Under no circumstances will they be alluded to in my hearing. We start with a clean sheet. And we shall end with one.'

This admonition was unnecessary. At mess on the open sea that dusk, with the few little lights of Auckland disappearing astern, I was astonished to find no talk at all of the coming campaign, indeed of anything martial. After Hulme had retired to his cabin there was brandy and backgammon and conversation concerning the paucity of willing womenfolk in the capital. We might have been relaxing in the regiment's Rutlandshire barracks rather than rocking on the Pacific with war ahead. Taking a turn on the deck with Cyprian, with stars of the South Sea flecking the sky, I finally expressed my wonder.

'Does no one,' I asked, 'give thought to what is before us?'

'I do,' he said.

'But not aloud.'

'That,' he explained, 'is bad form.'

I was not sure I understood. 'Bad form?'

'It is not something I necessarily agree with,' he hastened to add. 'I would certainly wish the army other in many respects. But mine is a lone voice. The prevailing view is that ours is an occupation for gentlemen, not tradesmen. We employ sergeants to attend to menial matters. Discussion of a practical nature is unseemly, not least in the mess.'

'We are talking of the eve of a fight,' I pointed out. 'Also of strange terrain and an unfamiliar enemy. Not to speak of your rockets.'

'I daresay lower ranks discuss such matters at length. The feeling is that we are not obliged to make ourselves intimate with their tattle.'

'There would be advantage, would there not, in making yourself familiar with their feelings, and fears?'

'I have sometimes argued so,' Cyprian admitted, 'this side of heresy.'

'And?'

'The sentiment is seen as dangerously democratic. I have, heaven forbid, even been accused of purveying Chartist rubbish about votes for tradesmen and labourers.'

A figure loomed out of the dark to rescue us from further consideration of military affairs. Lone and thoughtful George Philpotts was taking a turn on the deck too. This time he couldn't duck me; we shook hands.

'All's well?' he asked anxiously.

'That ends well,' I assured him.

He flinched nevertheless. Nor was he slow passing on his way.

'Poor George,' Cyprian said. 'He judges himself too harshly.'

'Perhaps so,' I agreed.

'I daresay he will have the chance to redeem himself. Not least in the eyes of his despairing father.'

'I daresay,' I said.

Powerfully scented land rose murky to port. Elsewhere there was sea and more sea, all of it deep.

Thirteen

*T*he Bay was as bewitching as ever I had seen it. One by one, on a sunny autumn afternoon, the vessels of our expedition dropped anchor off Blackguard Beach, with the blasted and blackened remains of the town in near view. Cyprian was engrossed. 'What a shame Louisa isn't here,' he said. 'Or perhaps not. Henry Youngman's *Belle of Blackguard Beach* moved her to tears. To see the place ravished might start her off again.'

Premature veterans of the campaign continued to cringe. George Philpotts judged it desirable to remain inconspicuous while the scene of disaster was studied through telescopes and opinions on loss of the town aired rather cruelly. Young officers were sobered; even their seniors were shaken. For captains and lieutenants alike this was something new. They were like clerics of diminished faith receiving a sign from on high. War was no longer hearsay. Some had waited half a lifetime for sight of a cooling battlefield; this one suggested sites of warmer character ahead. Then an unnerved subaltern shouted, 'The enemy!'

He had reason for fright. On high points about the beach warriors were rising with firearms aloft. Before a rush to the ship's guns began, and more misfortune took form, I identified the tribesmen as friendly. For one thing, Timothy Walker Nene could be seen on horseback, leading them down to the shore. A telescope informed me that beyond his facial tattoo he was no happier with the world. I deduced that he had left off harassing John Heke in favour of welcoming the red tribe to the realm of the warrior. Cyprian hastened to Colonel Hulme's side with my intelligence. Sighs of relief soon spread through all ranks on deck. Cyprian returned to me and said, 'Colonel Hulme is greatly obliged. He is now convinced of your value to this enterprise. You have made an excellent beginning.'

'As what?' I asked in alarm.

'Guide, interpreter, and gleaner of intelligence. He asks that you report directly to him in future.'

'That,' I protested, 'is not what I bargained for.'

'It is what you have,' Cyprian said tersely. 'Colonel Hulme is empowered to conscript all able-bodied male colonists in defence of the realm.'

'Dare I speak,' I asked, ' of obligations elsewhere?'

'You would surely not place an amorous adventure in the scales against duty?'

I distinctly would, with disadvantage to the latter. It was not, however, the setting to say so. Besides, I had a livelier shot in my locker.

'The fact is, Cyprian, I am a most unreliable fellow. My record, in matters of veracity, is infamously poor.'

'Infamously?'

'Notoriously,' I claimed with more modesty.

'What on earth are you talking about?'

'Henry Youngman,' I told him.

'What of him?'

'I know you to be a reader of his work. But I am also sure that you do not take his romances seriously.'

'What of that?' he allowed reluctantly.

'Would you,' I persisted, 'rely on his findings in matters of life and death?'

'Dear fellow, what are you telling me?'

The answer slowly became plain. Several expressions battled across his face. Wonder proved the winner. 'No,' he whispered.

'Exactly,' I said. 'The truth of the matter, Cyprian, is that I have lived more life than one.'

'And you are he? Henry Youngman?'

'Or have been. I must ask you not to trumpet it abroad.'

A further and final expression made a showing. I should have foreseen it. To my dismay it was delight.

'How extraordinary,' he said.

'In a way,' I had to agree.

'And how fabulous.'

'So I am free?'

'Free?'

'To go my own way. An untrustworthy tale-teller is no fit associate of sincere fighting men.'

Cyprian considered this, but not for long. 'Who does not draw the long bow on occasion, in peace and in war?'

'That is hardly the point,' I protested.

'I can't wait to tell Louisa,' he went on. She will never believe it. Henry Youngman my comrade in arms? She will think me unhinged.'

I found the suggestion intemperate too. Meanwhile I was gazing across the Bay at Williams's missionary settlement. What might Angela be about at this hour? Though she was now no more than a nautical mile away, there seemed all the Pacific between us.

'Don't be downcast,' Cyprian said quietly in my ear. 'Far be it from me to deny you compassionate leave as circumstances warrant.'

Colonel Hulme ordered a detachment of men landed. He took the first longboat. The band of the 58th, with shiny instruments and sturdy drums, filled a second. Cyprian and I found passage in a third. Ashore, theatrical preliminaries to war waxed apace. A phalanx of soldiers, marines and ratings formed on the seafront. Nene and his tribesmen listened attentively while Hulme proclaimed martial law in the Bay of Islands. He disclosed that Maori who were not with the Queen might soon be judged against her, with deeply disagreeable consequences. This especially seemed to please Nene; it suggested that Heke might win no further allies, that the days of his young rival were numbered. Shipboard guns then rang out a deafening royal salute. After a burp or two the band located the national anthem in its repertoire. The Union Jack fluttered nobly up an improvised flagstaff. Soldiers presented arms; officers saluted. Finally the Bay rocked with three British cheers. The message was unmistakable. Blackguard Beach was again Queen Victoria's. The campaign had begun. War was no longer a warrior romp.

In matters of ceremony, however, the Maori was not to be outshone. In reply to Hulme's message, Nene's tribesmen took the stage, heaving Britons aside as they arranged themselves in ranks. Their sulky mood was such that Britannia's best backed off hastily.

Hulme bawled, 'Fetch your friend here, Major Bridge.' Cyprian raced me to the colonel's side.

'What in damnation is going on now, Wildblood?' he asked.

'Maori formalities,' I informed him.

'Of a Christian kind?'

'I daresay not, sir.'

'Must it be suffered?' he asked.

'As ours has been,' I suggested. 'Theirs is also of rousing nature.'

That was to do it less than justice. Four hundred chanting warriors rolled rhythmically at Hulme's scattering force, then rolled back. At their head, with shiny club in hand, was Nene's Amazonian wife. It was her task not only to determine the tempo of the dance, but also to watch for flaws in warrior performance that might be warnings of weakness. Men likely to let death into Nene's ranks could be returned to their villages in disgrace. Meanwhile the dance thundered on. There was a stamping of feet; a slapping of muscles; and finally, most vividly, a rolling of eyes and baring of tongues. Then weapons were held high. There was a nervous silence.

'Is it finished?' Hulme asked in a hoarse whisper.

'But for speeches,' I promised.

'And you are sure they are with us?'

'Reliably, sir,' I assured him.

'There is a God,' he announced.

I saw it as no part of my business to inform our commander that Maori oratory might prove more fearful. It took Nene much of the afternoon to make the point that his interests were identical with those of Britain's young Queen. He paced back and forward, calling up a roster of ancestors to witness his words, and not least the Almighty. He pointed a ceremonial spear menacingly at bystanders and let his silences speak louder than words. There were many such silences. There were no fewer words. In one form and another, and then many more, most of his monologue was to the effect that he had begun battling John Heke without benefit of Britain. It was therefore now Hulme's duty to hasten his men to the fight.

I translated these sentiments into serviceable English.

'Duty?' Hulme bristled. 'He tells me my duty?'

'In short, sir,' I said.

'And attempts to give me orders?'

'Merely those you might give to advantage,' I explained.

Hulme was in further difficulty when he rose to announce common cause with Nene. He had orders from FitzRoy on the course to be followed in the coming campaign. These were that the Bay of Islands was to be made secure, and suspiciously neutral chiefs subdued lest they think to give comfort to rebels. John Heke would thus be isolated. His humiliation would follow in the fullness of war.

Nene could make no sense of this lacklustre procedure. Was John Heke to be left unmolested while tribesmen of no account were silenced? Was John Heke to be left bragging inland in his fortress?

That, Hulme admitted, was provisionally the case.

Nene rose and turned his back on the assembly.

Through me, Hulme asked what was amiss.

'Tell the colonel he is fortunate I still talk to him,' Nene said.

Hulme, in a sweat, informed Nene that orders were sacrosanct.

'Then let us see the governor lead,' Nene said. 'Not his juniors.'

That, Hulme replied, was impossible. Governor FitzRoy, responsible for the entire colony, had far more on his mind than a feckless Maori named Heke.

Nene spat. It was not to serve caution, he explained, that he gave allegiance to Britain. Caution? Its correct name was cowardice.

Hulme toiled on. In furtherance of orders, he announced, he meant first to strike at a settlement upriver from Blackguard Beach. The chief residing there, by name of Pomare, had been ambiguous in past dealings with Britain. He had not been heard to denounce John Heke.

'Pomare?' Nene asked.

'Pomare,' Hulme agreed.

'He is a card-playing drunk,' Nene said with disgust. 'A womaniser. And old.' He produced his trump. 'And not worth fighting.'

Nonetheless, Hulme insisted, a beginning had to be made, and an example.

Nene stood again. This time, to his curt order, his aides also stood. Then his hundreds.

'Make your beginning,' he challenged Hulme. 'Make your example.'

'Without you?' Hulme asked.

'I would insult myself by warring with such as Pomare,' Nene added. 'When you are serious, I may be there.'

'May?'

'If it pleases me,' Nene explained.

Ten minutes later his force was gone. Seekers of omens had a surfeit that afternoon.

The next day of soldiering began rowdy, with bugles rousing men before dawn. Chains were soon rattling and anchors drawn from the seabed. By daybreak the expedition's four vessels, with flags drifting aft, were travelling slowly up the Bay. It might be surmised that Providence had mixed feelings about the venture. Though the tide was helpful, the wind was weak.

Hulme gathered his officers. 'The nature of this initiative is no secret,' he informed them. 'It will be sharp. It will be short. It will be punitive. Should Pomare fail to submit we shall knock his village about his ears and raze it to the ground. Not only will the sorry affair of Blackguard Beach be avenged. The Bay of Islands will be left with an unsettling reminder of the consequences of native dissidence. Is that understood?'

It appeared to be. And especially by George Philpotts, at a distance; he made it appear that he was more interested in maritime business than martial. No one was deceived.

The sails, meanwhile, refused to fill. As day drew on, the vessels began fighting the tide. Fewer than five miles had been won before dark. Finally we moored a mile short of our goal. Unfamiliar lights on the water would doubtless warn Pomare and his neutral henchmen that the next day might be the least serene in their lives. They might already be pondering the perils of lukewarm loyalty to the Queen.

Next morning the sun showed Pomare's village to be a pretty little place, half on hillside, half along a crescent of beach, with buildings of European character rising among thatched native dwellings. Scrub and forest veiled it on three sides. There were cultivations, grazing beasts, drying nets, and canoes drawn up on the sand. Nothing could be less menacing. Smoke drifted from cooking fires. And to confirm first impressions a white flag flew from the highest point in the village.

Hulme viewed it with contempt.

'What do you make of that, Wildblood?' he asked.

There was only one thing to be made of it, but I was not so insensitive as to point this out to the colonel. 'Peaceful intention, sir,' I suggested.

'Martial law now prevails in the Bay.'

'As I understand it, sir,' I replied.

'It takes no account of pious intent. A white flag is now acceptable only in the hands of Maori actively loyal in character.'

'Such as Nene?'

'If the devil is to be trusted.'

'Word may not have reached Pomare yet,' I pointed out.

'Perhaps not,' Hulme allowed.

'So how is he to know?'

'When he discovers himself spirited off to captivity in Auckland,' Hulme explained.

He summoned Cyprian. 'Take Mr Wildblood ashore, Major Bridge,' he ordered. 'Have him explain to Pomare that he is to surrender himself to me or face the consequences.'

'Surrender?' Cyprian queried.

'Or suffer,' Hulme vowed.

Minutes later Cyprian and I were ferrying that message ashore. No warrior rose in our path. There were curious women and children in plenty. The earth seemed to have opened up and swallowed all men sound of limb. We had a sense, however, of being viewed from nearby vegetation. There were shadows stirring, possibly muskets trained. We climbed uphill and found a fat, elderly and amiable chief sunning himself on the veranda of his dwelling in the company of family and friends. Pomare appeared to be relishing the spectacle of British might ranged before his village. 'Does the Queen think me worth four warships?' he asked.

'Most sincerely,' I said.

'What is her problem?'

'Heke and those who think sympathetically of him.'

'Do I?'

'The thought is that you may.'

'Me?' His surprise seemed genuine.

'There are Maori waiting to learn which way the wind blows.'

He drew my attention to the pale length of calico floating above his village.

'That flag knows,' he argued.

Cyprian nudged me. 'Hurry,' he urged. 'Be frank with the fellow. Tell him formal surrender is required.'

'That might not be diplomatic,' I argued.

'We are not here to be discreet,' he pointed out.

'Nor is it incumbent upon us to perish,' I informed him. I was even more aware of possible presences in vegetation around.

'The longer this takes, the worse matters may be,' Cyprian insisted. 'Be honest. Get it over with now.'

I cleared my throat, trusting to inspiration. My faith in the sound of my own voice was not misplaced.

'The Governor,' I told Pomare, 'wishes you to be his guest in Auckland.'

He was impressed. 'The Governor?'

'It would give him great pleasure if you took advantage of his hospitality. One of our vessels is at your disposal. He hopes your voyage to join him in the capital proves pleasing.'

Pomare mused on this, with mounting interest. 'Are other chiefs in the Bay thus invited?'

'Not even Nene,' I said.

He mused further. 'Then I must go,' he concluded.

Cyprian asked me for a translation.

'No bonds will be required,' I said. 'Nor guns and guards.'

We retired from the village in orderly fashion. Hobbling along on a stick, Pomare led the way to our long boat. He remained in cheerful mood as ratings rowed us out to our vessel.

'That,' Cyprian whispered, 'was all rather marvellous. How did you win him over?'

'You may not wish to know.'

'By deception?'

'Better me than you,' I proposed. 'I have no uniform to discredit.'

'All the same,' he said.

'I admit only to bedecking truth a little,' I explained. 'Not, I must add, with pride in myself.'

Cyprian mourned for no more than a minute.

'Then it seems I must swallow mine too,' he decided. After a time he added, 'You must think me an innocent, Henry.'

'Ferdinand,' I insisted.

Colonel Hulme was not one for niceties. After a curt welcome he made it plain to Pomare that he was now in custody. It would be to his credit with the Queen if he ordered his people to give up their arms within the hour. Otherwise the village would be levelled. Pomare needed no thought. 'The order is given,' he announced, before hanging his head in humiliation.

Cyprian and I went ashore with a detachment of men to take charge of firearms as they were delivered up. It was a vain wait. The village was emptying. Not only had men gone. Women and children were absconding too. Cyprian was obliged to report himself empty-handed.

'So let us get on with it,' Hulme sighed.

'Sir?' Cyprian asked.

'Tell men foraging is now permitted,' Hulme announced.

'Is that to be seen as part of their duty?' Cyprian asked.

'It may sharpen their taste for soldiering,' Hulme said. 'I am not one to argue with the needs of human nature.'

'Might it not be said, sir, that Pomare's people have been terrified enough?'

'It might well be said. But not by you, Major Bridge. See that fire follows within the hour.'

Men of Colonel Hulme's regiment, the 96th, were first to the charge. Boat after boat beached under Pomare's village, spilling out scavengers. They sprinted uphill, racing from dwelling to dwelling, grabbing up anything useful and much that wasn't. No arms were located, nor kegs of powder. Such items had disappeared with the male population, doubtless in John Heke's direction. Livestock aside, looters found little of an enriching nature. Officers and men sped off in pursuit of pigs and chickens, goats and geese. Some creatures were shot down; others were put to the sword. There was mortal squealing and squawking, with flesh and feather flying, and founts of gore. Anguished Cyprian contrived not to launch his own men ashore till last. 'Indiscipline breeds indiscipline,' he whispered. 'The 58th will not behave as bandits.'

He held his regiment aloof from temptation, putting men in place to ensure that plunder was fairly divided and returned to the ships for commissariat purpose. This did not make him popular with men of Hulme's 96th. Arguments flourished between soldier and soldier with fisticuffs near. Cyprian stood firm and gave the order to torch the village. Soon the hillside was lively with flame; smoke hid the sun.

By nightfall it was over. The village was smouldering, Pomare on his way to confinement in the capital, and Hulme had Maori poultry on his table.

Cyprian and I took the evening air together. The powerful smell of smoke from shore diminished that pleasure. There were spurts of flame and sputters of sparks as last beams dropped and fragments of wall fell.

'So endeth my first action,' he mourned.

'With no loss of life,' I reminded him.

'With one decrepit chief lured into captivity, a tribe pauperised, and more volunteers sped to John Heke.'

'Much might have been worse.'

'It is difficult to see how.'

'Anyway,' I argued, 'it is not on your head alone.'

'What does that mean?'

'Your superiors were party to this too, as I recall. And, for that matter, me.'

'Nonetheless,' Cyprian said.

Someone sidled out of shipboard shadows to join us. George Philpotts took shape. He examined Cyprian through his monocle, then me. The three of us stood silent. It seemed we had something in common. It was not affection for ourselves.

Fourteen

*A*gain I find myself a reluctant visitor at my desk. Another week of my life has rippled past since I last made myself apparent here. I have even done my best, with bottle and glass, to forget this narrative. Yet it refuses to be extinguished. As soon as I sit the story rolls on. I have the powerful sense that I have been taking dictation, transcribing a tale spirited back from the misty approach to Valhalla. It is of course true that other hands have been been at work before me, mostly to make the tale tasteful. (I have even seen it featured boldly in a book titled *Wars That Won the Empire*, author anonymous, designed to edify bloodthirsty young Britons.) I am not, you understand, here to be edifying. Time is short, and winter days dark. I am talking of a far and faint melody only I live to hear, a bittersweet ballad of soldier and warrior in a homespun war of which even Queen Victoria may never have heard. The present year, by the way, is 1886. In another year she will have been five decades enthroned. British feats of arms have reddened the world's maps. The deeds of Rome's legions now look puny. The sun never dims on her Empire. Our good monarch has aged, though optimists claim she could outlive the century. It is to the point that I am some years her senior. I have no reason to imagine that I will survive her story; my modest ambition is to see my own in fetching shape.

While Hulme thought on the wisdom of singeing suspect Maori, and allowing rebel Heke to remain at large, I managed an excursion around the Bay for an hour in Angela's company. Major Cyprian's view was that I had earned it. There was a flaw in the arrangement, however. The hour was spent in proximity to Williams. His welcome was short of warm. 'I thought we might have seen the last of you, Mr Wildblood,' he observed.

'I trust disappointment is not too great, sir.'

'The New Zealand interior has been a graveyard for many more robust. Naturally we feared the worst.'

'Would that I were returning in triumph, sir.'

'I already have an account of yesterday's detestable enterprise,' Williams said. 'Britain must learn to live and let live. If left to his own devices John Heke will soon find his posturing unprofitable. Why speed more men to his side?'

'It is not for me to say,' I claimed.

'Yet, unless I am mistaken, you are now part of this ill-considered campaign.'

'Reluctantly,' I explained. 'I retain the hope that I may find a peacemaking role.'

'My view of things no longer makes provision for hope,' Williams said. It did, on the other hand, provide for his keeping an eye peeled for innocent intimacies between Angela and myself. We could do little more than exchange wistful glances when Williams's gaze wandered elsewhere. It was not often elsewhere. As craftsmen know the possibilities inherent in wood and stone, Williams knew the potential of the flesh for depravity. Even martial news did not divert him sufficiently. Angela and I risked no more than a furtive touch of hands as she set tea before me. Her lips shaped themselves into a silent kiss. That all but unhinged me.

'Was it fulfilling?' Cyprian asked on my return to duty.

'It might have been more so,' I confessed.

'Put it behind you,' he advised. 'There is work ahead.'

'Work?'

'Worthy of us,' Cyprian said with satisfaction. 'No stratagems, no subterfuges, no games.'

Timothy Walker Nene had descended on Colonel Hulme with an ultimatum. He announced that he had returned most of his battle-tried tribesmen to advantageous positions in the interior. They kept watch on John Heke, observing his fortress and all departures and arrivals. There were many such; it seemed the countryside seethed with inflammatory Maori messengers and footloose men with firearms. Immature malcontents were joining John Heke daily. Heke had to be attacked now or he, Nene, would wash his hands of the British, as would any wise warrior.

Within the minute Hulme concluded that continued dalliance in the Bay of Islands was unbecoming. Loss of Nene to neutrality would not read well in the most compassionate account of his expedition. 'A swift strike at Heke now,' he informed his officers, 'may well terminate native stirrings forever in the colony.'

To keep Heke guessing, and confuse spies, Hulme moved the three remaining vessels of his force under darkness to the north of the Bay of Islands, disembarking his men at daybreak and entering conference with Nene on the route to be taken. It was Nene's belief that the shortest path to Heke, some thirteen miles, served best. Hulme preferred an approach five miles longer. Military lore said that obvious routes tempted ambush.

'There are trees?' he asked.

'And rivers,' Nene agreed.

'There you are. You are saying that the region is roadless.'

'The longer way too,' Nene told Hulme.

'So what is the difference? Eighteen miles against thirteen? A mere five.'

He was not going to have it suggested by a half-heathen like Nene that Britons might not be up to exertion. 'I have always believed that a brisk tramp concentrates men's minds,' the colonel disclosed. 'A longer hike might invigorate them still more.'

With a sorrowful shake of head Nene finally gave way. If Britons needed to punish themselves, that was their business. His was to interest Britons in fracas with John Heke, not argue the merits of a moderate march through wilderness.

Cyprian was also troubled. 'Rations, sir?' he asked Hulme.

'Two days' salt meat and five days' biscuit,' Hulme announced.

'Rum, sir?'

'Men may toast the Queen's health before and after battle, and otherwise as circumstances require. Further sustenance would be a needless burden. An ample supply of shot is more to the point.'

'With respect, sir, so modest a ration does not provide for contingencies.'

'Contingencies, Major Bridge?'

'Delays, sir. Difficulties.'

'Which you foresee?'

'Not necessarily, sir.'

'Good,' Hulme grunted.

'Nevertheless, sir, I am trying to make the point that this is New Zealand. This is the first inland march Britons have made.'

'And you are thinking of your men.'

'That might be said, sir.'

'By all means think of them. Your are under no obligation, however, to voice your thoughts on the subject.'

'Yes, sir,' Cyprian said.

'There will be no delays,' Hulme disclosed. 'There will be no difficulties.'

'No, sir,' Cyprian said contritely.

'Let me enlighten you in matters of morale, Major Bridge. Were we to travel with foodstuff in greater quantity, men might begin to suspect that there is more to this war than they supposed; that there are hardships ahead, and their commanders dishonest. We must not allow them to entertain such notions, Major Bridge. We must not allow them vexation. We are here to make short work of John Heke and anyone who undermines our enterprise may face a court martial. Are we understood?'

'It would seem so, sir.'

Having chastened Cyprian, Hulme returned to winning over Nene, this time with a gift of apparel conjured up overnight by a naval tailor. There was a cocked hat, a blue naval coat with gold epaulettes, and striped military trousers and boots. He made a lavish sight as he took up a place beside Hulme at the head of the column. Other ranks fell in behind. Soldiers were in forage caps, with red jackets and grey trousers; and hung about with muskets, bayonets, ammunition pouches, water bottles, haversacks with biscuit and further rounds, topped off with bundled greatcoats and blankets. These shuffling mountains of *matériel* were followed by dourly dark-clad marines burdened by the new and hellish rockets. Hard behind were straw-hatted ratings, in wide white trousers, moving with a gait more suited to a rolling deck. Undaunted by British livery, Nene's warriors brought up the rear in blankets and kilts. Then the rum ration made its appearance in the form of casks in a cart. Lest men be tempted to drink the Queen's health prematurely, it was flanked by heartless guards. All told there were something like six hundred men on show. One stood out in this company. Tall and willowy George Philpotts, especially not with his monocle, had small hope of making himself unobtrusive in the ranks.

'I rather think,' Hulme announced, 'that we are not in need of your services, Lieutenant Philpotts.'

George fell out and returned disconsolate to his vessel. Like Nene, Hulme wanted none of poor omen in his column.

He waited for his moment. Then he raised his sword. A bugle sounded, summoning men to war. I own to a shiver of soul. After decades of indolence Britain was on the march again.

For much of the day I was at Cyprian's shoulder and seldom more than a pace behind Hulme and Nene. The terrain remained villainous in character. Where there was not swamp there was marsh. Where there was not hillock there was hill. Where there was not gully there was gorge. The autumn sunlight became uncomfortably warm. The grunts and sly curses of burdened men became more audible. So did the sound of cajoling sergeants. Nene began to find his uniform inconvenient. First he slung away his cocked hat, then his boots, finally trousers and frock coat. Before long he was defiantly barefoot in a blanket again. It was Hulme's supposition that the day's march would carry his men to the door of John Heke's domain. By late afternoon he had to concede that his limping contingent was miles short of its goal. Men may or may not have been more concentrated of mind; they were certainly muttering sentiments of a black character. Camp was finally pitched in a valley less cheerless than most, beside a serene stream. Piquets were put out, rough bivouacs built, and fires lit. After charring their allowance of meat to make it edible, soldiers chewed on biscuit; Maori made the most of cold potato.

Before he retired Colonel Hulme inspected the camp; and paused before the fire I shared with footsore Cyprian.

'It has not been the most fulfilling of days,' Hulme said.

'On one view of the matter, sir,' Cyprian agreed cautiously.

'The chances of war are many and uncertain,' Hulme confided. With his gift for second-hand wisdom, he added, 'There are good days, Major Bridge. And there are bad.'

Nevertheless that was as good a day as any Colonel Hulme was to know in the campaign. Nene's men thought to sweeten it with an evening hymn. Hibernians in the camp returned the compliment with a rousing Irish air. For a time there was a mirthful atmosphere with Maori and Briton taking turn to perform. There were jigs which would not have disgraced County Wexford, and made even a Maori war dance seem inhibited. New Zealand, however, had the last word. After we climbed into our blankets the firmament fell apart and unloaded enough of a deluge to unnerve Noah. Bivouacs were soon awash. Men shivering miserably under blankets saw out the night beside feeble fires. Morning confirmed the rout. Food was sodden. Powder was damp. The serene stream was a broad cataract. The pitiless sky offered more of the same.

Hulme uttered the only sentiment useful. 'My God,' he said in disbelief.

'Is the march to be resumed, sir?' Cyprian asked.

'Without pause,' Hulme announced.

'Am I at liberty to inform men as to the likely duration of today's proceedings?'

'Tell them four hours should see us within range of the enemy.'

'Four hours, sir?'

'Even should we swim, Major Bridge.'

For the most part we did. Four days later we finished with mire, mad rivers and dripping forest. We remained only in range of heaven's artillery. Thunder storms were interspersed with hail and drifting drizzle. At length, through mist, a familiar vista grew, one composed of extinct volcanoes and patchily open country. Heke's fortified ridge then became distinct in the distance. Hulme called a halt to enter conference with Nene. They made frequent use of Hulme's telescope. Differences were soon apparent. Nene wished to press on. Hulme wished to consider the terrain.

'This,' he argued, 'is no petty tribal feud. This is war as a nation fights it.'

Nene stormed off to join his own contingent. Hulme then called me to his side.

'I am given to understand, Wildblood, that the enemy is before us,' he said.

'That is also my impression, sir,' I said.

'My instructions are that an attack is to be launched only if John Heke remains intransigent. In short, he must be given a last chance before bayonets are fixed. This is not to Nene's liking, nor much to mine. Nene, however, does not answer to superiors. I reluctantly do.'

'What is this to me, sir?'

'Heke's mood must be determined. There is no one better suited to the task in this vicinity.'

'Than me, sir?'

'While you detour to Heke's fortress, the army will make camp with Nene's men. We shall expect you to rejoin us when you are able. I am most touched, if I may say so, by the speed with which you volunteer your services.'

An armed escort — which looked suspiciously like a guard — kept me company for the lesser half of the journey. I was left alone for the larger, musing on the likely invisibility of the muddy item of naval apparel I flew from a stick. The entire colony seemed to be holding its breath as I plodded on solo. At length I heard hoofbeats closing with me. I looked up from my muddy feet and met Moses' eye.

'Good,' he said. 'I win the bet.'

'What bet?'

'Heke wagered that only Williams would be fool enough to walk alone between armies. I put my money on you.'

An hour later I was in Heke's camp again.

'Tell me more slowly,' John Heke said.

Still breathless, I explained, 'I am here to ask if I can bear any message to Colonel Hulme or your tribesman Nene.'

'Message? Of what nature?'

'Of peace terms, perhaps. If you have some proposal Colonel Hulme might be pleased to hear it. Nene, possibly, less so. Nevertheless now is the time to say anything you have in mind to say. At least I can promise Colonel Hulme will listen.'

Heke was thoughtful.

'A kind word could yet calm matters,' I argued.

'Such as submission?' he suggested slyly.

'Nothing so fanciful. A promise of less mischief might be music to most British ears.'

'Inform the Colonel that we walk in the ways of virtue. Let him ask himself why his soldiers have not been ambushed; why they have met no skirmisher; why they have found a free path into our territory.'

'What would you wish the Colonel to conclude?'

'That true Christians cannot fire the first shot. The second may be ours. Never the first. Inform him also that he who strikes the first blow asks misfortune; that the worst of war will be on his head.'

'That does not sound scriptural.'

'Maori proverbs are not meant to,' he said.

I had the feeling that he had just minted another maxim to enrich his race's extensive store. Meanwhile he was resolved on the least irreligious route to ruin.

'If he attacks, we fight,' he explained. 'If he does not, we do not.'

'I shall enlighten the Colonel accordingly,' I promised.

I stood as if to leave. This was unduly hopeful.

'If he is awaiting your return, there is no haste,' he said.

'What does that mean?'

'He will not attack until you have returned to his line.'

'Who knows?' I said with discomfort.

'And I may be in the mood for a story,' he explained.

'What story?'

'Mine,' he ventured.

'That is a little premature.'

'So how many more flagstaffs must I fell?' he sighed.

'I think the present question is how many Britons. Not to speak of how many Nenes.'

'Or the flagstaffs will be forgotten?'

'Or poorly recalled.'

'Why must that be?'

'There is no accounting for human nature,' I argued. 'Meanwhile I am no seer. A storyteller needs to be familiar with his plot. This one remains unreasonably reticent.'

In the same minute, however, a narrative complication materialised noisily nearby. The Duke and two hundred armed associates were making an unexpected appearance. They had the dishevelled look of men who had been journeying far and fast.

'We are back,' the Duke announced.

The Duke distinctly was. Heke might have looked more appreciative. The Duke was in no mood to mince words.

'You mean to halt the red tribe with this fortress?' he mocked.

'We mean to fight,' Heke said.

'You mean to die,' the Duke said with contempt. 'It is the work of women.'

'This fortress?'

'It may be the work of those who think Christian prayer a protection. It is not the work of men who have looked a musket in the mouth.'

'Nene has not challenged it,' Heke protested.

'Because he wishes to see what the red tribe does with you. Has Nene held you in one place or has he not?'

Heke was silent.

'Give me your men,' the Duke demanded.

'For what?'

'To show you what a fortress may be.'

It was not a joyous reunion. To add to John Heke's unhappiness, the Duke had pagan priests in his retinue. Their role was to make men more comfortable with the notion of leaving this life. I foresaw protracted debate, a lengthy night of theological nature. While the Duke continued to find fault with his junior, men of his party swarmed over the fortress, ripping out palisades of vulnerable character, rolling sturdier logs into place, reinforcing the defences with rock, and dressing loopholes with curtains of flax. Entrenchments were also being deepened efficiently with spades. The Duke was diverted from his denunciations of Heke only by the need to shout orders at his workmen. Pandemonium did not promise to diminish. Everywhere the fortress was finding fresh shape.

I was allowed to see no more of business in hand. Moses said sidelong, 'It becomes desirable to get you out of here. Look at your feet as we pass among the Duke's men. Do not let them see your face. They may find it difficult to understand why you are not dead.'

He smuggled me through the Duke's combatants and presented me with open ground. 'Run rather fast,' he suggested.

'So Heke wishes to fight?' Colonel Hulme said.
　'There is no turning back,' I informed him.
　'And he remains at odds with his freshly arrived ally?'
　'With the Duke, sir. Most unhappily so.'
　'There is no chance, perhaps, that they might war with each other?'
　'Circumstances do not suggest so hopeful a view, sir.'
　'Meaning what?'
　'They would clash only for the privilege of battling you, sir.'
　Hulme grunted.
　'Sir?' I asked.
　'On your way, Wildblood,' he ordered.

Major Cyprian welcomed me back to our overnight quarters. 'Good fellow,' he said glumly. He had just returned from verifying the existence of his piquets. The day had turned cold again, with a faint drizzle. Rain dripped from his nose as he gazed toward Heke's eyrie, and tomorrow's enemy. 'Perhaps a little strife will warm us.'
　'Depend on it,' I said.

Fifteen

*F*ires burned on Heke's ridge nightlong. Or was it now the Duke's? Either way flames leapt bright. Midnight downpour did not diminish the glow.

Morning arrived faint, with bugles calling men from damp beds of bracken. Colonel Hulme was the first to his feet, with Cyprian soon dutiful beside him. There were all of eight hundred Briton and Maori battling for space in which to urinate and bush in which to defecate, and otherwise fighting for water and nourishment. There was much water, especially in the form of saturating showers, and next to no nourishment. Hulme contemplated Heke's fortress through a telescope. Then he passed it to Cyprian.

'Do you observe overnight change?' he asked.

Cyprian looked lengthily. 'Their numbers remain impossible to determine, sir,' he announced.

'Changes of a material nature, man.'

'Their defences would seem rather dense, sir. The front and left faces look particularly strong. I notice flanking angles not in evidence yesterday. These could bring crossfire to bear on storming parties. Palisades also seem of less pliant nature, if I am not mistaken. There has been extravagant use made of native flax, presumably to curtain marksmen, and rock to buttress their position.'

'Is that all?'

'Roughly, sir.'

'All sticks and stones, eh?'

'In a manner of speaking, sir.'

'It worries you?'

'It gives me thought, sir.'

'Then I must let you into a secret, Major Bridge. A fortress is only as good as the men who man it.'

'Perhaps so, sir.'

'And what manner of men do we confront here, Major?'

'That remains to be seen, sir.'

'Then let me enlighten you. Savages, Major. Innocent savages. Children playing with fire. It is almost indecent to intrude on their picturesque charade. Nevertheless their defences will be underfoot by noon.'

'So today is the day, sir,' Cyprian said.

'Delay would be inexcusable,' Hulme argued. 'We have the intelligence of your butterfly friend Wildblood. The rebel leaders are at odds with each other. Their henchmen possibly likewise. Morale might be still poorer this morning.'

'Not on the evidence of their fortress, if I may say so, sir.'

'Speak your mind this once, Major, and then let us hear no more of it.'

'I note the absence of artillery in our arsenal, sir.'

'We have rockets, have we not?'

'Much as we might wish them more familiar, sir.'

'By morning's end they will be,' Hulme promised.

'I had not thought of them as a substitute for honest guns and gunners, sir. Rather as a crowning glory.'

'Have you said all you wish to, Major Bridge?'

'For the larger part, sir.'

'Then get on with it,' Hulme ordered. 'Have men report to their storming parties. Allot them rum as required. We move within the hour.'

Having taken his time with toiletries, Nene wandered into Hulme's company. 'There is a problem?' he asked.

'Not of an engrossing nature,' Hulme told him.

'Heke is to be humbled today?'

'Forever.'

'That is a word I like to hear,' Nene said.

'What fighting man does not?' Hulme asked.

Finished with eavesdropping, I watched Cyprian coax men of his regiment, and residue of others, into belligerent formation. Pannikins of rum were passed from man to man and refilled frequently by compassionate corporals. This procedure did not allow for large ceremony or audible toasts to the monarch; men were preoccupied with licking the last drops from their moist moustaches. That finished, they faced again to the front. His officers and sergeants seemed to know his orders before he gave them and did their work well. One moment he was commanding a band of rank-smelling and foul-mouthed ne'er-do-wells; the next he was at the head of a column stiff with menace. Britain's Empire had a future with such as Major Cyprian Bridge.

That, nonetheless, was when trouble began. Nene's warriors, perceptive viewers of soldierly procedure, were taken aback by one item carried by already encumbered infantrymen. These were furled stretchers on which wounded and fallen would be recovered in the wake of battle. When the function of stretchers was explained, disbelief and outrage dawned on Maori faces. Such items could only tempt death into taking an interest in events. Declining to be party to their own decease, senior tribesmen waited in deputation on Hulme and Nene.

'This is not a war party,' they complained. 'This is a funeral march.'

Hulme and other Britons snickered unhelpfully.

Nene, though by no means aloof from omen himself, argued that it might be a mark of the British clan's courage that they were willing to play fast and loose with fate.

This impressed no one. Nene's less loyal tribesmen huddled in bitter conclave, like jurymen pondering the evidence. This sight was not pleasing to Nene. Nor was he happy when a further grievance manifested. Britons had been seen on their feet that morning while they consumed the little sustenance on hand. This also was ominous. Men about to do battle should sit and eat quietly, as if it were just another day in their lives; and not likely their last. From the Maori point of view, Britons were immature in such matters. With indifference to etiquette, and contempt for omens, Colonel Hulme's contingent made perilous allies. Indeed they were already dead. Who could trust fighting men who ate on their feet before battle and carried receptacles for the dead? Who would wish alliance with men doomed?

An elderly chief delivered the majority view. His fellows saw no reason to fight alongside Britons, and much reason not to. They were willing to provide vocal encouragement from a distance, if so desired.

Seeing his prestige slip away, and especially his standing with the Queen, Nene demanded that his fellows stand by him. He raged in vain. In minutes most of his contingent melted away into muddy terrain. He now mustered no more than two or three dozen men, all intimates and relatives; they did not appear any more ecstatic about martial enterprise than those departed. Meanwhile Hulme's force was thinned by a third without a shot fired.

Hulme was torn between astonishment, disgust and fury, and in the throes of all three. 'Damn me,' he got out. 'I thought the wretches were common-sense Christians.'

'That was also my impression, sir,' Cyprian said. He risked a suggestion. 'Perhaps we might delay matters a day, sir. Tomorrow we might better accommodate our allies.'

'Accommodate?' Hulme said. 'Accommodate?'

'Our allies. In respect of custom, sir.'

'I do not, Major Bridge, harken to pagan superstition in any shape or form. Nor do I mean to provide the occasion for it.'

'No, sir.'

'Furthermore, Major, you will favour me by informing Nene that we have no need of his services today.'

'Surely he has suffered enough humiliation this morning.'

'A little more, nevertheless, may not go amiss. Let his kind see how Britons battle; they may well find heart to join us.'

Nene was huddled among the few warriors left at his side. He remained sullen and silent as Cyprian salted his wound.

'Tell Colonel Hulme I pray for him,' he said unconvincingly.

Hulme was inspirited by news from a shivering scout. This venturesome fellow had scrambled through scrub and fern to win a view of rugged ground to the rear of Heke's ridge. It was his impression that the fortress was far less forbidding from that quarter. Palisades appeared leaner, rocks smaller, and earthworks rather more rudimentary.

'Are you telling me that such as we see of the fortress is a facade?' Hulme asked.

'It could be construed as such,' the scout allowed.

'Good,' Hulme said. 'Let us call their bluff.'

There was news even more melodious. The scout had observed warriors stealing off into woodland patching the vicinity. He had glimpsed between fifty and a hundred furtively on the move; he deduced that there might be many more making their way from the fortress.

'Deserting?' Hulme said.

'It is the only possible construction to be placed upon it, sir.'

'There is a further one,' Hulme argued. 'They are fed up with their leaders feuding.' He caught my eye. 'Wildblood? You have been in their camp. How would you interpret it?'

'I am no student of military matters,' I protested.

'But you would agree that there is no love lost between Heke and whatever the old pagan's name is.'

'The Duke, sir.'

'Might a last-minute parting of the ways be likely?'

'It cannot be ruled out,' I acknowledged.

'But you would agree that at the least the spirit of their followers may be gone?'

'In fraught circumstances anything is possible, sir.'

'Excellent,' he said.

That might apply both ways. I deemed it not the time to suggest so to Colonel Hulme.

He called officers up for a last conference. 'Gentlemen,' he said, 'here is my plan. We close with such of the fortress as we can observe. The rockets will then be loosed. The ensuing panic will do our work. Should resistance remain, one storming party will work its way about the fortress, to its vulnerable rear, and then give fight. The others will contrive to dampen the spirits of those defenders manning the front face of the fortress. I would expect surrender before that point is reached. Are we agreed?'

No one said not.

'Excellent,' Hulme said. 'Prepare to move on my signal.'

Before Cyprian took command of his chafing men again, he felt a need to express himself to me. 'I suspect matters may not be as simple as the colonel supposes. Yet who am I to say? I am about to look an armed foe in the face for the first time; I have to presume superiors know best. Make me a promise, Wildblood. Should I fall today, inform my lovely Louisa that I fell unflinching.'

As a story it was mellifluous enough, if lacking in invention.

'It would be my privilege,' I vowed.

'And see she does not grieve unhealthily.'

'You have my word on that too,' I said.

Rain continued to rustle between us. His nose resumed dripping. Then again, no one was a picture of courage that day.

'As for your own person,' he suggested, 'do keep it beyond musket range. Remember that a stray ball can damage a bystander at four hundred paces. It is an ignominious way to die. And, for that matter, an undesirable day on which to do so.'

'It is,' I agreed, 'a pity about the weather.'

We shook hands. I would have liked Cyprian's grip firmer. Mine might also have been less shaky.

Hulme's bugler sounded a watery summons to the battlefield. Cyprian unsheathed his sword, and took pistol in hand. The colours of the 58th lifted and fluttered overhead. With stiff step and stern faces, their muskets aslant, the men of his red-coated column advanced rank on rank to their drummer's beat. Something heaved in my stomach; I felt a thrill in my throat. Cyprian was a lyricist too.

Thereafter my view of matters was limited to what a telescope told me. Hulme launched his army across low ground and lakeside and ensconced half his number at the foot of the ridge harbouring Heke's fortress. Much of the other half moved off to the right where they might, if necessary, begin investment of the stronghold. Meanwhile marines took charge of a knoll beyond musket range and set up the stand from which their incapacitating rockets would fire. At this point I became aware that I was a far from lone witness of events. Several of Nene's defecting combatants had risen from scrub, as wide-eyed as I about the business in hand; they were particularly anxious for news from my telescope. I endeavoured to wave them away, with no success. One bold ruffian asked, 'Is it true that this new weapon will pursue a man wherever he flees?'

'It is possible,' I judged.

'Then how do we know it will not change its mind about Heke and chase us?'

'You do not,' I said severely.

This was effective. Most backed off a dozen yards, some more than a score. I was enabled to train the telescope without being jostled. Heavy breathing grew audible as a lieutenant of marines prepared to write history by giving warfare new form. Hulme lifted his sword as a signal. The lieutenant ignited his rocket.

How to put it benevolently? As a spectacle it proved magical. Smoke seethed from its rear. With spits of flame it flew left and right. It even appeared to be looking for the fortress. Short of Heke's palisades, however, it skipped from the ground and veered off to the eastern horizon, never again to be seen.

There was, I surmised, always a first time.

Nene's men peered out from the bushes into which they had plunged. They were still protecting their heads and blocking their ears. They wished to know whether the demonic business was over.

'No,' I informed them.

They dived deep into the landscape again.

The marine lieutenant, expressing himself coarsely, was completing a transaction with a second rocket. Hulme could be seen nearby, in some agitation. This time the rocket lifted with a lively bang which promised much. It too, however, proved coy. Once it had risen it began circling the fortress and then, with something of a sigh, soared away to the west. The third was even less robust of character. It farted unpromisingly before hitting an invisible wall and falling back among fleeing marines. By this time Heke's men were crowding every vantage point to watch the pyrotechnic performance. Heke himself, growing bolder, threw open a gate to get a better view. Standing there defiantly, he lit his pipe and waved the rockets away as he might mosquitoes. (Later, in the best tradition of legend, it was said that he stayed them with a fearless gaze and a devout prayer.) Whatever was apparent, it was not panic, other than among highly strung dogs. Maori cheering mounted as rocket after rocket was launched. Only the seventh could be counted a modest success. With the best of intentions it clipped a palisade, unleashed sparks, and lurched lukewarmly into the interior of the fortress. There was a frantic barking, then silence. Soon afterwards the defenders were holding up a canine carcass to encourage the besiegers below. 'Britons are good to kill dogs,' they taunted. The missiles fired thereafter may have been useful in fatiguing the vocal chords of the foe. For the most part, however, they confirmed that science was not going to end the worries of warfare overnight.

While rocketeers exhausted their store, I allowed my telescope to rove among rebel faces and figures on show. Something was missing; or someone. Then I saw or, rather, didn't. Unlike John Heke, the Duke was not a conspicuous spectator, perhaps not even a party to proceedings. Nor was I able to identify the more familiar and ferocious warriors of his retinue; only Heke's young and raucous followers were flaunting themselves. The Duke's invisibility might be good news for Hulme; it might also be bad. While I weighed the merits of reporting this observation to the colonel, the matter was removed from my hands. The final rocket flashed off into the overcast firmament. Hulme was left with no option but to feel for his foe. With sword high he urged his bristling army forward. Woe was in the making. So was Hulme's story, Heke's, the Duke's, and not least Cyprian's. How play cool chronicler here? I had a huge longing for a simpler life, for the days in World's End when I watched with wonder as Henry Youngman fluently moved deadly armies upon the page, managing to make Armageddon appear moderate before we padded off to a public house. As if in deference to my dilemma, the first shot was slow coming. As promised, it was not Heke's. Hulme, discharging his pistol, was merely seeking to invigorate his force with a sample of intoxications to come.

The frontal storming party, so far in strife only with rocks and rough terrain, was brought to a standstill by the fire beginning to issue from the fortress. Smoke soon made the scene misty, which was helpful for military reputations. Later Hulme would tell the world, or the little of it in hearing, that he had never been in doubt for a moment that the fortress was too strong to be taken without artillery; that it was never his intention to assault the confounded place. If so, why at this moment was he permitting his men to push hazardously uphill and make targets of themselves at a range of fifty paces? And why the party of pioneers to their rear, equipped to hack a tunnel through rebel defences? Was it his hope that they might be there to lend a hand when the Almighty considerately intervened and puffed away the rebel palisades? Unfortunately for Hulme, it was a day more notable for muddle than miracle. Hulme's frontal advance was finally halted by fire from the fortress. The route taken by the first storming party was already marked by fallen men. From a distance they seemed remarkably discreet as they toppled. The sound of shooting was barely to be heard above the boastful shouts of the combatants, not to speak of the cries of Nene's non-combatants ranged around me. They appeared most fairly to be urging both sides on. A win for Heke would prove them right in respect of retirement from the field. A triumph for Britain might be equally instructive; it would suggest that the red tribe was a worthy ally. I was not without mixed feelings myself, though I hoped Cyprian would survive the day unscarred.

So far as I could determine, however, he was doing his diligent best to fall. To reach the rear of the fortress his party had to traverse skyline with discouragingly little cover. Clusters of his men had gained the ridge; they were shaking themselves competently into line for attack as Heke's shot fell grievously among them. But the colours of the 58th continued to flutter while Cyprian, with sword swinging, called on his men to answer their enemy.

I heard a sigh at my side. An elderly cohort of Nene's was pointing toward the fortress, asking me to observe the flag risen there. Darkish in hue, it could not be mistaken for a truce flag.

'What does that mean?' I asked.

'Trouble,' he predicted.

'Of what kind?'

'The worst,' he suggested.

He was not inclined to be informative; the fact of the matter is that the fellow knew no more than I did. When I reflect moderately on events, however, I have to allow that his guess was as inspired as any. The bizarre truth is that the two men most seasoned in war — the Duke and Nene — were absent from the field. They were both watching to see if the noisy new boys in their neighbourhood had a bite to match their bark.

British cheers drifted downhill. Cyprian's men were rallying themselves for assault. Aimed heroically along the ridge, thus to rout Heke's men, they were unaware of menace mounting to their rear. In short, scores of Maori were cascading from hitherto harmless forest. By the time Cyprian sighted this force there must have been two hundred warriors anxious to make themselves felt. They were shooting as they came. I trained the telescope shakily on these proceedings. Even with the naked eye one could see Cyprian's difficulty all too plain. Before him were entrenched Maori in strength, and behind him a great many more crossing open ground. Plainer still was the fact that the new and unsuspected force was entirely the Duke's. Speeding ahead of his warriors, on his thin legs, he wielded no more than an ancestral club. This modest weapon did not make his appearance any the more heartwarming. The flag flown from Heke's fortress was a desperate plea for the Duke to enter the fray. The men Hulme's scout had observed creeping off from fortress to forest, earlier in the morning, had not been deserters; they had been obeying the Duke's order to stand aside and let Heke show himself to advantage. Should Heke find matters beyond him — in the form of envenomed Britons — he was to call up the Duke and his men with a flag. That was the arrangement between rebels. Heke, however, had lost his nerve prematurely; he asked the Duke's help before battle had been joined.

In effect, if not in intention, this placed Cyprian between the devil and the deep blue sea. Others may argue, as others infernally will, that this was intended; I can imagine some earnest historian arguing that it was nothing less than a craftsmanlike manoeuvre meant to entrap a storming party such as Cyprian's. Such a version of events might even assert that the the rear of the fortress had been left weak to tempt a storming party on to exposed ground between two firing lines. So be it. Historians require such riddles to enliven lethargic days at their desks. Intuition tells me that the Duke cared not a fig for Heke's distress flag; that when the first Britons fell he saw danger in Heke claiming credit for too many corpses. The result was that he raced jealously into battle to improve the scrappy look of his own ledger.

With Cyprian's demise more certain by the second I was left to think on how best to phrase his eulogy. I reckoned without other things, not least the discipline of his regiment. He had not drilled his men in vain. To his order — 'Right about', 'Fix bayonets' — they turned abruptly to face the Duke's challenge. They not only refused their foe a flank. They charged. Never in battle was there a sight more breathtaking. In what should have been the last minute of their lives, they were comporting themselves as coolly as tried and true veterans; not as skinny and motherless juveniles, felons better suited to breaking rock than splitting torsos, or lacklustre labourers looking for roast beef and rum in the Queen's army. Loud intakes and expulsions of breath about me suggested that Nene's men were similarly awed. The red tribe was after all a force to be reckoned with. They were not only determined to die; they were doing it with distinction.

When the foremost of the combatants met, a cruel crush grew; red jackets here, brown skins there, tomahawks swinging and bayonets thrusting. Men unable to win a footing rolled off the ridge; others reeled out from the fight and lay prone. Cyprian might literally have lost his head at that moment. He did not. He called upon his men to withdraw in orderly fashion, while marksmen kept the rebels at bay. Then, with order regained in the ranks, he called for another bayonet charge. This was no less fearful than the first. Indeed it would long be recalled by the Maori who survived it. As Moses told me indignantly later, 'The red tribe came with a rush, yelling horribly, grinding their teeth and cursing. It was unfair of the red tribe to curse us. We were doing no harm; we were merely fighting them.' Man after man in the Duke's entourage found life losing interest in him, or his feet taking an independent role in proceedings. Flight became more conspicuous than fight. Even the Duke was no longer visible. That might have been the end of the matter. It wasn't. The devil might be dumbfounded, but the deep blue sea rolled in. A wave of John Heke's warriors spilled from his fortress with the intention of engulfing Cyprian's men from the rear and relieving the Duke's harassed band.

Cyprian's answer came in the shape of an L. One arm of the L was to give the Duke second thoughts; the other arm was to hold off Heke. Again Cyprian calmed his men; again they braced. The impetus of John Heke's first warriors was such that they literally hurled themselves on the bayonets of the 58th. All Cyprian's men had to do was withdraw their steel and wait on the next candidates for carnage. These, as they came, were speared efficiently too. The formerly smooth skyline grew lumpy with the figures of the fallen. Before long the only men seriously on the move were John Heke's, returning fast to their fortress. Cyprian's men spurred them with a volley. Then, little by little, combat ceased. The fortress was silent, but for infrequent muskets discharged from loopholes. Survivors of the Duke's attack were limping off to less imperilled ground. Cyprian's band threw their forage caps in the air in triumph, and cheered themselves with passion; the flag of the 58th streamed boldly above. I could take breath again, it seemed. So ended the last open battle of John Heke's feud with Queen Victoria. Lest small mercies be mistaken for large, let me hasten to put the record right. The war was still unwon. John Heke still camped sturdily on the bloodied ridge, as even Colonel Hulme must have been aware.

There was a breathless voice to my rear. 'Am I too late, Wildblood?' it was saying.

The Reverend Williams had made his usual unpunctual appearance.

'Not to bury the dead, sir,' I informed him.

He surveyed the battle scene through my telescope. His sighs were frequent.

'Need it have been?' he asked.

As well ask why Troy.

By four in the afternoon Colonel Hulme concluded that there was no more he could fairly ask of his men. Which may be to say that he found his casualty count displeasingly large. 'I was right from the first,' he told those who had failed to notice. 'Such a fortress can be won only with artillery.'

There was not an officer willing to differ.

Finally Cyprian's party was also called down from its difficult perch. Heke's men rose from their ramparts to cheer them on their way. Desperate to involve himself in the events of the day, Nene made a last-minute appearance with his loyal few. They took up positions to the right and left of Cyprian's retiring party, and fired off shotguns and muskets to deter potential pursuers. As grimy and bloody as his men, with a distinguished gash on his forehead, Cyprian presented himself to Hulme.

'We gave as good as we got, sir,' he reported.

'That might be said, Major Bridge. Indeed.'

Might? *Might*? If elated Cyprian was fishing for congratulation, his line came up empty. Hulme had much else on his mind, and not least the prose of his battlefield dispatch to the Governor. Heroism might only muddy the case for artillery.

'If reinforced, sir, we might have pressed them still more,' Cyprian ventured even more vainly. 'And could yet tomorrow.'

'Your disappointment will weigh on my conscience,' Hulme promised. 'Nevertheless we begin return to the Bay of Islands in the morning.'

'Without forcing the issue, sir?'

'With honour,' Hulme disclosed.

Hulme moved off. Cyprian leaned heavily on my shoulder.

'With honour shared,' he said bitterly. 'Or shame.'

'You take it too personally,' I suggested.

'How can I not?'

'I daresay it was as terrifying as it looked.'

'The fact of the matter, Wildblood, is that a shot fired in earnest makes no more than a small discordant sound when it passes close to the ear. After a time one gets quite accustomed to it. Indeed one welcomes the sound; one knows that it is speeding elsewhere. As for the bayonet, it is no more than a test of one's calling.'

'Why are you telling me?' I asked.

'In the hope that Henry Youngman may get it right in his next narrative.'

'With a gallant young British officer as protagonist, perhaps?'

'Perhaps,' he agreed modestly.

Casualties argued that a meaty engagement had been fought. There were fourteen British dead and fifty wounded. Heke and the Duke might have lost thrice that number. Balancing his need for artillery against arousing the suspicion of command ineptitude, Colonel Hulme preferred a round figure; he settled for two hundred rebel Maori slain and as many wounded. A good tale if told in Greek.

Sixteen

*I*n the morning a shy young Maori materialised on the ground between Hulme's camp and Heke's ridge. In one hand he carried a truce flag; in the other, a letter. Williams hastened to the trembling youth before some irritable soldier thought to make him a target. The letter was, of course, from Heke. It told Colonel Hulme that there were British dead deserving a Christian farewell. His own dead, he informed Hulme, had been decently interred; he had thought it better to leave Britons untouched until their commander had an opportunity to lament their passing.

Hulme saw native impertinence in the message. '*Lament*?' he said.

'If you so choose,' Williams said mildly.

'He also expects me to dispose of our dead,' Hulme complained.

'Not personally,' Williams pointed out.

'Then what the devil is he saying?'

'That he still endeavours to behave well,' Williams suggested.

'While deploying his ruffians against us?'

'That is not necessarily at odds with Christian goodwill, sir.'

'Get on with you, Williams,' the colonel said. 'While I think of it, however, you have my permission to visit Heke's hill and conduct a service for our dead. I would be grateful if you limited your conversation with John Heke to the vagaries of the weather. On no account is he to be left with the impression that we are conceding the field. On no account. You hear?'

'Distinctly,' Williams said.

'And should he persist in trying to win intelligence, inform him that Britain will be back. By God we will, and with guns.'

'I shall make a point of serving such notice upon him,' Williams promised.

'I can provide a detachment of men for your safety,' Hulme offered.

'I think not, sir. Soldiers might prove inflammatory. This had best be a civilian enterprise.' He turned serenely to me. 'Wildblood?'

I endeavoured not to hear him.

'You might,' he went on, 'do me the favour of accompanying me to John Heke's camp. On the other hand, you are under no obligation to volunteer your services. It would be remiss of me to pretend there is no risk.'

It would be even more remiss not to acknowledge here that I needed Williams's good opinion.

We trudged up the ridge to Heke's trenches. Warriors appeared above us and extended a helping hand. Finally they made a respectful and silent escort as we walked the last level yards to Heke. He stood at the gate of the fortress with a wary face, the expression of a mission boy caught with his hand in a biscuit barrel. It was impossible not to notice that many of his novice warriors were in poor repair, sporting crude bandages. Heke himself, however, did not have a hair out of place; he was even clean shaven. With some relief I spied Moses in the throng; his smile was less sanguine than customary.

'Another sad day, Heke,' Williams sighed.

'As the Lord wills it,' Heke said.

'As you have,' Williams insisted.

'Sir?' Heke seemed honestly surprised.

'You take our Maker's name in vain,' Williams persisted. 'None of this need have been.'

'Tell the Governor. He marched soldiers here. I did not.'

'Though I urged against it, he sought retribution for your raid on Blackguard Beach, as many a prudent ruler would.'

'He has retribution. Let the dead be counted.'

'His or yours?'

Heke was silent.

'I understand your loss to be large too,' Williams said shrewdly.

Heke wasn't admitting so. 'If his are the price of ours, it is a price we must pay.'

'What are you saying?'

'We prayed before battle. Did the red tribe?'

'Not to my knowledge. No.'

'There,' Heke said. 'This war will be won by the godly.'

'I should not rely on it,' Williams warned.

Heke summoned Moses. 'Take them to their work. Provide warriors for the digging.'

Heke made a fastidious departure before the burial party began work. This could be construed as encouraging. It suggested that his heart wasn't yet sufficiently in war; that while the din of battle won his approval, he preferred bullets doing no damage and cadavers making no mess.

Before the fortress, on the fatal ridge, Britons were still strewn where they fell. Flies had not yet arrived in force. Save for their blackening wounds the men were unmutilated. Though warrior temptation must have been large, they had not been relieved of their uniforms; even of forage caps and firearms. Their appearance suggested they might still rise to a rousing order, if not in this world. There were several pitifully young faces, and some sadly old. Otherwise they had everything in common.

'To business, then,' Williams said.

The afternoon's work was no pleasure. One by one the dead were lowered into rough holes; one by one Williams prayed them into God's care. Warriors obligingly fetched wood for makeshift crosses.

Once I chanced a look uphill. Heke stood there silent, overlooking our enterprise, at a tactful distance. His expression continued to say that he found it difficult to rejoice in what he saw.

Nor did I, on another viewing of Heke. Someone who should have been at his side wasn't. Where was the Duke?

I whispered the question to Moses when the heavy-breathing burial party, feeling need of gravediggers' repartee, paused to light pipes.

'The Duke has lost his favoured son,' Moses confided.

'Does that mean his war may be over?'

Moses gazed at me, through billowing pipe smoke, as if contemplating a cretin.

'I see,' I said.

Before the last grave was filled Moses saw fit to afflict me with further information. It was not of the kind to allay apprehension. It seemed the Duke was even more disgusted with himself than with Heke. Yesterday's events had proved his warriors no match for Britons on open ground. He had gone into retreat to see what this might mean.

'Well?' I asked. 'What do you think it might?'

'When his wound has healed, and his grief?'

'Just so,' I said.

'Graves in greater number,' Moses predicted. 'More than that I cannot tell you.'

More than that he didn't need to.

The march back to the Bay of Islands was light on pomp and laboured in character. Sodden and sleepless for four days or more, men were feeble from lack of sustenance. They were also coughing and sneezing, and collapsing with grippe and fever. The wounded had to be nursed, their stretchers nudged up and down rough and wooded inclines. Then there were long delays while Colonel Hulme put out scouts to determine our route free of ambushers. So much for martial melodrama. Britain's first crusade in the antipodes ended in a crawl.

It is just to add, however, that disgrace was not discriminating. Hulme might have a liberal share, likewise Governor FitzRoy, who ordered the expedition; but so also did Heke and the Duke, with their failure to turn teeth-grinding British infantry. But no one was more humiliated than Timothy Walker Nene, the man who led his warhorses to water and failed to make them drink. He did not join Hulme on the retirement to the Bay of Islands. He needed to lick his wounds elsewhere. That they were more of the spirit than the flesh didn't make them less disabling.

When we carried the day against the vegetable kingdom we came in sight of an idyllic estuary and three British vessels moored: there was the familiar *Hazard*, but also the *North Star*, and a merchantman called *Rainbow*. Cyprian, beside me, gave a hoarse cry of delight. 'I do believe that is Lousia's vessel,' he announced.

Sure enough, an elegant young Englishwoman made her appearance on deck, parasol above her head. Louisa looked to be everything Cyprian said. She was petite, blonde and doll-like and waved a dainty hankerchief in the direction of her hero.

Cyprian was lost to me from that moment. For once he took only a negligible interest in military affairs, hastily settling his men into overnight camp, and leaving it to sergeants to see them victualled. He was far less perfunctory about finding a rating to row him out to the *Rainbow* and shamelessly falling into Louisa's embrace. He was seldom to be seen again that day in his official capacity, and not at all after dark. The prurient ruffians who crewed *Rainbow* later reported that their vessel rocked nightlong with the joyous reunion of Major Cyprian Bridge and his good wife. Fortune, as is well known, never favours the feeble.

In more melancholy vein, Hulme commandeered the *North Star* for more than a soft bed. He meant to return post-haste to Auckland before rumours of disaster diminished his standing with colonial authorities. His departure was so precipitate that he left most of his wounded behind; they were a poor advertisment for a colonel looking for compliments.

As commotion dwindled to commonplace clamour, I found a familiar figure at my side. George Philpotts was examining my soiled person merrily through his monocle.

'Dear fellow,' he said. 'You have been in the wars.'

I chose not to reply.

'I daresay this is worth a jolly verse or two,' he went on.

That failed to win my smile either.

'Tell me,' he said. 'Was it more fast and furious than the affray at Blackguard Beach?'

'It was seldom less than animated,' I admitted.

'So John Heke's manners are no better?'

'Not in the vicinity of red uniforms.'

'In other words, he is still all he thinks himself to be.'

'Loosely speaking.'

'Pity,' Philpotts said. 'Only one conclusion is possible.'

'What might that be?' I asked wearily.

'You need the navy,' George said recklessly.

I let loose a sneeze large enough to blow open death's door.

'While I prime the guns,' George said,' I suggest a hot tub and a hotter toddy.'

'Lead the way,' I whispered.

A friend in need was a friend indeed; I still had one to count on.

Williams was not in that category. To his credit, however, he made a Christian point of establishing that I was in good hands before he began the journey home to his mission station. He appeared mistily before me as I sank into soapy water.

'I wish not to appear heartless in this matter, Wildblood,' he said. 'The truth, however, is that I am not inviting you to join me as a guest. I must leave you to your friends in the military.'

'I am sorry about that, sir,' I found voice to say.

'Angela,' he went on, 'is always in an unnatural state of disturbance in consequence of your visits. She fails to keep her mind on domestic duties. Not to put too fine a point upon it, she is a hazard in the household. Crockery is more and more frequently broken, not to speak of food burned in the oven and beds left unmade. More than that, she is sullen, reverting to native type. Only one conclusion is possible. She is better off in your absence.'

'Have you asked for her opinion, sir?'

'I have not,' he admitted.

'Should her feelings not be taken into account?'

'The next thing you will be telling me that yours should be.'

'Modesty forbids it, sir. Also the fact is I find my intentions toward Angela more and more honourable.'

'Honourable?'

'You heard me, sir.'

'You appear to concede that they have not been.'

'At this point, sir, I admit nothing of the sort. Believe it or not, Reverend Williams, I am a changed man.'

'Far be it from me to suggest that you have not acted with credit in matters of peace and war. We are talking here, however, of a Christian soul at risk. And a literary libertine.'

'Would that I could convince you otherwise, sir.'

'Would that you could, Wildblood,' he sighed.

Williams departed. George Philpotts resumed watch on my person.

'What' he asked, 'does that add up to?'

'Heartbreak,' I informed him.

'Seek no further,' he said. 'I have the cure.'

I detest those dramatists, even our most distinguished, even our good and great Shakespeare, who place gripping spectacles off-stage: wrecks on stormy sea coasts, armies swaying in giant battles, items which some pedestrian actor, posing as a breathless messenger from afar, has the privilege of shouting to the cheated audience.

All this is to show, in what follows, that I am in good company. Life is at its most potent off stage, leaving imagination room to work on the worst. Nevertheless I confess a tinge of regret. Henry Youngman in his prime had no scruples; his towering waves, turbulent battles, and other acts of God and man, were all before the footlights. It would be easy to follow Henry's example, and God's for that matter, by pretending to be eyewitness of events in the Bay of Islands after Colonel Hulme disappeared from the stage.

For the first days after our return from the interior it was plain that Cyprian suffered much anguish when parted more than a minute from his young wife.

'She is a joy to behold,' I had to admit.

'I knew you would approve,' he said with a mischievous smile.

How could I not? Louisa's limpid eyes were aweing. Her smile was sweet. Her voice was attractively husky. When she extended her little gloved hand to me for the first time, I was at an unusual loss for words. For my money, there was only one female in the world more ravishing, or more available to be, though I pushed that painful thought aside.

'And you are Henry Youngman,' she said.

'I have been mistaken for him,' I allowed.

'I fear you are too modest,' she said. 'Cyprian tells me all.'

'Intimates, I explained, 'know me better as Ferdinand.'

'And I am to be seen as such? As an intimate?'

'It is my hope,' I said with passion.

'How thrilling.' Her lifting eyes made my heart leap. 'When next you commune with your associate, please inform him that I read *The Belle of Blackguard Beach* until the tear-stained pages fell apart. He has no more fervent an admirer.'

That might not be helpful, I decided, not least for Cyprian's marriage. Life was tangled enough in the Bay of Islands without tempting Henry back.

I said, 'His appearances have been few and far between since firearms were first discharged. He leaves such mundane matters to me.'

'I shall believe you,' she trilled.

Her innocence was alarming; I do believe she had no notion of what she did to men. Unless I was mistaken, even recumbent Henry twitched.

Marital matters aside, Cyprian fiddled in frustration. He had charge of three hundred men or more. Hulme had left him with no instruction other than to pacify unruly Maori should they show themselves near. Heke and the Duke, however, were not to be challenged. Hulme meant to dispose of them to lasting effect on his return. Meanwhile days passed fruitlessly. Had Hulme's vessel been blown past Auckland and out to sea? Had Governor FitzRoy suffered a seizure on hearing Hulme's news?

Meanwhile Cyprian's army idled. Drill sergeants did their best to instil a sense of vocation in restive soldiery, with indifferent result.

Forming fours was a formidable enterprise on slippery Bay of Islands ground. Floggings also failed to make an impression. Drunkenness, the result of fraternisation with overfriendly natives, became rampant; so also did pig-stealing and petty feuding with locals.

'Is this,' Cyprian grieved, 'to be yet another colonial war in which men are left to rot?'

The fact that it was his first independent command made his chagrin greater. The temptation to have a little war of his own, in Hulme's absence, proved impossible to resist; it would confirm the gallantry of the 58th and especially its major. So he saw his duty plain. If not to fight an enemy, it was to find one. Upriver there was a clan said to have furtively egged on John Heke. Though they had made no formal appearance on a battlefield, they had been helpful to the rebels in respect of provender and powder, and had also, as late-coming looters, picked the bones of Blackguard Beach clean. That qualified them for a punitive expedition. Moreover, a mite of danger might keep Cyprian's men up to the mark. From loyal natives he established the location of the untrustworthy clan's waterside haven. He selected three companies of the 58th for the assault; and recruited a party of seemingly reliable locals to lead the way.

'It will all be a morning's brisk labour,' he promised his lieutenants as he presented his plan of attack. Longboats, canoes and pinnaces filled with belligerents would proceed upriver under cover of dark. Their occupants would disembark at agreed points so as to cut off escape routes from the stronghold. Then attack would be launched, surprised malcontents put to flight, and their stronghold destroyed. 'What the rebels and their allies need is a modest whipping,' he explained. 'Are there questions?'

His lieutenants were impressed. Hulme had not been disposed to take juniors into his confidence. Nor had he been interested in questions.

'One further thing,' Cyprian told them. 'Do not treat men as mulish fools. Give them an understanding of what we are about. Don't merely bully them from afar. Allow them initiative. Perhaps even listen to advice. Most of them have been trained to this longer than you. Am I heard?'

He was. There was a shocked silence.

'You did say the men, sir?' an ensign asked.

'Sergeants and soldiers alike,' Cyprian confirmed.

The silence this time was even more profound.

Afterwards Cyprian walked me off a little way. 'How did that sound?' he asked.

'I see a new army in the making,' I said.

'None too soon,' he said. 'Perhaps this war, if it does nothing more, will hasten matters.'

He then looked me over.

'As for you,' he went on, 'this action does not provide for peaceful spectators. All will be in the firing line, I fear. I should be much in your debt were you to see that Louisa does not fret during my absence.'

With a surfeit of the New Zealand interior, my first reaction was relief. My second, however, was fright. Louisa in my care?

'You seem troubled,' he said.

'I am not the liveliest company,' I argued.

'Recite her some verse,' he suggested. 'That will surely charm her.'

The man did not know what he was saying. How explain that lyrics often had an unfortunate effect on the most moral of women? Charm her indeed.

'You might also,' he winked, 'tell her what a fine fellow you think her husband to be.'

'That will be the least of my problems,' I promised.

And here was my woe. I might guarantee Ferdinand Wildblood's behaviour. Henry Youngman was another matter. Defunct he might be; he was far from decently interred. That suave serpent was better not given the freedom of this antipodean Eden again. The dearest of friends was not to be cuckolded while dutifully serving Queen and Country.

In short, the difficulty was lust. My loyalty to Cyprian could not be put at risk; I was not to be left alone with Louisa. My vexation grew as martial preliminaries multiplied. Men were shuffled into companies, inspected by Cyprian, and given to understand their tasks when they moved upriver and met up with insurgents real or de facto. Preparations were better viewed from the foredeck of the *Hazard*. George Philpotts stood forlorn beside me. Yet again he was a bridesmaid at war's wedding. His bizarre behaviour at Blackguard Beach had neither been forgiven nor forgotten, not even by charitable Cyprian. George might be tempted to regain his good name with dangerous bravado; he was better left to fly the flag safely at base.

Across thirty yards of water, on the *Rainbow*, Louisa was also viewing the beginnings of the expedition. Though her eyes seldom shifted from Cyprian, she once or twice, with an affectionate smile, waved a gay, gloved hand in my direction. I felt a dismaying tremor in my knees.

I thought to confide in George. 'Cyprian,' I said, 'has asked me to attend to Louisa's needs during his absence upriver.'

'Lucky fellow,' George said with a sly smile.

'You misunderstand,' I said.

'What is there to misunderstand?'

'I am far from suited to the task.'

'To entertaining a pretty woman?' George said with incredulity.

'The fact of the matter is that I cannot trust myself in female company.'

George laughed rather crudely.

'So I have a favour to ask,' I explained. 'Could you ensure that she is not bored in the course of Cyprian's absence?'

'And what do you want me to tell her, when she asks after you?'

'Tell her I am indisposed,' I explained.

'You do not look in the least so to me.'

'I will be if Cyprian fails to find his wife in good repair,' I suggested.

With final waves and laughs, Cyprian's force climbed into longboats and pinnaces and began rowing sturdily on the tide. Soon the last craft of his fleet vanished beyond a bend in the river. Minutes later Ferdinand Wildblood likewise disappeared from view. My errand may not have been as perilous, but it was also compatible with honour. Helpful Maori pointed me toward the neighbourhood of the Bay of Islands I knew best. I was travelling, need I say, into forbidden territory: toward Williams's mission station, and Angela. On second thought I need say it. The truth is that I was killing two birds with one stone. On the one hand I was keeping Henry out of harm's way, and certainly out of arm's reach of Louisa. On the other I was giving Ferdinand a larger interest in life. This may seem an unnecessarily complicated manoeuvre. It was.

My route was as entangled. Tracks looped and sputtered out when they met salt water, of which there was more and more. I swam creeks and survived rousing encounters with marine mud. Finally a small river canoe, tied to a tree, proved my deliverance. By mid-afternoon, paddling with tender hands, I had the mission station in far view. By dusk I was drawing the canoe surreptitiously up on sand

and taking cover under large-limbed coastal vegetation. There was nothing for it now but to bide my time, to wait on lights to be extinguished, and for Williams and his wife to be bedded. Cyprian and his men, similarly secretive, were no doubt inching about a Maori stronghold in readiness for dawn attack. I also had a bout of cut and thrust in mind, if of kinder character. The dining room lamp was soon dimmed, but that in Williams's study began to glow infernally long. Then I realised the day was Saturday; Williams would be penning tomorrow's sermon. This one promised to be particularly long-winded; no soldier of a storming party lived in crueller suspense.

At last the study light was gone. With a suitable interval for prayer, the lamp in the marital bedroom was snuffed out too; dark prevailed. When I estimated enough minutes gone, I crept closer to the Williamses' dwelling. There were no sounds in the night save my heartbeat and distant Maori dogs. There was enough moonlight to spare me collisions with fences and foliage. Then, in a few bounds, I was at Angela's window. I scratched, rattled and rapped the glass. It seemed the wretched girl might never waken. It also seemed likely that I might soon have Williams heating my rear with shotgun pellets.

At excruciating length there was a shadow beyond the glass; the window rose cautiously. 'Yes?' Angela whispered.

'It is I,' or so I claimed.

'Ferdinand?' she asked with disbelief.

'Who else?'

With only a window ledge in the way of consummation, I charged. The upper half of my torso found its way into her room. My lower half, however, took another view of this tactic; my legs were left dangling in the night. There was also an all but unmanning encounter with a careless carpenter's nail. My arrival on her floor was less than glorious, but at least I was there.

'Quiet,' she pleaded, coolly fondling my brow.

'With pleasure,' I whispered.

Words were not our strong suit. Deliriously at rest in her arms, I wished Cyprian similar success. He could return to an unsullied marriage, never dreaming of the pains purity had put me to.

Dawn came sadly soon. I dressed with its first glimmer.

'Where are you going?' she asked.

'Where duty bids.'
'Must you?'
'You know as well as I that I am forbidden your company.'
'Then I will come with you,' she announced.
Here was a pickle.
'Impossible,' it pained me to answer.
'Why?'
'There is a war on,' I pointed out.
'It doesn't need you.'
I thought on that.
'I may need it,' I suggested.
'What for?'
'There is a ballad looking for a bard,' I explained. 'At the moment it is running about like a headless chicken.'

She declined to hear. 'We could escape into the forest together,' she added. 'No one could find us.'

That plot sounded familiar. I had no desire to relive *The Belle of Blackguard Beach* again; it had been painful enough pushing it from Henry's pen the first time. Anyway I was alert to the potential of a less sentimental narrative, with *Farewell the Warrior* presently the most promising title. Heke would surely be hurrying his goodbyes when Hulme returned with his gunners. When such stout-hearted fellows began work in New Zealand no rebel fortress would be safe. My problem was seeing an uplifting *finale*; it had to be more than a mountain of corpses.

Meanwhile I was detaching myself from Angela. 'When this woe is over,' I promised, 'I will be back to fetch you.'
'When will that be?'
'At most,' I argued, 'a week or two more.'
'It had better be,' she said. 'Or I will drag you off by the hair.'
Foreboding informed me that she meant it.

I laboured home by land and water through the day, and made my reappearance as Cyprian arrived downriver. My mission might have left room for mixed feelings, but in terms of winning high ground it could be counted a success. Cyprian's could not. He gazed bitterly at the world through a mask of mud. His slimy uniform was in need of a dedicated laundress.

'What happened?' I was reckless enough to ask.
'It is,' he explained, 'what didn't.'

His amphibious adventure had gone well so long as it was based on a respectable body of brine. But before midnight one waterway became several, most of them winding and all of them narrow. Cyprian refused to be daunted; he urged his force on. In this roulette of rivers boat after boat hurtled into foul mire; others rose high and dry on debris; some simply headed blind into parts unknown. Loss of the tide meant even more men marooned. Dawn was slow to make a showing. Mustering such men as he could in the murk, or something fewer than fifty of his original two hundred, Cyprian waded on to the objective. First light showed the Maori village misty beyond foliage. But catastrophe trumped him there too. Nesting duck took wing, leaping and lamenting overhead, informing the entire Bay of Islands that armed Britons were abroad. This gave the inhabitants of the village time to complete their Sunday prayers before decamping at a dignified pace. A few marksmen were left in place to slow intruders in their territory. This was managed with success for much of the morning. When marksmen too disappeared, presumably to pledge themselves to John Heke, Cyprian had another undistinguished and unpopulated fortress on his hands. With no satisfaction, and less loot, he ordered the place torched. The only good news was that the tide had returned, making the rivers navigable and a bedraggled return to base possible. All the day long sodden soldiery drifted back from the wilderness, some of them swimming. There was no disguising debacle. Cyprian had been the one commander to survive the battle for Heke's ridge with distinction. He should have left well alone. The attempt to confirm his audacity had been his undoing; he not only had reason to expect a cruel martial reprimand. He had also joined Hulme, Heke, Nene and the Duke in disgrace. And for that matter long-suffering George Philpotts.

George had the final say, sotto voce, as shamed Cyprian disappeared in the direction of his wife. 'I said all along it was a job for the navy,' he announced.

Next day brought poor Cyprian no peace of mind either. It certainly brought him a message from Timothy Walker Nene in the interior. Nene reported that Heke was continuing to recruit men for troublemaking. Tribesmen were further dividing, yet more of the young defecting from their fathers to bear muskets for Heke. This, Nene announced, had to be terminated. He asked Major Bridge to return his army to the field forthwith. He, Nene, was waiting. He,

Nene, would be a man of diminished faith in Britain should Major Bridge not make an appearance with his men. Was Major Bridge a fighting chief or was he not?

Cyprian was shaken. 'It is,' he concluded, 'a challenge.'

'Just so,' I had to agree.

'British subtleties of rank appear to be beyond him. The rascal obstinately refuses to understand that I am not my own man in such matters. I answer to superiors.'

He might have added that he already had much to answer for. He did not.

There was a PS to Nene's letter. Would Major Bridge's men not bring stretchers with them the next time? If they must, would they conceal them from Maori sight?

Cyprian found it necessary to walk off alone into the woods, possibly to meditate on the lesser griefs of life in a convict colony.

No one was winning euphoria on the wings of this war. The fact of the matter is that John Heke and Timothy Walker Nene were trying to recover their reputations. For a time their two bands did little more than circle each other, firing off shot and spitting taunts while teetering tribesmen decided who better to side with. The Duke had no part in this. He may have been nursing more than grief for a lost son. He may also have been harbouring the suspicion that warrior life had little to be said for it in alliance with a sonorous larrikin. Brimming with new boasts, Heke had convinced himself that fifty dead and disabled Britons made a triumph. The Duke knew better. By his reckoning nothing short of a hundred would give Britain pause.

That was for the future, and the return of the red tribe to the field. Meanwhile the duel between Heke and Nene had to be played out. Heke felt obliged to provide some theatre for his swelling band of understudies. This meant a mad dawn rush at a hill on which Nene was camped. It turned into a mad dawn rout as Nene's marksmen lifted from hiding and launched volleys into Heke's youthful line. But for a few veterans, who stood their ground, matters might have been worse. As it was, the affray was uncomfortably calamitous. Heke, trying to woo retiring men back to the fight, ran this way and that, mislaying his musket and ammunition and most of his apparel. His lack of sophistication showed itself when he permitted himself to grieve at immoderate length over a stricken cousin, meanwhile letting his men wander where they would. Finally he recalled himself to the task of generalship. Urging another charge at Nene, he grabbed up a musket from one dead man and a cartridge box from another. Those more familiar with the conventions of combat judged making free with dead men's property a harmful procedure, the more so when it was seen that the cartridge box, now buckled about his waist, was stained with the blood of its former owner. Heke, in their estimation, was asking a bullet. This was proved within a minute. A shot shattered Heke's thigh. Panic followed. As his dismayed men retired from the left, right and rear of the attack, a pagan priest, presumably mislaid by the Duke, made an enigmatic appearance. This wizened old fellow had never been impressed by Heke's Christian fervour.

'Where is your merciful Jesus now?' he asked Heke.

Heke groaned.

Rather than gloat further the priest informed him of a simple prayer which would render him invisible to the foe.

'Invisible?' Heke said.

'Exactly,' the old man replied. 'Repeat it after me carefully. Should you miss a word, we are dead.'

Fugitives cannot be finicky on a smoky battlefield. Heke gave his exclusive attention to the wording of the prayer. Moses and some undamaged companions then made a timely arrival. Taking up the prayer too, as who would not, they bore John Heke from the battle, passing through Nene's murderous throng without being sighted. Sceptics might say that the height of the fern abetted invisibility more than the priest's prayer. There is a powerful case, however, to be made for the latter. For Heke failed to shed the spell; he became even more immaterial. He was not seen leading his warriors, not noticed challenging a foe to fight. With the passing of weeks his condition began to look incurable.

With such sorrow, what price Cyprian's?

Seventeen

*T*he Duke's day had come. He had been waiting on John Heke to make an unworldly fool of himself in war. Heke had now obliged. His wound, aggravated by adventurous Maori surgery, ensured his silence while the Duke took over the war. Without a whimper of scruple from Heke, the Duke could now deploy warriors as he wished. He was not without thoughts in this matter. Having seen that the red tribe was not to be toyed with on open ground, he deduced that it must be wooed to a less salubrious location. To a fortress, perhaps, but not of the customary kind; one designed less to inhibit an enemy than invite him in. With that fashioned, he would bait it with rebels and depend on frustration undoing his foe.

On the coast the days and weeks passed benignly enough. Fish were plentiful. We foraged for oysters, and wreaked havoc on waterfowl. Muddy May became misty June. A vessel named *Surprise* made an appearance, with dispatches from Auckland and Sydney. These left Cyprian speechless. He found it necessary to sit down and go through them again with shaky hands.

'Colonel Hulme has been dismissed,' he finally reported. 'He made unreasonable proposals, such as postponing the war until summer. The result is that he is posted back, poor fellow, to Van Diemen's Land.'

I failed to see why this should agitate Cyprian. 'That gives you command,' I pointed out.

'Would that were so,' he mourned.

'We have another colonel, then?'

'Indeed,' he said. 'We may soon recall Colonel Hulme as rather endearing.'

'What are you saying?'

'Our new commander's name is Despard. Known far and wide

in the army as Despicable Despard. He has never felt at home in the nineteenth century. He confiscates current army manuals when he sights them in the hands of his juniors. He sees no cause to modify the predilections of a lifetime because some damnable pen-pusher tells him so. Perhaps his mother once loved him, but I am by no means sure of that.'

I felt gloom growing too. 'You omit one particular,' I said. 'You say nothing of his virtues as a soldier.'

'I believe he showed promise in 1799,' Cyprian said.

Despard arrived on HMS *British Sovereign* two days after dispatches announced his coming. He was a lean, cadaverous man whose frosty face was never thawed by anything akin to a smile. He had an extensive retinue, including a couple of seedy manservants of the ex-convict kind, an unhappy personal surgeon, and a bitter-tongued wife. With him were three flanking companies of his 99th, and some venerable artillerymen. With the 58th tallied too, he had six hundred troops. Despard made no secret of his desire to get the war won so that he could return to his leafy rural retreat in New South Wales. He appeared to nurse no misgivings about meeting up with an enemy of whom he had never heard; nor about campaigning in a country only just drawn to his attention. Moreover, he felt under no compulsion to remedy these shortcomings. Though he had not seen a campaign of substance in thirty years, he saw no good reason why this one should not be as lusty as his last. He rejected Cyprian's suggestion that he might care to make himself familiar with the ground, with the Maori, and for that matter with the men in his command. He was not one to let facts interfere with first impressions. These were to the effect that a New Zealand expedition hardly merited his time and talent. He let it be known that he was taking command from the goodness of his heart.

Charity was not otherwise evident. Cyprian attempted to arrange a dinner party to welcome Despicable Despard to the Bay of Islands. That proposition was not well received. 'When I require the company of subordinates,' Despard announced, 'I ask it.'

'Yes, sir,' Cyprian said meekly.

'And by the way, Bridge, I take it you regularly inspect the wine accounts of junior officers in your mess.'

'Wine accounts, sir?'

'There is a tendency, in isolated circumstances, for officers to become unnecessarily debilitated and unhealthily in debt. Isolation is no excuse. Circumstances are ever a test of a man's character. Make a point of going over their accounts in future, will you? And report outstanding delinquents to me.'

So much for command decree. Despard sequestered himself aboard the *British Sovereign*, far from his lessers, until he judged it time for the campaign to begin. This involved no long calculation, no requests for intelligence. Nor did it involve conferences with officers. Sooner, he disclosed, was better than later. The new march into the New Zealand interior would begin in the first fitting dawn. Cyprian didn't even have time to tally the wine accounts.

As Despard's army took form he noted, not before time, brown faces. 'What the devil have we here?' he asked.

'Maori, sir,' Cyprian helpfully explained.

'Maori?'

'The natives of New Zealand, sir.'

'Is that what they look like?'

'For the most part, sir.'

'They are rather large fellows,' Despard mused.

'Maori physique is not on the modest side, sir.'

'Do I or do I not discern that they are carrying weapons?'

'You are not mistaken, sir.'

'You mean they are not merely hired porters?'

'They are not hired at all, sir.'

'That is confounded odd.'

'Sir?'

'I thought we were fighting the rogues.'

'Of the unrulier kind,' Cyprian said. 'Fortunately for us, many wish to war for the Queen.'

Despard evinced a tendency to grumble. 'Since when has a British commander had need of savages?'

'In New Zealand, I respectfully suggest, sir. To refuse their wish might be unfortunate.'

'Unfortunate?'

'Those in need of a fight might, for example, take it into their heads to join John Heke.'

That made Despard no happier. 'What are you telling me, Bridge? That their devotion is skin deep?'

'Their loyalty is to their good name, sir. We wish the same of our regiments in the field.'

Despard gazed heavenward. Finally he said, 'In that case, Bridge, I will make you answerable for their behaviour. Should discipline require it, in the heat of battle, push lead into the buggers. Understood?'

'Sir,' Cyprian said, and saluted.

Where was I in these proceedings? The answer is nowhere. With the arrival of Despard an unobtrusive role in events appeared desirable. This meant sharing George Philpotts's cabin and seldom showing myself on the deck of the *Hazard*. It was not to last. Before the new march inland began, I was asked to report to Cyprian on the *Rainbow*. 'Your services are again required,' he announced.

My face must have said that I feared as much.

'I am sorry,' he said. 'But with a commander playing bull at a gate, you may be all the more necessary. We need someone capable of communicating with both allies and enemies. Also someone with a nose for intelligence.'

I did not care for the sound of that. Presentiment was justified.

Cyprian went on, 'I should like you to proceed ahead of the army. Your first task will be to mollify Timothy Walker Nene in respect of our delay. Your second will be to establish the whereabouts of the rebel force. You will favour me by not putting your life at larger risk than necessary.'

'Alone?' I said faintly.

'I daresay you can find a trustworthy Maori guide.'

At that point there was commotion on the deck above our heads. Feet thundered this way and that. There was grunting and masculine cursing. A female voice rose above the rest. 'Let me see him,' she shouted before being efficiently muffled.

There was more thumping. Then a distressed sergeant at arms appeared at the door of our cabin. 'There's a woman, sir,' he reported to Cyprian. 'A regular fire-eater.'

'So I hear,' Cyprian said coolly. 'What does she want?'

'Mr Wildblood, sir.'

'Me?' I said with wonder.

'Bring her down,' Cyprian ordered.

So it was that a sergeant at arms and two scratched and bruised marines wrestled their captive into our presence. Angela ceased struggling and stood there disarrayed and defiant.

'I told you I was coming,' she reminded me.

'Indeed,' I dared say.

Cyprian, to his credit, had a tolerant smile. 'I think introductions may be in order,' he suggested.

These were no feat. Gallant Cyprian even kissed Angela's hand.

'Well, well,' Cyprian said genially. 'I suspected all along there was more to you, Wildblood, than most might imagine.'

I was still, let me admit, in a state of intestinal agitation.

'Where is the Reverend Williams?' I asked Angela.

'Perhaps not far behind,' she suggested.

'Perhaps?'

'With a good wind, quite close. We must run.'

'Run?'

'He knows all,' she explained. 'He also carries a horsewhip.'

'Williams,' I protested, 'is a man of peace.'

She appeared to think that observation humorous. 'Not since he found your sonnets,' she said.

Cyprian rose tactfully. 'I think the word for this is elopement,' he informed me. 'Perhaps I should give you time to put your affairs in order.'

'That,' I insisted, 'will not be necessary.'

'No?' he said with surprise.

The pace of events persuaded me to think nimbly. 'Angela's proposition is not at odds with your request,' I claimed.

Cyprian was bemused. 'To proceed ahead of the army?' he said.

'I now have my trustworthy Maori guide,' I pointed out.

'Dear fellow,' Cyprian said. 'I have no call on your services in present circumstances. I would not hear of it. Never.'

He did, of course. We may have been the first lovers in history to elope into war. The originality of the notion made *The Belle of Blackguard Beach* look limp. Meanwhile George Philpotts, ever the soul of kindness, assigned ratings to row us upriver. Fearful of Williams cracking a whip to our rear, Angela and I scrambled still deeper into the New Zealand interior. Not until nightfall were we sure of our safety. Canvas and fern made a passable bivouac. Her arms made a better.

In the morning, as mist cleared, we breakfasted before a small fire. Before we moved on I made a point of unpacking my two-barrelled pistol and checking powder and shot required for its function; its time might have come.

'What,' she asked, 'do you mean to do with that?'

'It interests me too,' I said.

One of Timothy Walker Nene's patrols rounded us up without a shot fired. He was none too impressed when we appeared with Cyprian's message; but then Nene seldom was with anyone or anything. With three hundred warriors he had been waiting weeks for the red tribe to resume hostilities against John Heke. While waiting, and with no thanks to Britain, he had fought off Heke and, better still, silenced him. Nene was by no means persuaded that Britons were on their way even now.

'You have our word,' I said.

He looked dubious. What price the pledge of a transient poet and a missionary's maid?

'And who is this new colonel?' he asked. 'This Despard?'

There seemed no harm in trying to cheer Nene. 'A man famed for his fury,' I promised.

'He will need all he has,' Nene said. 'He now fights the Duke.'

'I daresay Colonel Despard has been apprised of the peril.'

I had no authority for this. Despard might have been; he might not. Either way the campaigning colonel would not have been anxious for larger enlightenment. One rebel savage was as good as another. As it happened, however, Despard *had* been encouraged by news of Heke's wound. No one had dared discourage him with intelligence of the Duke.

'We have another mission,' I informed Nene. 'It is to establish the circumstances of the enemy.'

Nene snorted. 'Is it thought that I don't know?'

'With respect, I am instructed to see with my own eyes.'

'Then see. They are camped no more than six miles from here. If you hope to sight Heke, you will not.'

'Not?'

'The Duke alone resides there.'

With an escort of Nene's men we ventured still further next day. From a hilltop we looked out on the location the Duke had chosen to site the next collision between the rebels and the red tribe. It was difficult to see advantage in the place. It was all low and largely level ground of motley character, patched with cultivations. Even my untutored eye saw that it was overlooked by knolls and hillocks from which British guns might direct damaging fire. Indifferent to such danger, tribesmen were swarming this way and that, digging trenches and pits, and raising sturdy palisades. Parties were arriving in burdened by foodstuffs; others were optimistically laying them in store for the forthcoming seige. A telescope showed me the distinctively wiry figure of the Duke at the heart of activity. Otherwise it disclosed young rebels and old. Grime made Heke's youngsters and the Duke's veterans all but indistinguishable.

'What do you see?' Angela asked.

I gazed again into the Duke's rising citadel. A shiver rose through me. Though the alphabet was unfamiliar, I could see what the fortress might spell. The Duke was taking his stance in deep water, where the fattest fish swam.

So what did I see?

'Melancholy,' I reported.

With mission done, we journeyed back to Nene's camp.

'Was it as I told you,' Nene asked, 'or was it not?'

'The Duke was there,' I agreed.

'And no Heke?'

'As you said.'

'Good,' Nene said with satisfaction. 'He has lost his hunger for war.'

'So it would seem.'

'Some say Heke is dying. I think not. I think he merely finds a deathbed a safe place to be. Should he rise from it like Lazarus, he might have to show fight again.'

'I take your word for it,' I said.

'What of yours?' he asked. 'Where is this man of miracles you promised? This Colonel Despard? Does he wish war or does he not?'

'It is not for me to know his mind,' I answered.

'I have two fresh horses,' Nene said. 'Find him. Speed him here.'

Angela and I rode warily north. There was no telling what the misty landscape might unveil. There were too many men about with guns for our ride to be romantic. The inclement weather was also conducive to a monkish existence. From a high point, the next day, we looked out on some miles of the feebly forested district Despard should by now have been crossing. Though I used it extensively, my telescope failed to find a flicker of movement in the vicinity. I sighed; Angela sulked. We lunched on stale bread and cold potato.

'When I came to you,' she pointed out, 'I expected better than this.'

'That was my thought too,' I said.

The fact of the matter, however, was that I had nothing superior on offer. North there were soldiers. South there were warriors. There was no bliss east or west either. Northern New Zealand, alas for elopers, is narrow.

'Let me get duty over with,' I proposed. 'Then we can think again.'

'Duty?'

'Informing Colonel Despard of Nene's impatience.'

'And of the Duke's fortress.'

'That too,' I agreed.

She made a sound of disgust. 'It will be all the same,' she judged astutely.

Nevertheless we climbed wearily back into our saddles. I let my telescope roam again. Caution was justified. This time I picked up three horsemen journeying slowly across open ground. They may have been half a mile off; they may have been less. Their direction meant that we were about to see more of them.

'Remove yourself from the skyline,' I ordered Angela, and was swift to set an example. We tugged our beasts into a neighbouring gully.

'What now?' she asked breathless.

'Don't talk,' I said. 'Pray if you must.'

She prayed. It was difficult to fault her judgement.

I climbed uphill, using scrub for concealment, and again deployed my telescope to advantage. The riders were neither in uniform nor warrior garb. Arms were not apparent either. That was the good news. Then came the bad. The three were mixed in race. The two to the rear were Maori. The one leading the way had Europe's hue. He also had a clerical collar.

'Dear God,' I choked.

'God?' Angela asked, clawing uphill to tumble beside me in fright.

'His deputy,' I explained. 'Your godfather appears to be on his own warpath.'

'What do we do?' she asked.

As if I had any notion. Soldiers and warriors had it simpler in that territory.

'This calls for a tactical movement to the rear,' I decided.

'What does that mean?'

'Translated from army parlance, disappearance.'

'To where?'

'You must have cousins in this neighbourhood.'

'Cousins?'

'My understanding is that a Maori with fewer than a hundred cousins is a person of no standing. Where are yours?'

'Some are with Heke, some with the Duke. Many are with Nene.'

'And none neutral?'

'Not that I have heard.'

'That is unlucky. You mean we are not likely to fall in with tribesmen of serene character?'

'There is Heke,' she suggested.

I thought on that. 'True,' I had to agree. Whatever else might be said of Heke, he now appeared the one party in the locality who saw no future in the grave.

I peered through scrub at Williams and his companions again. With relief I saw them dismounting and tethering their horses. Preparations for a camp fire — perhaps a lunch of missionary mutton — were soon begun. They were halting for an hour or better.

'To our horses,' I whispered to Angela.

'Horses?'

'We are riding back the way we came,' I explained.

'To Nene?'

'To Heke.'

'You are sure of this?' she asked.

'Not particularly,' I confessed.

'To reach Heke we must first pass Nene's warriors. Then the Duke's. Heke is far to their rear.'

'That is my impression too,' I informed her.

'Then what are you saying?'

'Better impassioned muskets than the slings and arrows of the righteous.'

I couldn't allow her to muse. Our discomforts might suggest that a return to the role of model mission girl was in her best interests.

We stole away from our observation point, renewed our acquaintance with our horses, and rode. This manuscript is sufficiently burdened with accounts of ingenious journeys through the New Zealand interior. Instinct tells me that enough is a feast, especially when this narrative touches on New Zealand terrain. Who needs to know how we bypassed Nene by travelling warily west of his camp, and circumspectly detoured to the east of the Duke's fortress? It appears that we did, though I am by no means willing to swear to it.

Lest I lose sight of the large picture, however, I have to record that Despicable Despard was at the same time adding to history's increasingly rich store of martial encounters with the antipodean landscape; his guns were being hauled in and out of mire by steaming oxen and blasphemous gunners. The drays and ox-carts were falling apart under the weight of weaponry. Infantrymen by the hundred were milling about helpless and hungry. The more anarchic were wandering off to plunder the livestock of Maori and missionary settlements. A spectator might have concluded that he was also witness to an army falling apart. Such a spectator would not have been far wrong. Despard was lamenting that no one had informed him that New Zealand had no leafy highways and no cobbled lanes; and no amiable inns where he might enjoy the produce of local vineyards and dine amply before bedding down for the night. This was not war as he had known it in Napoleon's vicinity. He even began suspecting treachery on the part of subordinates, a plot to discredit him by leading him into wildwood. Had the Duke been underhand enough to arrange an ambush, he would have scattered the army and taken possession of its food and firepower there and then; it would have been another and not necessarily lesser edition of the disaster in India's Khyber Pass. Fortunately for Britons it was essential to the Duke's scheme that the red tribe did not abandon their march; he required them in the location he had prepared. The absence of ambush suggested to some that warrior honour was at work. Not so. Chivalry was not conspicuous in the Duke's arsenal. A modest triumph was not on his mind either.

During premature disarray no one derided the inefficient soldiery, and the expedition's choleric commander, more than Lieutenant George Philpotts. Determined to put dishonour behind, George assumed command of the sailors and marines of the naval contingent. Despard learned too late of George's unconventional conduct at Blackguard Beach; too late, that is, to send him packing. The chances were that something like a hundred tars might insubordinately retire from the field in sympathy with their rollicking and rebellious lieutenant. Meanwhile George craftily placed himself alongside sane Cyprian and the disciplined 58th. Always unharmoniously attired, unbuttoned and half-buckled, George became more so; he jauntily capped off his patchwork costume with a soldier's forage cap, the better to infuriate Despard. No longer bashful — after all, there were now Britons with reputations muddier than his — George made free with naval advice. 'Let off a broadside now,' he urged. 'Let the enemy know we are on the horizon. They may even see virtue in tacking away fast.' George's extravagant representations to Despard on that score were met with a stony gaze.

'What makes you think I am in need of your wisdom, young man?' the colonel inquired.

'You are welcome to it,' George said generously.

'I expect that you also entertain other notions about the nature of this enterprise.'

'Only one of moment, sir.'

'And what would that be, lieutenant?'

'That this, sir, has the makings of farce.'

'You, young man, have the ingredients of a mutineer.'

'Better than of a blind fool, sir.'

'Who is that insolent wretch with a monocle?' Despard afterwards asked Cyprian.

'George Philpotts, sir,' Cyprian answered. 'A versatile fellow.'

'That description,' Despard justly observed, 'could disguise a multitude of sins.'

'Perhaps, sir,' Cyprian shrugged.

'There is something missing in the man; his words have a less than respectful ring in my presence.'

'That may be due to naval service, sir. I can vouch, on the whole, for his good intentions as a combatant.'

'Is it your impression, Bridge, that I require versatility from my juniors?'

'Not conspicuously, sir.'

'And as for good intentions, it is known that the way to hell is paved with them.'

'If you say so, sir.'

'In point of fact, Major Bridge, I see to it. Especially to stoking hell to intolerable temperature. Alluring as I find the prospect of making an example of the fellow here and now, I hold you responsible for his behaviour. Let him be seen and not heard.'

As if Cyprian didn't have enough to vex him. George Philpotts meant to remain visible and audible to his last breath. He wasn't a bishop's son for nothing.

I have wandered. While madness fed on muddle in the north, Angela and I rode into John Heke's place of refuge in the south. It was a small village, lacking in outward distinction and an indifferent location for a hero between battles. One obvious merit was that it was not liable to be caught in crossfire; it sat far from Despard's cannon and the Duke's muskets. Another, less apparent, was that Williams was unlikely to hunt us down here. Meanwhile it was tranquil. There were fewer than a dozen warriors on show, most of them engrossed in the fall of grubby playing cards; the more desultory didn't even note our approach until we were upon them. Even then there was no large interest in our appearance, still less any reaching for firearms. Had we been a British column, they would have been captive without a shot fired. The first to bestir himself was Moses. I had never seen his face less animated; his smile was jaded.

'This is a surprise,' he said.

'To us too,' I admitted.

'How are we to see you? As spies or friends?'

'As in need of sanctuary,' I told him.

'This is true?'

'Should you doubt it, look for the Reverend Williams riding fast.'

That intelligence put Moses in better humour. 'If you wish it,' he proposed, 'I can arrange a Maori marriage.'

'What form does that take?'

'Of the simplest. The man and the woman must be seen under the same blanket. If you wish it, I shall be your witness.'

'I have the impression,' I said nervously, 'that matters may be past that point.'

'It is never too late to be lawful,' Moses argued. 'If you are not talking marriage, why are you here?'

'If reports are to be credited, John Heke has allied himself with sanity. There is no present prospect of a quiet life elsewhere.'

'If you have good news from the north,' he said, 'let us hear it. If it is bad, perhaps not.'

'Not?'

'Heke has enough of the bad.'

'He still suffers?'

'Alas. Until now he has known only triumph. He is still getting used to the notion that tribulation is also the lot of the warrior.'

'You are telling me his grief is of the spirit?'

'The flesh is no friend to him either.'

Moses led us into one of the dwellings. Womenfolk tending Heke withdrew when we entered. We found him bedded in gloom; there was a weak candle by a bedside table, and a Bible. The man was unmixed misery. His skin was slack, his eyes bleak. A sour odour rose from his blankets and bandages; the smell of sweat was compounded by reeking discharge from his thigh wound. It was difficult to recall the imperious young horseman I had first seen in the forest. Was this convalescent the warrior who had left Britons in confusion?

'Friends,' Moses informed him.

At first Heke found it difficult to muster interest. The slightest of movements, even a shift of his head, appeared to bring pain. So might world-conquering Alexander have been seen as the poison plundered his flesh.

'Henry Youngman?' he asked.

Who was I to deny him? 'The same,' I said.

'I think we are neither of us the same, Henry,' he suggested.

That was more true than he knew. 'Who knows?' I said.

'I know,' he said hoarsely. Then he thought to ask, 'What went wrong?'

'Perhaps one flagstaff too many. The mightiest of men have been undone by success.'

He was quiet. His eyes closed.

'That sounds well,' he decided.

'It might read better,' I argued.

'I have the Bible beside me, Henry.'

'It has not escaped my attention.'

'Does it not have the best stories?'

'It has moments,' I agreed.

'Moments?'

'I prefer not to pass judgement on literary rivals.'

'It tells me that all things pass.'

'When of a mind to.'

'What are you saying?'

'That such is not presently the case. The Duke is building his fortress. Despard is marching. Yet they still call it John Heke's war.'

It was cruel to remind him. But it had to be said.

'I think on that too,' he confessed.

'And where does thought take you?'

'I have twice sent messages to the Duke. I have told him that there is no need for more dead.'

'His reply?'

'He laughs. You have looked on his fortress?'

'And seen it as less than ideal.'

'As he wishes it seen.'

'How else might it be?'

'It is made of more than rock and wood; of more than pits and trenches.'

'More? What more?'

'Vengeance,' Heke warned.

There was a silence.

'The Duke,' Heke explained, 'cannot have it said that he ignored the death of his son. Insult began this war. Injury will end it. The pagan priests in his camp never tire of telling him so.'

'How much vengeance does the Duke require?'

'A field of British dead.'

'A large field or small?'

'One to remember. You understand?'

I felt a chill. 'I am trying to,' I said.

Heke stirred in anguish, lifted a hand, and grasped mine feebly. 'Tell the British they must march no further,' he pleaded. 'Tell them to turn back. All things say that they will end badly.'

'You are talking omens?'

'Omens are unnecessary. The Duke is fighting his last war.'

I was silent.

'If you desire friends in the army long in this life, tell them now.'

'Would you wish them to understand that the war is over?'

'That is for Britain to say. If the Duke is left idle in his fortress, fighting will finish; his warriors will wander home to their villages with no shot fired.'

'You think this?'

'I know it. Tell the British that Christ bids me speak.'

Heke now saw the possibilities of residence in another story. The apprentice devil was making a winsome return as a candidate saint.

An hour later I was to be seen saddled again, ready to ride north. I left protesting Angela in Moses' care. 'How do I know you will be back?' she asked.

'Somewhere out there firearms may soon be discharging in number. Worse yet, your godfather may remain on the rampage. I do not mean to loiter.'

This was true. I knew my task hopeless. I had as much chance of stopping Despard — or Nene, for that matter — as I had of halting one of George Stephenson's smoky locomotives on the London-Brighton run. I was benevolently humouring a man in need of good news. Personal warnings to such as Cyprian and George Philpotts might not go amiss either. Meanwhile I was growing ever more intimate with the uncharitable terrain; I was certainly carrying much of it with me.

Dark halted me in uncomfortable proximity to the Duke's current domain. I could see dozens of fires burning in the locality where his fortress had risen; it was fair to conclude that his fighting men were no fewer.

At first light I pressed on. I did not have to travel far. Only two or three miles now separated the ambitious adversaries. Ahead, beyond a scattering of skirmishers, the army was fanning out on gently rolling ground, regimental colours floating overhead, a lone drum sounding the beat. George Philpotts's naval contingent marched to their own. There too was Nene's swaggering Maori contingent, casual in kilts, with muskets held horizontal across their shoulders. Then there was an ill-sorted ensemble of civilian militia, fetched from Auckland at the last moment, bowed under with pioneer equipment meant to take the mightiest fortress apart. Rumbling drays and creaking ox-carts, with munitions and cannon, brought up the rear. It was a sight to silence those tempted to think the war frivolous in character. Humiliation had been a tonic: Britons had never been more earnestly disposed on a battlefield. No matter that they numbered short of a thousand; they seemed, in that dawn hour, ten times as many. Some might have seen this disciplined advance to the fight as Despard's doing. The fact is that Cyprian, his lieutenants, and his trusted sergeants, had been toiling for days — with Despard querulous or indifferent — to hound even the least enthusiastic ranker into lethal form. Cyprian had drilled them again and again, in the hope that they might see intercourse with an armed enemy as restful. Maori viewers of such fatiguing activity coined a new proverb: 'The patience of the soldier is greater than God's.' Despard complained that Cyprian ignored such time-honoured British formations as the column and the square, configurations which had served well at Waterloo. 'There is nothing *pretty* about your drill,' he complained to Cyprian. 'Your men amble forward like Farmer Brown's cows when they hear your bugler.'

'That is open order,' Cyprian explained.

'Another name for sloppiness,' Despard said. 'Where is the bliss?'

'In allowing unfriendly shot passage between my men, sir.'

'Between?'

'Rather than through their vitals, sir,' Cyprian said patiently. 'I instruct them to make use of cover and irregular ground as they move forward. I ask imagination and enterprise of those in my command. They are not dumb machines, sir. Treat them as human and they respond appropriately.'

'Human did you say?'

'Indeed, sir.'

'That is original. I daresay you will soon be telling me that the buggers need no longer be whipped well to fight.'

'Not more than thirty lashes, sir.'

'Enough,' Despard said. 'Heresy must stop somewhere.'

The fruit of Cyprian's detour from perennial martial forms was ripely on show that morning: his briskly moving men looked as if they had an interest in events. Not far to the rear of the skirmishing line Cyprian was striding along beside Despard and Nene; there was a cluster of underlings at their heels. As soon as I saw my way safe, and the skirmishers clear, I pointed my beast toward them and endeavoured to establish my peaceful character with cheerful waves.

'Who in damnation are you?' Despard demanded.

I found myself too breathless to reply.

Cyprian intervened. 'His name is Wildblood, sir. He has been on my strength, on and off, for some time past.'

Despard made no secret of his distaste for my condition. Recent circumstances had made no provision for toiletries, even for rudimentary grooming. My breeches and jacket were stiff with dried mud and forest filth; I had the impression that dead leaves were floating from my hair as I dismounted.

'Remarkable,' Despard pronounced. 'Do you send him out to terrify the foe?'

'To win intelligence, sir. On this occasion we had begun to believe him lost.' Cyprian turned to me. 'Well, what is it? Have you news?'

I looked him in the eye, then Despard too. 'I come from John Heke,' I informed them.

That silenced banter. It certainly put Despard off his stride. Officers and men began to bank up behind.

'Did I hear right?' Despard asked. 'You have had commerce with the enemy?'

Cyprian, sensing menace, stepped in again. 'It is nothing new in this campaign, sir,' he explained. 'Battle lines have often been crossed by non-belligerents. Not only by men of the cloth; by Mr Wildblood too. The intelligence he wins has seldom been other than enlightening.'

'Such traffic with the enemy will stop here,' Despard announced. 'Such traffic will stop now.'

'With respect, sir, should we not first hear what Wildblood has to say?'

'If we must,' Despard grumbled.

I addressed myself to him. 'John Heke asks a favour of you, sir.'

'Favour?'

'From his sickbed, sir.'

'Mercy may be considered when war has done its worst.'

'You miss the point, sir. John Heke has your welfare in mind.'

'Mine?'

'And that of your officers, allies, and men.'

'What cheek is this?'

'It is sincerely meant, sir. He asks that you return your army from whence it came.'

'He what?'

'He wishes you to know that there is misfortune ahead. Not to speak of pagan priests and vengeance. This war, in brief, is losing its compassionate character. The Duke is out to wrest it from Heke, sir. His interest is less in feuding with Britain than in confirming his competence to kill. Means have become ends. He cannot be kindly.'

Despard was strangely speechless. Finally he lifted a finger and pointed at me. 'Are you implying that we are to be undone by a mob of unwholesome savages?'

'I am suggesting they could be troublesome,' I told him.

'I wish this man watched,' he announced. To Cyprian he said. 'Have a guard placed on him. He is capable of panicking all ranks.'

Any fright I might promote was dwarfed by an outbreak of musketry ahead, with spurts of smoke rising. British skirmishers had blundered into ground commanded by the Duke's marksmen. The ambush confirmed John Heke's despairing plea. If deception was now acceptable, everything might be. 'You may have to do something about this, major,' Despard informed Cyprian.

'I will, sir,' Cyprian promised.

He whispered to me, 'Get yourself clear, for God's sake. There is no need for you here.'

He must have observed me looking pensively to my rear. If he imagined I was estimating the distance to some leafy sanctuary, he was mistaken. I was watching three horsemen close with the hindquarters of Despard's host, Williams at their centre. I could not afford to drift rearward. Ahead was woe; behind was sorrow. I wagered on woe.

'Can't you hear me?' Cyprian said. 'Go, man, go.'

'Impossible,' I reported.

'This,' Cyprian explained, 'is a task for professionals.'

I gave my horse its freedom, and found my pistol. Cyprian looked even more aghast when I cocked it.

'It is customary to load it first,' he pointed out.

He grabbed the weapon irritably from me and primed it in seconds. 'If you must, then,' he sighed. 'Stay close to me.'

As a hundred men hastened to the fight, I fitted myself into the space to Cyprian's rear. Racing across clear ground to cover, we began quarrelling more with tall scrub and treefern than vengeful warriors. Lieutenants began hacking a way through with their swords and urging men on at the double. Musket balls cracking through growth, however, persuaded Britons that a cautious canter served best. Finally leaf and frond fell away and revealed a small village a hundred yards off. Arrayed before it, discharging muskets as they withdrew, were some two score warriors.

Cyprian pointed his sword. 'Bravo, my bold boys!' he cried. 'At them!' (Indeed he did. Life is often a Henry Youngman tale.) Thereupon he sprinted, leaving me perilously exposed. The press of soldiery made retirement impractical; besides I had the sensation that my back might make a broad target.

I was aware of sound building within me long before it issued from my vocal chords; in the same instant a similar baying surged from a hundred throats around me. Modest though my contribution to this cacophony may have been, it was unnerving enough. For we were all racing forward with Cyprian. To my astonishment, I was even pointing my pistol with menace. A soldier to my left fell away with a groan; and one of Nene's kilted Maori, rather more silently, to my right. And still we sped on, hurdling creek and cultivation, until Cyprian called upon combatants to stand firm and deliver a volley.

I would sooner not make much of my own complicity in events. Yet the fact is that in the moment I tested my weapon the enemy melted away as one; those who thought Ferdinand Wildblood a mere rhymester might well think twice. Cyprian, anxious to establish supremacy, called on his men to fire at will. It soon became clear that the Duke had only put out warriors to draw Despard on. They were now retiring as instructed. The excitement was for nothing.

After an altercation with a malevolent log, I discerned that I was alive and intact. There was a hand on my shoulder and a familiar voice in my ear. 'Good Lord, Ferdie old fellow,' it said. 'What are you doing here?' George Philpotts was examining me quizzically through his monocle. 'There is no call for you to be in the thick of it.'

'That is now my impression too,' I confessed.

He put his hand under my arm and lifted me clear of clamour. 'So favour me with an explanation.'

'There,' I said.

I indicated black-clad Williams, in the middle distance, leading his horse. He was looking at faces in the throng and so far not finding mine. Circumstances suggested he soon would.

'That wretched cleric again?' George asked. 'Is he still on your tail?'

'If this goes on, he could be the death of me,' I explained.

'Stay low,' George urged. 'Leave him to me.'

'You may find him difficult to placate.'

'Not at all. In Despard's hearing I shall comment loudly on Williams's Christian courage, and his endearing intimacy with the enemy. I shall praise the fellow to the skies. Despard's dislike of me should ensure a result.'

George was as good as his word. Long before nightfall a protesting Williams was borne off to the rear of Despard's army by a pair of apologetic lieutenants; he was instructed to stay away until worldly matters had been decided. This left me free to wander within the limits prescribed by hostilities. Some might see my vantage point on events as privileged. Far be it from me to remind them that war grants no indulgences. For one thing Angela was on the far side of the duel between the Duke and Despard; I was destined to sleep alone as long as it lasted.

Eighteen

Serendipity no longer surprises me. It tells me that life has a strategy, and God knows it needs one. This is by way of interpreting yesterday's upheaval in my routine. As I dawdle from chapter to chapter of this memoir, correcting here, amplifying there, I frequently have the feeling that I am the sole repository of the events imparted to these pages; that no one else now living knows or cares about happenings in northernmost New Zealand in the year 1845. Let me confess myself in error. My visitor this morning was a tall, fair and rather sweet-faced young fellow. The faint antipodean sound in his vowels confirmed the distant address on his visiting card. At first I imagined he might be a colonial publisher looking to rekindle Henry Youngman's questionable reputation; I was ready to give him short shrift. Not a bit of it. Henry Youngman was not on his mind, nor his neglected works. My guest wished gossip about John Heke and his war. Looking for those who had known Heke, or might have, he had chanced upon the name Ferdinand Wildblood in some crinkled record; he saw it as his great luck that I was alive in London. Seldom a day passes without my reflecting on the same item of good fortune. It would have been all too easy for an informal Maori bullet to trim four decades from my span.

'How is it out in New Zealand now?' I asked politely.

'No British colony is making greater strides,' he claimed. 'Roads, railways and sunny farms grace every vista. The population is growing. Many of its citizens are now New Zealand born — as indeed I am myself, sir. Who knows but that we may one day be seen as the people of a proud and independent nation?'

His rhetoric sounded suspiciously republican. 'On its own?' I asked.

'Without necessarily neglecting its imperial connection,' he hastened to add. 'I daresay we shall be slow to surrender the authority inherent in the Union Jack.'

'As John Heke reluctantly saw,' I suggested.

'Just so, sir,' he agreed. 'He must have been a remarkable fellow.'

'If pandemonium is a measure,' I said.

'One might more usefully say, sir, that he made the most of an otherwise tawdry time.'

'What are you looking for, young fellow? A hero?'

'A patriot, perhaps.'

'A New Zealand patriot?' I began getting his gist.

'Whatever his colour, it is difficult to deny John Heke that description. He thumbed his nose at Britain's might.'

'With help from friends,' I suggested.

'Friends, sir?'

'I had the Duke in mind.'

He was baffled. 'The Duke?' He was seeing me as an old man in a muddle. 'My understanding, sir, is that the Duke of Wellington had no hand in the New Zealand campaign. My recollection is that, from his London residence, he announced that distance alone precluded him from bringing Colonel Despard before a court martial.'

'I have another nobleman in mind,' I explained. 'Kawiti was his native name. His demeanour, not least on the battlefield, won him the alias.'

'Of Duke?'

'Exactly,' I said.

'Fascinating,' he announced, though not believing a word. 'And you suggest this fellow was of importance?'

'I have been endeavouring to leave that impression.'

'And he fought alongside Heke?'

'Some might say Heke fought somewhat to his rear.'

'I will keep it in mind,' he promised. 'The Duke indeed. It makes the affray all the more colourful.'

'If blood can be seen so before it blackens,' I said, and pushed to the point. 'What fires your interest in this war?' I asked.

'A feeling for my country's past,' he claimed.

'New Zealand's?'

'I fear we own too little of our story, and even that is likely to be lost. Friends tell me I am a romantic. I am willing to allow that I may be a decade or two premature. But a start must be made.'

'Though many might say New Zealand was now welcome to it, I rather thought the episode belonged to Britain.'

'Perhaps, sir. But we surely have claim on the events which went into our making.'

'You are less than forthcoming,' I suggested. 'You have hardly journeyed twelve thousand miles to gossip idly with old buffers like me.'

'True,' he agreed.

'So what is your purpose?'

'Why, sir, to write of it,' he said in tolerant tone.

I should have had the wit to see it sooner. Perhaps I was reluctant to relinquish the fantasy that it was all my own. Anyway I was shaken. I have for some years been aware that I didn't have all the time in the world to put the record right. It was now no longer a one-horse race.

The rest of the difficult visitation had one redeeming feature. I had someone to talk to about matters long on my mind. In fact, assisted by a rather fine sherry, I talked rather more than I should to a rival. He could be observed listening, from time to time, when I ventured my account of events. There was, however, no place for it in his inventory. He seldom troubled to take a note and then perhaps to humour me. With documents and maps he offered proof positive that I could not have seen what I saw. For example, in the engagement I have begun chronicling, he had a dozen accounts to the effect that John Heke was in the fight from the first shot. These placed him everywhere in the ensuing siege. There was a better story in warring with an outlaw of reckless reputation than with an unromantic old heathen.

I protested, but it was pointless. My assertion that Heke was on his sickbed and far from the field when matters took a homicidal turn was received with a shake of the head and considerable sympathy. It seemed that I had my chronology wrong. I had everything wrong.

'Young man,' I asked, 'are you familiar with the *Song of Roland* ?'

'The song of what, sir?'

'Never mind. Let us just say that it is an anonymous narrative which celebrates a fight between Christian and Moor in the French Pyrenees much of a thousand years ago. It is as stirring a story as any in the literature of France. Frenchmen on the eve of fray have sung for centuries. Who needs to know whether there was such a battle?'

'Are you saying there was not, sir?'

'I am saying there was, young man,' I said severely. 'Unedifyingly, and alas for literature, it was a domestic spat between Christian and

Christian, with but a few hundred involved. Some balladist, a century on, discerned that a battle with Moors sounded superior. So he peppered his account with thousands of the villains.'

'You are saying the story is all a wicked lie, sir?' Despite his unfamiliarity with French epics my visitor was shocked.

'*The Song of Roland* a lie? A lie?'

'That seems the sum of what you are telling me.'

'Never,' I said.

'Then what is the point?'

I had no wish to spell out my allegory. 'I may be saying that it doesn't matter where John Heke was, or was not; what he did, or did not.'

'Doesn't *matter*?' he said, in even deeper distress.

'It's all the same in a thousand years. Some men perish poorly, others die well. We are all of the company of cowards and heroes when the last trump sounds.'

'With respect, sir, that is rather cavalier.'

'Much as we wish to be on the side of the angels, Homer wins over Herodotus. Everything you say rather proves the point.'

My companion was now in a pleasing state of confusion.

'Forgive me,' he said. 'What is it you are telling me?'

'I too wish I knew,' I confessed.

'I am taxing you unforgivably, sir,' he said nervously.

This was true. Exhaustion, however, was mutual. He asked no more questions of contentious nature and soon took his leave. Seeing him to my door was as much as I could manage; there were twinges in my legs and aches in my rump. Though I haven't been aboard a horse in three decades, I seemed as saddlesore as I was the day I rode in to save Despard's good men from death and disgrace. Nonsensical of course, but there we are. When my faithful cabman called at five, to bear me off to my club, I sped him away with a consolation sixpence. More good drinking time gone forever. John Heke's war could still take its toll. Worse still, when I retired early with malt whisky and milk, I dreamed muskets and cannon. I was marooned in the stifling miasma of war. Eventually I woke shivering to dark and silence. Who was trying to contact me? Experimentally, I called, 'Cyprian?'

No answer.

'George? George Philpotts?'

No word from him either.

Finally I asked, 'Heke? John Heke?'

I swear to it. I heard a deep sigh.

Thereafter I slept as a child. This morning I am back at my desk, much the better for it. The teller may yet catch up with the tale.

By evening Despard's army was arrayed on high ground before the Duke's fortress. The reader may wonder, as indeed Despard should have, why the Duke left this attractive terrain to his enemy. There is no mystery. The Duke not only wished himself seen as a negligent strategist; he required the British in euphoric mood as they swam as fish to a net. The more euphoria first, the more frustration later. The more frustration, the more hope of foolhardy foemen. In respect of Colonel Despard he was successful. Elation was less apparent among other ranks. They teetered this way and that on slimy ground, struggling to raise their few tents in the frosty dusk. Most would have the moist sky as roof and dripping bracken for blanket. All would find hard biscuit and a miserly ration of rum their only fare. They would not have been impressed with their commander's finding that the war was as good as won.

The colonel determined that such was the case when he climbed a conical hill with Timothy Walker Nene and gazed into the Duke's fortress. He could not believe that fortune was presenting him with so foolish a foe. The place sat in easy musket range. Not that muskets bulked large on his mind at that moment, or even artillery. He was seeking uplift.

'We shall,' he announced, 'fly the Union Jack here. Let it greet the buggers in the morning. Let it signal that retribution is at hand.'

'What of your guns?' Nene asked.

'All in good time,' Despard said. 'In my experience nothing puts infidels to flight faster than Britain's colours.'

This did much to suggest that Despard was suffering some confusion about which war he was fighting; he was certainly missing the point of this one.

'As for the guns,' Despard informed Nene, 'they will scatter those indiscreet enough to remain entrenched. I daresay they will be suing for peace by dusk tomorrow. What, by the way, is this place called?'

'Ohaeawai,' Nene told him.

'A name for the history books,' Despard decided. 'Has it a meaning?'

'Most surely,' Nene disclosed. 'The place of hot water.'

Who needed omens?

The army was brisk from first light. Buglers roused sullen and saturated soldiers from pillows of fern. They were not detained by breakfast nor by their need for dry apparel. There was no breakfast; there was no dry apparel. There was thus no delay in their standing to arms. The flag rose on the eminence Despard had chosen. The infidels not only failed to flee; they irreverently perforated it with a volley. To reaffirm that message cries carried up from the rebel line. 'Come, soldiers,' they invited. 'Join your friends cold in the grave.'

Despard was thoughtful.

'They appear single of mind,' he said reluctantly. 'Major Bridge, have you a view?'

'Of the obvious kind, sir,' Cyprian said. 'We bring the guns to bear and establish a breach.'

'Into which we push.'

'With the enemy suitably diminished,' Cyprian agreed.

'A day's work, would you say?'

'If sufficiently fervent, sir.'

'See to it,' Despard ordered.

Under Cyprian's direction men rolled rocks and logs into place; others rearranged hillside with pick and shovel. The result of their endeavours was a platform for a four-gun battery. These 6-pounders and 12-pounders, last seen unseating Bonaparte's cavalry, were manhandled uphill and trained on the fortress. By now morning mist had cleared. Weak winter sunlight brightened the vista. Warriors could be seen thick on the ground. Merriment was apparent and musketry absent. The inhabitants of the fortress were as much engrossed by the preliminaries as any Briton with a beating heart. As the preface to battle lengthened, impatience made itself heard. 'Hurry with your guns, soldiers,' rebels challenged.

Cyprian's men argued the last gun into position, then sited some world-weary mortars on neighbouring eminences. Shells were brought forward and guns primed. Ranging shots were not deemed necessary. A blind gunner couldn't fail to score.

'Are our visiting cards ready?' Despard asked Cyprian.

'Tolerably, sir.'

'Then send them,' the colonel ordered.

'At what intervals, sir?'

'Don't stint,' Despard suggested. 'The larger the uproar, the faster we will be free of the villains.'

Cyprian signalled gunnery sergeants. Whatever the next minutes lacked, it was not uproar. The four-gun battery discharged impeccably. Mortars followed with their own distinctive thudding. Smoke streamed up from empty barrels as shell, ball, grape and canisters of shot flew at the fortress. As commotion mounted, gunners were to be seen stripped to the waist and sooty enough to pass as negroes. Their industry — and the ensuing tempest of dust, dirt and smoke — soon rendered their target invisible. For that matter they too were coughing, cursing phantoms in a mist of ignited powder as they stoked their muzzles with fresh cargo and torched fuses. Cyprian, whatever his colonel's wish, had to call a pause. Little by little the fortress took form again in the gloom. It was a sight to bemuse the most competent commander. On the one hand there was not a living soul to be seen. On the other there was not a corpse on view. Even more magically, the fortress was as before; the place was intact. Telescopes determined that shells from the battery had at best embedded themselves in a forest of stout palisades; at worst they had vanished altogether. If timbers had been shaken, it was not showing; at most they had been chipped. Mortars had made an even more modest impression; their elderly projectiles had failed to detonate, thereby contributing further powder and shot to the rebel armoury. In short, fiasco. There was no other construction to be placed on the scene before us. Scores of mocking rebels appeared from nowhere, filling the fortress again. Unexploded missiles were being retrieved and borne off in glee. Other warriors were examining the palisades and judging them sound. More discouragingly still, many were discharging muskets. There were enough Britons making targets on the skyline for their shot to be useful. Even Despard bent the knee to the Duke's marksmen; a pair of gunners slower to stoop slumped to the ground, one deathly quiet and the other desperately wheezing.

'How would you interpret this, Major Bridge?' Despard asked.

'As interesting, sir,' Cyprian said.

'Where were the fiends hiding?'

'Underground, I daresay,' Cyprian said.

'Are you telling me we war with troglodytes?'

'Certainly with men who fancy themselves as fortress builders, sir.'

Despard was silent for a minute. 'Remarkable,' he judged. 'Have I more surprise in store?'

'That is for you to say, sir.'

'Me?'

'Most men in your command are past awe,' Cyprian explained.

Colonel Despard mused for a time, ducking briefly as another shot promised to part his scalp. 'Well,' he said to Cyprian. 'What are you waiting for?'

'Your orders, sir.'

'I was under the impression that they had been given, major. They have not been countermanded.'

'Sir?'

'Keep up the good work. Bombard the buggers. If you can't destroy them, dispirit them; deafen them. Wear and tear at their walls until they begin to tumble.'

'And if the procedure again proves ineffective, sir?'

'It has never been my custom to listen to defeatist talk, Major Bridge.'

'No, sir. But in such an event?'

'You move the guns nearer, Bridge. And if necessary, nearer still.'

'That might prove expensive in terms of men, sir.'

'Are you are saying there are not sufficient replacements?'

'I am questioning the need to dig graves prematurely.'

'Is it asked, then?'

'Sir?'

'Your question, Bridge.'

'It would seem so, sir.'

'Good, then. Continue seeing shells fall where they should.'

On Despard's instruction Cyprian moved guns and gunners three times that day, each time to a site closer to the fortress. Maori musketry fell away, apparently on order, whenever the guns were moved into greater intimacy with the defence works. There was only one deduction to be made. To dispirit Despard still more, the Duke actually *wanted* the artillery at short range. It meant his marksmen could pick off gunners without wasteful expenditure of powder and shot. There was a further bonus. Each move of guns meant shot fell in a different quarter of the fortress; defences were seldom tested long in the same place. Where damage was done, it was repaired painlessly by defenders.

That first day of siege was one of the least exhilarating of Despard's life. At dusk, in need of solace beyond that offered by a bottle, he called Cyprian to his tent.

'Underground, did you say?'

'Deeper than one might surmise, sir. I deduce all manner of

bunkers and tunnels reinforced overhead by logs. As for their marksmen, they are impossible to silence. Their loopholes are curtained with flax; our shot slides harmlessly away.'

'So what are we to conclude?'

'That no breach has been made, sir.'

His own evaluation confirmed, Despard summoned other subordinates to his side. 'It would appear,' he informed them, 'that our enemy must henceforward be treated with some respect.'

His juniors shuffled, and were silent.

'There will be nothing reckless,' he announced. 'I do not mean to tolerate false heroics.'

Heroics, even of the authorised kind, were not much on the mind of those assembled. Food, warmth and a respite from racket were larger issues.

'From tomorrow we proceed with due care and deliberation,' Despard ruled. 'Furthermore there will be no extravagant dissipation of munitions.'

That caused many a gunnery officer to gape.

'If I may, sir,' Cyprian said, 'I should like to raise the issue of our own security.'

'Ours?'

'If the enemy is not to be underestimated.'

'Speak your mind, Major Bridge.'

'We are in unfamiliar territory, sir.'

'That has not escaped my attention. And?'

'I suggest ample piquets, sir.'

'Are you suggesting we are to be terrified?'

'Inconvenienced possibly, sir.'

'Permit me to remind you, Major, that we are not cowering within fortress walls. Our foe is.'

'On one view of the matter, sir.'

'Is there another?'

'Insecure perimeters might tempt them to become venturesome.'

With splendid timing, muskets became noisy nearby. There was a ripping sound overhead. Sergeants were shouting, Nene's Maori baying, and more shots ringing around. It was soon clear, however, that the British camp was being teased rather than attacked. As disorder diminished several officers rose shamefaced from the muddy floor of Despard's command tent, where panic had placed them; there was a distinct smell of fresh faeces. Colonel Despard continued to gaze with fascination at punctured canvas above his head.

'I judge that to have been a stray ball,' he said.

'Indeed, sir,' Cyprian said.

'See to it, then, Bridge.'

'To what, sir?'

'What else, man? Don't stint with piquets.'

Next day dawned quiet. Due care and deliberation was much in evidence. So was stalemate. On Despard's order cannon and mortar disturbed the peace on the half hour. 'Regularity,' he announced, 'is the handmaiden of success. Our men know where they are. The enemy knows we mean to persist.'

The generous intervals between salvoes allowed rebels the run of their fortress. On the half hour, give or take a minute, they made a leisurely disappearance underground. Between times the Duke's marksmen were in competition, challenging each other to bring down Britons. Their fusillades ensured that surgeons were busy. So passed the second day of siege, then the third. On the fourth Despard ordered oxen slain for sustenance; it was that or command a contingent of skeletons. His unappreciative troops, hungry though they were, had mixed feelings. Without oxen they would have to manhandle weaponry back to the coast unaided. That might be as debilitating as Despard's present strategy.

Nights did not improve either. There was seldom an evening without a sortie from the fortress designed to leave Britons fretful. For every genuine skirmish there were a dozen false alarms; the Duke need not have bothered pushing out parties. Sleep remained on meagre ration behind British lines. Piquet duty, nonetheless, became popular. Timothy Walker Nene, never a leader to neglect fighting men, or to starve them, sent warriors out to forage for potatoes and, while they were at it, friendly womenfolk. These warmed many a Briton on nightlong vigil.

The bivouac I shared with Cyprian and George Philpotts may have been poor in comfort; it remained, however, rich with mutiny.

'Your clown of a colonel,' George predicted, 'will get us all killed.'

'Perhaps,' Cyprian said wearily.

'No breach has been made. Nor is one likely to be at the present rate.'

'What is your point?'

'The fortress must be taken.'

'True,' Cyprian sighed.

'If Despard would cease fidgeting with his guns, and train fire on the one site, we might see a gap appear. Until then, never.'

'George, dear fellow, do you think I have not the same thought?'

'It is difficult to detect it,' George said.

Next morning George presented himself to Colonel Despard with a daring proposition. This was that the palisades be mined and blown up with gunpowder. The colonel was no more impressed by the scheme than by George's irregular appearance. Since siege began George had seen even less virtue in formal attire. In a medley of costume old and new — blue shirt, white naval belltopper, red scarf and purloined army trousers — he looked more a pirate than a man in pursuit of the Queen's enemies. That is, until he flipped his monocle nonchalantly to his eye. That was his procedure when of a mind to disconcert Despard.

'I am not interested in representations from a nautical vagabond,' Despard announced. 'Button yourself up, man. You are a disgrace to your service.'

'In which case, sir, I am not the only one present with that distinction.'

After a further fraught minute, in which they failed to stare each other out, Despard said, 'I take it you are volunteering for this lunatic enterprise.'

'Naturally, sir. As I imagine others might.'

'Others?'

'Who no longer wish to be made fools of.'

'Fools?' Despard bristled. 'Fools?'

'One and all, sir. And by a few scapegrace Maori. The fact of the matter is that we are deceiving ourselves. We are not besieging the fortress; we are ourselves besieged. We must fight our way out. That fortress stands between us and self respect. If the palisades are not to be moved by artillery, we must improvise.'

'If your notion is to redeem yourself, Philpotts, you may lay it to rest.'

'Sir?'

'Tempted as I am to be rid of you, I have no wish to burden the navy with further disgrace.'

'Not for the first time, sir, I fail to read your mind. Or hear a plain answer.'

'I am telling you, Philpotts, that your proposition is rejected. I don't believe you mean it seriously yourself. Cowards are notorious braggarts.'

George was silent. Then he said, 'In that case, sir, would you fancy a wager?'

'Of what nature, man?'

'The simplest, sir. You will surrender a bottle of your best claret to me should I present myself in full view of rebel marksmen five minutes hence. Should I fail to do so you will be one guinea richer.'

'It has never been my custom to countenance madness, Philpotts. Nor is it my intention to begin today.'

'Very well, sir. In that case my left hand must challenge my right.'

George moored his monocle and withdrew. A minute or two passed. To Despard's alarm, and that of his army, George then made an appearance between battle lines; it looked as if both his left hand and right might be luckless. Still sartorially spellbinding, he had no weapon more alarming than a riding crop. As he scrambled downhill, toward the fortress, hostilities diminished; finally they ceased. George's aberrant appearance may have been the saving of him; it is possible that theologically dizzied Maori — with Wesleyan, Anglican and Catholic contesting their souls — might have mistaken him for yet another costumed clergyman wishing to interfere with a fight. In any event no bullet brought him down. He was permitted passage to the first row of palisades and even allowed to examine them closely. Before long an armed warrior rose some feet above him. 'What,' this burly fellow asked, 'do you think you are doing?'

'I might ask the same of you,' George said.

'We are challenging your flag,' the Maori explained.

'And we are here to ensure it flies,' George said.

'Do you wish to be shot, then?'

'Not especially,' George had to confess.

'Then why are you here?'

'To congratulate you on your defence works. Convey my compliments to your commander. He is worth a hundred of ours.'

His point made with polish, George strolled back to British lines without Maori marksmen objecting. Despard was nowhere in view; he remained quiet in his command tent for the rest of the day. He failed to offer George even an inferior claret. His written messages to Cyprian concerned greater punctuality in the launching of salvoes. They were to continue on the half hour, not a minute more, not a minute less. He suggested all timepieces be checked to this end. A glance at the calendar might have been more constructive. Was it the ninth or tenth day of siege? No matter; there were more.

A poor tradesman blames his tools. Despard judged his armaments deficient. He sent a message back to the Bay of Islands asking the commander of the *Hazard* for a 32-pounder. Twenty men were dispatched to drag this two-ton engine of war inland.

'That,' he predicted, 'will give the buggers something to think about. We will take the smile off their faces.'

'When elephants fly,' George Philpotts whispered.

'I will settle for pigs,' Cyprian sighed.

In need of a recipe for triumph, Despard was receptive to a proposition put to him by an unduly imaginative artillery lieutenant. This was to the effect that the Duke's fortress might be abandoned if the place were sufficiently befouled.

'Befouled, sir?' Cyprian asked.

Cyprian and I had been ordered into Despard's presence as the wait for the 32-pounder grew longer.

'Be rendered obnoxious,' Despard explained. 'In short, unfit for human habitation.'

'That is a large order,' Cyprian protested. 'It is also my feeling that we have been endeavouring to do just that.'

Despard ignored this intervention. His gaze moved coolly to me. 'Is it your impression, Wildblood, that our foe cares greatly for hygiene?'

'Hygiene, sir?' I was baffled.

'Just so,' Despard said. 'Does the Maori feel that cleanliness and godliness go hand and hand? Are they sanitary by nature?'

'Let me put it this way, sir. They find water a welcome sight at the end of a muddy hike. They also set their latrines at a distance from living quarters.'

'Good,' Despard said. 'That is encouraging.'

'How so, sir?' I ventured.

'For our purposes,' Despard said enigmatically. 'I have in mind a project which, with God's help, should inhibit the enemy. We have an accumulation of empty shell cases of which use may be made. I am thinking to fill them with substances possibly more potent than shot. Fitted with short time-fuses, they can be discharged from our mortars.'

'I still fail to follow you, sir,' Cyprian complained. 'Potent substances?'

'Think, man, think,' Despard urged. 'Dedicate yourself to the problem of disheartening the enemy.'

'I am trying to, sir. And have been for days.'

'You disappoint me, Bridge. If I am not mistaken, you are an officer who argues that the British army should be more inventive in character.'

'At times, sir,' Cyprian admitted.

'Why not make use of our mortars to rain a toxic cargo down on Maori heads? Give me a good reason why not, Bridge.'

Poor Cyprian was even more at sea.

'Toxic, sir?'

'Poisonous,' Despard agreed. 'Or potentially so.'

'It is still unclear to me, sir.'

'Then I shall be brief, Bridge. What happened to the guts of the oxen we slew?'

'I daresay unappetising innards were decently interred, sir.'

'And should have a healthy reek of rot by now?'

'Indeed,' Cyprian allowed.

'Have your men dig them up,' Despard ordered.

Cyprian was distinctly apprehensive.

'The guts, sir?'

'The choicest,' Despard said. 'And when that task is done, have your men empty the latrine pits. The fresher the dung, the better for our purpose.'

Cyprian paled still more.

'I trust I understand you right, sir,' he managed to say.

'You do indeed,' Despard confirmed. 'Furthermore, with the mentioned materials, you will whip up an unpalatable stew. It should not be too watery. There must be sufficient solid to pack easily into shells.'

'To be fired into the fortress?'

'We understand each other,' Despard said.

His eyes were aglow. Let us be fair. The originality of the notion promised to make conventional projectiles *passe*. The new genre could even be named for our colonel. A salvo of Despards might henceforward pave the way for triumph wherever Britain was vexed.

He went on to explain, 'On impact the shells will distribute their malodorous contents the length and breadth of the fortress. Life within will become exceedingly unpleasant. By tomorrow there will be an even more vile miasma. At that point we can expect poisonous vapours to produce disease. Our foe will be enfeebled, deprived of all animation, and prey to infantrymen with bared steel. Do you follow me now, Major Bridge?'

'To the letter, sir,' Cyprian said, though his face was a picture.

'Excellent,' Despard said. 'There is no one I would sooner trust with the task.'

The meaning was plain. Despard meant to put both turbulent rebels and troublesome subordinates in their place. If he wasn't killing two birds with one stone, he was certainly dumping them in the same dunghill.

Let it be said that Major Cyprian Bridge never behaved more gallantly, on the battlefield or off, than he did that aromatic morning. Officers and men with a keen olfactory sense positioned themselves far from the scene, insensitively looking on and laughing as Cyprian and a team of loyal men went about their labours. No one was heard more hysterical than George Philpotts. 'I knew it,' he announced. 'The British army doesn't just march on its stomach. It attacks with its arse.'

He afforded Cyprian no comfort either. 'Henceforward,' he predicted, 'the 58th will be known as the Rutlandshire shit-shovellers. The knights of night soil.'

Matters were cool between George and Cyprian for some time thereafter.

At four that afternoon, with shells ripe for discharge, mortar crews more than ready to rid themselves of their pungent missiles, spectators gathered on vantage points overlooking the fortress. To a man they were willing to be bewitched by the promised spectacle: goodwill abounded, and perhaps clandestine rum. Fresh-faced Cyprian paused beside George Philpotts and me for a time, considering the scene, though I rather wished he might move himself downwind. After his exertions he had not been sparing with soap and water, and equally liberal with eau de cologne. He still fell short of fragrant. To my relief he moved on to the mortar emplacement. George caught my eye mischievously. We had the same thought: that Cyprian would not be a comfortable companion in our bivouac that night.

Last to take up position was Despard himself, climbing uphill at stately pace. In full uniform he lent a sense of occasion to proceedings. It was his notion to delay firing till toward day's end. Rebels would have less light in which to determine what had fallen among them and take appropriate action. Vapours would begin pestilential work under the cover of dark; the inhabitants of the fortress would wake in an evil cesspit.

So much for theory. In practice, it has to be said, the shells flew up impeccably, at a 45-degree angle, dropping more or less on target. There was no reason why they should not; the mortarmen had been perfecting this trajectory for days. As usual, when British guns were in business, the fortress was deserted; not a rebel in view. The first round caught the place amidships. The second and third too. The first plopped; the second plipped. The third made a sound even more obscure. Despard deemed charges damp and shells in need of refilling. This did not endear him to reeking gunners as they hastened on with the Queen's work. The sky was dull, the day darkening early. 'Keep at it,' Despard urged. 'We have not many minutes more.'

Success of a sort followed. One missile detonated with a dull sound; it was the signal for several more to scatter their freight in and about the fortress. A mirthless smile hovered on Despard's features; for a moment he even looked human. Finally he called off fire. 'We shall see what we see,' he said with satisfaction.

What we saw, in the fading light, was difficult to interpret. Rebels were slow making their customary appearance to mock British gunners. A bemused dog did. It sniffed left, sniffed right, and then took centre stage. It appeared, for a time, to consider something amiss. Finally it lifted its leg, as if to join in the sport, and let loose a spirited stream. It proved the scout for several more canine roamers. They too sniffed here and there and contributed their mite. These creatures held the entire army spellbound. Minutes passed. No ill effects were discernible. With dusk beginning to veil the scene, Despard called a halt to proceedings. Where were the Duke's rebels? One might conclude that they had more to fear from British faeces than British firepower. Another inference is possible: that the Duke's spies had seen Cyprian and his band at their weird work and had decided not to interfere with British ritual until it was seen harmful. Who is to say? This principled scribe cannot.

Despard was undiminished. 'They may begin dropping with maladies tomorrow,' he said. 'There will be a gold sovereign for the first confirmed report.'

Watchers were many next day. Not a rebel Maori was sighted sickening, though some were seen collapsing with laughter as they interred turd and tattered intestine with cheeky indifference. Despard's sovereign went begging. The following day was also empty of spectacle; the one highlight was a cleansing downpour. By the third day the promised plague was even less apparent. Poisonous vapours were not noticeably afflicting the Duke's marksmen. They were, if anything, wilier. One ball blew away a button of Despard's jacket.

The colonel ruled out long discussion of events. 'Let us look on this as a constructive episode, gentlemen,' he suggested to his officers. 'If nothing else we have, at no small sacrifice, confirmed that poisonous vapours are of no value in warfare.'

George Philpotts had to be assisted from the assembly with some abdominal difficulty; it proved to be levity.

There never was a campaign so fraught with constructive episodes; the largest was now in the making.

Nineteen

Reluctant as I am to infringe on the narrative at this point, the fact is that I had begun to feel I was in the wrong story; certainly in an uninspired one. Gloom was the prevailing mood in the British camp. Doom, in one form or another, was daily more sure. Honour required it. The Duke did not mean to relinquish his fortress until he had a memorable tally of Britons. Despard, for his part, had no intention of capping his career with an inglorious scamper back to the Bay of Islands while Maori lead whipped about his heels. Nonetheless he was at the end of his tether. He had never heard of a fortress which failed to succumb to single-minded assault; and refused to recognise that he had met with one. His ammunition was growing short: he added frugality to regularity in his orders of the day. Long days of shellfire had not diminished the fortress an inch; the Duke's marksmen remained potent. More, Despard feared he was losing Nene and his loyal Maori. Their role this far had been menial. They might find more to animate them in the Duke's ranks; so might many neutral Maori spectators. The fruits of further standstill were plain. It might mean more armies of Maori marauders out to insult the Union Jack.

It can be seen that Colonel Despard had more than enough to think on in June's gentle drizzle. The arrival of the 32-pounder from the coast, however, had a medicinal effect. Aside from its greater potency, it had longer range; gunners would be less afflicted by musketry as they went about their work. Meanwhile it took all of a day to heave it on to that height from which Despard had first envisaged countryside carpeted with slain rebels. He was again privy to that vision.

'I think,' he observed to Cyprian, 'we can begin warming enemy arses. A ranging shot, before dark falls, will serve them with notice of what to expect tomorrow.'

'Indeed, sir,' Cyprian said.

The fact is optimism had begun infecting even the level-headed. Nothing beguiles tired troops more than a noisy new toy.

The Duke had been observing preparations with interest and ordering men to battle stations. Clear ground within the fortress had emptied of all but a pair of dawdling warriors by the time the order was given to discharge the new weapon. Just one of the two was unlucky. His head flew off like a cricket ball; the rest of him sagged slowly to earth. For Despard this was a sign from on high.

'There,' he said with satisfaction. 'We resume execution at eight tomorrow.'

Evening passed slowly in the leafy bivouac I shared with Cyprian and George. Even backgammon was out of favour. Cyprian finally gave notice of his feelings. 'I hear fate hastening near,' he said.

'Fate?' George asked.

'If our new gun does not persuade a few timbers to fall.'

'You think Despard will give the order to storm?'

'I cannot hear him ordering retirement this side of Judgement Day.'

Cyprian was silent again, and George morose. In need of night air and an empty bladder I left them to their thoughts. As it happened, I failed to unbutton; I had not moved more than five paces from the bivouac when I was taken powerfully from behind. A rough hand planted itself across my mouth before I could express myself with feeling. My assailant dragged me away and dumped me unceremoniously into fern. Cyprian's day of judgement was mere hypothesis; I had met mine. I waited on a tomahawk's fall.

'Quiet,' a friendly voice advised me.

The hand over my mouth allowed me a chance to muster a whisper.

'Moses?' I asked in awe.

'The same,' he acknowledged.

'What are you doing here?'

'I also wonder,' he said.

We crawled inconspicuously away from bivouacs, tents, and feeble campfires. Piquets were thinner that night, many of them amorously entwined with sociable tribeswomen. Finally Moses judged us safe; he even risked lighting his pipe.

'Well?' I said breathless.

'Angela needs to know what has happened to you.'

'It is by no means clear to me either.'

'She fears Williams might have caught up with you. Even that you might have fled the colony.'

'Much as events may be conspiring to that end, that is not yet the case.'

'I could smuggle you back to her.'

'Across battle lines?'

'As I came. I have cousins among Nene's men. They guaranteed me passage so long as my mission was personal. When I explained that I was here on behalf of a lamenting woman they even pointed me to your quarters. I daresay they would not object to you keeping me company on my return to Heke.'

I thought on Angela's arms. Temptation was cruel. In the end, however, I proved incorruptible. 'My disappearance would cause my friend Cyprian Bridge grave embarrassment,' I explained. 'He is answerable to my behaviour. Furthermore, he needs me to witness his.'

'Pity,' Moses said.

'Anyway I suspect you are not here merely to bear tidings from Angela.'

'True,' he admitted. 'I have also been trying to interest men in living longer lives.'

'You have been talking for Heke.'

'Just so,' he sighed. 'My first mission was to plead with the Duke. Heke still hopes the old man might leave off making Britons miserable.'

'The Duke's reply?'

'Not until a hundred red tribesmen have fallen.'

'That may be ambitious. Colonel Despard has a new gun.'

'The Duke has known of its coming for days. He has never been seen happier. He instructed his men not to slow it. He even has a kind reply to Heke's plea. He asks me to inform Heke that, in fairness, peace may better be talked after the big gun speaks.'

'In fairness?'

'Those are his words.'

'What does that mean?'

'When the Duke talks fairness it is best to go to ground. You will please Angela if you do so tomorrow.'

'Tomorrow?'

'Especially tomorrow.'

'You are telling me something.'

'On the contrary,' he said. 'I am not telling you something.'

Moses tapped ash from his pipe, shook my hand, and peered out from vegetation. Judging his path free of piquets, he leapt from one scrap of scrub to another. A rustle or two later and he was gone. I was left to confer with premonition.

My dark thoughts were no less eloquent when I returned to our bivouac; it was suddenly and surprisingly crowded with solemn young Britons waiting their turn to make use of their major's pen, paper and ink. Cyprian, as his last duty that eve, was calling in junior officers of the 58th to make their wills in his presence. God knows what Nene's sensitive Maori might have made of that.

One officer, a young, gentle and fair-haired captain named Grant, lingered longer than most of his peers. His face was troubled. 'You judge matters to be serious, sir?' he finally got out.

'All martial matters are serious,' Cyprian said crisply.

'Then perhaps I mean fatal, sir.'

'It is always a likelihood,' Cyprian agreed.'What are you saying?'

'That I have my parents in mind, sir. I am their only child. My mother was too frail to bear another.'

'Your point still eludes me, Captain Grant.'

'I fancy their old age would be lonely without me, sir.'

'I daresay, Grant.' Cyprian's face was impatient; perhaps he had his Louisa in mind. He went on, 'What is it you wish of me, then?'

The shy young captain was silent.

'You could be relieved of duty,' Cyprian suggested. 'I could arrange for a surgeon to pronounce your health poor. With inducement he might even recommend a speedy return to your parents.'

Grant's answer was quick. 'No, sir.'

'Then we are on the horns of a dilemma, are we not?'

'I expect we are, sir,' Grant agreed, and looked at the ground.

There was compassion in Cyprian's voice at last. 'If it helps, Grant, I shall pray that you come to no harm.'

'Thank you, sir.'

'Goodnight, Captain Grant.'

When Grant had gone Cyprian looked me in the eye for a considerable time. We did not speak.

I woke to a bugler, dawn light, and thudding boots. My timepiece said seven. Breakfast was brief. The day was sunny, without a whisper of wind or rain. By fifteen minutes to eight Despard's army was waiting on his wish. At that point he thought to make the most of the bewitching quiet before bombardment began. He posted himself on the summit where the flag flew, and on which the 32-pounder was now primed. From that eminence he looked into the fortress and was astonished to see a rival flag being hoisted by an amiable assembly of the Duke's warriors. As it unfurled in the wind, it colourfully disclosed sun, moon, and star.

'That,' Despard observed to Cyprian, 'is no ordinary ensign.'

'Indeed not, sir,' Cyprian said.

'How is one to construe it?'

'As cosmic in character,' Cyprian decided.

'But what the deuce is it saying?'

'As elsewhere in the world, sir, I imagine it acknowledges that fight has begun.'

'Impudence,' Colonel Despard diagnosed. 'Are they telling us that the past two weeks count for nothing?'

'Apparently so, sir.'

There were now ten minutes left to the hour. Rather than disturb prior arrangements, and order his new gun discharged early, Colonel Despard strode irritably downhill and ordered an idle 12-pounder crew to push shot in the vicinity of the rebel flag. This abrupt departure from plan saved his hide. In that respect it was the most unfortunate walk of the war. Had he not surrendered to indignation many a gallant young Briton might have survived to compose lively memoirs of the New Zealand campaign, thereby making my present enterprise redundant.

For at that moment there were cries and shots from the summit he had just vacated. Unbelievably, it was seen infested with the Duke's warriors. While Britons in full muster faced the fortress, a powerful party of the enemy had crept to their rear. This sly sortie not only put a piquet of the 58th to flight; it also scattered a defensive ring of Nene's men. In less than a minute the summit was in rebel grip. So also was the 32-pounder and the Union Jack. The Duke, not Despard, was serving notice that battle was joined. To spread dismay even more, musketry banged out from the fortress. This did much to confirm George Philpotts's finding that the besiegers were themselves besieged.

When Despard found voice, he ordered his bugler to sound alarm. Cyprian was the first officer to make sense. While Despard bellowed, he calmly rallied such of the 58th as he found on hand and, without waiting on reinforcement, pushed men uphill with fixed bayonets. No matter that shot was showering from two sides. Moving in open order, his men made it plain that they were not of a mind to be slowed, especially when they won enough footing to press forward with Sheffield's best steel. Many of the Duke's warriors were astute enough to discern that they had been here before; they recognised the cursing and grinding molars of Britain's infantry in mass. Emptying their weapons for the last time, they began to decamp. Cyprian's men snapped hard on their heels until they disappeared among trees. But the rebel task was accomplished, the damage done. Not only was there more work for surgeons and the need for a gravedigging detail. The 32-pounder had been toppled from its perch and left belly up in ooze. More dispiriting still, the Union Jack was gone.

Cyprian rested his men until Despard made a breathless appearance. He reluctantly offered congratulations.

'That was a tolerable performance, Major Bridge,' he observed.

'It had to be, sir,' Cyprian pointed out.

Other officers were roving about in a daze, many of them shamefaced, some still looking for their similarly panicked men. Despard called them together for a summary of their situation.

'Let there be no mistake,' he announced. 'We are in contest with a treacherous foe. They will stop at nothing to degrade us. Let there be no more talk of mercy.'

Talk of mercy had not been been apparent in the British camp for some time, if ever. But no matter.

'Sir?' said a discreet young subaltern.

'What is it, man?'

'You would do well to look over your right shoulder, sir.'

Despard was unmoved. 'My right shoulder?'

'Indeed, sir.'

Despard looked. His eyes, as did those of his dishevelled juniors, eventually came to rest on the Duke's fortress. The fate of the Union Jack was no longer a mystery. It flew from the fortress flagstaff at half mast and upside down. The Duke's celestial pennant flapped belittlingly above it. There was a poignant moment before Despard thought to confide his thoughts. Every hair on his hirsute face was bristling.

'Bloody savages,' he breathed.

Those were his last sober words of the day.

There was no further talk of lowering the palisades with firepower; and none of demoralising the Duke with din.

'We storm,' Despard said.

'Today, sir?' Cyprian said faintly.

'At three,' Despard decided.

'No breach has been made, sir,' Cyprian pointed out.

'True,' Despard said with indifference.

'And we are left with hardly six hours to ready our ranks, sir.'

'Just so,' Despard agreed from a distance.

He was, it appeared, no longer of our company.

Officers and men began gathering up personal effects for safekeeping. Those hitherto slow to make wills, or write letters to next of kin, needed no further encouragement. Cyprian and George left such of themselves as they wished to bequeath to posterity in my non-combatant hands.

'Kiss Louisa for me should I fail to survive this lunacy,' Cyprian asked. 'And if such proves the case, tell her I shall haunt her until our reunion in a world sweeter than this.'

I felt he was unduly optimistic on that score. The pleasures of heaven, as I understood them, precluded reunions likely to shake ships' timbers. But far be it from me, at this late hour, to draw his attention to the insipid theological view of the hereafter.

George had his own request. Unable to make pen and paper useful, he begged me to make full account of his fate to his father, the distinguished Bishop of Exeter; this entreaty also plumbed pessimism more than circumstances so far warranted.

'You are not dead yet,' I pointed out.

'Oh, but I soon shall be,' he insisted.

There was no playful smile. His certainty was aweing.

'Come,' I urged feebly.

'I wish to leave this life with one happy thought,' he explained. 'As a bishop my father sits of right in the House of Lords. My hope is that he may rise to his feet and do Britain service by denouncing Despard and his cretinous kind. Better still, the entire British army — a service in which advancement is won with money rather than merit. My demise must serve some useful purpose.'

'That is a modest ambition,' I suggested.

'I have another. Quite frankly, Ferdie, I have been a disappointment as a son. Pater has never seen me as more than a drunken gambler and fornicator. The tale of my gallant death might cheer the old boy no end. Promise to tell him a good one.'

I felt heartsick. 'I will be shaking your hand after the fortress has fallen,' I argued.

He seemed not to hear.

Twenty

Muster of men for the storming parties began at two. The Duke's pinpricks were having the desired outcome. The British lion, with ruffled mane, was about to lumber into his field of fire. Silence grew in the fortress, taunts and challenges fading away. One might surmise that firearms were being cleaned and shot tallied. Behind British lines men had been fed with such edibles as harassed cooks could summon; Despard was insistent that storming parties served their monarch best with full bellies.

Timothy Walker Nene, after fretting through the morning, made a last appeal to Despard. He requested an interpreter so that Despard should not mistake his meaning. That meant me. The assault was insane, Nene said; the mere thought of it left him sick at heart. Better that Despard personally shot his own soldiers one by one, he argued, than that he push brave young men into an abyss. I ensured that this plea lost nothing in translation.

'What is he saying?' Despard demanded. 'That he wishes no part of this?'

'Nor his Maori,' I explained.

'I knew all along natives were not to be trusted,' Despard said. 'Bloody cowards one and all.'

I endeavoured to express this more charitably. It proved impossible to launder it.

'Tell the colonel that he is a very stupid man,' Nene said.

I found that no feat; I even coloured it a little.

'Tell the savage to march his men off,' Despard roared. 'I regret that it is not in my power to have him arrested and flogged.'

I conveyed such of this as suited the occasion. Nene withdrew a few yards to confer with lieutenants. Then he planted himself before the colonel again.

'What does he want now?' Despard asked. 'Hasn't he heard me?'

'Indeed he has, sir,' I said. 'He offers you a favour.'

'Favour?'

'Of bold nature, if I am not mistaken.'

'Continue,' Despard ordered.

'He says that if madness must be, he will do his best to see that disaster is kept within bounds. In brief, sir, he offers to lead his Maori in a feint to the rear of the fortress. That may not only distract the Duke; it might also lessen the damage his muskets can do from the front.'

'What do you hear in that, Wildblood?'

'A philanthropic proposition,' I risked saying.

'I hear the bleat of a spineless barbarian who wishes to keep a finger in the British pie. I am no fool. I suspect his hope is to wrest land from the rebels from behind British guns.'

'Is that your reply, sir?'

'Indeed,' Despard said.

I did not interpret. Mayhem, at this point, would serve no purpose. 'The colonel,' I advised Nene, 'does not request your services.'

'Then may he request God's,' Nene said.

He marched his Maori to the rear. With him went the last prospect of an unpretentious bloodletting.

The remaining hour was the longest in the lives of most present; for the imaginative it also looked to be the last. I climbed to the least imperilled location in the vicinity. It afforded me a view of preliminaries. The silence was ventilated by shots from the rejuvenated 32-pounder. In the end it proved no better than its leaner cousins in demolishing the palisades. At five minutes to three, when the last round fell, the Duke's defences were as forbidding as before. Then the Duke made himself heard. He was steeling his men for the fray. 'Stand firm,' he called. 'Let the red tribe march into our ovens.'

He may have been expressing himself figuratively; but who was I to say? I did not offer to interpret. The men of the forlorn hope, the martial euphemism for those foremost in a storming party, had enough to contemplate. Most of the volunteers for that fateful role were men of Cyprian's beloved 58th. He managed to watch them without wincing as they filed into place. So that honours might be divided, however, the front ranks were interspersed with ageing workhorses of Despard's 99th. Despard gave command of the first storming party to a sufficiently obsequious major of his own regiment. Cyprian, to his chagrin, had to make do with the second. Last to make a showing was a mixed contingent of sailors and militia equipped with axes, hatchets, grappling hooks, ropes and ladders, implements to ensure that the palisades presented no further obstacle. This nondescript group was in the command of George Philpotts; Despard mistakenly imagined him out of harm's way among military merchandise.

All in all, Despard's army could not have presented a worrying sight to the Duke's warriors. Men were ragged and filthy, their uniforms soiled and faces drawn; many were barefoot, or had their crumbling boots tied together with strips of flax. Their trousers were tattered and patched; their red jackets were dulled to the colour of brick. Their bayonets alone suggested them serious.

Men finally assembled in dead ground, in a broad gully a hundred paces short of the fortress. Judging a short pause adequate, Despard instructed his bugler to sound advance. The problem was that he had neglected to notify most of those in his command of his intentions; even lieutenants had been overlooked. Sergeants, corporals and rankers were meant to be clairvoyant. For the first five minutes, as a result, the bugler's sound produced an unhappy melee. Officers tended to move off in one direction, their men elsewhere, until recalled and persuaded to find each other. Fortunately most of this confusion was out of view of those entrenched in the fortress; otherwise the Duke's marksmen might have had an even more noteworthy day.

The bugler sounded advance again. This time the result was less mixed. 'Prepare to charge,' officers commanded. Then 'Charge'. Men of the forlorn hope moved off at a trot, rank after rank, in close order. Their elbows were touching; there were no more than the regulation twenty-three inches between ranks. Despard was not going to countenance unsightly procedure in this battle: there were no untidy probes, messy feints, or ambling skirmishers. There was merely infantry in tight formation, muskets loaded and bayonets bristling, about to war as well as they knew.

In the hollow a second storming party formed as the first lifted away. The pioneer and naval party was preparing too. Among tradesmen George Philpotts was as conspicuous as ever. His attire for the day included not only a forage cap but also army issue black trousers with a red stripe, and a blue sailor's tunic; a sword swung from his waist. On first sight of proceedings ahead he had second thoughts about his garb. 'Damn me if I'm going to die a soldier,' he decided. With that he tossed away the cap, divested himself of the trousers, freed his sword, and hurried forward to give fight in flannel drawers, his monocle still marvellously in place.

Meanwhile the first party was closing steadily with the fortress. Fifty paces out, men heaved into a run with a hearty British hurrah. It was a signal to death to begin reaping. The citadel of vengeance came to life, with fire flashing along its front face. Then bastions right and left flared too. Finally there was a boom loud enough to speed the devil back to Bible class. As smoke cleared, it became apparent that the fortress was defended by more than muskets. Hidden in a flanking angle until that moment was a veteran 9-pounder purloined from a passing whaler. Liberally stuffed with old chains in lieu of conventional shot, it trimmed away most of the men of the first storming party; the second had to pick a path through bodies sundered and sometimes headless. Then they began toppling too. Not a man of them saw a Maori face. Rank after rank cheered themselves on; rank after rank reeled off into eternity or, if they were luckier, lifelong infirmity. Their uniforms smoked as shot burned into them again and again at short range. The few men who reached the fortress wall began slashing at ties ineffectually with bayonets, or tearing at timber with bare hands.

Militia and sailors were ordered forward to force an entrance. Most of the militia, on meeting a tide of metal, went judiciously to earth. George led a small group of sailors on with a lone scaling ladder. Miraculously ducking shot, they managed to prop it against the fortress wall. George then dismissed the party and urged them to do something happier with their lives. With a last salute to things of this world, George mounted the ladder and flourished his sword. Even in his long flannels, even as he filled with the lead of a Maori fusillade, he managed to cut a monumental figure; he seemed to float above the palisades before winging into the fortress. His fear of dying the undistinguished death of a ranker was baseless. The stain of Blackguard Beach was forgiven and forgotten. To this day, as I understand it, the Maori of northern New Zealand recount the tale of George Philpotts's demise with awe; he was the only Briton that day to view the interior of the Duke's fortress, albeit in his last moment. Passing travellers even place flowers on his grave, under a tall English oak. They believe it brings luck. There are too few heroes in this world, they say, for such as he to be unremembered. Amen.

By then in de facto command of the assault — with Despard's favoured officers immobile or breathing their last — Cyprian was making equally stylish efforts to win fame and a funeral. With a few men of muscle he even hauled away some of the fortress's lighter fencing only to find two fences more. Despard himself, jigging from one foot to the other, appeared to be petitioning heaven as he watched much of his army mince itself on Maori architecture. In an absent-minded fit of diligence, he suggested to his bugler that retirement might be sounded. As the notes fluttered above the battle, he turned to the bugler in poor temper.

'Who ordered that?' he demanded.
'Why, you did yourself, sir,' the baffled bugler pointed out.
'Did I indeed?'
'I fear so, sir.'
'That is damned curious. Tell me, young fellow, do you observe the fortress taken?'
'Not at this juncture, sir,' the bugler confessed.
Despard mused while more men died. 'So why should I have done that, pray?'
In fear of court martial, the bugler replied, 'I cannot imagine, sir.'
'Very well. Call the buggers back if you must.'
So much for generalship. The ensuing retreat was no more masterful. Britons had forgotten how to depart a battlefield in disciplined fashion. Soldiers bolting from blazing loopholes found their weapons an impediment and discarded them as they ran. This did not necessarily save them. Feuding over proprietorship of loopholes, Maori marksmen placed shot among a forest of fleeing legs. A few brave Britons staggered home with wounded and dying on their shoulders. The Duke's men crept from the palisades and among Britons abandoned. Their swinging tomahawks won an impressive silence.

The attack lasted no longer than five minutes. At its end there were forty Britons lifeless on the field and others slowly expiring. More than a hundred were mangled in ways large and small. Not a rebel could be heard suffering.
Quiet grew. Both sides seemed dumbfounded.

I found Cyprian resting such of his regiment as he managed to retrieve from the inferno. The seriously damaged were being borne off to surgeons in stretchers and makeshift litters. Short range shooting meant minor wounds were few. Cyprian himself was intact, though this was not apparent. His uniform was bloody and blackened, his voice a bleak whisper.

'George too?' he asked.

'George too,' I confirmed.

'Is this war?' He was still breathing hard.

'Our wishes sometimes confound us,' I suggested.

'Tell me it is not true,' he pleaded.

At his most venturesome Henry Youngman would have found that difficult. The best that could be expected from Ferdinand Wildblood was a civilised elegy for the fallen. The fact is that the day was as desperate as any in the history of British arms.

Nor was it finished. The Duke's recipe for humble pie required him to assemble his men where they were most visible to the red tribe and there lead them in an athletic war dance. The picturesque character of this performance — the stamping feet and flashing tongues, the pitiless chanting and wild leaps with weapons high — eluded me as dead cooled by the dozen under the winter sun. I knew what it meant at last. There was nothing in the least quaint in this pagan polka. It spoke defiance, exultation, triumph, and above all contempt of death; it spoke of men mastering the world and the worst it could do. Need I say that my soul shrivelled? My genitals likewise? Consider it said.

Cyprian, reluctant to leave the field, shepherded the last of his casualties to safety. His eyes were still stunned.

'Come,' I said, and offered my shoulder.

'I am not a victim,' he protested.

'I am the best judge of that,' I argued.

He leaned on me after all as we limped after his men. Engrossed in finding a path unmenaced by shot, I failed to note another impediment. Freed from Despard's quarantine by the sound of strife, the Reverend Williams had arrived to do his duty by Christendom's dead. His face said he was still struggling to comprehend the magnitude of his task. He acknowledged my presence only so far as I formed part of a charmless spectacle.

'I cannot believe it, Wildblood,' he confided.

'Your difficulty is shared,' I told him.

'Meanwhile we have a familiar mission.'

'We, sir?'

'You and I,' he agreed.

'If you mean recovering the dead, sir, you would be well advised to let battlefield fever pass.'

'Never,' he said. 'Strike while the iron is hot. The Duke may be a pagan, but many in his entourage are more enlightened. Should we approach the fortress they may hear our plea charitably.'

'If John Heke were among them, perhaps.'

'Confound the fellow,' Williams said. 'I am beginning to miss him.'

Later that afternoon we approached the fortress in full view of the Duke's marksmen. A shot discharged in the air stopped us short of our goal.

'Say your business,' an authoritative voice shouted.

'I come for Christian heroes of all colours,' Williams replied.

There was a lengthy silence. A conference was evidently in progress. Meanwhile we were marooned in a sea of human fragments. Soldiers and sailors were strewn among streamers of viscera and a slime of drying blood. Shock lingered on the few faces intact, resignation on others. And that is not to tally the least agreeable sight of all. George Philpotts's monocle dangled poignantly from the point of a palisade. The rest of him was missing.

The same voice said, 'Come for the dead when your Colonel withdraws his army and promises peace for a month.'

'You ask him to confess defeat.'

'He cannot boast victory.'

'In that respect he may amaze you,' Williams promised.

'Then peace for a week,' the rebel bargained generously. 'Return with the colonel's answer tomorrow.'

Midwinter dusk was falling as we made our way back to the camp. 'Thank you, Wildblood,' Williams said. 'I daresay you have been expecting harsh words from me.'

'Such words should not have surprised me, sir.'

'You will not hear them today,' Williams explained. 'Mortality on such a scale encourages a different perspective.'

'Indeed, sir.'

'Angela is well?'

'Safe in Heke's camp.'

'You would do well to think of her soul,' he suggested. 'And for that matter of yours.'

'I shall give it thought,' I promised.

'The communion rail is ready for you. Similarly the altar. Not to put too fine a point on it, God is.'

'That is a tall order, sir.'

'May you soon hear it,' Williams said.

'What is it now?' Despard asked.

Relieved of his boots, if not of command misery, he sat in his tent. An attentive manservant filled his glass to brimming, plainly not for the first time.

'It is in respect of the dead, sir,' Williams said.

'Been counting them, have you?'

'My brief is to ensure Christian burial.'

'Shall I tell you what I think?' Despard downed his grog and indicated his need for more.

'By all means,' Williams said.

'There is more to this than meets the eye.'

'God's intentions are seldom apparent,' Williams agreed.

'I talk of perfidy,' Despard explained.

'Perfidy, sir?'

'Rank treachery. Whoever heard of natives who refused to back away from Britain's bayonets? Whoever heard of a heathen fortress halting us? I smell renegades at work.'

Williams was as nonplussed as I.

'Renegades?' he asked quietly.

'White men,' Despard disclosed. 'Mercenaries. Traffickers with the enemy. Perhaps treason-loving Yankees.'

'This far,' Williams observed gently, 'such renegades have failed to make themselves apparent.'

'That is their cunning,' Despard explained. 'Would you expect such fiends to show their faces? The proof of their existence is before us.'

'Proof, sir?'

'On the battlefield. The good men fallen there cry betrayal by their own kind. This has not been the work of untutored savages.'

'Who knows?' Williams asked, as piously as he could.

'I know,' said Despard, beginning to quiver.

'And you will confide as much in your report?' Williams said.

'You understand me,' Despard said. 'To argue otherwise would be disloyal to our dead.'

'Speaking of the dead,' Williams said,'I bear a rebel proposition.'

'It is not my intention to offer mercy,' Despard announced.

Wherever he was campaigning, it was still elsewhere.

The day had been bitter; night was no improvement. The busiest location in the British camp was the surgeon's tent. Bullets were extracted, bones set, and limbs amputated. The surgeons slaved in a soup of mud and blood. Elsewhere, in tent after silent tent, men lay felled by rheumatism, cramp and shock. Many a young lieutenant lost interest in his vocation that day; many a captain began contemplating the sale of his commission.

As if there were not enough to unnerve them, there was war dance after war dance performed in the fortress; there were no uplifting hymns of the kind John Heke favoured. There was also, from time to time, satanic shrieking, which may or may not have been pagan priests possessed by spirits. At all events it was preferable to think so. Terrified men on piquet duty deserted their posts and had to be persuaded back again by officers still capable of pointing a pistol.

Despard's lamp burned till late. For his superiors he dictated the following to a tactfully silent subaltern: 'It would be difficult to give an impression of the enthusiasm with which troops advanced to the attack. The struggle was who would be foremost. My troops returned to camp undaunted in mind and spirit, wishing only that another opportunity of attack might be offered them.'

You think that dispatch this chronicler's invention? Not a syllable is mine.

The Duke had composed a more reliable report for tribesmen far and near. It was short of flourishes and succinct in character: 'One wing of Britain is broken and hangs dangling on the ground. Who will help break the other?'

Cyprian, after touring tents and consoling his wounded, finally made his appearance in the accommodation we shared with George Philpotts; the silence there was crushing. He sat for a time with head in hands.

'If it is any comfort,' I finally informed him, 'you were not beaten by mere savages.'

'No?'

'Your commander attributes today's disaster to renegades.'
Cyprian remained silent for a time.
'That means he may have to find one,' he pointed out.
'Like whom?' I asked.
'Like you,' he warned.
My interest in colonial warfare appeared to be on the wane.

Twenty One

I am here again. At my desk, that is, in 1886, a year which tends to dart displeasingly past when I pick up my pen. The reek of that luckless day fills my nostrils only in imagination. I am here, home, in reach of a reputable whisky and in no peril; it is all over, and a long time ago. No one need live through it again, as I have been obliged to, sometimes with tears misting the ink.

I performed George's last request, writing to his father and reporting his death in incandescent prose. Did the good Bishop of Exeter then rise to his feet in the House of Lords to denounce martial imbeciles? Would that I could say so. Report of such an incident never came my way. And the world went on *its* way. I imagine it likelier that the bishop brooded for a time, as bereaved fathers do, and before proceeding to evensong ordered a tactfully worded headstone raised in a New Zealand churchyard. This wreath of words is the most I can do for George's memory.

It is not easy to take up the tale again. Easier, perhaps, to close it off here and now with some soothing summation. But this is not George's tale. Not Cyprian's, Despard's, or for that matter mine. It begins, though it may not end, with John Heke; we should attempt to see it through at his side, if we can establish his whereabouts. Mystifying though it may be, this was still his war.

It is said that when news of the battle reached Heke he was in what seemed his last coma, his commerce with this world complete. There was debate among his aides about whether he should be informed of events in the place of hot water. Some held that the shock of the news might launch him into the afterlife; others argued that intelligence of British disaster might be the medicine he needed. After long conference the latter view prevailed. Moses was given the task of delivering the news, in as loud a voice as possible; he stood by Heke's bedside and boomed.

At first there was no response. Then, as Moses' report grew starker, Heke's left eye magically opened. Then, after a time, his right. Much the same happened with his hands. The left twitched and the right followed suit. By the time Moses had finished Heke had his full complement of senses and limbs. He even swung his legs from the bed and stood upright. He reached for his Bible and placed it firmly under his arm. The shrinking of his flesh, evident for weeks, seemed to cease in that moment; he grew an inch or two before the eyes of those assembled. Interpret this how you will. Let Heke not be seen, however, as just another of war's weaklings; this was not the resurrection of a coward. Heke, as no other party in this affair, had a war to win with his stars before he could aspire to terrestrial triumph.

'Now,' he said, 'must God's battle begin.'

There was a puzzled silence.

Then, 'Lead me to the sun. Lead me to the light.'

Even his most loyal followers were confused. They tried taking his arm, as he seemed to request, but were shaken off. Children sped out into the world to inform outlying tribesmen that John Heke was again in the land of the living.

So for that matter were most of the characters in this chronicle. Williams had begun winkling Britain's dead from the fatal front face of the fortress; Cyprian and fellow survivors of the 58th were proving proficient gravediggers. Despard remained austerely out of view in the command tent until martial housekeeping was done. In his view the siege was still proceeding. The enemy was still there to be overpowered. Spasmodic gunnery may have argued that such was the case. Nothing else did. Boredom became the victor on both fronts. Even with shells falling squarely rebels grew lethargic in running to cover. Rebel marksmen no longer performed with accuracy; they seemed to discharge their weapons mainly for the bliss of seeing Britons jump.

To be fair, however, this impasse was not solely of Despard's making. The colonel's initial inclination, in the dawn following his darkest day, had been to make a seemly retreat to the Bay of Islands. He ordered tents and tools and stores destroyed and ammunition buried. Before the order was carried out Timothy Walker Nene and lesser chiefs put in an appearance. Through my good offices as interpreter, Despard harangued them for playing no part in the assault on the fortress; they in their turn suggested their wisdom confirmed. In a brisk about face, however, they argued the folly of retreat at this point. Retirement so long as dead were unburied would leave a dangerous impression in the minds of both enemies and neutrals.

'Dangerous?' Despard said.

'Deserting one's dead is as shameful to the Maori as rank cowardice,' I explained. 'Should you not retrieve your distinguished men, no Maori would follow you from this day forward.'

'Never in my life, Wildblood, have I embraced pagan custom.'

'In current circumstances, sir, it might be happier to bend habit. It is that or lose native allies. You may well have need of them should retirement from the field begin. Without Nene's protection your men would be prey to ambushers. He also points out that such ammunition as you bury would fast be recovered by the rebels and used to effect.'

'God damn it,' Despard said.

'Sir?'

'The order is countermanded.'

'You wish me to convey this to Major Bridge, sir?'

'Tell him it is my intention to persist with the siege — not out of respect for native sensibilities, but until the part played by renegades is clarified.'

'Renegades, sir?'

'The vile creatures who this far have failed to show their faces. That we have not sighted them is testimony to their cunning hand in this.'

As reasoning this was remarkably circular. No matter; it was not for me to enlighten him.

Despard leaned close to my ear, 'Furthermore, Wildblood,' he said, 'only someone familiar with martial procedure could have foreseen the nature of yesterday's battle and arranged rebels accordingly.'

I hiked off in Cyprian's direction.

'You are in need of a rest,' my dear friend observed.

'I see someone needier.'

'I have responsibilities,' he pointed out. 'My men must be nursed back to health for the next debacle. If Despard thinks to remain here, there is no reason why you should. Why not look out your dusky sweetheart while there is a chance? Information concerning John

Heke might also be useful. One hears that he is dead again. It would be helpful if one report of his demise could be verified.'

'You mean this?'

'Of course. Would that I could restore myself in Louisa's arms.'

I was overwhelmed. 'How can I repay you?'

'By considering it an order,' he said.

I may not have raised dust in my rush south; I must have left mud flying astern.

It was my luck to happen on Heke's camp the day after he dramatically shook off the cloak of invisibility and returned to the corporeal world. That meant uproar. Rowdy tribesmen were crowding in to view the miracle. The younger were flourishing their neglected weapons. The meaning of the event was much debated. It suggested to many that God had revived Heke in order to demonstrate his displeasure with the Duke. Sceptics said that if such were the case God might worthily have acted sooner.

It was not for me to interpret the Almighty. Moses whisked me clear of the throng. 'You saw the battle?' he asked.

'All,' I said.

'Was it as terrible as told?'

'It was never sightly.'

We turned into a quiet corner of the camp. A sublime vision cancelled memory of carnage. For there stood Angela clad in meagre native garb, not a curve disguised. She gave out a faint cry and opened her arms wide. That was the signal for Moses to vanish. Angela led me to her dwelling. Would that I could account for the next hour of delirium. I beg the reader not to feel cheated; I too, needless to say, would love to relive it. I never understood why Sophocles, in the long eve of his life, rejoiced in loss of erotic function, claiming that it was like ridding himself of a lunatic companion. Even in memory — second hand, so to speak — I celebrate with a sigh.

The hour ended not with sweet conversation of the *après* kind, but with banging on the door of Angela's dwelling.

'Do you share a blanket?' Moses was asking.

Though I failed at first to see why, we modestly ensured that we did.

'Your witness is here,' he announced.

The door swung open. Moses looked down on us gravely, determining that our situation was all circumstances suggested.

'Congratulations,' he said.

I was slow to understand. 'Congratulations?'

'I have never seen two more married.'

Dear God. I was a long way from Lovelady and Pettiworth. Literary life was ever hazardous.

'There is nothing to stop a repeat in Williams's church,' Moses explained. 'Christian ceremony is far more social.'

I was slow getting my breath.

'Meanwhile,' Moses went on, 'Heke wishes to see you.'

Heke said, 'Not for the first time, I gave Britons warning.'

'As before, no one listened,' I explained.

He was leaner, his eyes moodier.

I thought to add, 'What happens now?'

'I was hoping to hear your suggestion.'

'Mine?'

'Is the tale written?'

I couldn't disappoint him. 'What would you wish to hear?'

He was silent.

'That Britons have disappeared?' I proposed. 'That sanity and civility now prevail?'

He looked skyward.

'That is not the case,' I said.

It was not my intention to encourage him, but it was truth. There was still a war. Absentee though he may have been, it was not too late for John Heke to affix his signature to such strife as remained.

I had as large a problem with Angela. She failed to see why I should feel obliged to return to companions of my own colour and kind.

'You are now of my tribe,' she pointed out.

'I might have difficulty making myself understood on that score.'

'Not if you remain. Who is to care?'

'Honour cares. It may come hunting for me.'

'Here?'

'Even here.'

She was unimpressed. 'Very well. A week more. No longer. You might think we were married fast. We can be unmarried faster.'

Despard's mixed feelings were as nothing to mine.

Combat was not conspicuous. Williams was. He grew in my path as

I picked my way back into British lines. The Bible under his arm was sticky with New Zealand clay in consequence of numerous graveside ceremonies. 'The task is all but done,' he disclosed, 'with virtually none left as carrion.'

'*Virtually* none, sir? What is your meaning there?'

'There are exceptions. Your friend Philpotts for one. And the 58th's Captain Grant.'

'Grant?' I said with sick feeling, remembering the nervous young man in Cyprian's tent, too fearful to confess fear.

'The rebels refuse to surrender their bodies. Indeed they deny that such exist. To be frank, Wildblood, I am uneasy. It bodes nothing good.'

'What are you saying? That George is to have no earthly dwelling?'

Williams shrugged. 'Without a cadaver, Wildblood, I cannot work miracles.'

'See that he has at least a heavenly mansion,' I suggested.

In yet poorer humour I strode on to Cyprian. He lay in our bivouac as a man felled. His colour was waxy, his tunic and trousers stiffly coated with terra firma. He barely had strength to raise himself on an elbow.

'What possessed me to think I was made for this?' he whispered.

'This?'

'The army.'

'Doubt,' I suggested, 'is a little late in the day.'

'On the contrary,' he said. 'I might yet make more of myself.'

'As what?' I asked sympathetically.

'As an artist,' he claimed. 'When young, I had a rare gift for watercolours. On my fifteenth birthday, as time approached to take up the family trade, my father bade me put childish things aside; my brushes and paints were destroyed.'

'And you think to begin again?'

'I do,' he confirmed.

Wonders in this war were not to cease. John Heke might yet join Islam and the Duke embrace Buddha.

'What of yourself?' he said croakily. 'Did it go well?'

'Tolerably,' I answered.

'What does that mean?'

'In all confidence,' I told him, 'I appear to be married.'

That, and the explanation which followed, revived Cyprian considerably. He found a smile in his diminished repertoire of expression and fetched a bottle from under his pillow.

'The way I see it,' he said, 'there is only one person who can get you out of this.'

'Who might that be?'

'Henry Youngman,' he said. 'He would free you in a poignant paragraph.'

'Did I mishear myself?' I asked. 'Did I say I wished to get out of it?'

'You don't?'

'I appear,' I confessed, 'to be getting used to the notion.'

Cyprian's face was all shock. 'Come, dear boy,' he said. 'Dalliance with a native girl is one thing. Matrimony is madness. Think what you are saying. I know poets are small respecters of convention, but this is pushing idiosyncrasy too far. Further, I see reefs to port and starboard. God has defined races quite clearly. We are not to interfere. Think what your children would be.'

'Of interesting hue,' I suggested.

'You amaze me,' he said.

He brooded for a time on the bottle we were emptying, and decided a change of subject tactful. 'And Heke?' he asked.

'Alive and revived,' I reported. 'And in a characteristic state of perplexity.'

'Is he again to be counted a menace?'

'If his prayers are answered.'

Dark came soon. Also quiet. That evening was remarkable for the latter. A shot from the fortress would have been welcome. The silence made for suspicion; Cyprian, fearing a nocturnal *coup de grâce* from the Duke, ordered piquets doubled. Even Despard, afoot among British fires, was uncommonly fretful.

'How would you interpret this, Wildblood?' he asked.

'As loss of interest, sir,' I suggested.

'I suspect terror,' he said. 'Common sense may be telling them to come to heel.'

'That is a happy thought, sir.'

'Think it,' he ordered.

The only alarms, that long night, were due to piquets using powder and shot to battle with rocks and branches assuming warrior form in the fitful moonlight. Silence grew again in morning's first gleam.

Despard's slumber was ended by Nene brushing guards aside

to win an audience with the colonel. 'The fortress awaits us,' he announced.

Despard, having drunk himself into deep sleep, found it difficult to take an interest. 'What is it now?' he groaned. 'Another confounded omen?'

'Listen,' Nene said.

They listened. Save for gossiping soldiers there was little to be heard.

'Well?' Despard said.

'It is time to move forward,' Nene argued.

'I give such orders,' Despard pointed out.

'And I do not wait on them,' Nene replied.

His exit was abrupt.

A man of his word, Nene took fewer than five minutes to muster his men in view of red-eyed Britons. Then he ordered his contingent forward. On the part of Britons there was a race to vantage points lest another massacre be missed. With no conspicuous caution the warriors bounded across the terrain before the fortress, separating into four parties. The central parties moved forward slowly; the two wings spread wide, to tempt rebel fire. Such fire was slow coming.

Cyprian, beside me, was bewitched by proceedings; I heard a deep intake of breath. 'I see a commander worth serving,' he announced.

There was still no shot or warrior challenge. The meaning soon dawned on many faces.

'They have gone?' Cyprian said, not daring to believe it. 'Gone?'

With wild cries, Nene's men were scrambling over the palisades and dropping into the fortress. Though excitable tribesmen dashed right and left, no sound of resistance rose.

'Indeed,' I said.

The place of hot water was lukewarm; Britain's bath was over.

A few minutes later we too stood within the fortress. Despard was not far behind. The place was already shrinking to sober dimension: it may have been the work of illusionists, but it was also the work of men. One marvelled that it had been an agent of anguish; that it had ever looked invulnerable. Nene's people were already retiring from the place burdened by plunder. The cornucopia of loot deepened the mystery of the Duke's disappearance. He had the wherewithal to fight on for most of a year. There was no shortage of sustenance. There were potatoes by the ton, and Indian corn. There was ammunition. There were arms and accoutrements recovered from Britain's dead and booty dating back to Blackguard Beach. There was something of everything for those now streaming noisily into the fortress. How had it fallen into their hands, and why?

'Like the Arabs,' Despard judged, 'our foemen have folded their tents and fled away.'

Cyprian's expression said he did not see desert nomads of much pertinence here. Nevertheless he held his tongue.

'A conquest is a conquest,' Despard continued. 'The rest is but detail.'

'Conquest, sir?' Cyprian said with some awe.

'Conquest,' Despard confirmed. 'If there is a word more helpful, Bridge, I am free to hear it.'

Not in the mood to sink a buoyant superior, Cyprian was silent. Nor did I feel obliged to point out to the colonel that for the Maori departure from a fortress was no disgrace. It was no lasting city and never meant to be. A fortress was built, as this one plainly had been, for a particular fight. With the fight finished, the site blooded, it was of no further use. (See Henry Youngman's knowledgeable *The Vengeance of The Tattooed Trojans*.) Triumph was in fallen foemen, not in possession of a fortress. The Duke had wanted a hundred Britons toppled. A hundred he had, and a good dozen more. My surmise was that he had loitered here only to see what the British thought to do next; there was always the prospect of another hundred making themselves available to his marksmen. This evaluation would not have been welcome to Colonel Despard. Cyprian and I looked at our feet while he rejoiced inventively.

'Rally your rabble, Major Bridge,' he ordered. 'Bring them to heel.'

'For what purpose, sir?' Cyprian asked.

'There is work to be done,' Despard said. 'I wish disturbances in the ground carefully examined. I wish anything looking like a grave opened up. I need their dead numbered accurately for my dispatch to the Governor. It might also be helpful if the nature of their wounds was noted.'

'Yes, sir,' Cyprian with straight face.

'Furthermore, Bridge,' Despard went on, 'you will pay especial attention to the hue of the corpses.'

'The hue, sir?' Cyprian was baffled.

'Their colour, man. Their race. Need I spell it out? One of those graves may hold a clue to our difficulties here. A dead renegade would be most desirable.'

'I imagine it might, sir,' Cyprian allowed.

'And when you have done with that, proceed with torching the fortress. I wish not a stick of it left.'

That at least was a worthy enterprise. 'With pleasure, sir,' Cyprian said.

What Cyprian didn't know, what Despard couldn't, was that this campaign had lost the last of its cordial character; Despard's orders ensured that horror would not remain in hiding.

I was standing with Cyprian when an agitated ensign arrived running. Cyprian's men, supervised by officers, had been digging fruitlessly in all corners of the fortress for some time. Cyprian had only just predicted, 'We will find no rebel dead this side of Judgement Day.'

He spoke too soon. The ensign was breathless and shuddering.

'Two corpses, sir,' he reported. 'Both of them white.'

'White? White men?'

'Indeed, sir.'

Dear God. Despard had his renegades after all. Cyprian was showing shock too.

'My men have ceased digging, waiting on your inspection of the grave,' the ensign explained. 'The bodies are only part uncovered.'

Cyprian, with every evidence of distaste, said, 'Fetch the colonel too. They are his trophies.'

'Yes, sir,' the ensign said. He dashed obediently to the colonel with his unsavoury tidings.

Meanwhile we advanced on the location, the hole in the earth, the diggers standing idle.

'If you don't have the stomach,' Cyprian said, 'I would not think the worse of you if you beat a retreat.'

He did a brave job of disguising that his interior was as much at risk as mine.

We arrived at the shallow grave. The stench obliged us to use hankerchiefs. With a borrowed spade Cyprian peeled away clay clinging to the corpses. Then, with greater delicacy, he knelt and brushed the last of it away from their faces. We looked not on anonymous renegades, but on familiar features. One of the two was Lieutenant George Philpotts, late of the Royal Navy. The second was the 58th's missing Captain Grant.

Distressed Cyprian stood back. 'Fetch them out,' he ordered.

Despard's arrival coincided with the exhumation. 'Didn't I say renegades?' he shouted ecstatically at Cyprian as he came. 'Didn't I say?'

Cyprian wasn't saying anything. No one near the grave was. The two deceased at our feet had been mangled. George Philpotts's scalp had been hacked away clumsily. The buttocks of Captain Grant, and the flesh of his thighs, had been sliced off with more authority.

I was looking skyward. Cyprian was convulsively emptying his stomach. Even vexed Despard fell quiet. For my part, I would like to record no more of this. But there was more. Nene's men had found an elderly, frail and half-deaf associate of the Duke's slumbering in a bunker; this bemused fellow had been mislaid when the fortress was evacuated. In present company he was fortunate not to have been sped to his forebears by bayonet or bullet. Correctly recognising that his situation remained perilous, he was prepared to babble the rest of the day away, especially when brought before the chief of the red tribe.

'See what the wretch has to say for himself,' Despard ordered me. 'Ask him, for example, to account for the indignities to our dead. If the fellow refuses to impart information, tell him we shall hold him personally responsible. If he does, we may let him live.'

There was no need of incentives. The shaky fellow continued to have more than enough to say for himself. It appeared that there had been loud dispute in the Duke's camp in the course of the siege. Christians of Heke's stripe had been tetchy with the pagan priests in the Duke's entourage; and pagans vice versa. Bickering was brought to a head by Despard's assault, and the consignment of dead Britons delivered to their door. This was the signal for the feud to become earnest. Christians thought to leave well alone. Pagans considered the corpses to be legitimate booty of the battlefield. Foliage of war — human flesh, in short — was necessary for festivity, and invocations to the war god Tu, to ensure continuing good fortune in battle. As men of rank, and unmistakably of courage, poor George and his innocent companion in catastrophe had been deemed suitable for ceremony: George's scalp was used for purposes of divination, and Grant's flesh, when roasted, for ritual consumption. The pagans triumphed and Christians sulked. Spokesmen for the latter prophesied that only ill could result from such acts; they saw evil unleash itself across the land as a black cloud. Old fears took fire in the form of uneasy dreams; the place began boiling with omens.

That was the poetry. The old man's prose was also consistent with such as we knew. The uproar from the squeamish in the Duke's band did not diminish; open desertions began. Dissension grew so enfeebling that the Duke, rather than preside over armed riot in his ranks, ordered the fortress abandoned between one day and the next. Other qualms weighed the Duke's garrison down too: 'We were told,' the old fellow said, 'that the soldiers would go wherever they were ordered, even to certain death, but we did not believe it. We did not know there were such warriors in the world. Now we know it. Many have grown fearful, thinking more kindly of their fellow men, and especially of the red tribe.'

He hung his head in shamed emphasis.

I translated as little of this as possible to Colonel Despard; he required no encouragement.

Saddling his hobby horse again, Despard most fortunately missed much of the point. 'Renegades,' he whispered. 'Ask him about the renegades who built this fortress.'

I asked. The old fellow replied at intolerable length.

'He reports that there are no such renegades,' I said.

'None?'

'None, sir. And he takes it amiss that credit should not go where credit is due; his tribesmen are carpenters of competence and pride. Their fortresses have dictated the course of many a battle.'

'Confound the old bugger,' Despard said. 'We may have to cast our net wider.'

'What is to be done, then, sir?'

'With renegades? A bullet would be kind. A rope would be better.'

'With the old man, sir,' I said.

'Ask him for a guarantee of good conduct in future,' Despard said.

'There is no risk of his giving further offence to the Queen,' I judged.

'Good. So kick his arse memorably, Wildblood, and then set him free.'

An interpreter is under no obligation to serve sentiments of a coarse kind. I set him free.

Three devilish days of labour were necessary to rid the world of the Duke's fortress. The driving devil was Despard. He resolved that not a chip of it would remain to perplex posterity. Maori figures were seen on nearby heights as the chopping and burning went on, and the bloodstained terrain was meticulously levelled. These bystanders were doing no more than marvel at men so determined to banish all memory of a battle. Nothing became Britons more than their departure from the place of hot water. Had they the seed, they would have grassed it over too.

There was a striking omission in Despard's report to the Governor. He provided no count of rebel dead. This, given the circumstances, was wise. Felled rebels could not have tallied more than ten; some said fewer than five. For connoisseurs of the curious, there is one other detail. The report was headed *Camp at John Heke's fortress*.

What more did the Duke have to do?

Twenty Two

*I*f there is urgency in my prose today, there is a reason. After a few days' absence, the consequence of a fatiguing fever, I took a cab to my club again last night. It was not a pleasing experience. Faces are growing unfamiliar there, and younger; faces once regular are vanishing. It is considered poor form to refer to these defections, and I am not one to quarrel with custom. Last night, for the first time, there was not a single intimate of long standing in view. For continuity's sake I reluctantly seated myself near a fellow for whom I have never much cared. I mean Sebastian Goodfellow.

Those who peruse forgotten anthologies of English verse may recall the name above some limply Byronic pastiche or Wordsworthian potpourri; others may remember it attached to defamatory reviews of his literary betters. Those who have never encountered Goodfellow on the printed page need not feel deprived. In a half century of refined festering, he has been no ornament to English letters. His bald and shiny pate is a beacon in any bookish gathering: it advertises reefs with a razor edge. When he was younger, his bitter smile had something in common with that of a savaging shark. With age it has become the centrepiece of a death's head. Last night, more threadbare than ever, he was half-hidden behind *The Illustrated London News*, which is more or less his level; he now prefers pictures to print. For my part I pretended an interest in *Punch*, while continuing to hope for congenial company. We sat with our backs to each other. But I knew he was there; he surely knew I was. It was only a matter of time before the first word was exchanged. On my reckoning it would arrive as I finished my first brandy; Goodfellow would likewise be in need of another and seedily looking for someone to help him raise the price. He spoke a sip short of my calculation.

'The name Dinwiddie familiar to you, Wildblood?' he grunted.

'Dinwiddie?' I uttered.

A funereal bell tolled at the back of my head. My mouth was dry; the tremble in my hand owed nothing to fever. I hadn't heard the name in forty years. Dinwiddie had to be all of a hundred years old or dead. Desirably dead. At that moment I effectively was. Goodfellow didn't shift his chair or look over his shoulder; he spoke into space.

'What,' I said with pain, 'makes you ask, Goodfellow?'

With considerable effort I also refrained from looking around.

'There was a fellow about yesterday of that name,' Goodfellow explained.

'Here?'

'Kicking up a fearful fuss. Asking for you at the door. Said he'd come to collect. I trust there is nothing to it. This club prides itself on its reputation for quiet. It doesn't do to have creditors of depraved and deranged nature banging at the door.'

Goodfellow pressed his advantage. If he imagined he could use Dinwiddie or his impersonator to winkle a conscience drink from me, he was about to learn better.

'Fortunately,' he went on, 'there were few members in earshot. The doorman heaved the vile old wretch back into the street, though not before a number of profanities were heard. As it turned out, there was no need to call a constable. He made no return, though one was promised.'

'And his name was Dinwiddie, did you say?'

'He uttered it loudly enough. Along with menaces meant for you.'

'I have never heard the name,' I claimed.

'He certainly makes free with yours.'

Stalemate. Silence. Lest Goodfellow was sharpening a stiletto, I looked around and reviewed the situation to my rear. So far as I could see my ancient adversary was in conversation with a large-leafed indoor plant of tropical character. At all events I moved briskly. I killed my brandy, signed my bill, and made for the door. Goodfellow was still cheerfully talking to himself. I was conversing with no one, though the doorman eyed me inquisitively as he held an umbrella over my head and called up my cab. Had he been the one who dealt with Dinwiddie? I had the impression he was about to give me a sly wink. 'More foul weather, sir,' he suggested.

'Without doubt,' I agreed tersely.

I made it plain that I did not welcome further intimacy.

At home, before laying siege to my private stockpile of liquor, I sat heavy-breathing in the first chair I found. Attacked by inspiration, I finally went to my desk and unlocked a lower drawer. Within, as good as the day it was purchased, was the two-barrelled pistol which had seen out New Zealand in my company: in terms of damage done it was all but virgin. I am aware that an American gentleman named Colt has long since devised a quick-firing weapon that makes mine antique. Nevertheless tried friends are true friends. I was not one to discard an old companion now. And Dinwiddie was unlikely to be possessed of a Colt. I also had powder and shot in a neat package. I endeavoured to remember how Cyprian had loaded the weapon, on a faraway day, and for that matter how to discharge it. My sight is not what it was when I scanned New Zealand skylines, and my fingers even less cooperative than they were a decade ago. Nevertheless, with patience and remarkably little blasphemy I made the thing functional and gave it a polish. What now? After some reflection I placed the weapon next to this manuscript. It cannot be said that I undervalue my work.

The pistol was still beside my pen when I resumed my desk this morning. I had a choice of implements. I took up the pen. It was that or sit with a pistol in my lap the day long. Among other things it might unhinge my housekeeper. She has problem enough with the fierce Maori carvings, venerable souvenirs of my New Zealand excursion, which gaze idolatrously from my walls. She refuses to dust these antipodean *objets d'art*; she suspects me to be a satanist of sorts. For her to see me ready as if for war, among those gaunt reminders of human mortality, might mean screams to rouse the neighbourhood.

So. I begin to speed this story. Someone must.

Martial lore has it that there is only one thing worse than the minutes passed in the dust and delirium of battle. That is, surviving the weeks and months between battles. In this instance there was a half year of ennui. It is not my intention to become a servant of chronology; I am not on this earth to explain its whims. Nor can I reveal how Colonel Despard retained command of the Queen's men in New Zealand. Since good news is always more convenient than bad, even the level-headed Governor FitzRoy was beguiled by Despard's communications from the front; and when Despard returned to Auckland, as he very soon did, he was cheered as a hero by joyous colonists and rapturous clerks. No matter that his communications, written or oral, had no more than a momentary association with reality. No matter that such as Cyprian muttered mutinously; their reservations were seen as envy.

Another battle, you ask? Need there have been one? That is an unintelligent question. Of course there had to be. Neither soldier nor warrior cares for an unkempt climax. Nor, thinking of Dinwiddie, do I at this moment.

All the same, it has to be allowed the peace was a possibility. All claimed to desire it. Words were soon flying as thickly as shot had lately been; almost as much ink expended as blood on the battlefields. Northern New Zealand swarmed with messengers on the march bearing claim, counter-claim, petitions and entreaties. There were unrealistic requests. Governor FitzRoy, for example, wanted all plunder to be returned to its rightful owners as a condition of peace. John Heke correctly pointed out that the plunder had been plundered; that such as survived was now in the possession of Timothy Walker Nene and his Queen-loving cohorts. Governor FitzRoy also wished both John Heke and the Duke to surrender certain lands to the Queen in compensation for mischief done and disrespect for the Union Jack shown. Heke's reply came in the form of enigmatic poetry: 'Land,' he announced, 'was given by God for a dwelling place for man in this world, a resting place for painful feet, a burial place for weary strangers wandering the earth.' This might have meant anything. The Governor's aides mused over this missive, looking for a yes or no, and found neither. The Duke, though acknowledging that he now had no quarrel with peace, was downright baffled by the Governor's unworldly proposition. Having fought what should have been his last fight, and taken an unforgettable toll of Britons, he failed to see why he should not be permitted to retire from the field with the honours of war; or why he should be obliged to behave as one beaten, suffering the pains and penalties of failure. No one could fairly ask that of him. Must he make his point again? He also observed that most of the land the Governor wished him to surrender was not his to relinquish; he offered to fight for it all the same.

It has to be said that, in the confusion following on battle, the Duke was one of the few participants who remained less than lunatic. From his point of view the vengeance taken was ample. After evacuation of the fortress he had been happy to see his warriors disappear back to dwellings by river and sea with a sumptuous anthology of tales for their children's children. For his part he trudged home, in the company of a few close kinsmen, with the impression that he had heard the last of Britain.

In this he was in error. Continuing bombardments of British documents—proclamations, pleas and proposals for peace—began testing his patience more than Despard's artillery. John Heke's pious shouting, right and left, compounded the clamour. Sometimes it seemed Heke was willing to settle with the British; sometimes he adamantly was not. Perhaps it depended on where his prose took him when he dictated a letter. He managed to be both bellicose and contrite in the space of an eloquent paragraph. His tale was in tatters. Not even the Duke could read Heke's mind. The government needed a team of translators, and they finished confessing themselves mystified.

So passed July, August, September, and some of October. In that month the Duke concluded that the fidgety peace was failing to improve anyone's character. Britons had no intention of conceding a victory; he was required to be a remorseful loser. An insensitive British promise of a pardon made matters even more intolerable. A pardon? For refusing to shame ancestors? He deduced that it was impossible to drum sanity into the heads of the Britons. While continuing to talk peace, insofar as the subject interested him, he instructed warriors to begin gathering again, this time not in John Heke's neighbourhood; this time there would be no mistake about whose war it was. When the news reached Heke an unusual silence prevailed. There was suspicion of another failure in health. Next day he came down on the side of belligerence. It was that or lose Christians to the company of the shameless pagans among the Duke's fighting men. Upheaval ensued. Heke's people marched into the leafy interior, soon joined by others of his old flagstaff-fellers, and there began building a stronghold while the Duke scouted terrain for his own. Differences between them were manifest again. The Duke needed another battle to the death. John Heke still wished an engagement of glory in which the virtuous were victors and no Christian killed.

It is only fair to point out that the colonial authorities were also not of one voice. Having begun to believe his own dispatches, Despard claimed to have proven that rebel Maori could only be talked to at the point of the bayonet; that negotiations were wasteful of time and energy and debilitating to boot. Governor FitzRoy differed. He had an entire colony to administer, not just the lean limb of land which gladiator Despard saw as his coliseum; FitzRoy's concern was that ill-will be contained. He did not want to turn rebels into roaming bands of brigands. He did not wish other tribesmen led into temptation either. Sweet reason was better than the sword. His superiors, however, were supping on sour. Before spring was gone FitzRoy was given notice of his recall from New Zealand; and of the appointment of a new Governor, a sometime explorer of the Australian desert who might not flinch, as a sensible seafarer like FitzRoy had, from wading into New Zealand's wilds. This was a man named Grey, said to have a hearty way with aborigines.

A firm Governor, then. A fire-eating commander. A friendly chieftain. All that remained was men and munitions. More than a thousand men were soon available; ships began arriving with munitions from Sydney.

Some observed these proceedings with a cool eye. Not the least of them was Cyprian, still in mourning for companions lost. He remained aloof from garrison gossip. Also, as threatened, he took up watercolours again. One might have expected him to flee into scenes of serenity, of New Zealand fern, tree and sea. Not so. His busy brush depicted the events he had lately survived, battlefields frilled with warring men, flashing muskets, and smoke billowing from embattled fortresses. Very prettily too. Posterity may yet judge his paintings kindly, less as art than chronicle. Posterity, however, will never know the heartsick soldier beneath. Louisa was bewildered by the loss of her once ardent husband. His libido had gone along with his love of war. Nothing had been learned. News of another punitive expedition confirmed it. Cyprian foresaw the extinction of the 58th; it would disappear into the limbo reserved for British regiments lost and better forgotten. So might he, along with his hope of an enlightened army. Despard, in short, was due to do the same again.

My situation remained as muddled. Colonel Despard was unwilling to relinquish the proposition that renegades, rather than rebel Maori, presented the largest threat to his well-being. He even appeared to hold them responsible for his loudly advertised constipation. The fact that there had been no sighting of such renegades continued to spur him. Reluctantly acknowledging that renegades may not have been active in rebel ranks, he began turning a cold eye on likely culprits nearer to hand. First he scanned missionary faces for twitches of treason, especially Wesleyans and Catholics, men who might have provided spiritual uplift for Maori rebels. Then his suspicion fell on passing Yankee skippers and Auckland mercantile colonists who might have a pecuniary interest in lengthening the war; many were rumoured to be trading weapons, powder and shot to the rebels. With most eliminated — and Nene's Maori deemed loyal — there was only one possible candidate for the role of renegade. Cyprian had foreseen it. That candidate was me.

Summoned by Despard, I found no welcoming smile. He announced, 'I require you, Wildblood, to account for all your movements, and activities, in recent time.'

'In detail, sir?'

'In considerable detail,' he confirmed.

'That is a large order, sir.'

Despard's expression suggested he was indifferent to the dimension of the task.

'Moreover,' I protested, 'some of it might not be seemly.'

'As I surmised,' Despard said, clapping his hands with relish.

'Is this in the nature of a court martial, sir?'

'It is in the nature of an interview. A court martial could well follow. God may be the best judge of that. Meanwhile I am.'

That was ominous.

'Begin,' he ordered.

He knew not what he asked. I was not Henry Youngman's mentor for nothing. Several hours later, with my narrative still to reach floodtide, I had begun a meticulous description of my second day in New Zealand. (Food had come, drink, and frequent opportunities to relieve ourselves in his personal latrine.) Along with other symptoms of impending paralysis, his eyes were beginning to flutter; even to close. Finally he shook himself into consciousness again.

'Pray tell me, Wildblood,' he said. 'Does this go on?'

'I fear it does, sir,' I reported.

His eyes closed again. Minutes later his frame fell gently forward. Then, as if propelled by some invisible force, he pitched abruptly to the floor. There was a manservant near at hand, and an aide. They raced to return the colonel to an upright posture. His eyes, however, were slow opening. Finally they rested on me.

'This interview,' he said unpromisingly, 'will be resumed in the morning. In the meantime have Major Bridge place this man under guard.'

Two armed men of the 99th delivered me to Cyprian. His face was solemn as he heard me out. 'There is only one thing for it,' he diagnosed.

'That is my view of the matter too,' I said.

There were no goodbyes of an audible kind. Cyprian chivalrously looked the other way when I took my leave of matters military. There was only one direction to take. With leaps and lengthy bounds, then in a discreet canter, I was pointed at the camp where I had last seen Heke, Moses and Angela. Fighting off foliage, and battling through swamp, I arrived in sight of the place in dawn's light. There was a lone fire burning. Otherwise it appeared deserted. Fearing that I might meet up with a rogue tribesman, and be seen as one surviving Briton too many, I approached the place warily with pistol in hand. My apprehensions were groundless. Tending the fire and cooking a modest breakfast was Moses. My appearance did not occasion large surprise. Nor did my wild eyes and fugitive condition.

'Put that away,' he said in respect of my pistol. 'You might give someone the notion you can use it.'

I did so, if somewhat shamefaced. 'Angela?' I asked.

'Here,' he said.

I felt faint with relief. 'And Heke?'

'Moved inland with most of his men. He judges deep forest desirable until Britons decide when to war. I remain here to tell stragglers which direction to take. Angela remains to see whether she has a man.'

'Which she has,' I suggested.

'Not a day soon,' he said. 'I am about to pack up here. Tomorrow she might also have gone. Meanwhile, what is your problem?'

'Did I say I had one?'

'Who hasn't?' he said.

I admitted my current difficulty with Colonel Despard.

'You mean you are a bird with no branch on which to rest?'

Maori imagery no longer left me at a loss. 'And when a bird has feathers, it flies,' I agreed.

'You cannot show your face near Heke now,' he pointed out.

'Nor anywhere else in the colony,' I noted.

'I must think on this,' he said.

'I think of nothing else,' I confessed.

Thought of a sober nature was terminated when Angela, roused by our voices, and with a fine sense of timing, made a shapely appearance from a nearby dwelling. In respect of storytelling tempo the Author of All Things is seldom surpassed.

Moses put a premature stop to utterances of affection.
'Blackguard Beach,' he said.
I failed to take his meaning. 'Blackguard Beach?'
'Where better?'
I still failed to comprehend.
'The place is empty,' he pointed out. 'Ships no longer call. Who would look for you there?'
'For me?'
'And your wife.'
I was still unfamiliar with that homely description of Angela. Perhaps, for a moment, I looked puzzled.
'This woman here,' Moses said.
'This woman here,' Angela said.
'Indeed,' I hastened to agree.
Later that day Moses broke camp. Before hiking off to join Heke he set our feet on a safe path to Blackguard Beach.

What can I say of the months ensuing? Nirvana has never had need of embellishment. Spring came warmly and gently to the Bay of Islands that year; nowhere was it sweeter than at Blackguard Beach. Picking a path through debris, spent shrapnel and shot, we camped in a cottage less ravaged than most in the village. It sat some way back from the beach, overlooking the Bay of Islands at its balmy best. There we played Eden with no serpent in sight. Clothes were not a need. Eve was first to discard them and soon afterwards Adam. A fishing net served most of our culinary wants; we dug potatoes from colonists' abandoned plots. Summer followed fast on spring. It was possible to surmise that it might last forever. The absence of news, of shipping, surly tribesmen and sullen soldiers, tended to encourage this notion. Distant smoke rising from Williams's mission station up harbour reminded us that Christ still had an outpost in the Bay; and that next to no one else had.

I know that there are many poets who are ill disposed to happiness; who think nothing becomes their vocation more than a choleric gaze on the world. I am not of their number (see for example Ferdinand Wildblood's neglected *Ballad of Blackguard Beach*, born of this episode).

Let it be seen as a reward for perseverance. Patience is not a flower which grows in everyone's garden. Angela and I had lived our lives for such a season as this.

And then, you ask. And then? There is no pleasing everyone. I sense the reader waiting on the fruit of the tree to ripen ruinously. I cannot satisfy cynical need. The more I look back on those months, the more blissful they appear. Unfashionable it may be, but our idyll was flawless. That is my problem. Bliss is not conducive to narrative interest.

There was of course an end. Otherwise I would not be playing memoirist here; I might still be beside Angela above Blackguard Beach, turning fresh fish on our fire and watching the sun redden hill and harbour at day's end. We had no calendar or need of one; our dawns and dusks might have added up to a year. Historians say not. They tell me that the morning Eden ended was November 24, 1845, with summer barely broached. Penning that date brings on a deep fit of melancholy.

That morning something must have woken me. Whatever it was, I refused to acknowledge it. I lifted, shifted and fell back into Angela's warm arms. The something, however, persisted. I opened my eyes. Light told me that the sun was already high. Then I heard voices. Faint, but voices. They refused to be dismissed as an auditory illusion. I left Angela asleep, pulled on what was left of my tunic, and tugged up trousers long in disuse. Then, creeping off quietly, I opened our door.

I may never perish of stoppage of the heart. Had I the propensity for so sudden an end, I should have suffered it that minute. For there was the Bay of Islands — a tapestry of blue sea, green archipelago, and wave-lapped ribs of rock — as exquisite as ever. Only one thing marred the spectacle. That was man. There were as many as five hundred lusty fellows in military red or naval blue swarming on the shore. Out on the water sat three British vessels. Combatants and cargo were still being ferried to land. On the hill above the town a new flagstaff was rising as two score tars heaved muscularly on rope. Had I a telescope I might have seen more. I had no wish for a telescope; I did not need to see more. I shook myself and failed to awaken. This was a nightmare with no escape. War was walking heavy-booted into Eden. Britain was back.

I went to warn Angela. That was a useful first step. The problem was finding a second.

'Here?' she said.

'By the hundred,' I said.

'So what do we do?'

'Put a brave face on it, perhaps.'

'What does a brave face mean?'

'In England we use the French expression. Sang froid. Coolness. Absence of excitement.'

'Why isn't English good enough for Englishmen?'

This was no time to explain. In very few minutes I was going to personify sang froid or perish.

She clothed herself in haste. Eve disappeared in the folds of her garments. When she finally went to the door she too was awed by the host assembling below.

'At least,' I suggested optimistically, 'we will learn what is happening.'

That didn't impress her. Women, by and large, have no feeling for history; they merely see it as hurtful.

We hiked downhill. Contrary to expectation, we were in luck. The first soldiers we met up with were of Cyprian's 58th, not of Despard's 99th; they briskly led us to their major.

'Good God,' Cyprian managed to say. 'You? Here?'

'Alas,' I said.

'I thought you might at least have fled a prudent distance.'

'I am throwing myself on the mercy of the fates,' I explained, if rather imperfectly.

'If you mean Colonel Despard,' he said, 'you can rest your mind. He has forgotten he ever mentioned renegades. His mind is too miniature to hold more than one notion at a time. In respect of British deficiencies, real or fancied, Governor FitzRoy makes a far more formidable scapegoat than a pen-pushing poet. Meanwhile Despard is on the scent of another distinguished duel with rebels before someone has second thoughts about his sanity.'

'What are you saying then?' I asked. 'That I am safe?'

'It is true that you escaped from informal custody. I have explained to the Colonel that you are of a nervous and normally retiring disposition, unaccustomed to military discipline. And that you must have taken fright on the day in question. I daresay he has even forgotten your name. Consider your knuckles rapped and remain close to me.'

'For what?'

'War,' Cyprian said bitterly. 'An end to disgrace, one way or the other.'

'What if I say that I have seen my share?'

'I would say I didn't hear you,' Cyprian replied.

In that unceremonious manner I returned to the ranks. Cyprian didn't press the point that I was still a conscript; he preferred me to feel I was volunteering. Nothing was simple, however. Nothing pertaining to Angela ever was. It became necessary, over her protests, to speed her off to Williams's mission station. Blackguard Beach, as it filled with loud and lewd males, was no longer a place for a woman of character. We ventured across the Bay in a leaky dinghy and beached on Williams's sinless shore. Williams examined our approach through a telescope; he drew a faulty conclusion. This became evident as he helped us to land.

'I am not disappointed,' he said with satisfaction.'I knew today would come.'

'Sir?'

I imagined he was talking of the return of his prodigal goddaughter.

He went on, 'If ever I doubted your sense of honour, Wildblood, forgive me.'

This was baffling too, if not for long.

'The church is in good order,' he explained. 'My parishioners even decked it with flowers this morning, as if they knew something was afoot. As for the civil details, they should not detain us unduly.'

That was true. They didn't. Though I had to borrow an uncomfortably tight suit from Williams, the ceremony was almost as painless. Inside the hour we were one in the eyes of God.

That night Angela and I shared something more than a tribal blanket; we sank into our first lawful bed. Few further details are available. Memory cruelly reminds me that something akin to paralysis followed. However much I wished his guidance, even Henry Youngman refused to rise to the occasion.

Cyprian and I now had something in common. On the other hand, he had the war as excuse.

Next morning I rowed back to Blackguard Beach with more than war to reflect on. In the still afternoon a pall of domestic smoke hung over the foreshore where Britain's regiments were camped. It was possible to see it as a harbinger of hellfire.

'Louisa?' I asked Cyprian.

'Don't ask,' he said.

'Meaning?'

'I have sent her off to Auckland. Her irritation with me is beginnning to mount. There may be more there to charm her.'

Womanless, then, we were ready for war.

Despite the passionate efforts Angela and I had made to that end, the world hadn't stood still. During the term of our defection matters had come to a head and aggrieved belligerents had shaken themselves into injurious form. Their motives, as always, were mixed. Despard needed a crushing blow to ensure nay-sayers were never again heard questioning his aptitude. Timothy Walker Nene wished that blow to ensure that Maori remained under the sway of traditional leaders and not delinquents old and new. The Duke and John Heke needed merely to demonstrate that they were undefeated. But they were unable to agree on how and where to confirm that this was so. Heke, in his boldest voice, had begun challenging all comers from far forest, far too far for British artillery to be dragged in. The Duke, with less uproar, had also established a headquarters high in the interior, but near enough to tempt Britons. With an impressive panorama of forest and fierce hills on all sides, the site was a warrior's dream before the first sod was dug and the first palisade heaved into position. It had a suitably sinister name: The Bat's Nest.

There. All is in place. Dare I set it in motion?

Despard soon did.

The 58th, reinforced with platoons of innocents from Sydney, was subject to much bitter drilling. Unusually, Cyprian appeared to be giving sadistic sergeants free rein. Long floggings were heard.

'Is harshness desirable?' I protested.

'Necessary,' Cyprian explained. 'We are not here from whim. We are here to challenge the Duke.'

'Not John Heke?'

'He is to be bypassed. The new Governor deduces that Heke is less harmful than the Duke.'

I felt relief. A perceptive Governor was something.

'If the Duke's nuisance is ended, Heke's fall must follow,' Cyprian explained. 'At least that is the theory. With the Duke's new fortress levelled, his warriors scattered, the colony is ours.'

'It begins to sound familiar.'

'Just so,' Cyprian said with great gloom.

By the first day of December, Despard had his men mustered and artillery unloaded. With a naval brigade and friendly natives tallied too, he had sixteen hundred men, a third of them from the 58th. A surfeit of firepower might compensate for lack of experience in the ranks. There were two naval 32-pounders, one 18-pounder, two 12-pounders, one 6-pounder, and four mortars. Or ten muzzles ready to deliver destruction and death. Munitions were sufficient to clear Constantinople of Turks. At first sight, at least, the Duke was due to be overwhelmed by the abundance of men and machines of war. First sight, however, failed to take the Duke into account. His mind marched more nimbly than any assault force. And Despard's delay in striking meant that the Duke had time to rid his fortress of imperfections and make warrior quarters invulnerable. Meanwhile, when the march inland began, the Duke let the forest and fear war for him. He didn't put out ambush parties; he didn't need to. Britons nervously pushed lead at anything that moved on their route; many a stray cow, pig or dog met its end. Some premature heroes, disposed to think that they were under fire, returned bullets in kind. Others fell victim to purloined rum; floggings were even more frequent. There were eighteen serpentine miles to travel, most of them uphill; men could only move as fast as fern-felling infantry and cursing road-builders allowed. It took more days than miles. Each filled with the sounds of tramping men, unhappy oxen, and banging drays. Rain or shine, the march was impressive. From high points I watched the army winding up into the hills, sometimes as heaving shadows in morning mist, often as sweaty beasts of burden under noon sun. There was no mistaking British steel unsheathed. By December 23 the head of the column was in hailing distance of The Bat's Nest.

On Christmas Eve, the command party, which now included the colony's new consul, took stance on a convenient ridge. Through a gap in greenery the good Governor Grey gazed with fascination at the Duke's masterwork. Its situation and robust character suggested that the Duke's earlier citadels had been rehearsals for this. (Do I exaggerate? Very well, then. But in model or plan The Bat's Nest is still studied in Britain's halls of martial learning.) The Governor, however, took Despard's word that it was as manageable as the last fortress he levelled. He also listened in silence when Despard gave the order for seven hundred men to move forward the next morning with just two 12-pound howitzers. Cyprian was dismayed.

'He is incapable of thinking,' he said. 'We have hardly mustered and he orders assault.'

Timothy Walker Nene objected on another count. 'Tomorrow,' he pointed out, 'is Christmas Day.'

'What are you saying?' Despard asked.

'My men respect the day of Christ's birth, even if Britons do not,' Nene explained.

Despard was frustrated. 'This is war,' he disclosed.

'It will not be ours,' Nene said. 'Not tomorrow.'

As it happened, however, the Almighty overruled Colonel Despard. He aimed a cloudburst at the British camp, effectively silencing disrespect for his only begotten son. Lest the message be misread, he underlined it with lightning.

The weather gave Cyprian a chance to circumvent his superior; he went over Despard's head to appeal to Governor Grey. 'Far be it from me to question orders, sir,' he said. 'But it does seem to me that it would be desirable to think before rushing in.'

'You have my full attention, Bridge,' the Governor said.

'And even more desirable, sir, to have our heavier guns working beforehand. Charging a Maori fortress before a breach is made can have unfortunate result, as recent casualties might suggest to an enlightened eye.'

That was as near as Cyprian came to mutiny.

'And you wish me to be counted with the enlightened?' the Governor asked.

'That is my hope, sir,' Cyprian confessed. 'Colonel Despard's battlefield repertoire is limited.'

'I shall recall what you say, Bridge. However, I can do no more than instruct Colonel Despard to manage this war to Britain's advantage. I ask only that he looks sufficiently fearsome. My hope, to be frank, is that a bold show of belligerence will make the wretches retire with no further loss of life. Humiliation may be sufficient punishment.'

'That is compassionate of you, sir.'

'Charity never goes amiss,' Grey said.

'I have mercy to our own in mind, sir.'

'No doubt you have, Bridge.'

So there Cyprian was. With an incompetent commander and a compassionate Governor. It was not an auspicious mix. It certainly brought no tear of joy to Cyprian's eye.

Nevertheless he must have made some impression. Next day the 32-pounders were brought forward to provide the show of power the Governor required. So were several other pieces. After Timothy Walker's brisk tribesmen had cleared the area of rebel marksmen, a battery was sited on an untimbered knoll; it began discharging across a deep ravine at the Duke's fortress. There was no further talk of a sudden rush. On the other hand, there was no large talk of anything, least of all strategy. So long as there was sufficient din Despard could dream the day away. So also, with laudanum to sweeten the long hours, could the Governor. Gunners made do with cold tea and dry biscuit. Others merely made do. Musket balls flying out from the fortress, however harmless, suggested that the enemy was not disposed to retire.

Yet the siege was begun, the last battle.

There was a familiar blemish, however. There was no John Heke.

Twenty Three

Last evening, with this narrative nearing its close, I judged that I had earned a reprieve. To reward myself for diligence I took my life in my hands, more or less literally, and journeyed to the club in the care of my customary cabman. Nevertheless, I deposited my pistol in a deep pocket of my coat. Dinwiddie, should he be waiting in ambush, was never going to find me short of offensive spirit.

Within the club I again had the problem of unfamiliar faces; my difficulty in that respect now grows daily. Sebastian Goodfellow, alas, was again in his favoured armchair, engaged with the same *Illustrated London News*; he appeared not to have shifted an inch in the forty-eight hours since I left him. Evidence suggested that he was still in senile conversation with me. I collapsed into a nearby chair and beckoned for brandy. Without looking in my direction, Goodfellow asked, 'Catch up with him, did you, Wildblood?'

'With whom, Goodfellow?'

'The Dinwiddie fellow.'

I again feigned ignorance of the name.

'Good Lord,' Goodfellow said. 'I was only just telling you about him.'

'Him?'

'Dinwiddie. The fellow the doorman heaved out.'

'In that case,' I suggested, 'one of us appears to have a memory problem. Or a fitful grip on the world. I can vouch for it not being me.'

That did not demolish him. I wheeled in a bigger gun.

'I have a yard of fine prose to show for myself today,' I pointed out. 'What have you?'

I regretted that. It was cruel. It is all of a decade since he published his last libellous line.

Goodfellow gazed into his dry glass. After a longish silence, he said, 'I don't suppose you could help a fellow out with a drink.'

'I might manage that,' I said with no warmth.

'I've upset you with this Dinwiddie nonsense,' he suggested.

'Not at all,' I claimed.

There was another considerable pause.

'There aren't many of us left,' he said.

'Us? Left? '

'Literary men of the first water. Boys of the old brigade. Our numbers are fewer.'

'Perhaps so. What are you saying?'

'We should stand or fall together,' he proposed.

'I am willing to grieve charitably at your grave, Goodfellow. Jumping in to share it is another matter.'

'Don't mock,' he said. 'We all have something on our conscience.'

Was he in league with Dinwiddie? If so he was making a fair fist of it. If not he was arousing that suspicion.

'Meaning what, Goodfellow?'

'It is time to lay old scores to rest.'

'It is for you to make a beginning.'

'Very well, then,' he sighed. 'I daresay you recall my review of *South Sea Sonnets.*'

'Every foul word,' I agreed.

'And not one I don't regret,' he said. 'That youthful misdemeanour has haunted me many a long night.'

'That is decent of you, Goodfellow. Though I would have preferred your *mea culpa* heard at the time.'

'You forgive me, then?'

'If it helps you. I have larger matters in mind.'

That was true. One was evading Dinwiddie. Another was getting this told.

'That warms me, Wildblood. It truly does.'

The man, possibly on the strength of one drink, was maudlin. To speed oblivion I ordered him another.

'Perhaps I could help you similarly,' he said.

'Similarly?'

'In respect of emptying your conscience.'

'What makes you think it encumbered?'

'Come,' Goodfellow said. 'What literary man survives half a century free of envy and malice? And, for that matter, of worse?'

'What, pray, does that mean?'

'Theft, perhaps. Enthusiastic imitation. Bare-faced pastiche.

Borrowed thoughts. Pilfered phrases. Purloined images. Erudite larceny. Not to speak of commonplace plagiarism.'

That catalogue of iniquity heralded a rich silence.

'Are you still confessing, Goodfellow? Or is this meant for me?'

'If the cap fits,' he said slyly.

I appeared to be on my feet. Otherwise I remained moderate. 'Confound you, Goodfellow,' I said. 'Damn you to hell.' Even more commendably, I refrained from dashing my drink in his face.

Fellow clubmen halted their conversation to look and stare. Having ascertained that it was just a couple of the old literary contingent feuding again, with no fisticuffs likely, they turned their backs. By that time I was closing with the door. I retrieved my unnaturally heavy coat; the doorman helped me heave it on and signalled for a cab. 'Rain again, sir,' he observed.

'Indeed,' I hissed. The truth is that I was still shaking. I descended the steps to the street all but blind, the doorman's arm on mine; he helped me across slippery cobbles and passed me into a cabman's care. Had I been less harassed, perhaps, I might have taken more interest in who was seeing me home. As things were I had none.

At least the unfamiliar fellow made brief work of the journey. In impressively quick time we were pulling into my street, stopping at my gate. The door of the cab opened. Again there was a helping hand. It was then that my senses began saying that all wasn't well with the world. The first sense to suggest this was smell; a faint but rank odour, human rather than horse. The second was touch; the grip on my arm was firmer than warranted. Then sight told me more. In the faint gaslight, as my feet encountered carriageway, the cabman came into clear view. His livery was unprofessionally dishevelled. Mostly buried under a hat and a grey bush of beard, his face was not easily recognisable; nevertheless the eyes were Dinwiddie's. The toothless smile confirmed nemesis.

'At your service, Mr Wildblood,' he said.

I endeavoured, as who wouldn't, to separate from the fellow. The surprise of the thing was that he released his grip with no extensive prompting; he even allowed me to reach for my pistol, though my efforts in this respect were clumsy. 'There won't be no need for that, sir,' he suggested. When I persisted in the project, he did no more than place a restraining hand on mine. 'With two barrels you could shoot yourself in both feet, sir,' he pointed out.

'What do you want?' I managed to ask.

'You,' he informed me.

I failed to take him at his word. 'If it's a matter of money,' I said, 'something might soon be arranged.'

'Too late for that now, sir. What is money to me?'

'I observe that the years have taken their toll of you too. Money might mean your last days spent in more comfort.'

He shook his head. 'I've seen them out,' he disclosed.

I made no sense of this. 'If that is the case,' I said, 'perhaps you will let me go my way.'

'I can't do that, sir,' Dinwiddie said.

'Why not, pray?'

'It's not in the yarn.'

'Yarn? Whose yarn?'

'Ours, sir. We have to see it through.'

'Your meaning eludes me, Dinwiddie.'

'I'm saying I'll be back tomorrow night, sir.'

'The devil you will.'

'In a manner of speaking, sir,' he agreed. 'And between seven and eight.'

'What makes you think I'll be here?'

'Oh, but you shall be, sir. Unless you wish me to pick you up at your club.'

'There is a choice, then?'

'Only in where I pick you up, sir. Not in when. That is decided.'

'Decided? By whom?'

'By the boss of this fancy song and dance, sir. Come, sir. We're both old hands at this. We know it don't pay to ask questions. Not about where yarns come from, or who spins them. I won't make a point of arriving before seven, sir. And I won't be no later than eight. You'll have a day to get your things tidy. Not that you'll be needing baggage. I reckon as you know all that, sir.'

I was beginning to.

'Who gave you the chore?'

He shrugged. 'Someone must have seen me suited, sir.'

'Someone? Who?'

'Maybe some old mate of yours, sir.'

A chill crept up from my feet. It spoke of a winter longer than London's.

'Mate?'

'Crony, sir. Someone you knew well.'

I eliminated most candidates in a moment. That exercise left me with one.

'Heke? John Heke?'

'Who else, sir?' Dinwiddie said slyly.

'I have a story to end,' I protested.

'Heke's keen on hearing it too.'

'Inform him, if you will, that it is still far from finished.'

'Don't fret, sir. That's why you've got tomorrow. Get yourself a good sleep.'

He mounted his cab and, with a crack of whip, steered his horse off into the mist. He hadn't even troubled me for the fare. Had he been there or had he not? There was evidence, however, that his beast had; there was a steamy dollop of turd at my feet. And I could hear, in the distance, his empty cab rattling away.

On the last day of 1845, after a week of British bombardment, the Duke hoisted his flag. He was impolitely telling Despard that battle had only just begun. It was the same flag as before, featuring sun, moon and stars; a reminder, if one were needed, that the warrior's business was to carve his name on the cosmos.

The Duke's indifference to Britain's best efforts did nothing to lift martial morale. Colonel Despard was reminded of his role in proceedings. With memory of the last disastrous day the Duke's flag had unfurled, he ordered a gunnery lieutenant to bring the flagstaff down. It was the luckiest shot of the war. Flagstaff and flag disappeared in a swirl of smoke. When it cleared, there was only debris and shreds of calico to be seen. British cheers were loud. Though no human casualty was visible, it seemed a helpful portent. Next morning there was one of more enigmatic nature. With the sun brilliant above, the moon miraculously became visible in the sky, with a star bright beside it. No one had seen the like before. A medley of Maori voices said that the Duke's flag had gone to heaven, there to look down on the fray. It was a good omen or bad; there was nothing between. Perhaps the Duke and his army were due to follow their flag skyward. On the other hand much attention was given the position of the star. It was on the Duke's side of the daydreaming moon. That might argue British disaster; who knew?

Awash in freakish events, the Duke called in lieutenants. 'My thought,' he disclosed, 'is that we give the red tribe one good day of battle. That will be enough.'

'One day?' asked a querulous comrade. 'Enough?'

'They have only one skill,' he explained. 'That is to rush. It must be as before. Then it is over. We may kill a hundred. We cannot kill a thousand. Not if roasted with iron day after day, and warriors not hearing themselves speak. We slay such as we can, and then say sufficient. Our last battle will be our best.'

'Will Heke be told?' someone asked.

'He will be,' the Duke promised.

Soon after, a messenger raced to deliver the Duke's decision to John Heke in his deep forest hide. A day or two later Heke's reply arrived. It lacked nothing in noise.

The heart knoweth not when the soldiers will come, he announced. *Let there be no sign of fear. Take care that your judgement is not trampled on by the many. Let not the slack of the fishing line be in the damp till it rot. Oh friend, oh sire, put aside this folly, the end thereof is child's play, but keep a sharp lookout for the dust of that thing — the soldiers. Let the one day, the only day, be warm; let it not be cold. If we do fail, continue to the last. Oh, tribe, behold the house of strife. Enough. Amen. Go, this my letter, to hearken to the cry of the guns.*

This dispatch left the impression that Heke rather than the Duke was in the firing line, his sleep shattered by British shells. Who can say where he was domiciled? The house of strife has many mansions; human fancy lodges in the least humble of all. The message was as difficult to interpret as moon and star in a sunlit sky. The Duke shook his head. 'When Heke's letter says we,' he mused, 'does it mean he?'

No one could oblige with an answer.

'Is he to hearken to the cry of the guns or just his letter?'

The Duke looked at his lieutenants. They looked as baffled.

In that moment the Duke appeared to deduce, not for the first time, that he was in league less with a warrior than a long-winded wordsmith. He wasn't seen to lament long. He was waiting for triumph's hour.

So was Despard. Fresh reconnaissance located ferny ground sheltered by woodland just four hundred yards from the Duke's fortress. If cleared of the enemy, it would make an ideal site for breaching batteries. Despard gave Nene the chore of making it safe. 'Let me see if you are in earnest,' he said.

Nene proved his sincerity with a dozen rebel dead. So three stout stockades rose with no interference and the Duke's warriors looking on in frustration. Some urged action on the Duke as the stockades grew more menacing. He refused them the pleasure. 'They change nothing,' he said. 'It must end the same. First bombardment, then storming. We will get the soldiers on our day, in our way.'

After seven days' labour the stockades were finished and fitted with artillery. Despard, however, was still shy about pushing big guns forward; presumably he was recalling the fate of a certain 32-pounder lost to a sly sortie. (Despard and the Duke had one thing in common; they were both fighting, as fighting men will, their last affray.) The Governor, impatient with preliminaries, and especially caution, eventually overruled Despard. 'I have the reins of the entire colony in my hands,' he announced. 'If you, sir, cannot end this local nuisance, I shall.' Humiliated Despard was given one day to push his bigger guns forward and train them at the Duke's palisades; two to deliver the least merciful barrage Britain could muster. That was on a Thursday, the siege seventeen days' old. Friday, however, produced rather more sensation. Indeed it put all else in the shade.

John Heke, after many months truant, returned to his war.

'Impossible,' I said to Cyprian when rumour first arrived from the front. 'He chances spoiling everything.'

'Everything?' Cyprian was puzzled.

'Certainly his hard-won renown. It is at risk near a battlefield.'

'Nevertheless it appears to be true,' Cyprian went on. 'Timothy Walker has spies in the forest, in and around the fortress, eavesdropping on rebel affairs. According to them Heke and sixty warlike companions crept in at first light. Anyway it seems I am not to be disappointed. I am to meet with the rebel incarnate at last.'

'Experience suggests you would do better to keep your eye on the Duke.'

'All the same,' Cyprian said.

Indeed. But it was not all the same. Hunting for his story, John Heke had found it searching for him; its hoarse summons said there was life in it still.

'What are you thinking on?' Cyprian asked, after rumour had been confirmed.

'On Heke,' I confessed.

'Do I hear sympathy for the enemy?'

'You hear tomorrow's guns,' I said.

'Meaning?'

'No one on that side or this will hear them louder than Heke.'
'But he will see them out?'
'There can now be none braver,' I explained.

Three batteries of guns began execution soon after Saturday dawned. One battery stood six hundred yards from the fortress; the second three hundred; and the third and most menacing a mere one hundred and fifty. Guns and gunners, hidden behind high stockades, were immune to Maori musketry. For once most guns were trained on the one point, the western wall of the fortress; Nene's intelligence had determined it the most likely site for a breach to be made. Remaining firepower was dedicated to demoralising the enemy. As gun after gun came into play, mortar after mortar, the roar made past British barrages appear frivolous. Never had the unsophisticated South Pacific seen its like; never had Britons launched themselves on any land with larger authority. The unholy storm of shot and shell didn't stop; it raged on for hour after hour. The air hummed with cannon balls and cruel metal; the ground, even at a distance, shook with bursting explosive. It was unthinkable that anyone could long survive the fire and brimstone of that hilltop in hell. The optimistic Governor waited for the truce flag which would permit him to begin work as a compassionate benefactor, healer of wounds and forgiver of rebels, the father of the colony. His cue failed to come. Even when guns began lowering the western face of the fortress, no truce flag flew.

The outer row of palisades dispersed like a bank of fog in morning breeze. Meritorious though this shooting was, it was short of heartening; the outer palisades crumpled only to reveal others as thick. Sometimes warriors could be glimpsed in the haze, snuffing out fires or collecting fizzing fuses from shells before they exploded. Otherwise the place looked lifeless. But as the battle-seasoned reader might surmise by now, and dim-witted Despard still didn't, rebel dead were few. Hours of barrage produced just four corpses, one of them a harmless old woman, two of them juveniles quarrelling over possession of late-detonating shell when it engulfed them. The fourth was a poorly disciplined warrior from the peaceful south, with no great grievance against Britons, here on a fighting holiday. When a round shot parted him from a limb he managed to take it in good humour before he expired. 'What playful creatures these cannon balls are,' he said. 'This one has run away with my leg.'

In mid-afternoon bombardment ended. A cool breeze cleared

smoke. Warriors didn't show themselves outside their bunkers; the fortress looked temptingly deserted. It had to be a ploy. Colonel Despard was unwilling to see it so. Recognising a rendezvous with glory, and a rapid return to New South Wales, he ordered up a storming party. 'Ahead we have the two rebel leaders for the price of one,' he announced. 'Victory is ours.'

I heard Cyprian's intake of breath. 'It cannot be,' he said.

It was. The location promised to be as scalding as the place of hot water; this time Despard had hundreds more to herd to the grave. As the storming party of ten score formed, ranks of infantry readied themselves to follow. Cyprian, after shaking my hand silently, took his place with his men. Heralded by bugle and drumbeat, the storming party began moving forward. The beginnings of disaster did not pass Timothy Walker Nene by. He leapt out of a watching throng. Then he stood with arms outstretched before the men of the forlorn hope. 'Stop,' he ordered.

Despard was outraged. 'Stand to one side,' he roared.

Nene was indifferent. 'No further,' he said. 'Or it must be over my body.'

He appeared to mean it. He bared his chest before Britain's bayonets.

'I need no tuition from savages,' Despard said, not for the first time, but certainly the last.

'Why lose your army for a bundle of sticks?' Timothy Walker said. 'Soon it will be yours for nothing. And your men alive.'

Rebuke followed reprimand, spiced with slight and slur, while the storming party remained stationary. In those fraught minutes the war was decided. For Governor Grey arrived in from the rear. He too saw no merit in making men targets for the Duke's entrenched warriors; at least not in his presence. Loss of an army would not read well in his first report as governor. In short, he sided with Timothy Walker. Despard, the picture of a man deprived, ordered his bugler to sound retirement. Retirement? Reprieve.

Cyprian materialised at my side again. 'How many more lives do I have?' he asked.

It was an uneasy night, with shells lofted regularly into the fortress to deter tribal tradesmen from renovating their defence works. The sabbath dawned fair and warm. As a summer day it could not be bettered. Was it to be rich with theatre as the last? Unknown to us that day's histrionics were elsewhere. Within the fortress, the Duke, still waiting on the British rush, ordered his men to remain at their posts with weapons ready. John Heke, never one to neglect the calendar, pointed out that it was Sunday.

'What of that?' the Duke asked.

'It is the Lord's day.'

'To you perhaps. I know of no Lord.'

'Nevertheless it is not a day for toil.'

'Any day, with the red tribe before us, may be a day for warrior work.'

Ignoring this wisdom, Heke called up Christians for a prayer meeting. Rather than risk an assembly within range of Despard's guns, he decided a bush clearing to the rear of the fortress served best for worship. The Duke looked on in dismay as warriors rose from battle positions and trooped off with Heke. Not all were Christian. Many were men of no large faith sickened with siege and looking for a peaceful pastime after Saturday's shellfire. The Duke made a vain appeal for them to return. As thwarted as Despard had been, the Duke was left with hardly more than a dozen stubborn heathen standing to arms.

Quiet grew on both sides of the battle line. That on the British side was not especially pious. As many a half-civilised foe has learned to his grief, British soldiers have never minded doing injury on Sunday; only when there is nothing better are they inclined to occupy themselves long with prayers.

Meanwhile the devil was finding work for Timothy Walker Nene. Soon deciding that the rebel silence had promise, he followed British example and dismissed his tribesmen with the most perfunctory of prayers. Then he crawled toward the fortress with a few trusted fellows. No shot singed them. There wasn't even a rebel shout. Sentries were absent, even where palisades had been thinned by shells. Suddenly and silently, he began beckoning, urging Despard's army to follow. Cyprian was the first officer to act. Without waiting on an order, he gathered up such men as he could muster and hurtled after Nene. Others began pounding behind.

What stealthy Nene had seen was apparent to all who followed. With Heke still busy with the Lord's day, the fortress was all but empty of defenders. Timothy Walker's men were not detained long by the palisades; they quietly wormed through them wherever they found weakness. Then they charged in. It was only a matter of time before exuberance got the better of a warrior and betrayed the fact that hand-to-hand battle had begun. The Duke had an alarm bell at the heart of the fortress. One of Timothy Walker's warriors, powerfully tempted to prove it in working order, found he couldn't race past without ringing it. This woke the Duke and his staunchly pagan dozen from their dispirited doze in a rear trench. They found the British army bursting through their front door.

The Duke called up a volley, then another, to check the red tide. It was too little; half the fortress was deluged with soldiers, and the other half about to be inundated. Meanwhile a messenger scurried off to John Heke. It requested him to forsake the sabbath and show his warrior face. That was also too late, though it has to be said that nothing became Heke more than his rapid arrival on the scene with three hundred remorseful Christians. Having lost the Duke's fortress, they recognised that it was their duty to regain it. With lips still warm with hymns they began discharging their muskets. Britons and their equally murderous allies were halted, but not for long. They merely made use of the defensive features of the fortress — pit, trench and bunker — until they reloaded their weapons and were ready to charge on again. Designed to entrap the red tribe, the fortress was now a net for rebels. John Heke, some say, was first to recognise that they were ensnared in the Duke's masterpiece. He urged retirement on his senior. If Britons were drawn out of the fortress, into the woods, they might be ambushed in a time-honoured way. The Duke was slow hearing. Dire bursts of musketry — left, right, and centre — interested him more. Whenever there was a slothful gap in the shooting, he raced to fill it personally. There was no one more determined to die on that day. Soon rumour said he had. At that point all hope of Heke imposing authority on the rebel force was gone. Even when the Duke was located alive there was no stopping suicidal tribesmen. Warrior after warrior fell, and too few Britons.

The remaining hours of the day were no more beneficial. Yard by enfeebling yard the fortress was conceded. With no hope left of a reversal of fortune, rebels fought less to win back the Duke's fortress than to rescue their dead and dying. As for the rest, far from enough Britons were tempted into the trees to be toppled by ambush. Sufficient were shot, however, to give Despard pause in respect of ordering pursuit. Survivors of the rebel force made an unmolested departure. Few spoke; even fewer looked their fellows in the eye.

This was especially true of those who claimed to be Christian.

By sabbath's end the war had a winner. It was not virtue.

'It seems John Heke survived,' Cyprian reported. 'At least he was seen departing the field intact.'

Unbuttoned after battle, his face filthy, Cyprian was propped against a tree. Pistol and sword lay beside him. He was putting a pannikin of soldiers' rum to use. Drops dribbled from each side of his mouth as he gulped.

'The Duke?' I asked.

'The same,' he said. 'He was also seen taking to the woods with large reluctance. There is no doubt who carried the day.'

'In a sense,' I admitted.

'In a sense?' he said irritably. 'Didn't we take the fortress?'

'With a little help from on high,' I suggested.

'You are giving the Almighty credit?'

'For surprising negligence.'

Cyprian was shocked. 'In what way?'

'In allowing his faithful to lose the war as they sang his praises. What does that say to you?'

Cyprian hesitated before joining me in heresy. 'That he has an original turn of mind,' he suggested.

'To take a charitable view.'

'I must also revise my earlier judgement,' Cyprian confessed. 'Conversion before conquest has something to be said for it.'

'Perhaps,' I said.

Among soiled soldiers and sailors retiring rowdily from the fortress with loot was a distinctive figure with a British forage cap tipped to the back of his head. In the company of recent foemen, his rebel musket shouldered, Moses limped by with a confidential wink. It should not have surprised me. The first commandment of the warrior tells him to be on the winning side. In the blood and blast of the battle for The Bat's Nest, Moses had found the injunction unusually compelling.

'Perhaps?' Cyprian replied indignantly. 'There is no perhaps about it. We belled the Maori cat. I rather think this signals the last of the warrior world.'

I watched Moses amble away with his new comrades.

'I think not,' I said.

Twenty Four

*H*ere we are then; the last chapter. And here I am, or otherwise. As I labour down a clean page I sense my exit line lifting to meet me. Though watchful, I fail to sight it yet. Is it waiting in ambush beyond my next word? To war with it I have just this weary pen.

Burdened with afterthoughts, hobbled by loose ends, most literary postscripts are poor, stumbling creatures. It is not my intention to encumber this one more than the reader's curiosity warrants. Even a thrice told tale is never free of imperfections. It is too late to ride to the rescue of this one. Anyway what story was ever more than a fretful excuse for our flaws? They make what we are — and, more to the point, what we are not — more tolerable. They suggest that we might be worth someone's attention. Are we? Then whose? That of the prolix and overpraised Author of All Things? His answers are brusque where benevolence would become him best; he does not even seem interested in hearing the question. Nevertheless, when Judgement Day dawns, our stories may be as fig-leaves in Eden's wild garden; they will be all we have to show for our sins.

It is time for a roll call of my companions in war. First John Heke. Rapidly finding the fugitive life unrewarding, he rode out of the hills with the last of his entourage and surrendered himself to Williams, committing himself afresh to Christ at the communion rail. That wasn't all. Within three weeks of the fall of The Bat's Nest he was wined and dined by British officers and pronounced the best of fine fellows, as merry a rebel as the British army had ever subdued. Many a story of gallantry was told in that reunion of enemies. There were peals of mirth as finer points of recent fray were related; no one laughed more heartily than John Heke as the bottles emptied. This event did nothing to harm his reputation; and much to confirm it. The Duke, for example, was never discussed. Nor was Nene much mentioned. Britons were too mesmerised by heroic and handsome Heke to notice that there had been other warriors abroad. In this respect they were anticipating the scribblers and illustrators who found Heke inspirational. Their fancies made even Henry Youngman seem a model of integrity. Legend is what we have when history is on holiday, which means most of the time.

After he formally sued for peace and found forgiveness, John Heke had just four years left to him. It cannot be said that he lived them with large peace of mind. They were often as anguished as those which had gone before. For the sake of his reputation he occasionally uttered sentiments of a combative kind. But his heart wasn't in it. When in difficulty with colonists he stopped short of urging a fresh war on his fellows. Contrarily, he seemed most to crave a formal meal with the new Governor; for local purposes this was as good as dining with Queen Victoria. Finally a breakfast was arranged aboard a British ship. At the last moment he became fearful about the occasion; he felt he might be kidnapped and carried off. Anyway stage fright prevailed; he failed to put in an appearance. It was to be another year before he broke bread with the Governor and toasted Queen Victoria. The occasion was lively and loud. John Heke pronounced himself pleased. He pledged that no more flagstaffs would fall. (Not that they were thought likely to, at this late stage, but no matter.)

I saw less of him in those years; he was difficult company. He slowly dwindled. He continued to imagine that his story needed him to die boldly at The Bat's Nest, in some mad solo lunge at Britons. He failed to see that it required him to do no more than he did, to be no more than he was; that he was the principal in a narrative of a less conventional character. The world's timepieces ticked past his mysterious minute in war's arena. Existence was now one day after another. He did not appear anxious to know what Henry Youngman might make of him; he feared the worst. Such fear was unjustified. Henry was long out of business. And Heke himself was walking proof of James' Biblical proposition (chapter four, verse fourteen). What, asked that apostle, is a man's life? A vapour that appeareth for a little time and then vanisheth away.

Appeareth he had. Vanisheth he did. Inaction never became warriors. Without purpose to their lives, his followers fell into scandalous habits. They played cards, drank to excess, womanised, and stole horses. They even grew indifferent to sabbath observance. Heke would once have banished such sinners from his band. He no longer did. Indeed, in his final year, he joined them in disgrace. With his loyal and long-suffering wife elsewhere, he took up with a flirtatious mission girl. This episode was short and shaming. His wife, learning of the alliance, rode into his camp. She dragged him from his dwelling and beat him without mercy. Though he cried out in pain as he bruised, he did no more than turn the other cheek in the approved Christian manner. When she judged retribution sufficient she cast him aside, aiming a last and unmanning kick between his legs as he lay groaning.

This did not impress those remaining in his retinue. These were soon fewer. A man who couldn't win a fight with a woman was no warrior; the mystery was that he had ever been seen as one. Some say this altercation hastened his end; it certainly heralded it. He took to his bed and never rose from it again. A doctor diagnosed consumption; tribesmen judged loss of mana the source of his woe. A year later, in 1850, now deserted by all but his forgiving spouse, he drew his last breath; he was just forty years old. His faults were forgotten overnight. After formal Christian ceremony his corpse was handed over to sorrowing tribesmen. It was costumed richly in fine-woven Maori garments and hung about with precious jade adornments. His head was bedecked with white feathers, signalling a man of merit. On one side of his bier was a whalebone weapon which his ancestors had borne into battle. On the other side was a musket which he had. Though wasted, his face remained handsome. As for the mourners, even Timothy Walker Nene was rumoured present.

The Duke? Alas. Unlike Heke, he had been too preoccupied with warring well to attend to the needs of his tribe. The potato crop had not been planted; his plantations grew weeds. His followers did not have enough gunpowder to make much impression on bird or beast. Soon his people were dwelling in dour poverty, on a diet of stringy fernroot and skinny eel. For a time Britons lived in fear of his return to rebellion. They were mistaken. His last battle had been fought. 'I have done with John Heke,' he announced. 'I have done with war.' More enigmatically he added, 'There are hidden places in houses which all men do not see. There are places in men's hearts which are also not seen. There are such hidden spots in my heart where wounds, grief and disappointment dwell.'

He lived his last days with dignity. He never quite bowed his head to Britain, though he did to a greater power. Seven years after The Bat's Nest fell, three after John Heke died, he capitulated to Christ, perhaps the last pagan Maori to succumb. Some might say not before time. He died a year later, in 1854.

He found it no problem to pardon a grandson who had fought against him with conspicuous courage; there is nothing to suggest that he forgave John Heke for wrecking his best battle and robbing him of the rest.

Colonel Despard, the alleged victor, departed New Zealand after the battle of The Bat's Nest and made no appearance in those islands again; nor were his services sought. He rather miraculously retained command of the 99th until his seventy-first year, never heard aknowledging that the nineteenth century had arrived. Luckily for his lessers, he was never allowed a battlefield again. He was promoted to major-general shortly before his demise in 1858. In his last years he disclaimed all knowledge of New Zealand and a war rumoured to have been fought there. This was no memory lapse. It had more to do with former subordinates beginning to express themselves in unfettered fashion. Yet it has to be said that no commander in military history had Christ more useful on his strength.

Timothy Walker Nene, whose largest triumph lay in saving Britain from itself, lived longer then most. He died in 1871, not far from his hundredth year. After The Bat's Nest he interceded with the colonial government to ensure that rebellious fellow Maori were treated fairly, with no forfeiture of land. Britons provided for him handsomely. There were regular gifts of blankets, flour, sugar, tobacco and pipes. A large cottage was built for him at Blackguard Beach as settlement there grew again; and a brick seat from which he could view the sunsets of the Bay of Islands. He was also awarded an annual pension of £100, with another £100 to be distributed among retainers. Some might see this as a bribe. Not so. A warrior never scorns reward for services rendered. An annuity is more lasting than loot.

Missionary Williams had as bitter an end as any. Accused of caring more for his Maori parishioners than for his fellow countrymen — in short, of disloyalty — he was eventually hounded from the Church

Missionary Society on the grounds that his large purchases of Maori land did not become a cleric. It was even claimed that his purchases provoked the war. No one believed this, of course, but then no one was especially expected to. He died in 1867, twenty years after the war, still mired in scandal.

Major Cyprian Bridge had to wait many years more for promotion. He was in his fifty-second year before he assumed command of the 58th; by then he had lost interest in reforming the British army and rescuing it from error. Bluff and bewhiskered, he was indistinguishable from most men of his martial station. He was never given another war to fight and did not seek one. His beloved Louisa bore him two sons and three daughters; the females failed to survive infancy. Then, in 1860, Louisa herself died. Stricken Cyprian sold off his commission a year later. His sons settled in New Zealand; Cyprian himself returned to England, where he married again and died only last year, in 1885, at the age of seventy-eight. I journeyed sometimes to Cheltenham to see him in his final years. He remained clever with watercolours until his sight began failing. Our war faded too, as wars do. 'Ferdie,' he sometimes confided, after a third brandy, 'it's all been a deuced confusing business, wouldn't you say?'

'What has, Cyprian?' I asked.

He would fail to remember.

There is no escaping it. Finally I must account for Ferdinand Wildblood too. After the fall of The Bat's Nest I went into the timber business with Moses. I did the accounts; Moses supervised axemen and sawyers, among them several who had cut their teeth on British flagstaffs. The colony needed timber — for houses, ships and post and rail fences — and we energetically met market demand. Two years later, with our pockets full and more than enough forest levelled forever (much as the unfairly mocked Governor FitzRoy feared) Moses and I amicably dissolved our partnership. Moses wished to settle into Blackguard Beach as owner of a small and respectable hostelry; he reckoned that sooner or later people might begin visiting it again because of its unholy reputation; and to relive the life and times of John Heke. Who better as guide than one of Heke's retired rebels?

For my part, I judged a return to England now in order. There was no place for a peddler of poems in the colony and for that matter no one to print them. Angela had her doubts about the wisdom of farewelling the Bay of Islands forever. It was not a happy decision. We landed in England in 1850. I expected life to be a large struggle. Lovelady and Pettiworth were long out of business; I foresaw an existence on the unfashionable fringe of London's literary world. I reckoned without life or, for that matter, my onetime accomplice. The unloved manuscript Henry Youngman had left behind, *Death By a Thousand Muskets*, had scored a surprising success in my absence, if not in its original form. Enriched with rather sweet melodies, the tale of the Maori Napoleon had become a music hall triumph called *Jolly King Hongi*. While I lived perilously among the hills and rivers of northern New Zealand — while guns roared, muskets flashed, and fortresses flamed — pennies, shillings and pounds had been cascading into my London coffers. My sleepy and surprisingly honest lawyer found it difficult to believe the sum he held to my credit. Henry Youngman, before he departed the material world, had ensured me an affluent middle age.

'I imagine you'll give us another one now,' my lawyer said, meaning another music hall coup.

'I fear not,' I informed him.

Henry had determined that my old age would not be impoverished either. So, unless this last-minute manuscript is one day made amusing, there will never be a melodious sequel called *Happy John Heke*. In the fullness of time my antipodean verse made an appearance, if largely at my expense. Alfred Lord Tennyson, who in a kind note acknowledged receipt of the copies I sent him, was not unimpressed. The likes of Sebastian Goodfellow can be ignored.

I pass to less happy matters, i.e. marital. The reader, having noted that I live alone, will have inferred the worst. In the version Henry might have written, the worst would go something like this: on arrival in England, Angela, far from her native soil, is afflicted by homesickness; in London's melancholy seasons she pines for the ferny forest and tranquil tides of her birthplace. The heart-wrenching finale would have her taking ship back to New Zealand, leaving me bereft in London's cold streets.

Alas for the above, Angela thrived from the moment she set her feet on English soil. Not to put too fine a point on it, her feet soared out of sight. There was little in London that failed to intrigue her. The daily din, the foodstuffs and the finery of a great city were all bewitching. Not for her the longing, which I fast had, for the simple life of the South Sea. When I proposed a return to the Bay of Islands, if only for a fond visit, she looked at me as if at a lunatic; and shuddered. 'What is there for me?' she demanded. She had, of course, a point. By then she was already a celebrity in London, familiar at the theatre and opera (in the company of her prematurely decrepit spouse and sometimes of men younger) and known in London society as the Maori princess. Aided by my capital she had gone into business on her own account. Never having seen women in other than flax capes and missionary-sanctioned garments before, it was the world of *haute couture* which thrilled her most. The needlework she had learned at mission school now came into its own. When she finished bedecking herself regally, she found much pleasure and profit in costuming others of her sex in high fashion. Children? Her frivolous life permitted no time for maternity, though a traditional Maori recipe may also be suspected. Meanwhile there was no dressmaker more coveted in London than Princess Angela; she soon had a score of women in her employ.

I must be forgiven mixed feelings; this remunerative episode may have been destined to end badly. A daylong idler at a desk was not Angela's notion of a husband. (Henry Youngman, where are you?) It was the scandal of the summer season, in the middle 1850s, when she ran off with a horse-riding and hunting French nobleman. More than that I cannot say. More than that I do not wish to. Her salon closed; London's Maori princess became a memory. My understanding is that she and her marquis live in a chilly castle in the vicinity of Fontainebleu with a litter of grandchildren. At any rate I have not heard different. All things pass.

Enough. This memoir must not meander. It is only on loan.

That brings me, with not many minutes to spare, to Dinwiddie. (When he has done his duty I hope that I might perform similar service for Sebastian Goodfellow.) In less than an hour the counterfeit cabman will be halting his conveyance at my door. I stole Dinwiddie's stolen story as others have mine. The custom is not confined to the realm of the written word. Those who dwell in war's domain are even more familiar with it. John Heke, without putting pen to paper, made off with the Duke's tale. In respect of robbing reputations Colonel Despard proved himself no mean felon either. It seems we are all strands of the one story. The Author of All Things isn't disposed to part with the copyright.

All the same, I suspect that he may have writer's cramp, that form of palsy that comes from persisting too long with the pen when invention begins to fail. Perhaps the effort of fancying humankind upon this planet, and then filling the sky with sun, moon and stars, proved his downfall. He hasn't the dimmest notion of what to do with us next. So here we are, blundering about brutally, killing our own kind and often our own kin, waiting on him to resume his knotty narrative. Until then, until a celestial bugle calls belligerents back from their last battle, mourn the men — soldier and warrior — whose once luminous lives are now no more than dust in a dark universe.

Yes. No. Yes. I am not mistaken. It is time to take my place in the story of stories. That is the whinny of a waiting horse beyond my window. That is a young Maori tenor ventilating his hymn with a wild warrior cry. That is Dinwiddie's businesslike bang on my door.